GREAT SHORT WORKS OF

Willa Cather

GREAT SHORT WORKS OF

Willa Cather

ROBERT K. MILLER, EDITOR

PERENNIAL LIBRARY

Harper & Row, Publishers, New York
Grand Rapids, Philadelphia, St. Louis, San Francisco
London, Singapore, Sydney, Tokyo

FIRST EDITION

Designer: Cassandra J. Pappas

Library of Congress Cataloging-in-Publication Data

Cather, Willa, 1873–1947.
  The great short works of Willa Cather.
  "Perennial Library."
  Bibliography: p.
  I. Miller, Robert Keith, 1949- . II. Title.
PS3505.A87A6 1989 813'.52 88-45964
ISBN 0-06-080970-1

89 90 91 92 93 WB/OPM 10 9 8 7 6 5 4 3 2 1

CONTENTS

INTRODUCTION

When a thirty-five-year-old farmer named Charles Cather decided to move to Nebraska from the Back Creek Valley of Virginia in 1883, he could not have foreseen how this decision would help enrich American literature. Accompanied by his wife, four children, his mother-in-law, a nephew, a niece, a hired girl and her brother, he was part of a nineteenth-century phenomenon: the great movement west to settle the seemingly endless land of a vast continent. Much of Nebraska was still a prairie covered by unbroken waves of grass, but new arrivals were common and the population was growing rapidly. That Charles Cather and his family were among the new settlers is important because of the effect this move had upon the oldest child in the family, the nine-year-old Willa Cather.

Although Willa Cather would live in Nebraska for

only thirteen years, her life there became the well-spring from which she drew the inspiration for much of her work. Longing for the hills and trees of Virginia, and observing her adopted state initially from the perspective of a displaced person, Cather would eventually teach the world to see the beauty of open grassland. Cut off from the history and traditions of Virginia, she would find an abiding interest in the Old World customs preserved in farmhouse kitchens by Czech, Swedish, Danish, Norwegian, French, and German immigrants. Uprooted at an early age, she would develop a passionate attachment to place that would inform all of her work. These factors, among others, would eventually combine to make Willa Cather one of the most eloquent and thoughtful writers in the history of American literature.

The young Willa Cather also had the great advantage of growing up with books. Her parents were cultivated and sensitive people whose reading included the nineteenth-century English and American classics, as well as Shakespeare and the Bible. Other resources were soon within Willa's reach. After a year and a half in Nebraska, her father decided to give up farming—moving his family to Red Cloud, which was then a lively and prosperous town linked to Chicago, Denver, and Kansas City by eight passenger trains a day. Charles Cather opened an office where he would sell sufficient real estate and insurance to support a growing family, and his eldest daughter entered into the life of the town, forming a number of important relationships.

Foremost among these relationships was the friendship that grew up between Willa and the family of Mr. and Mrs. James Miner. Mr. Miner, who owned one of the principal stores in Red Cloud, became the prototype for Mr. Dillon in "Two Friends" (1932), and his wife has been immortalized as Mrs. Harling in *My Antonia* (1918). Willa Cather's lifelong passion for serious music, which is evident in so much of her work, can be traced in part to the influence of Mrs. Miner, who was a talented pianist. And it was in this home that Cather met Annie Sadilek—then a hired girl, but eventually to become the inspiration for both Antonia Shimerda in *My Antonia* and Mary Rosicky in "Neighbour Rosicky" (1928), one of the most beautiful of all Cather's stories.

Another window to a larger world was provided by Mr. and Mrs. Charles Wiener, who lived next door to the Cathers in Red Cloud. The prototypes for Mr. and Mrs. Rosen in "Old Mrs. Harris" (1932), they introduced Willa to French literature and made their extensive library available to her. Other important influences during Cather's years in Red Cloud include William Ducker, an Englishman who tutored her in both Latin and Greek; Dr. McKeeby, the family physician who would eventually become Dr. Archie in *The Song of the Lark* (1915); Evangeline King, the gifted teacher upon whom Cather would base the character of Miss Knightly in "The Best Years" (1948); and Silas Garber, a former governor of Nebraska whose marriage to a much younger woman would inspire *A Lost Lady* (1923).

A sense of what it was like to live in Red Cloud during the late 1880s can be obtained from reading "Old Mrs. Harris," a story with a strong autobiographical dimension. But so much of Cather's fiction is rooted in her memories of Red Cloud that it is difficult to imagine her work without her experiences there. Red Cloud reappears, in various works, as Hanover, Moonstone, Black Hawk, Sweet Water, Haverford, and Skyline. Long after she was an internationally celebrated novelist living in New York, Cather continued to think of Red Cloud as her hometown. Her parents lived there until her father's death in 1928, and her visits with them were of great importance to her.

By 1890, however, the sixteen-year-old Willa Cather had outgrown Red Cloud. In September of that year she arrived in Lincoln, where she would prepare to attend the University of Nebraska. Her friends during the next few years included Louise Pound, who would one day become the first woman president of the Modern Language Association, and Dorothy Canfield, the daughter of the university chancellor. In addition to being a frequent guest of both the Pounds and the Canfields, two of the most prominent families in Lincoln, Cather was also friendly with the Westermanns, a highly cultivated German family who would provide the model for the Erlichs in *One of Ours* (1922). Another important friendship developed with Mariel, Frances, and Ellen Gere—fellow students whose father owned the *Nebraska State Journal*, Lincoln's leading newspaper —and Will Owen Jones, who was managing editor of the *Journal*.

Willa Cather's career as a writer began during her first year in Lincoln. Her English professor assigned an essay on Thomas Carlyle and was so impressed by the one Cather wrote in response to this assignment that he arranged for its publication. Once having tasted the excitement of publication, Cather continued to write. Within the next two years she would take numerous literature courses and become one of the editors and principal contributors of a student literary magazine. She would also see her first story published: "Peter," which she would one day rework for a central episode in *My Antonia*, was published by a Boston magazine in May 1892.

In the following year, Cather began to focus her energy in a new direction. She took a course in journalism from Will Owen Jones and was subsequently invited to contribute a regular column to the *Journal*. The offer was timely; 1893 was a year of drought and financial depression. Cather's family in Red Cloud was struggling to meet expenses, and she was glad to become partially self-supporting. Not yet twenty years old, Willa Cather had begun the career of a professional journalist that would eventually take her to Pittsburgh and then to New York.

Lincoln provided ample topics to fill Cather's columns. The state capital as well as the home of the university, it was also a railroad center that had tripled in size within the previous decade. Although the population was still only thirty-five thousand, the city supported two theaters and attracted many traveling theatrical companies each year. By her senior year in college, Cather was contributing an average of at least four columns a week to the *Journal* and beginning to acquire a reputation beyond Nebraska. Many of her columns were devoted to the theater, and her reviews provided her with a vehicle for defining the artistic standards that would characterize her later work. These reviews could be acerbic when the young critic was displeased, but Cather found much to enjoy in her new role. She had become a public authority while still a full-time student, and the pleasure she found in attending plays and concerts can be inferred from stories like "A

Wagner Matinee" and "Paul's Case."

After her graduation in June 1895, Cather continued to contribute reviews to Lincoln newspapers, but she worried about not having a a permanent, full-time job. She need not have worried long. Only one year after she graduated from college, she was offered the chance to edit the *Home Monthly*, a new magazine being published in Pittsburgh—then a wealthy city more than ten times the size of Lincoln and an important cultural center. Cather did not hesitate to accept this opportunity. She headed East, and for the rest of her life would return to Nebraska only to visit.

Cather would live in Pittsburgh for the next ten years, but her tenure on the *Home Monthly* was limited to little more than a year. Although she was managing editor in all but name, she was unable to change the magazine's editorial policy, which insisted that the *Monthly's* pages would be "kept clean and pure in tone." Cather thought little of much of the material she was expected to print, and she resigned during the summer of 1897. Within a few months, however, she obtained an important staff position on the *Daily Leader*, the largest evening paper in Pennsylvania. Soon afterward, she met Ethelbert Nevin, the brother of her new employers. A talented composer who would die young—although not before he had dedicated a love song to Cather—Nevin would become the prototype for Valentine Ramsay in "Uncle Valentine" (1925).

While fulfilling her many responsibilities as an editor, Cather also reviewed plays and concerts and continued to send regular columns back to Nebraska. This heavy load of journalism left her little time for writing fiction, but in 1900, while still employed by the *Leader*, she published "Eric Hermannson's Soul"; the first of the stories in the following collection, it anticipates the great works of the Cather canon in both subject matter and narrative technique. Cather successfully sold "Eric Hermannson's Soul" to a large national magazine, and this sale, coupled with the realization that journalism was keeping her from doing writing of her own, encouraged her to make an important career change: She resigned from the *Leader*, and, in 1901, became a teacher at Pittsburgh's Central High School.

From Cather's experience as a teacher comes one of her most famous stories: "Paul's Case," the concluding story in *The Troll Garden* (1905). Although Cather was a dedicated teacher, she now had her summers free to write, and her writing at this time was facilitated by a new friend who was to become one of the most important people in her life.

Isabelle McClung was the daughter of a conservative and affluent Pittsburgh judge. Deeply interested in the arts, and destined eventually to marry an internationally acclaimed violinist, McClung first met Cather in 1901. They soon became close friends, and Cather eventually moved into the McClung house in a wealthy section of Pittsburgh. It was a large house, staffed with many servants; Cather was given a room on the third floor as her own study, and after years of living in various boarding houses, she thoroughly enjoyed the peace, comfort, and companionship she found in the McClung home. This would be Cather's home until she moved to New York in 1906, and she found it an ideal place to write. *The Troll Garden*, the collection of stories that marks the culmination of Cather's Pittsburgh years, is dedicated to Isabelle McClung—as is *The Song of the Lark*.

There are seven stories in *The Troll Garden*: "Flavia and Her Artists," "The Sculptor's Funeral," "The Garden Lodge," "A Death in the Desert," "The Marriage of Phaedra," "A Wagner Matinee," and "Paul's Case." As James Woodress and other Cather scholars have shown, the stories are arranged in a careful pattern, alternating between those that show the seduction of characters by art and those that show the defeat of artists by life. *The Troll Garden* attracted only limited notice in 1905, and Cather herself later condemned several of its stories. In 1920, however, when she published *Youth and the Bright Medusa*, her second collection of stories and her first book for Alfred Knopf, she reprinted four of *The Troll Garden* stories with only minor revisions: "Paul's Case," "A Wagner Matinee," "The Sculptor's Funeral," and "A Death in the Desert." Late in life, she returned to these stories when preparing Houghton Mifflin's Library Edition of her collected work, *The Novels and Stories of Willa Cather* (1937–1941). She dropped "A Death in the Desert" from the Library Edition, retaining only "Paul's Case," "A Wagner Matinee," and "The Sculptor's Funeral"—the three *Troll Garden* stories that are included in the following collection of her great short works.

The Troll Garden, however, was not Cather's first book. That distinction belongs to *April Twilights* (1903), a slim volume of verse—most of which had been already published in various magazines. In 1923 Cather would revise this collection, dropping several of the original poems and adding others. Neither the original nor the revised volume suggests that Cather could write poetry as distinguished as her fiction, and her poems are now of interest primarily to scholars concerned with establishing correlations among her works as a whole.

Having published two books, Cather was beginning to define herself as a writer during her last few years in Pittsburgh. In 1906, however, her career underwent another dramatic change. Samuel McClure, who had published *The Troll Garden*, invited her to come to New York and work on *McClure's Magazine*, which was then one of the best magazines in the country. Among the writers McClure published in his magazine were Rudyard Kipling, Robert Louis Stevenson, Thomas Hardy, Stephen Crane, Jack London, Bret Harte, and Mark Twain. He also encouraged his staff —which for several years included Ida Tarbell and Lincoln Steffens—to research long, thoughtful articles on American social issues. Although Cather had already turned away from newspaper journalism, she could reasonably expect to do less hurried work in taking up a position on *McClure's*. She would spend six years on the magazine and become managing editor—an unusual accomplishment for a woman in the early twentieth century. In addition to helping edit the magazine, Cather was also expected to recruit new writers and seek out new material. On assignment for *McClure's*, she traveled to England in 1909, where she attended the funeral of George Meredith, met H. G. Wells, and accompanied Lady Gregory to the Abbey Theatre's first London production of *The Playboy of the Western World* (which they enjoyed from the box of William Butler Yeats). This was experience of a different order from reviewing plays in Lincoln, Nebraska.

Cather's trips abroad were important in confirming

the great value she found in European culture—a value that can be detected in such works as *Alexander's Bridge* (1912), *One of Ours* (1922), *The Professor's House* (1925), *Death Comes for the Archbishop* (1927), and *Shadows on the Rock* (1931). But of all the trips Cather undertook as an editor of *McClure's*, the most important may well have been the first: She spent most of 1907 and part of 1908 on assignment in Boston, researching the life of Mary Baker Eddy, the founder of Christian Science. It was while she was in Boston that she met Sarah Orne Jewett, the author who would have the single greatest influence in Cather's subsequent development into a mature and enduring writer.

Jewett was the first important woman writer Cather had met, and while separated in age by more than a generation, the two women shared many of the same values. A New England regionalist who wrote subtle, deceptively simple stories (a collection of which Cather would edit in 1925), Jewett gave Cather what, in retrospect, was the very advice she needed. Cather was still unsure of herself as a writer and, as such stories as "Flavia and Her Artists" and "The Marriage of Phaedra" suggest, she was often inclined to imitate Henry James—who was then at the height of his major phase. Jewett praised such stories as "The Sculptor's Funeral" and encouraged Cather to continue in this vein. Concerned that Cather would not develop her talent while submerged in the tide of editorial obligations at *McClure's*, Jewett encouraged the younger writer to find her own "quiet center of life, and to write from that to the world." In what E. K. Brown, Cather's first biographer, called "the most important letter, beyond question, that Willa Cather ever received," Jewett warned Cather that she was not developing her talent:

> I cannot help saying what I think about your
> writing and its being hindered by such incessant,
> important, responsible work as you have in your
> hands now. I do think that it is impossible for
> you to work so hard and yet have your gifts
> mature as they should—when one's first
> working power has spent itself, nothing ever
> brings it back the same. . . . if you don't keep and
> guard and mature your force and, above all,
> have time and quiet to perfect your work, you
> will be writing things not much better than you
> did five years ago.

Jewett then cited Cather's life in Nebraska and her childhood in Virginia as two of the worlds she might write about best.

Jewett would die only six months after writing this letter, but Cather never forgot it. We can see Jewett's influence in "The Enchanted Bluff," a story with a western setting that Cather published in 1909. Jewett's influence is also apparent in "The Bohemian Girl" (1912), and in what critics agree to be Cather's great "breakthrough" novel—*O Pioneers!* (1913), which, significantly, Cather dedicated "To the memory of Sarah Orne Jewett in whose beautiful and delicate work there is the perfection that endures."

The need to make a living, however, kept Cather at *McClure's* until 1912, the year which may be said to mark the critical turning point in her career. This was the year she published *Alexander's Bridge*, her first novel and one that she would later come to disown.

Set in upper-middle-class Boston and London, it is the product of a writer who still saw literature in terms of urban sophistication. That Cather turned immediately from *Alexander's Bridge* to "The Bohemian Girl," which is set in rural Nebraska and published the same year as *Alexander's Bridge*, suggests that she was reacting against her first novel and remembering Jewett's advice. Although Cather never chose to reprint "The Bohemian Girl," it is still a powerful story that clearly foreshadows *O Pioneers!* in both its setting and its focus upon a strong woman who is unafraid to take chances.

It was in 1912 that Cather also took her first trip to the Southwest, a trip that lasted for several months and inspired her to return annually for the next several years. Deeply impressed by Indian and Hispanic culture, and fascinated by the beauty of the land itself, Cather would draw upon her love for the Southwest for important sections of both *The Song of the Lark* and *The Professor's House*—and, most centrally, for what is arguably her best novel, *Death Comes for the Archbishop*. It should be noted, however, that Cather's interest in the Southwest predates her first visit there. "The Enchanted Bluff"—which is included in the following collection—was written three years before Cather first visited Arizona and New Mexico. Although this wonderfully evocative story is set in Nebraska, it is focused upon the ambition of a group of boys to see where the Cliff-Dwellers had lived "down in New Mexico somewheres."

The rest of Cather's life was devoted to writing the works which the headstone on her grave accurately describes as "her enduring gift to her country and all its people." Although she would soften her resignation from *McClure's* by devoting much of 1913 to helping McClure write his *Autobiography* and contributing three more articles to his magazine, she was henceforth able to support herself by concentrating upon her fiction. By the mid twenties, her royalties would make her a wealthy woman.

The twenties were the decade of Cather's greatest accomplishment. Five of her twelve novels date from this decade. But of this and the remaining decades of her life, it can be said that Cather's work was her life. With a few important exceptions—such as Yehudi Menuhin—her friends were the friends of her childhood or—like Isabelle McClung, Edith Lewis, and Elizabeth Sergeant—friends from Pittsburgh and her early years in New York. She would continue to make her home in New York until her death in 1947, making annual visits to the places she loved —like Jaffrey, New Hampshire, where she is buried, and Grand Manan, a quiet island off the coast of New Brunswick where she built a simple cottage to which she liked to retreat. Disillusioned by American materialism and disheartened by both the Great Depression and the rise of fascism in Europe, Cather felt increasingly alienated from the modern world during the last twenty years of her life. She also suffered from gradually weakening health. Once gregarious, she became intensely private—declining interviews, rereading her favorite books, reflecting upon the past, and writing with more difficulty after 1935.

Once her long literary apprenticeship had come to an end, Cather enjoyed a high critical reputation. By the end of the First World War, she had become recognized as a new and important voice in American literature, and her stature grew with each of her subsequent publications, suffering only a temporary eclipse in the years immediately before and after her death. H. L. Mencken praised *My Antonia* as "one of the best [novels] that any American has ever done," and Edmund Wilson pronounced Cather the only writer "who has brought genuine distinction to the description of the West." Of all her novels, only *One of Ours* received a significant number of bad reviews, yet even this somewhat uneven novel earned her large royalties and a Pulitzer Prize in 1923.

Although Cather had the happy experience of seeing her work widely praised within her own lifetime, her reputation has grown in recent decades. Writing in the early fifties, E. K. Brown declared "no American novelist since the death of Henry James was Willa Cather's equal in vision or in design." More recently, James Woodress has written, "I know of no other American writer of this century who is more likely to go on being read than Cather." Cather's collected works include ample evidence to support such large claims. If they seem strange to readers who are unfamiliar with her work (or who can only remember being forced to read *My Antonia* in high school), it is because literary fashion for many years favored writers who were more relentlessly "modern." Compared to much of the literature produced by her contemporaries—especially in the twenties and thirties—Cather once seemed a little old-fashioned. She confidently ignored both Marx and Freud during the years they had their greatest influence upon American intellectuals. Most of her settings have the familiarity of an American landscape, and it is easy to undervalue whatever is close to home.

Her characters have clearly defined values, and sex is treated only obliquely. Most importantly, Cather's works often end in a spirit of affirmation, rather than ennui or despair. All this can be off-putting to readers who associate sophistication with alienated characters seducing each other in a foreign setting. But while many of Cather's contemporaries now seem to speak in the dated language of a period increasingly far removed from our own, Cather herself has aged well. Her fiction has the timelessness characteristic of great art.

The triumph of Willa Cather is that she is a master of making the difficult look easy. She does this so well, in fact, that it's easy to overlook how very good she is at what she is doing. Most of her work is immediately accessible to the general reader and can be enjoyed without critical commentary. On the other hand, anyone who has read widely should be able to recognize within Cather a wealth of unobtrusive allusion that can help open up innumerable layers of meaning. And anyone interested in narrative technique should come to see that few writers of fiction were Cather's equal in composition. All of the stories in the following collection deserve more than one reading, and they will repay anyone who returns to them prepared to linger and listen carefully.

As Cather noted in "The Novel Démeublé" (an important critical essay which is reprinted here), "The higher processes of art are all processes of simplification." With this thought in mind, consider the difference between the first story in the following collection and the last. "Eric Hermannson's Soul" is a fine story with two especially memorable scenes—the scene in which Margaret's pony is maddened by a herd of wild ponies immediately before

Eric declares that he loves her "more than Christ who died for me," and the later scene in which Eric and Margaret climb the windmill for a moment of deep communion. The story also reveals an early working out of themes that would become characteristic of Cather's mature work. But despite its many strengths, "Eric Hermannson's Soul" betrays signs of a writer anxious to make an impression. The reference to *Cavalleria Rusticana* is apt—for Eric is a rustic knight and music is at the heart of the story. References to *Peer Gynt*, Silenus, Siegfried, and "the Goths before the white marbles in the Roman Capitol" can also be defended on thematic grounds. But allusions to Bourget, Rossetti, Tennyson, "Nero in his seraglio" and "the stone Doryphorus, who stands in his perfect, reposeful strength in the Louvre" are harder to justify. Cather had not yet learned to wear her learning lightly. In "Old Mrs. Harris"—written thirty years later, at the height of Cather's creative ability—the references to Goethe and Michelet occur naturally within two scenes set in a roomful of books. There are no gratuitous allusions, and the entire story is told with what seems to be great simplicity. In Cather's short fiction, as in her novels, we see a gradual paring away of all nonessentials in order to leave "the scene bare for the play of emotions, great and little," the goal which Cather had set for herself in "The Novel Démeublé."

This goal is reflected in Cather's mastery of narrative technique. The young author of "Eric Hermannson's Soul" already knew a great deal about how to write fiction. The story begins and ends with a confrontation between Eric and Asa Skinner; Cather dramatically contrasts the love Eric has to offer with the relationship to which Margaret is destined to return by using a letter from Margaret's fiancé, and the dance with which the story ends provides an effective climax. Plot is important, however, and much of the story is focused upon resolving the question of whether or not the boy will get the girl—a potentially conventional story line that is handled with considerable originality. (Readers might note that this story of an upper-class woman who is sexually attracted to a strong man who is her social inferior predates by twenty-eight years the well-known use of this situation by D. H. Lawrence.) In "Old Mrs. Harris," on the other hand, plot has almost entirely disappeared. There is, to be sure, some suspense about whether Vickie will get to go to college, but this is only one thread within a complicated fabric. One sign of the complexity of this work is that the author is able to sustain a profoundly moving story of unusual length without, strictly speaking, telling a "story" at all. This is a narrative in which almost nothing happens; carefully chosen details and a shifting point of view enable us to learn a great deal about "emotions, great and little." The significance of "Old Mrs. Harris" comes from insight into character rather than curiosity generated by plot.

Because of her emphasis upon understanding character, Cather often employs a shifting point of view. In "Eric Hermannson's Soul" we see Eric from Margaret's point of view and Margaret from Eric's. "Paul's Case" is initially told from the point of view of Paul's teachers but then shifts to allow readers to see Paul's perspective. Although "The Bohemian Girl" is told primarily from Nils' point of view, individual scenes are told from Clara's. "Neighbour Rosicky" includes scenes that reflect the viewpoints of Mary,

Polly, Rudolph, and Dr. Ed even though the story as a whole is unified by Anton Rosicky's point of view. And "Old Mrs. Harris," Cather's greatest story, is structured around a constantly shifting point of view that reveals the limitations of perception among a group of closely related characters who never entirely understand one another. All of these shifts are handled so smoothly that one seldom detects any sign of strain.

Within the stories in the following collection, only "The Sculptor's Funeral" reveals a problem with point of view. The first part of the story is told primarily from the viewpoint of the young Bostonian who has accompanied the body of Harvey Merrick, a gifted sculptor, home to Kansas for burial. The small-minded and mercantile vulgarity of Merrick's hometown is effectively revealed long before Jim Laird begins the uninterrupted diatribe that dominates the last several pages of the story. This long speech—which is reminiscent of Col. Sherburn's in *Huckleberry Finn* (a work Cather much admired)—is not without impact, but it tends to encapsulate the meaning of the story a little too neatly. In later stories, like "The Enchanted Bluff," "Neighbour Rosicky," and "Old Mrs. Harris," Cather would be more subtle.

Cather's stories also reveal a persistent return to certain themes that are characteristic of her work as a whole. In "Eric Hermannson's Soul" we find a conflict between the rural West and the urban East in which Cather recognizes the appeal of Eastern sophistication even while celebrating the freedom and grandeur of the West. "A Wagner Matinee" offers a stark contrast between the rich civilization of the East and the cultural desolation of the West where "just outside the door of the concert hall, lay the black pond with the cattle-tracked bluffs; the tall, unpainted house, with weather-curled boards; naked as a tower, the crook-backed ash seedlings where the dish-cloths hung to dry; the gaunt, moulting turkeys picking up refuse about the kitchen door." (Not surprisingly, "A Wagner Matinee" offended many of Cather's readers in Nebraska—including her own family who recognized similarities between Aunt Georgiana and Cather's Aunt Franc.) Like "A Wagner Matinee," "The Sculptor's Funeral" also reveals a conflict between Eastern and Western values. Just as Aunt Georgiana could not hear good music without traveling to Boston, Harvey Merrick had been obliged to move East in order to become an artist. The two stories are almost inversions of one another: One is set in the West and the other in the East; each allows us to see close up a world invoked indirectly in the other.

In "Neighbour Rosicky," we find what may be Cather's finest treatment of this theme. Anton Rosicky comes to Nebraska by way of London and New York. After the poverty of his life in London, New York initially seems wonderful to him. He enjoys companionship, good food, and standing room at the opera—performances during "the great days of opera in New York" that "gave a fellow something to think about for the rest of the week." But after five years in the city, Rosicky becomes restless. A New York spring makes him long to run away, and he begins to drink too much "to get a temporary illusion of freedom and wide horizons." The scene in which he resolves to leave New York is worth quoting at length:

It was a Fourth of July afternoon, and he was sitting in Park Place in the sun. The lower part of New York was empty.... So much stone and asphalt with nothing going on, so many empty windows. The emptiness was intense, like the stillness in a great factory when the machinery stops and the belts and bands cease running. It was too great a change, it took all the strength out of one. Those blank buildings, without the stream of life pouring through them, were like empty jails. It struck young Rosicky that this was the trouble with big cities; they built you in from the earth itself, cemented you away from any contact with the ground. You lived in an unnatural world, like the fish in an aquarium, who were probably much more comfortable than they ever were in the sea.

There is nothing shrill about the indictment of urban life in this passage, which should be balanced against the description of a Nebraska graveyard with which the story ends:

For the first time it struck Doctor Ed that this was really a beautiful graveyard. He thought of city cemeteries; acres of shrubbery and heavy stone, so arranged and lonely and unlike anything in the living world. Cities of the dead, indeed; cities of the forgotten, of the "put away." But this was open and free, this little square of long grass which the wind forever stirred. Nothing but the sky overhead, and the many coloured fields running on until they met that sky. The horses worked here in summer; the neighbours passed on their way to town; and

over yonder, in the cornfield, Rosicky's own
cattle would be eating fodder as winter came on.
Nothing could be more undeathlike than this
place; nothing could be more right for a man
who had helped to do the work of great cities
and had always longed for the open country and
had got to it at last.

As these passages suggest, the conflict we find in
Cather's work between Eastern and Western values
merges with an equally important conflict between
the city and the country. In "Neighbour Rosicky"
the country is clearly preferable. Here, as in *O Pioneers!* and *My Ántonia*, Cather is the spiritual heir
of Emerson, Thoreau, and Whitman—the American
romantics who celebrated nature, self-reliance, and
the common man. But in Cather's early stories, the
city has much greater appeal. Readers of "A Wagner
Matinee" should readily understand why Cather
chose to live her own life in cities. And even though
New York, in "Paul's Case," is seen through the
eyes of a diseased imagination, the city nevertheless
had undeniable appeal. Within Cather's work as a
whole, it is the small town that is almost always
grim. The city can offer culture, and the country
freedom—but the small town offers neither. The
narrow-minded confinement of small town life is
one of the often-cited themes of *My Ántonia*, and
within the following collection it can be found in
"The Sculptor's Funeral."

Closely related to these themes is the critique of
mercantile values that runs throughout all of
Cather's work. In "The Sculptor's Funeral," we find
a gallery of financial scoundrels. One of the townspeople betrays his own father in a business partner-

ship, another wants an unmerited increase in his army pension, and yet another "wanted to wheedle old women up in Vermont into investing their annuities in real estate mortgages that are not worth the paper they are written on." A more subtle example of financial corruption can be found in "The Bohemian Girl," where Clara's husband Olaf and two of her brothers-in law profit from having legal control over the children of a dead cousin. According to Clara: "Olaf has to do something that looks like the square thing, now that he's a public man! ...But he makes a good commission out of it. He lets Peters and Anders put in big bills for the keep of the two boys, and he pays them out of the estate ...Olaf gets something out of it, too." And then there is the wealthy but repulsive Janet Oglethorpe in "Uncle Valentine" who finds pleasure in haggling about money and even "bargains in her sleep." After Janet buys up the land over which her ex-husband likes to roam, it is not surprising that "the wave of industrial expansion swept down that valley, and roaring mills belch their black smoke up to the heights where those lovely houses used to stand."

Against these characters whose lives revolve around profit and loss, Cather celebrates men and women who put other values first. The Rosickys, for example, refuse to sell their cream—preferring to give it to their children. When record-breaking heat destroys their corn crop, they respond by having a picnic. As Mary later recalls: "An' we enjoyed ourselves that year, poor as we was, an' our neighbours wasn't a bit better off for bein' miserable. Some of 'em grieved till they got poor digestions and couldn't relish what they did have." The neighbors, in return, note that the Rosickys don't get ahead financially, but as Dr. Burleigh reflects: "Maybe...people as generous and warm-hearted and affectionate as the Rosickys never got ahead much; maybe you couldn't enjoy your life and put it into the bank too."

Elsewhere in Cather's fiction we find other characters who also turn their back on wealth. In "Old Mrs. Harris" there is the cultivated Mr. Rosen who "was a reflective, unambitious man, who didn't mind keeping a clothing-store in a little Western town, so long as he had a great deal of time to read philosophy." Mr. Templeton, in the same story, is clearly more attractive than "the hard old money-grubbers on Main Street" who are much quicker to collect their debts. In "The Bohemian Girl," Nils Ericson willingly gives up a claim to his father's estate, and Clara Vavrika prefers music, spontaneity, and wit to her position as the wife of a wealthy man. Like the Rosickys, such characters know that you can't "enjoy your life and put it into the bank, too."

But if Cather was contemptuous of greed and petty economy, she nevertheless believed in the importance of hard work, finding particular value in the experience of the pioneers who made the wilderness into rich and productive farmland. The celebration of such characters, especially first-generation European immigrants, is a major theme in Cather's novels. It is anticipated in "The Bohemian Girl" when Nils studies the old women gathered to celebrate a barn-raising:

> The older women, having assured themselves
> that there were twenty kinds of cake, not
> counting cookies, and three dozen fat pies,
> repaired to the corner behind the pile of
> watermelons, put on their white aprons, and fell

to their knitting and fancywork. They were a fine company of old women, and a Dutch painter would have loved to find them there together, where the sun made bright patches on the floor and sent long, quivering shafts of gold through the dusky shade up among the rafters. There were fat, rosy old women who looked hot in their best black dresses; spare, alert old women with brown, dark-veined hands; and several of almost heroic frame.... Nils ... watched them as they sat chattering in four languages, their fingers never lagging behind their tongues.

"Look at them over there," he whispered ... "Aren't they the Old Guard? I've just counted thirty hands. I guess they've wrung many a chicken's neck and warmed many a boy's jacket for him in their time."

In reality he fell into amazement when he thought of the Herculean labours those fifteen pairs of hands had performed: of the cows they had milked, the butter they had made, the gardens they had planted, the children and grandchildren they had tended, the brooms they had worn out, the mountains of food they had cooked. It made him dizzy.

As words like "heroic" and "Herculean" suggest, these nurturing women have achieved great things, but there is a note of nostalgia here, a tendency to see these women as picturesque because their moment in history is rapidly passing. Clara expresses Cather's own view when she observes that by comparison "The second generation are a tame lot." This tendency to prefer the past to the present becomes increasingly evident in much of Cather's later fiction; within the following collection, it is most central to "Uncle Valentine," which is set in "a lovely time, in a bygone period of American life; just at the incoming of this century which has made all the world so different."

Old Mrs. Harris, in the story that bears her name, is another example of a hardworking woman associated with "a bygone period of American life." Her neighbors feel that her daughter allows her to work too hard, failing to understand that Mrs. Harris prefers the work to seeing her daughter become a drudge. Her old-fashioned Southern values are at odds with those of the "snappy little Western democracy" in which she now lives. She takes pride in having a well-dressed daughter ready to receive guests in a comfortable parlor and finds renewal in the love of her grandchildren:

> Sometimes, in the morning, if her feet ached more than usual, Mrs. Harris felt a little low.... She would hang up her towel with a sigh and go into the kitchen, feeling that it was hard to make a start. But the moment she heard the children running down the uncarpeted back stairs, she forgot to be low. Indeed, she ceased to be an individual, an old woman with aching feet; she became part of a group, became a relationship.

Once again, hard work is given dignity because it is associated with caring and growing. Like the old women in the Ericson barn, Mrs. Harris works hard not because she is trying to acquire wealth but because she is providing the loving attention that sustains the lives around her.

Cather repeatedly emphasizes the importance of relationships. It is Mrs. Harris's relationship to her family that gives meaning to her life, and a similar claim might be made for both Mary and Anton Rosicky. One of the most moving scenes in "Neighbour Rosicky" occurs when Rosicky is rescued by his daughter-in-law after having had a heart attack. She puts him to bed and as she watches him reflects that he "had a special gift for loving people, something that was like an ear for music or an eye for colour. It was quiet, unobtrusive; it was merely there." This realization subsequently "brought her to herself" by awakening her from the brooding discontent that was spoiling her life.

Cather was not, however, sentimental about family life. The description of Paul's life on Cordelia Street, with "the cold bathroom with the grimy zinc tub, the cracked mirror, the dripping spiggots," is anything but attractive. More importantly, there is no sympathy between Paul and his father, who seems totally incapable of understanding his extraordinary son. Cather's fiction also includes many examples of unhappy marriages. In "Eric Hermannson's Soul" Margaret Elliot seems destined for a loveless marriage upon her return to the East. The marriage between Martin and Annie Merrick in "The Sculptor's Funeral" seems to have degenerated long before the story begins. Tip Smith, in "The Enchanted Bluff," "married a slatternly, unthrifty country girl...and has grown stooped and grey from irregular meals and broken sleep." In "The Bohemian Girl," Clara and Olaf Ericson clearly have nothing in common. And Valentine Ramsay, in

"Uncle Valentine," is able to escape from an unhappy marriage only by acting, in his own words, like "a butcher."

Cather would describe unhappy marriages in such novels as *One of Ours*, *My Mortal Enemy*, and *The Professor's House*. But within the short fiction included in this collection, it is "The Bohemian Girl" that treats this subject most boldly. What is astonishing about this story from 1912 is that Clara's decision to run away with her husband's brother is presented without a hint of rebuke. The portrayal of her relationship with Nils, and the contrasting description of her relationship with Olaf, makes Clara's flight seem both courageous and just. She has saved herself from becoming a bitter old woman.

Although "The Bohemian Girl" has been much praised, several of Cather's critics have found fault with the conclusion, an epilogue in which Eric Ericson runs away from the farm in order to join his older brother but then decides to return home to his mother. The epilogue is important, however, because it reminds us that the relationships that give meaning to life come in different forms. Nils and Clara may find happiness by running away to Europe together, but anyone seeking to join them there may not be so fortunate. Clara herself had found it difficult to leave home: "The great, silent country seemed to lay a spell upon her. The ground seemed to hold her as if by roots." She breaks this spell in part because she is an extraordinary woman, but also in part because Nils is there to swing her into the saddle. By making Eric return to the farm, where he is reconciled with his mother, Cather is emphasizing that self-fulfillment can be found in one's own country. If some people flourish in a radically different environment, others have roots that go too deep to allow for transplanting. Compared to "A Wagner Matinee, "The Bohemian Girl" marks an important stage in Cather's coming to terms with Nebraska, and the conclusion simply reasserts a message that is implicit throughout the entire text. When we remember the description of the farm women gathered to celebrate Olaf Ericson's new barn, we should not be surprised that Eric Ericson can find happiness by returning to his mother's farm. The story wisely recognizes that different lives must have different resolutions.

Written at the turning point of her career, "The Bohemian Girl" is one of the most affirmative of all Cather's stories. All of the principal characters get what they want, yet no one is made to suffer as a result. Many of Cather's early stories are much more grim. "The Sculptor's Funeral" ends, like it begins, with a death. "A Wagner Matinee" closes with a bleak description of the world to which Aunt Georgiana is doomed to return. "Paul's Case" ends with a suicide. And the epilogue of "The Enchanted Bluff" records the defeat of childhood dreams. But as Cather began to see her own dreams fulfilled, her tone became more positive. Even when she sounds a melancholy note of loss, as she does in "Uncle Valentine" and *The Professor's House* (which were published the same year), Cather seldom sounds so bitter as she does in some of her earliest works. In "Uncle Valentine," for example, the emphasis is upon the beauty of a "golden year," not upon the smokestacks at the story's end. And while both "Neighbour Rosicky" and "Old Mrs. Harris" end with a death, both stories emphasize the continuity of life from one generation to another. These late stories are among the greatest achievements of a writer who had come to terms with her own experience and, in so doing, found her most enduring voice—a voice that eloquently testified to the importance of beauty, generosity, and creativity in a world in which such qualities are frequently endangered.

The following collection includes only nine of the more than fifty stories that Cather published. In addition to "Eric Hermannson's Soul," "The Enchanted Bluff," "The Bohemian Girl," and "Uncle Valentine," four critically important stories that Cather did not reprint in any of the collections of her short fiction published in her lifetime, this volume also includes what are widely considered to be the best of the stories in *The Troll Garden* and *Obscure Destinies*. Readers who enjoy this selection will find other Cather stories in *Youth and the Bright Medusa*, *The Old Beauty and Others*, *Willa Cather's Collected Short Fiction 1892–1912*, and *Uncle Valentine and Other Stories: Willa Cather's Uncollected Short Fiction, 1915–1929*. To read the stories of Willa Cather is to discover that her short fiction is an essential part of the great legacy she left to our country.

ROBERT K. MILLER
STEVENS POINT, WISCONSIN

A NOTE ON THE TEXT

The purpose of this edition is to provide general readers with an accurate and consistent text of works that were written over a thirty-year period and originally published by companies with different editorial policies. Three of these works, "The Sculptor's Funeral," "A Wagner Matinee," and "Paul's Case," were revised by Cather when they were reprinted during her lifetime. The text for these three stories as they are published here comes from the definitive edition of *The Troll Garden* (1905) published by the University of Nebraska Press in 1983.

The text for "Eric Hermannson's Soul," "The Enchanted Bluff," and "The Bohemian Girl" comes (with permission from the University of Nebraska Press) from *Willa Cather's Collected Short Fiction 1892–1912*, edited by Virginia Faulkner. The text for "Uncle Valentine" comes from its first publication, in the February and March 1925 issues of the *Woman's Home Companion*. The text for "Neighbour Rosicky" and "Old Mrs. Harris" comes from the first edition of *Obscure Destinies*, published by Alfred A. Knopf in 1932. These six stories, and the critical essay that completes the collection, have been edited as lightly as possible in order to respect the integrity of Cather's work.

Great Short Works of Willa Cather retains Cather's spelling even when it differs from forms that are now standard. Readers will note that Cather often favored British spelling (as in *neighbour* rather than neighbor). She also favored the use of double *ll*'s (as in *travelling*) where a single *l* would be sufficient. Spelling has been changed only when necessary to retain consistency from one story to the next (as in *grey* for gray), or to eliminate a definite misspelling (as in *rheum* for *rhume*) or typographical error (as in *told* for *hold*). Conflicts in spelling have been resolved by editing the stories that Cather did not reprint during her lifetime ("Eric Hermannson's Soul," "The Enchanted Bluff," "The Bohemian Girl," and "Uncle Valentine") to conform in spelling to those that she had the opportunity to review in proof ("The Sculptor's Funeral," "A Wagner Matinee," "Paul's Case," "Neighbour Rosicky," and "Old Mrs. Harris").

Cather's punctuation has also been retained, including her use of hyphens in words (like *by-stander* and *post-office*) that no longer require them. An exception has been made for *to-day*, *to-night*, and *to-morrow* and also for *school-house*. Since Cather chose to stop hyphenating these words in her later work, the hyphen has been dropped where its use would conflict with the form she came to prefer.

GREAT SHORT WORKS OF

Willa Cather

ERIC

HERMANNSON'S

SOUL

It was a great night at the Lone Star schoolhouse—a night when the Spirit was present with power and when God was very near to man. So it seemed to Asa Skinner, servant of God and Free Gospeller. The schoolhouse was crowded with the saved and sanctified, robust men and women, trembling and quailing before the power of some mysterious psychic force. Here and there among this cowering, sweating multitude crouched some poor wretch who had felt the pangs of an awakened conscience, but had not yet experienced that complete divestment of reason, that frenzy born of a convulsion of the mind, which, in the parlance of the Free Gospellers, is termed "the Light." On the floor before the mourners' bench lay the unconscious figure of a man in whom outraged nature had sought her last resort. This "trance" state is the highest evidence of grace among the Free Gospellers, and indicates a close walking with God.

Before the desk stood Asa Skinner, shouting of the mercy and vengeance of God, and in his eyes shone a terrible earnestness, an almost prophetic flame. Asa was a converted train gambler who used to run between Omaha and Denver. He was a man made for the extremes of life; from the most debauched of men he had become the most ascetic. His was a bestial face, a face that bore the stamp of Nature's eternal injustice. The forehead was low, projecting over the eyes, and the sandy hair was plastered down over it and then brushed back at an abrupt right angle. The chin was heavy, the nostrils were low and wide, and the lower lip hung loosely except in his moments of spasmodic earnestness, when it shut like a steel trap. Yet about those coarse features there were deep, rugged furrows, the scars of many a hand-to-hand struggle with the weakness of the flesh, and about that drooping lip were sharp, strenuous lines that had conquered it and taught it to pray. Over those seamed cheeks there was a certain pallor, a greyness caught from many a vigil. It was as though, after Nature had done her worst with that face, some fine chisel had gone over it, chastening and almost transfiguring it. Tonight, as his muscles twitched with emotion, and the perspiration dropped from his hair and chin, there was a certain convincing power in the man. For Asa Skinner was a man possessed of a belief, of that sentiment of the sublime before which all inequalities are leveled, that transport of conviction which seems superior to all laws of condition, under which debauchees have become martyrs; which made a tinker an artist and a camel-driver the founder of an empire. This was with Asa Skinner tonight, as he stood proclaiming the vengeance of God.

It might have occurred to an impartial observer that Asa Skinner's God was indeed a vengeful God if he could reserve vengeance for those of his creatures who were packed into the Lone Star schoolhouse that night. Poor exiles of all nations; men from the south and the north, peasants from almost every country of Europe, most of them from the mountainous, night-bound coast of Norway. Honest men for the most part, but men with whom the world had dealt hardly; the failures of all countries, men sobered by toil and saddened by exile, who had been driven to fight for the dominion of an untoward soil, to sow where others should gather, the advance guard of a mighty civilization to be.

Never had Asa Skinner spoken more earnestly than now. He felt that the Lord had this night a special work for him to do. Tonight Eric Hermannson, the wildest lad on all the Divide, sat in his audience with a fiddle on his knee, just as he had dropped in on his way to play for some dance. The violin is an object of particular abhorrence to the Free Gospellers. Their antagonism to the church organ is bitter enough, but the fiddle they regard as a very incarnation of evil desires, singing forever of worldly pleasures and inseparably associated with all forbidden things.

Eric Hermannson had long been the object of the prayers of the revivalists. His mother had felt the power of the Spirit weeks ago, and special prayer-meetings had been held at her house for her son. But Eric had only gone his ways laughing, the ways of youth, which are short enough at best, and none too flowery on the Divide. He slipped away from the prayer-meetings to meet the Campbell boys in Genereau's saloon, or hug the plump little French girls at Chevalier's dances, and sometimes, of a summer night, he even went across the dewy cornfields and through the wild-plum thicket to play the fiddle for Lena Hanson, whose name was a reproach through all the Divide country, where the women are usually too plain and too busy and too tired to depart from the ways of virtue. On such occasions Lena, attired in a pink wrapper and silk stockings and tiny pink slippers, would sing to him, accompanying herself on a battered guitar. It gave him a delicious sense of freedom and experience to be with a woman who, no matter how, had lived in big cities and knew the ways of town folk, who had never worked in the fields and had kept her hands white and soft, her throat fair and tender, who had heard great singers in Denver and Salt Lake, and who knew the strange language of flattery and idleness and mirth.

Yet, careless as he seemed, the frantic prayers of his mother were not altogether without their effect upon Eric. For days he had been fleeing before them as a criminal from his pursuers, and over his pleasures had fallen the shadow of something dark and terrible that dogged his steps. The harder he danced, the louder he sang, the more was he conscious that this phantom was gaining upon him, that in time it would track him down. One Sunday afternoon, late in the fall, when he had been drinking beer with Lena Hanson and listening to a song which made his cheeks burn, a rattlesnake had crawled out of the side of the sod house and thrust its ugly head in under the screen door. He was not afraid of snakes, but he knew enough of Gospellism to feel the significance of the reptile lying coiled there upon her doorstep. His lips were cold when he kissed Lena goodbye, and he went there no more.

The final barrier between Eric and his mother's

faith was his violin, and to that he clung as a man sometimes will cling to his dearest sin, to the weakness more precious to him than all his strength. In the great world beauty comes to men in many guises, and art in a hundred forms, but for Eric there was only his violin. It stood, to him, for all the manifestations of art; it was his only bridge into the kingdom of the soul.

It was to Eric Hermannson that the evangelist directed his impassioned pleading that night.

"Saul, Saul, why persecutest thou me? Is there a Saul here tonight who has stopped his ears to that gentle pleading, who has thrust a spear into that bleeding side? Think of it, my brother; you are offered this wonderful love and you prefer the worm that dieth not and the fire which will not be quenched. What right have you to lose one of God's precious souls? *Saul, Saul, why persecutest thou me?"*

A great joy dawned in Asa Skinner's pale face, for he saw that Eric Hermannson was swaying to and fro in his seat. The minister fell upon his knees and threw his long arms up over his head.

"O my brothers! I feel it coming, the blessing we have prayed for. I tell you the Spirit is coming! Just a little more prayer, brothers, a little more zeal, and he will be here. I can feel his cooling wing upon my brow. Glory be to God forever and ever, amen!"

The whole congregation groaned under the pressure of this spiritual panic. Shouts and hallelujahs went up from every lip. Another figure fell prostrate upon the floor. From the mourners' bench rose a chant of terror and rapture:

"Eating honey and drinking wine,
  Glory to the bleeding Lamb!

I am my Lord's and he is mine,
Glory to the bleeding Lamb!"

The hymn was sung in a dozen dialects and voiced all the vague yearning of these hungry lives, of these people who had starved all the passions so long, only to fall victims to the barest of them all, fear.

A groan of ultimate anguish rose from Eric Hermannson's bowed head, and the sound was like the groan of a great tree when it falls in the forest.

The minister rose suddenly to his feet and threw back his head, crying in a loud voice:

"Lazarus, come forth! Eric Hermannson, you are lost, going down at sea. In the name of God, and Jesus Christ his Son, I throw you the life line. Take hold! Almighty God, my soul for his!" The minister threw his arms out and lifted his quivering face.

Eric Hermannson rose to his feet; his lips were set and the lightning was in his eyes. He took his violin by the neck and crushed it to splinters across his knee, and to Asa Skinner the sound was like the shackles of sin broken audibly asunder.

II

For more than two years Eric Hermannson kept the austere faith to which he had sworn himself, kept it until a girl from the East came to spend a week on the Nebraska Divide. She was a girl of other manners and conditions, and there were greater distances between her life and Eric's than all the miles which separated Rattlesnake Creek from New York City. Indeed, she had no business to be in the West at all; but ah! across what leagues of land and sea, by what improbable chances, do the unrelenting gods bring to us our fate!

It was in a year of financial depression that Wyllis Elliot came to Nebraska to buy cheap land and revisit the country where he had spent a year of his youth. When he had graduated from Harvard it was still customary for moneyed gentlemen to send their scapegrace sons to rough it on ranches in the wilds of Nebraska or Dakota, or to consign them to a living death in the sagebrush of the Black Hills. These young men did not always return to the ways of civilized life. But Wyllis Elliot had not married a half-breed, nor been shot in a cowpunchers' brawl, nor wrecked by bad whisky, nor appropriated by a smirched adventuress. He had been saved from these things by a girl, his sister, who had been very near to his life ever since the days when they read fairy tales together and dreamed the dreams that never come true. On this, his first visit to his father's ranch since he left it six years before, he brought her with him. She had been laid up half the winter from a sprain received while skating, and had had too much time for reflection during those months. She was restless and filled with a desire to see something of the wild country of which her brother had told her so much. She was to be married the next winter, and Wyllis understood her when she begged him to take her with him on this long, aimless jaunt across the continent, to taste the last of their freedom together. It comes to all women of her type—that desire to taste the unknown which allures and terrifies, to run one's whole soul's length out to the wind—just once.

It had been an eventful journey. Wyllis somehow understood that strain of gypsy blood in his sister, and he knew where to take her. They had slept in sod houses on the Platte River, made the acquaintance of the personnel of a third-rate opera company on the train to Deadwood, dined in a camp of railroad constructors at the world's end beyond New Castle, gone through the Black Hills on horseback, fished for trout in Dome Lake, watched a dance at Cripple Creek, where the lost souls who hide in the hills gathered for their besotted revelry. And now, last of all, before the return to thraldom, there was this little shack, anchored on the windy crest of the Divide, a little black dot against the flaming sunsets, a scented sea of cornland bathed in opalescent air and blinding sunlight.

Margaret Elliot was one of those women of whom there are so many in this day, when old order, passing, giveth place to new; beautiful, talented, critical, unsatisfied, tired of the world at twenty-four. For the moment the life and people of the Divide interested her. She was there but a week; perhaps had she stayed longer, that inexorable ennui which travels faster even than the Vestibule Limited would have overtaken her. The week she tarried there was the week that Eric Hermannson was helping Jerry Lockhart thresh; a week earlier or a week later, and there would have been no story to write.

It was on Thursday and they were to leave on Saturday. Wyllis and his sister were sitting on the wide piazza of the ranchhouse, staring out into the afternoon sunlight and protesting against the gusts of hot wind that blew up from the sandy riverbottom twenty miles to the southward.

The young man pulled his cap lower over his eyes and remarked:

"This wind is the real thing; you don't strike it anywhere else. You remember we had a touch of it in Algiers and I told you it came from Kansas. It's the keynote of this country."

Wyllis touched her hand that lay on the hammock and continued gently:

"I hope it's paid you, Sis. Roughing it's dangerous business; it takes the taste out of things."

She shut her fingers firmly over the brown hand that was so like her own.

"Paid? Why, Wyllis, I haven't been so happy since we were children and were going to discover the ruins of Troy together some day. Do you know, I believe I could just stay on here forever and let the world go on its own gait. It seems as though the tension and strain we used to talk of last winter were gone for good, as though one could never give one's strength out to such petty things any more."

Wyllis brushed the ashes of his pipe away from the silk handkerchief that was knotted about his neck and stared moodily off at the skyline.

"No, you're mistaken. This would bore you after a while. You can't shake the fever of the other life. I've tried it. There was a time when the gay fellows of Rome could trot down into the Thebaid and burrow into the sandhills and get rid of it. But it's all too complex now. You see we've made our dissipations so dainty and respectable that they've gone further in than the flesh, and taken hold of the ego proper. You couldn't rest, even here. The war cry would follow you."

"You don't waste words, Wyllis, but you never miss fire. I talk more than you do, without saying half so much. You must have learned the art of silence from these taciturn Norwegians. I think I like silent men."

"Naturally," said Wyllis, "since you have decided to marry the most brilliant talker you know."

Both were silent for a time, listening to the sighing of the hot wind through the parched morning-glory vines. Margaret spoke first.

"Tell me, Wyllis, were many of the Norwegians you used to know as interesting as Eric Hermannson?"

"Who, Siegfried? Well, no. He used to be the flower of the Norwegian youth in my day, and he's rather an exception, even now. He has retrograded, though. The bonds of the soil have tightened on him, I fancy."

"Siegfried? Come, that's rather good, Wyllis. He looks like a dragon-slayer. What is it that makes him so different from the others? I can talk to him; he seems quite like a human being."

"Well," said Wyllis, meditatively, "I don't read Bourget as much as my cultured sister, and I'm not so well up in analysis, but I fancy it's because one keeps cherishing a perfectly unwarranted suspicion that under that big, hulking anatomy of his, he may conceal a soul somewhere. *Nicht wahr?*"

"Something like that," said Margaret, thoughtfully, "except that it's more than a suspicion, and it isn't groundless. He has one, and he makes it known, somehow, without speaking."

"I always have my doubts about loquacious souls," Wyllis remarked, with the unbelieving smile that had grown habitual with him.

Margaret went on, not heeding the interruption. "I knew it from the first, when he told me about the suicide of his cousin, the Bernstein boy. That kind of blunt pathos can't be summoned at will in anybody. The earlier novelists rose to it, sometimes, unconsciously. But last night when I sang for him I was doubly sure. Oh, I haven't told you about that yet! Better light your pipe again. You see, he stumbled in on me in the dark when I was pumping away at that old parlour organ to please Mrs. Lockhart. It's her household fetish and I've forgotten how many pounds of butter she made and sold to buy it. Well, Eric stumbled in, and in some inarticulate manner made me understand that he wanted me to sing for him. I sang just the old things, of course. It's queer to sing familiar things here at the world's end. It makes one think how the hearts of men have carried them around the world, into the wastes of Iceland and the jungles of Africa and the islands of the Pacific. I think if one lived here long enough one would quite forget how to be trivial, and would read only the great books that we never get time to read in the world, and would remember only the great music, and the things that are really worth while would stand out clearly against that horizon over there. And of course I played the intermezzo from *Cavalleria Rusticana* for him; it goes rather better on an organ than most things do. He shuffled his feet and twisted his big hands up into knots and blurted out that he didn't know there was any music like that in the world. Why, there were tears in his voice, Wyllis! Yes, like Rossetti, I *heard* his tears. Then it dawned upon me that it was probably the first good music he had ever heard in all his life. Think of it, to care for music as he does and never to hear it, never to know that it exists on earth! To long for it as we long for other perfect experiences that never come. I can't tell you what music means to that man. I never saw any one so susceptible to it. It gave him speech, he became alive. When I had finished the intermezzo, he began telling me about a little crippled brother who died and whom he loved and used to carry everywhere in his arms. He did not wait for encouragement. He took up the story and told it slowly, as if to himself, just sort of rose up and told his own woe to answer Mascagni's. It overcame me."

"Poor devil," said Wyllis, looking at her with mysterious eyes, "and so you've given him a new woe. Now he'll go on wanting Grieg and Schubert the rest of his days and never getting them. That's a girl's philanthropy for you!"

Jerry Lockhart came out of the house screwing his chin over the unusual luxury of a stiff white collar, which his wife insisted upon as a necessary article of toilet while Miss Elliot was at the house. Jerry sat down on the step and smiled his broad, red smile at Margaret.

"Well, I've got the music for your dance, Miss Elliot. Olaf Oleson will bring his accordion and Mollie will play the organ, when she isn't lookin' after the grub, and a little chap from Frenchtown will bring his fiddle—though the French don't mix with the Norwegians much."

"Delightful! Mr. Lockhart, that dance will be the feature of our trip, and it's so nice of you to get it up for us. We'll see the Norwegians in character at last," cried Margaret, cordially.

"See here, Lockhart, I'll settle with you for backing her in this scheme," said Wyllis, sitting up and knocking the ashes out of his pipe. "She's done crazy things enough on this trip, but to talk of dancing all night with a gang of half-mad Norwegians and taking the carriage at four to catch the six o'clock train out of Riverton—well, it's tommy-rot, that's what it is!"

"Wyllis, I leave it to your sovereign power of reason to decide whether it isn't easier to stay up all night than to get up at three in the morning. To get up at three, think what that means! No, sir, I prefer to keep my vigil and then get into a sleeper."

"But what do you want with the Norwegians? I thought you were tired of dancing."

"So I am, with some people. But I want to see a

Norwegian dance, and I intend to. Come, Wyllis, you know how seldom it is that one really wants to do anything nowadays. I wonder when I have really wanted to go to a party before. It will be something to remember next month at Newport, when we have to and don't want to. Remember your own theory that contrast is about the only thing that makes life endurable. This is my party and Mr. Lockhart's; your whole duty tomorrow night will consist in being nice to the Norwegian girls. I'll warrant you were adept enough at it once. And you'd better be very nice indeed, for if there are many such young Valkyries as Eric's sister among them, they would simply tie you up in a knot if they suspected you were guying them."

Wyllis groaned and sank back into the hammock to consider his fate, while his sister went on.

"And the guests, Mr. Lockhart, did they accept?"

Lockhart took out his knife and began sharpening it on the sole of his plowshoe.

"Well, I guess we'll have a couple dozen. You see it's pretty hard to get a crowd together here any more. Most of 'em have gone over to the Free Gospellers, and they'd rather put their feet in the fire than shake 'em to a fiddle."

Margaret made a gesture of impatience. "Those Free Gospellers have just cast an evil spell over this country, haven't they?"

"Well," said Lockhart, cautiously, "I don't just like to pass judgment on any Christian sect, but if you're to know the chosen by their works, the Gospellers can't make a very proud showin', an' that's a fact. They're responsible for a few suicides, and they've sent a good-sized delegation to the state insane asylum, an' I don't see as they've made the rest of us much better than we were before. I had a little herd-boy last spring, as square a little Dane as I want to work for me, but after the Gospellers got hold of him and sanctified him, the little beggar used to get down on his knees out on the prairie and pray by the hour and let the cattle get into the corn, an' I had to fire him. That's about the way it goes. Now there's Eric; that chap used to be a hustler and the spryest dancer in all this section—called all the dances. Now he's got no ambition and he's glum as a preacher. I don't suppose we can even get him to come in tomorrow night."

"Eric? Why, he must dance, we can't let him off," said Margaret, quickly. "Why, I intend to dance with him myself!"

"I'm afraid he won't dance. I asked him this morning if he'd help us out and he said, 'I don't dance now, any more,'" said Lockhart, imitating the laboured English of the Norwegian.

"'The Miller of Hofbau, the Miller of Hofbau, O my Princess!'" chirped Wyllis, cheerfully, from his hammock.

The red on his sister's cheek deepened a little, and she laughed mischievously. "We'll see about that, sir. I'll not admit that I am beaten until I have asked him myself."

Every night Eric rode over to St. Anne, a little village in the heart of the French settlement, for the mail. As the road lay through the most attractive part of the Divide country, on several occasions Margaret Elliot and her brother had accompanied him. Tonight Wyllis had business with Lockhart, and Margaret rode with Eric, mounted on a frisky little mustang that Mrs. Lockhart had broken to the sidesaddle. Margaret regarded her escort very much as she did the servant who always accompanied her on long rides at home, and the ride to the village was a silent one. She was occupied with thoughts of another world, and Eric was wrestling with more thoughts than had ever been crowded into his head before. He rode with his eyes riveted on that slight figure before him, as though he wished to absorb it through the optic nerves and hold it in his brain forever. He understood the situation perfectly. His brain worked slowly, but he had a keen sense of the values of things. This girl represented an entirely new species of humanity to him, but he knew where to place her. The prophets of old, when an angel first appeared unto them, never doubted its high origin.

Eric was patient under the adverse conditions of his life, but he was not servile. The Norse blood in him had not entirely lost its self-reliance. He came of a proud fisher line, men who were not afraid of anything but the ice and the devil, and he had prospects before him when his father went down off the North Cape in the long Arctic night, and his mother, seized by a violent horror of seafaring life, had followed her brother to America. Eric was eighteen then, handsome as young Siegfried, a giant in stature, with a skin singularly pure and delicate, like a Swede's; hair as yellow as the locks of Tennyson's amorous Prince, and eyes of a fierce, burning blue, whose flash was most dangerous to women. He had in those days a certain pride of bearing, a certain confidence of approach, that usually accompanies physical perfection. It was even said of him then that he was in love with life, and inclined to levity, a vice most unusual on the Divide. But the sad history of those Norwegian exiles, transplanted in an arid soil and under a scorching sun, had repeated itself in his case. Toil and isolation had sobered him, and he grew more and more like the clods among which he laboured. It was as though some red-hot instrument had touched for a moment those delicate fibers of the brain which respond to acute pain or pleasure, in which lies the power of exquisite sensation, and had seared them quite away. It is a painful thing to watch the light die out of the eyes of those Norsemen, leaving an expression of impenetrable sadness, quite passive, quite hopeless, a shadow that is never lifted. With some this change comes almost at once, in the first bitterness of homesickness, with others it comes more slowly, according to the time it takes each man's heart to die.

Oh, those poor Northmen of the Divide! They are dead many a year before they are put to rest in the little graveyard on the windy hill where exiles of all nations grow akin.

The peculiar species of hypochondria to which the exiles of his people sooner or later succumb had not developed in Eric until that night at the Lone Star schoolhouse, when he had broken his violin across his knee. After that, the gloom of his people settled down upon him, and the gospel of maceration began its work. *"If thine eye offend thee, pluck it out,"* et cetera. The pagan smile that once hovered about his lips was gone, and he was one with sorrow. Religion heals a hundred hearts for one that it embitters, but when it destroys, its work is quick and deadly, and where the agony of the cross has been, joy will not come again. This man understood things literally: one must live without pleasure to die without fear; to save the soul it was necessary to starve the soul.

The sun hung low above the cornfields when Margaret and her cavalier left St. Anne. South of the town there is a stretch of road that runs for some three miles through the French settlement, where the prairie is as level as the surface of a lake. There the fields of flax and wheat and rye are bordered by precise rows of slender, tapering Lombard poplars. It was a yellow world that Margaret Elliot saw under the wide light of the setting sun.

The girl gathered up her reins and called back to Eric, "It will be safe to run the horses here, won't it?"

"Yes, I think so, now," he answered, touching his spur to his pony's flank. They were off like the wind. It is an old saying in the West that newcomers always ride a horse or two to death before they get broken in to the country. They are tempted by the great open spaces and try to outride the horizon, to get to the end of something. Margaret galloped over the level road, and Eric, from behind, saw her long veil fluttering in the wind. It had fluttered just so in his dreams last night and the night before. With a sudden inspiration of courage he overtook her and rode beside her, looking intently at her half-averted face. Before, he had only stolen occasional glances at it, seen it in blinding flashes, always with more or less embarrassment, but now he determined to let every line of it sink into his memory. Men of the world would have said that it was an unusual face, nervous, finely cut, with clear, elegant lines that betokened ancestry. Men of letters would have called it a historic face, and would have conjectured at what old passions, long asleep, what old sorrows forgotten time out of mind, doing battle together in ages gone, had curved those delicate nostrils, left their unconscious memory in those eyes. But Eric read no meaning in these details. To him this beauty was something more than colour and line; it was a flash of white light, in which one cannot distinguish colour because all colours are there. To him it was a complete revelation, an embodiment of those dreams of impossible loveliness that linger by a young man's pillow on midsummer nights; yet, because it held something more than the attraction of health and youth and shapeliness, it troubled him, and in its presence he felt as the Goths before the white marbles in the Roman Capitol, not knowing whether they were men or gods. At times he felt like uncovering his head before it, again the fury seized him to break and despoil, to find the clay in this spirit-thing and stamp upon it. Away from her, he longed to strike out with his arms, and take and hold; it maddened him that this woman whom he could break in his hands should be so much stronger than he. But near her, he never questioned this strength; he admitted its potentiality as he admitted the miracles of the Bible; it enervated and conquered him. Tonight, when he rode so close to her that he could have touched her, he knew that he might as well reach out his hand to take a star.

Margaret stirred uneasily under his gaze and turned questioningly in her saddle.

"This wind puts me a little out of breath when we ride fast," she said.

Eric turned his eyes away.

"I want to ask you if I go to New York to work, if I maybe hear music like you sang last night? I been a purty good hand to work," he asked, timidly.

Margaret looked at him with surprise, and then, as she studied the outline of his face, pityingly.

"Well, you might—but you'd lose a good deal else. I shouldn't like you to go to New York—and be poor, you'd be out of atmosphere, some way," she said, slowly. Inwardly she was thinking: *There he would be altogether sordid, impossible—a machine who would carry one's trunks upstairs, perhaps. Here he is every inch a man, rather picturesque; why is it?* "No," she added aloud, "I shouldn't like that."

"Then I not go," said Eric, decidedly.

Margaret turned her face to hide a smile. She was a trifle amused and a trifle annoyed. Suddenly she spoke again.

"But I'll tell you what I do want you to do, Eric. I want you to dance with us tomorrow night and teach me some of the Norwegian dances; they say you know them all. Won't you?"

Eric straightened himself in his saddle and his eyes flashed as they had done in the Lone Star schoolhouse when he broke his violin across his knee.

"Yes, I will," he said, quietly, and he believed that he delivered his soul to hell as he said it.

They had reached the rougher country now, where the road wound through a narrow cut in one of the bluffs along the creek, when a beat of hoofs ahead and the sharp neighing of horses made the ponies start and Eric rose in his stirrups. Then down the gulch in front of them and over the steep clay banks thundered a herd of wild ponies, nimble as monkeys and wild as rabbits, such as horse-traders drive east from the plains of Montana to sell in the farming country. Margaret's pony made a shrill sound, a neigh that was almost a scream, and started up the clay bank to meet them, all the wild blood of the range breaking out in an instant. Margaret called to Eric just as he threw himself out of the saddle and caught her pony's bit. But the wiry little animal had gone mad and was kicking and biting like a devil. Her wild brothers of the range were all about her, neighing, and pawing the earth, and striking her with their forefeet and snapping at her flanks. It was the old liberty of the range that the little beast fought for.

"Drop the reins and hold tight, tight!" Eric called,

throwing all his weight upon the bit, struggling under those frantic forefeet that now beat at his breast, and now kicked at the wild mustangs that surged and tossed about him. He succeeded in wrenching the pony's head toward him and crowding her withers against the clay bank, so that she could not roll.

"Hold tight, tight!" he shouted again, launching a kick at a snorting animal that reared back against Margaret's saddle. If she should lose her courage and fall now, under those hoofs—He struck out again and again, kicking right and left with all his might. Already the negligent drivers had galloped into the cut, and their long quirts were whistling over the heads of the herd. As suddenly as it had come, the struggling, frantic wave of wild life swept up out of the gulch and on across the open prairie, and with a long despairing whinny of farewell the pony dropped her head and stood trembling in her sweat, shaking the foam and blood from her bit.

Eric stepped close to Margaret's side and laid his hand on her saddle. "You are not hurt?" he asked, hoarsely. As he raised his face in the soft starlight she saw that it was white and drawn and that his lips were working nervously.

"No, no, not at all. But you, you are suffering; they struck you!" she cried in sharp alarm.

He stepped back and drew his hand across his brow.

"No, it is not that," he spoke rapidly now, with his hands clenched at his side. "But if they had hurt you, I would beat their brains out with my hands, I would kill them all. I was never afraid before. You are the only beautiful thing that has ever come close to me. You came like an angel out of the sky. You are like the music you sing, you are like the stars and the snow on the mountains where I played when I was a little boy. You are like all that I wanted once and never had, you are all that they have killed in me. I die for you to-night, tomorrow, for all eternity. I am not a coward; I was afraid because I love you more than Christ who died for me, more than I am afraid of hell, or hope for heaven. I was never afraid before. If you had fallen— oh, my God!" He threw his arms out blindly and dropped his head upon the pony's mane, leaning limply against the animal like a man struck by some sickness. His shoulders rose and fell perceptibly with his laboured breathing. The horse stood cowed with exhaustion and fear. Presently Margaret laid her hand on Eric's head and said gently:

"You are better now, shall we go on? Can you get your horse?"

"No, he has gone with the herd. I will lead yours, she is not safe. I will not frighten you again." His voice was still husky, but it was steady now. He took hold of the bit and tramped home in silence.

When they reached the house, Eric stood stolidly by the pony's head until Wyllis came to lift his sister from the saddle.

"The horses were badly frightened, Wyllis. I think I was pretty thoroughly scared myself," she said as she took her brother's arm and went slowly up the hill toward the house. "No, I'm not hurt, thanks to Eric. You must thank him for taking such good care of me. He's a mighty fine fellow. I'll tell you all about it in the morning, dear. I was pretty well shaken up and I'm going right to bed now. Good night."

When she reached the low room in which she slept, she sank upon the bed in her riding dress, face down-ward.

"Oh, I pity him! I pity him!" she murmured, with a

long sigh of exhaustion. She must have slept a little. When she rose again, she took from her dress a letter that had been waiting for her at the village post-office. It was closely written in a long, angular hand, covering a dozen pages of foreign note-paper, and began:

My Dearest Margaret: If I should attempt to say *how like a winter hath thine absence been,* I should incur the risk of being tedious. Really, it takes the sparkle out of everything. Having nothing better to do, and not caring to go anywhere in particular without you, I remained in the city until Jack Courtwell noted my general despondency and brought me down here to his place on the sound to manage some open-air theatricals he is getting up. *As You Like It* is of course the piece selected. Miss Harrison plays Rosalind. I wish you had been here to take the part. Miss Harrison reads her lines well, but she is either a maiden-all-forlorn or a tomboy; insists on reading into the part all sorts of deeper meanings and highly coloured suggestions wholly out of harmony with the pastoral setting. Like most of the professionals, she exaggerates the emotional element and quite fails to do justice to Rosalind's facile wit and really brilliant mental qualities. Gerard will do Orlando, but rumor says he is *épris* of your sometime friend, Miss Meredith, and his memory is treacherous and his interest fitful.

My new pictures arrived last week on the *Gascogne.* The Puvis de Chavannes is even more beautiful than I thought it in Paris. A pale dream-maiden sits by a pale dream-cow and a stream of anemic water flows at her feet. The

Constant, you will remember, I got because you
admired it. It is here in all its florid splendour,
the whole dominated by a glowing sensuosity.
The drapery of the female figure is as wonderful
as you said; the fabric all barbaric pearl and
gold, painted with an easy, effortless
voluptuousness, and that white, gleaming line of
African coast in the background recalls
memories of you very precious to me. But it is
useless to deny that Constant irritates me.
Though I cannot prove the charge against him,
his brilliancy always makes me suspect him of
cheapness.

Here Margaret stopped and glanced at the remaining pages of this strange love-letter. They seemed to be
filled chiefly with discussions of pictures and books,
and with a slow smile she laid them by.

She rose and began undressing. Before she lay down
she went to open the window. With her hand on the
sill, she hesitated, feeling suddenly as though some
danger were lurking outside, some inordinate desire
waiting to spring upon her in the darkness. She stood
there for a long time, gazing at the infinite sweep of
the sky.

"Oh, it is all so little, so little there," she murmured.
"When everything else is so dwarfed, why should one
expect love to be great? Why should one try to read
highly coloured suggestions into a life like that? If only I
could find one thing in it all that mattered greatly, one
thing that would warm me when I am alone! Will life
never give me that one great moment?"

As she raised the window, she heard a sound in the
plum bushes outside. It was only the house-dog
roused from his sleep, but Margaret started violently

and trembled so that she caught the foot of the bed for support. Again she felt herself pursued by some overwhelming longing, some desperate necessity for herself, like the outstretching of helpless, unseen arms in the darkness, and the air seemed heavy with sighs of yearning. She fled to her bed with the words, "I love you more than Christ who died for me!" ringing in her ears.

III

About midnight the dance at Lockhart's was at its height. Even the old men who had come to "look on" caught the spirit of revelry and stamped the floor with the vigor of old Silenus. Eric took the violin from the Frenchmen, and Minna Oleson sat at the organ, and the music grew more and more characteristic—rude, half mournful music, made up of the folksongs of the North, that the villagers sing through the long night in hamlets by the sea, when they are thinking of the sun, and the spring, and the fishermen so long away. To Margaret some of it sounded like Grieg's *Peer Gynt* music. She found something irresistibly infectious in the mirth of these people who were so seldom merry, and she felt almost one of them. Something seemed struggling for freedom in them tonight, something of the joyous childhood of the nations which exile had not killed. The girls were all boisterous with delight. Pleasure came to them but rarely, and when it came, they caught at it wildly and crushed its fluttering wings in their strong brown fingers. They had a hard life enough, most of them. Torrid summers and freezing winters, labour and drudgery and ignorance, were the portion of their girlhood; a short wooing, a hasty, loveless marriage, unlimited maternity, thankless sons, premature age and ugliness, were the dower of their womanhood. But what matter? Tonight there was hot liquor in the glass and hot blood in the heart; tonight they danced.

Tonight Eric Hermannson had renewed his youth. He was no longer the big, silent Norwegian who had sat at Margaret's feet and looked hoplessly into her eyes. Tonight he was a man, with a man's rights and a man's power. Tonight he was Siegfried indeed. His hair was yellow as the heavy wheat in the ripe of summer, and his eyes flashed like the blue water between the ice packs in the north seas. He was not afraid of Margaret tonight, and when he danced with her he held her firmly. She was tired and dragged on his arm a little, but the strength of the man was like an all-pervading fluid, stealing through her veins, awakening under her heart some nameless, unsuspected existence that had slumbered there all these years and that went out through her throbbing finger-tips to his that answered. She wondered if the hoydenish blood of some lawless ancestor, long asleep, were calling out in her tonight, some drop of a hotter fluid that the centuries had failed to cool, and why, if this curse were in her, it had not spoken before. But was it a curse, this awakening, this wealth before undiscovered, this music set free? For the first time in her life her heart held something stronger than herself, was not this worth while? Then she ceased to wonder. She lost sight of the lights and the faces and the music was drowned by the beating of her own arteries. She saw only the blue eyes that flashed above her, felt only the warmth of that throbbing hand which held hers and which the blood of his heart fed. Dimly, as in a dream, she saw the drooping shoulders, high white forehead and tight, cynical mouth of the man she was to marry in December. For an hour she had been crowding back the memory of that face with all her strength.

"Let us stop, this is enough," she whispered. His only answer was to tighten the arm behind her. She sighed and let that masterful strength bear her where it would. She forgot that this man was little more than a savage, that they would part at dawn. The blood has no memories, no reflections, no regrets for the past, no consideration of the future.

"Let us go out where it is cooler," she said when the music stopped; thinking, *I am growing faint here, I shall be all right in the open air.* They stepped out into the cool, blue air of the night.

Since the older folk had begun dancing, the young Norwegians had been slipping out in couples to climb the windmill tower into the cooler atmosphere, as is their custom.

"You like to go up?" asked Eric, close to her ear.

She turned and looked at him with suppressed amusement. "How high is it?"

"Forty feet, about. I not let you fall." There was a note of irresistible pleading in his voice, and she felt that he tremendously wished her to go. Well, why not? This was a night of the unusual, when she was not herself at all, but was living an unreality. Tomorrow, yes, in a few hours, there would be the Vestibule Limited and the world.

"Well, if you'll take good care of me. I used to be able to climb, when I was a little girl."

Once at the top and seated on the platform, they were silent. Margaret wondered if she would not hunger for that scene all her life, through all the routine of the days to come. Above them stretched the great Western sky, serenely blue, even in the night, with its big, burning stars, never so cold and dead and far away as in denser atmospheres. The moon would not be up for twenty minutes yet, and all about the horizon, that wide horizon, which seemed to reach around the world, lingered a pale white light, as of a universal dawn. The weary wind brought up to them the heavy odours of the cornfields. The music of the dance sounded faintly from below. Eric leaned on his elbow beside her, his legs swinging down on the ladder. His great shoulders looked more than ever like those of the stone Doryphorus, who stands in his perfect, reposeful strength in the Louvre, and had often made her wonder if such men died forever with the youth of Greece.

"How sweet the corn smells at night," said Margaret nervously.

"Yes, like the flowers that grow in paradise, I think."

She was somewhat startled by this reply, and more startled when this taciturn man spoke again.

"You go away tomorrow?"

"Yes, we have stayed longer than we thought to now."

"You not come back any more?"

"No, I expect not. You see, it is a long trip halfway across the continent."

"You soon forget about this country, I guess." It seemed to him now a little thing to lose his soul for this woman, but that she should utterly forget this night into which he threw all his life and all his eternity, that was a bitter thought.

"No, Eric, I will not forget. You have all been too kind to me for that. And you won't be sorry you danced this one night, will you?"

"I never be sorry. I have not been so happy before. I not be so happy again, ever. You will be happy many nights yet, I only this one. I will dream sometimes, maybe."

The mighty resignation of his tone alarmed and touched her. It was as when some great animal composes itself for death, as when a great ship goes down at sea.

She sighed, but did not answer him. He drew a little closer and looked into her eyes.

"You are not always happy, too?" he asked.

"No, not always, Eric; not very often, I think."

"You have a trouble?"

"Yes, but I cannot put it into words. Perhaps if I could do that, I could cure it."

He clasped his hands together over his heart, as children do when they pray, and said falteringly, "If I own all the world, I give him you."

Margaret felt a sudden moisture in her eyes, and laid her hand on his.

"Thank you, Eric; I believe you would. But perhaps even then I should not be happy. Perhaps I have too much of it already."

She did not take her hand away from him; she did not dare. She sat still and waited for the traditions in which she had always believed to speak and save her. But they were dumb. She belonged to an ultra-refined civilization which tries to cheat nature with elegant sophistries. Cheat nature? Bah! One generation may do it, perhaps two, but the third—Can we ever rise above nature or sink below her? Did she not turn on Jerusalem as upon Sodom, upon St. Anthony in his desert as upon Nero in his seraglio? Does she not always cry in brutal triumph: "I am here still, at the bottom of things, warming the roots of life; you cannot starve me nor tame me nor thwart me; I made the world, I rule it, and I am its destiny."

This woman, on a windmill tower at the world's end with a giant barbarian, heard that cry tonight, and she was afraid! Ah! the terror and the delight of that moment when first we fear ourselves! Until then we have not lived.

"Come, Eric, let us go down; the moon is up and the music has begun again," she said.

He rose silently and stepped down upon the ladder, putting his arm about her to help her. That arm could have thrown Thor's hammer out in the cornfields yonder, yet it scarcely touched her, and his hand trembled as it had done in the dance. His face was level with hers now and the moonlight fell sharply upon it. All her life she had searched the faces of men for the look that lay in his eyes. She knew that that look had never shone for her before, would never shine for her on earth again, that such love comes to one only in dreams or in impossible places like this, unattainable always. This was Love's self, in a moment it would die. Stung by the agonized appeal that emanated from the man's whole being, she leaned forward and laid her lips on his. Once, twice and again she heard the deep respirations rattle in his throat while she held them there, and the riotous force under her heart became an engulfing weakness. He drew her up to him until he felt all the resistance go out of her body, until every nerve relaxed and yielded. When she drew her face back from his, it was white with fear.

"Let us go down, oh, my God! let us go down!" she muttered. And the drunken stars up yonder seemed reeling to some appointed doom as she clung to the rounds of the ladder. All that she was to know of love she had left upon his lips.

"The devil is loose again," whispered Olaf Oleson,

as he saw Eric dancing a moment later, his eyes blazing.

But Eric was thinking with an almost savage exultation of the time when he should pay for this. Ah, there would be no quailing then! If ever a soul went fearlessly, proudly down to the gates infernal, his should go. For a moment he fancied he was there already, treading down the tempest of flame, hugging the fiery hurricane to his breast. He wondered whether in ages gone, all the countless years of sinning in which men had sold and lost and flung their souls away, any man had ever so cheated Satan, had ever bartered his soul for so great a price.

It seemed but a little while till dawn.

The carriage was brought to the door and Wyllis Elliot and his sister said goodbye. She could not meet Eric's eyes as she gave him her hand, but as he stood by the horse's head, just as the carriage moved off, she gave him one swift glance that said, "I will not forget." In a moment the carriage was gone.

Eric changed his coat and plunged his head into the water tank and went to the barn to hook up his team. As he led his horses to the door, a shadow fell across his path, and he saw Skinner rising in his stirrups. His rugged face was pale and worn with looking after his wayward flock, with dragging men into the way of salvation.

"Good morning, Eric. There was a dance here last night?" he asked, sternly.

"A dance? Oh, yes, a dance," replied Eric, cheerfully.

"Certainly you did not dance, Eric?"

"Yes, I danced. I danced all the time."

The minister's shoulders drooped, and an expression of profound discouragement settled over his haggard face. There was almost anguish in the yearning he felt for this soul.

"Eric, I didn't look for this from you. I thought God had set his mark on you if he ever had on any man. And it is for things like this that you set your soul back a thousand years from God. O foolish and perverse generation!"

Eric drew himself up to his full height and looked off to where the new day was gilding the corn-tassels and flooding the uplands with light. As his nostrils drew in the breath of the dew and the morning, something from the only poetry he had ever read flashed across his mind, and he murmured, half to himself, with dreamy exultation:

"'And a day shall be as a thousand years, and a thousand years as a day.'"

THE SCULPTOR'S
FUNERAL

A group of the townspeople stood on the station siding of a little Kansas town, awaiting the coming of the
night train, which was already twenty minutes over-
due. The snow had fallen thick over everything; in the
pale starlight the lines of bluffs across the wide, white
meadows south of the town made soft, smoke-coloured curves against the clear sky. The men on the
siding stood first on one foot and then on the other,
their hands thrust deep into their trousers pockets,
their overcoats open, their shoulders screwed up with
the cold; and they glanced from time to time toward
the southeast, where the railroad track wound along
the river shore. They conversed in low tones and
moved about restlessly, seeming uncertain as to what
was expected of them. There was but one of the company who looked as though he knew exactly why he
was there; and he kept conspicuously apart; walking

to the far end of the platform, returning to the station door, then pacing up the track again, his chin sunk in the high collar of his overcoat, his burly shoulders drooping forward, his gait heavy and dogged. Presently he was approached by a tall, spare, grizzled man clad in a faded Grand Army suit, who shuffled out from the group and advanced with a certain deference, craning his neck forward until his back made the angle of a jack-knife three-quarters open.

"I reckon she's-agoin' to be pretty late agin tonight, Jim," he remarked in a squeaky falsetto. "S'pose it's the snow?"

"I don't know," responded the other man with a shade of annoyance, speaking from out an astonishing cataract of red beard that grew fiercely and thickly in all directions.

The spare man shifted the quill toothpick he was chewing to the other side of his mouth. "It ain't likely that anybody from the East will come with the corpse, I s'pose," he went on reflectively.

"I don't know," responded the other, more curtly than before.

"It's too bad he didn't belong to some lodge or other. I like an order funeral myself. They seem more appropriate for people of some repytation," the spare man continued, with an ingratiating concession in his shrill voice, as he carefully placed his toothpick in his vest pocket. He always carried the flag at the G.A.R. funerals in the town.

The heavy man turned on his heel, without replying, and walked up the siding. The spare man shuffled back to the uneasy group. "Jim's ez full ez a tick, ez ushel," he commented commiseratingly.

Just then a distant whistle sounded, and there was a shuffling of feet on the platform. A number of lanky boys of all ages appeared as suddenly and slimily as eels wakened by the crack of thunder; some came from the waiting-room, where they had been warming themselves by the red stove, or half asleep on the slat benches; others uncoiled themselves from baggage trucks or slid out of express wagons. Two clambered down from the driver's seat of a hearse that stood backed up against the siding. They straightened their stooping shoulders and lifted their heads, and a flash of momentary animation kindled their dull eyes at that cold, vibrant scream, the world-wide call for men. It stirred them like the note of a trumpet; just as it had often stirred the man who was coming home to-night, in his boyhood.

The night express shot, red as a rocket, from out the eastward marsh lands and wound along the river shore under the long lines of shivering poplars that sentinelled the meadows, the escaping steam hanging in grey masses against the pale sky and blotting out the Milky Way. In a moment the red glare from the headlight streamed up the snow-covered track before the siding and glittered on the wet, black rails. The burly man with the dishevelled red beard walked swiftly up the platform toward the approaching train, uncovering his head as he went. The group of men behind him hesitated, glanced questioningly at one another, and awkwardly followed his example. The train stopped, and the crowd shuffled up to the express car just as the door was thrown open, the spare man in the G.A.R. suit thrusting his head forward with curiosity. The express messenger appeared in the doorway, accompanied by a young man in a long ulster and travelling cap.

"Are Mr. Merrick's friends here?" inquired the young man.

The group on the platform swayed and shuffled uneasily. Philip Phelps, the banker, responded with dignity: "We have come to take charge of the body. Mr. Merrick's father is very feeble and can't be about."

"Send the agent out here," growled the express messenger, "and tell the operator to lend a hand."

The coffin was got out of its rough box and down on the snowy platform. The townspeople drew back enough to make room for it and then formed a close semicircle about it, looking curiously at the palm leaf which lay across the black cover. No one said anything. The baggage man stood by his truck, waiting to get at the trunks. The engine panted heavily, and the fireman dodged in and out among the wheels with his yellow torch and long oil-can, snapping the spindle boxes. The young Bostonian, one of the dead sculptor's pupils who had come with the body, looked about him helplessly. He turned to the banker, the only one of that black, uneasy, stoop-shouldered group who seemed enough of an individual to be addressed.

"None of Mr. Merrick's brothers are here?" he asked uncertainly.

The man with the red beard for the first time stepped up and joined the group. "No, they have not come yet; the family is scattered. The body will be taken directly to the house." He stooped and took hold of one of the handles of the coffin.

"Take the long hill road up, Thompson, it will be easier on the horses," called the liveryman as the undertaker snapped the door of the hearse and prepared to mount to the driver's seat.

Laird, the red-bearded lawyer, turned again to the stranger: "We didn't know whether there would be any one with him or not," he explained. "It's a long walk, so you'd better go up in the hack." He pointed to a single battered conveyance, but the young man replied stiffly: "Thank you, but I think I will go up with the hearse. If you don't object," turning to the undertaker, "I'll ride with you."

They clambered up over the wheels and drove off in the starlight up the long, white hill toward the town. The lamps in the still village were shining from under the low, snow-burdened roofs; and beyond, on every side, the plains reached out into emptiness, peaceful and wide as the soft sky itself, and wrapped in a tangible, white silence.

When the hearse backed up to a wooden sidewalk before a naked, weather-beaten frame house, the same composite, ill-defined group that had stood upon the station siding was huddled about the gate. The front yard was an icy swamp, and a couple of warped planks, extending from the sidewalk to the door, made a sort of rickety footbridge. The gate hung on one hinge, and was opened wide with difficulty. Steavens, the young stranger, noticed that something black was tied to the knob of the front door.

The grating sound made by the casket, as it was drawn from the hearse, was answered by a scream from the house; the front door was wrenched open, and a tall, corpulent woman rushed out bareheaded into the snow and flung herself upon the coffin, shrieking: "My boy, my boy! And this is how you've come home to me!"

As Steavens turned away and closed his eyes with a shudder of unutterable repulsion, another woman, also tall, but flat and angular dressed entirely in black, darted out of the house and caught Mrs. Merrick by the shoulders, crying sharply: "Come, come, mother; you mustn't go on like this!" Her tone changed to one of obsequious solemnity as she turned to the banker: "The parlour is ready, Mr. Phelps."

The bearers carried the coffin along the narrow boards, while the undertaker ran ahead with the coffin rests. They bore it into a large, unheated room that smelled of dampness and disuse and furniture polish, and set it down under a hanging lamp ornamented with jingling glass prisms and before a "Rogers group" of John Alden and Priscilla, wreathed with smilax. Henry Steavens stared about him with the sickening conviction that there had been some horrible mistake, and that he had somehow arrived at the wrong destination. He looked painfully about over the clover-green Brussels, the fat plush upholstery; among the hand-painted china placques and panels and vases, for some mark of identification, for something that might once conceivably have belonged to Harvey Merrick. It was not until he recognized his friend in the crayon portrait of a little boy in kilts and curls, hanging above the piano, that he felt willing to let any of these people approach the coffin.

"Take the lid off, Mr. Thompson; let me see my boy's face," wailed the elder woman between her sobs. This time Steavens looked fearfully, almost beseechingly into her face, red and swollen under its masses of strong, black, shiny hair. He flushed, dropped his eyes, and then, almost incredulously, looked again. There was a kind of power about her face—a kind of brutal handsomeness, even; but it was scarred and furrowed by violence, and so coloured and coarsened by fiercer passions that grief seemed never to have laid a gentle finger there. The long nose was distended and knobbed at the end, and there were deep lines on either side of it; her heavy, black brows almost met across her forehead, her teeth were large and square, and set far apart—teeth that could tear. She filled the room; the men were obliterated, seemed tossed about like twigs in an angry water, and even Steavens felt himself being drawn into the whirlpool.

The daughter—the tall, raw-boned woman in crêpe, with a mourning comb in her hair which curiously lengthened her long face—sat stiffly upon the sofa, her hands, conspicuous for their large knuckles, folded in her lap, her mouth and eyes drawn down, solemnly awaiting the opening of the coffin. Near the door stood a mulatto woman, evidently a servant in the house, with a timid bearing and an emaciated face pitifully sad and gentle. She was weeping silently, the corner of her calico apron lifted to her eyes, occasionally suppressing a long, quivering sob. Steavens walked over and stood beside her.

Feeble steps were heard on the stairs, and an old man, tall and frail, odorous of pipe smoke, with shaggy, unkept grey hair and a dingy beard, tobacco stained about the mouth, entered uncertainly. He went slowly up to the coffin and stood rolling a blue cotton handkerchief between his hands, seeming so pained and embarrassed by his wife's orgy of grief that he had no consciousness of anything else.

"There, there, Annie, dear, don't take on so," he quavered timidly, putting out a shaking hand and awkwardly patting her elbow. She turned with a cry, and sank upon his shoulder with such violence that he tottered a little. He did not even glance toward the coffin, but continued to look at her with a dull, frightened, appealing expression, as a spaniel looks at the whip. His sunken cheeks slowly reddened and burned with miserable shame. When his wife rushed from the room, her daughter strode after her with set lips. The servant stole up to the coffin, bent over it for a moment, and then slipped away to the kitchen, leaving Steavens, the lawyer, and the father to themselves. The old man stood trembling and looking down at his dead son's face. The sculptor's splendid head seemed even more noble in its rigid stillness than in life. The dark hair had crept down upon the wide forehead; the face seemed strangely long, but in it there was not that beautiful and chaste repose which we expect to find in the faces of the dead. The brows were so drawn that there were two deep lines above the beaked nose, and the chin was thrust forward defiantly. It was as though the strain of life had been so sharp and bitter that death could not at once wholly relax the tension and smooth the countenance into perfect peace—as though he were still guarding something precious and holy, which might even yet be wrested from him.

The old man's lips were working under his stained beard. He turned to the lawyer with timid deference: "Phelps and the rest are comin' back to set up with Harve, ain't they?" he asked. "Thank 'ee, Jim, thank 'ee." He brushed the hair back gently from his son's forehead. "He was a good boy, Jim; always a good boy. He was ez gentle ez a child and the kindest of 'em all—only we didn't none of us ever onderstand him." The tears trickled slowly down his beard and dropped upon the sculptor's coat.

"Martin, Martin. Oh, Martin! come here," his wife wailed from the top of the stairs. The old man started timorously: "Yes, Annie, I'm coming." He turned away, hesitated, stood for a moment in miserable indecision; then reached back and patted the dead man's hair softly, and stumbled from the room.

"Poor old man, I didn't think he had any tears left. Seems as if his eyes would have gone dry long ago. At his age nothing cuts very deep," remarked the lawyer.

Something in his tone made Steavens glance up. While the mother had been in the room, the young man had scarcely seen any one else; but now, from the moment he first glanced into Jim Laird's florid face and blood-shot eyes, he knew that he had found what he had been heartsick at not finding before—the feeling, the understanding, that must exist in some one, even here.

The man was red as his beard, with features swollen and blurred by dissipation, and a hot, blazing blue eye. His face was strained—that of a man who is controlling himself with difficulty—and he kept plucking at his beard with a sort of fierce resentment. Steavens, sitting by the window, watched him turn down the glaring lamp, still its jangling pendants with an angry gesture, and then stand with his hands locked behind him, staring down into the master's face. He could not help wondering what link there could have been between the porcelain vessel and so sooty a lump of potter's clay.

From the kitchen an uproar was sounding; when the dining-room door opened, the import of it was clear. The mother was abusing the maid for having forgotten to make the dressing for the chicken salad which had been prepared for the watchers. Steavens had never heard anything in the least like it; it was injured, emotional, dramatic abuse, unique and masterly in its excruciating cruelty, as violent and unrestrained as had been her grief of twenty minutes before. With a shudder of disgust the lawyer went into the dining-room and closed the door into the kitchen.

"Poor Roxy's getting it now," he remarked when he came back. "The Merricks took her out of the poorhouse years ago; and if her loyalty would let her, I guess the poor old thing could tell tales that would curdle your blood. She's the mulatto woman who was standing in here a while ago, with her apron to her eyes. The old woman is a fury; there never was anybody like her for demonstrative piety and ingenious cruelty. She made Harvey's life a hell for him when he lived at home; he was so sick ashamed of it. I never could see how he kept himself so sweet."

"He was wonderful," said Steavens slowly, "wonderful; but until to-night I have never known how wonderful."

"That is the true and eternal wonder of it, anyway; that it can come even from such a dung heap as this," the lawyer cried, with a sweeping gesture which seemed to indicate much more than the four walls within which they stood.

"I think I'll see whether I can get a little air. The room is so close I am beginning to feel rather faint," murmured Steavens, struggling with one of the windows. The sash was stuck, however, and would not yield, so he sat down dejectedly and began pulling at his collar. The lawyer came over, loosened the sash with one blow of his red fist and sent the window up a few inches. Steavens thanked him, but the nausea which had been gradually climbing into his throat for the last half hour left him with but one desire—a desperate feeling that he must get away from this place with what was left of Harvey Merrick. Oh, he comprehended well enough now the quiet bitterness of the smile that he had seen so often on his master's lips!

He remembered that once, when Merrick returned from a visit home, he brought with him a singularly feeling and suggestive bas-relief of a thin, faded old woman, sitting and sewing something pinned to her knee; while a full-lipped, full-blooded little urchin, his trousers held up by a single gallows, stood beside her, impatiently twitching her gown to call her attention to a butterfly he had caught. Steavens, impressed by the tender and delicate modelling of the thin, tired face, had asked him if it were his mother. He remembered the dull flush that had burned up in the sculptor's face.

The lawyer was sitting in a rocking-chair beside the coffin, his head thrown back and his eyes closed. Steavens looked at him earnestly, puzzled at the line of the chin, and wondering why a man should conceal a feature of such distinction under that disfiguring shock of beard. Suddenly, as though he felt the young sculptor's keen glance, he opened his eyes.

"Was he always a good deal of an oyster?" he asked abruptly. "He was terribly shy as a boy."

"Yes, he was an oyster, since you put it so," rejoined Steavens. "Although he could be very fond of people, he always gave one the impression of being detached. He disliked violent emotion; he was reflective, and rather distrustful of himself—except, of course, as regarded his work. He was sure-footed enough there. He distrusted men pretty thoroughly and women even more, yet somehow without believing ill of them. He was determined, indeed, to believe the best, but he seemed afraid to investigate."

"A burnt dog dreads the fire," said the lawyer grimly, and closed his eyes.

Steavens went on and on, reconstructing that whole miserable boyhood. All this raw, biting ugliness had been the portion of the man whose tastes were refined beyond the limits of the reasonable—whose mind was an exhaustless gallery of beautiful impressions, and so sensitive that the mere shadow of a poplar leaf flickering against a sunny wall would be etched and held there forever. Surely, if ever a man had the magic word in his finger tips, it was Merrick. Whatever he touched, he revealed its holiest secret; liberated it from enchantment and restored it to its pristine loveliness, like the Arabian prince who fought the enchantress spell for spell. Upon whatever he had come in contact with, he had left a beautiful record of the experience—a sort of ethereal signature; a scent, a sound, a colour that was his own.

Steavens understood now the real tragedy of his master's life; neither love nor wine, as many had conjectured; but a blow which had fallen earlier and cut deeper than these could have done—a shame not his, and yet so unescapably his, to hide in his heart from his very boyhood. And without—the frontier warfare; the yearning of a boy, cast ashore upon a desert of newness and ugliness and sordidness, for all that is chastened and old, and noble with traditions.

At eleven o'clock the tall, flat woman in black crêpe entered and announced that the watchers were arriving, and asked them "to step into the dining-room." As Steavens rose, the lawyer said dryly: "You go on—it'll be a good experience for you, doubtless; as for me, I'm not equal to that crowd to-night; I've had twenty years of them."

As Steavens closed the door after him he glanced back at the lawyer, sitting by the coffin in the dim light, with his chin resting on his hand.

The same misty group that had stood before the door of the express car shuffled into the dining-room. In the light of the kerosene lamp they separated and became individuals. The minister, a pale, feeble-looking man with white hair and blond chin-whiskers, took his seat beside a small side table and placed his Bible upon it. The Grand Army man sat down behind the stove and tilted his chair back comfortably against the wall, fishing his quill toothpick from his waistcoat pocket. The two bankers, Phelps and Elder, sat off in a corner behind the dinner-table, where they could finish their discussion of the new usury law and its effect on chattel security loans. The real estate agent, an old man with a smiling, hypocritical face, soon joined them. The coal and lumber dealer and the cattle shipper sat on opposite sides of the hard coal-burner, their feet on the nickel-work. Steavens took a book from his pocket and began to read. The talk around him ranged through various topics of local interest while the house was quieting down. When it was clear that the members of the family were in bed, the Grand Army man hitched his shoulders and, untangling his long legs, caught his heels on the rounds of his chair.

"S'pose there'll be a will, Phelps?" he queried in his weak falsetto.

The banker laughed disagreeably, and began trimming his nails with a pearl-handled pocket-knife.

"There'll scarcely be any need for one, will there?" he queried in his turn.

The restless Grand Army man shifted his position again, getting his knees still nearer his chin. "Why, the ole man says Harve's done right well lately," he chirped.

The other banker spoke up. "I reckon he means by that Harve ain't asked him to mortgage any more farms lately, so as he could go on with his education."

"Seems like my mind don't reach back to a time when Harve wasn't bein' edycated," tittered the Grand Army man.

There was a general chuckle. The minister took out his handkerchief and blew his nose sonorously.

Banker Phelps closed his knife with a snap. "It's too bad the old man's sons didn't turn out better," he remarked with reflective authority. "They never hung together. He spent money enough on Harve to stock a dozen cattle-farms, and he might as well have poured it into Sand Creek. If Harve had stayed at home and helped nurse what little they had, and gone into stock on the old man's bottom farm, they might all have been well fixed. But the old man had to trust everything to tenants and was cheated right and left."

"Harve never could have handled stock none," interposed the cattleman. "He hadn't it in him to be sharp. Do you remember when he bought Sander's mules for eight-year olds, when everybody in town knew that Sander's father-in-law give 'em to his wife for a wedding present eighteen years before, an' they was full-grown mules then?"

Every one chuckled, and the Grand Army man rubbed his knees with a spasm of childish delight.

"Harve never was much account for anything practical, and he shore was never fond of work," began the coal and lumber dealer. "I mind the last time he was home; the day he left, when the old man was out to the barn helpin' his hand hitch up to take Harve to the train, and Cal Moots was patchin' up the fence, Harve, he come out on the step and sings out, in his ladylike voice: 'Cal Moots, Cal Moots! please come cord my trunk.'"

"That's Harve for you," approved the Grand Army man gleefully. "I kin hear him howlin' yet, when he was a big feller in long pants and his mother used to whale him with a rawhide in the barn for lettin' the cows git foundered in the cornfield when he was drivin' 'em home from pasture. He killed a cow of mine that-a-way onct—a pure Jersey and the best milker I had, an' the ole man had to put up for her. Harve, he was watchin' the sun set acrost the marshes when the anamile got away; he argued that sunset was oncommon fine."

"Where the old man made his mistake was in sending the boy East to school," said Phelps, stroking his goatee and speaking in a deliberate, judicial tone. "There was where he got his head full of trapseing to Paris and all such folly. What Harve needed, of all people, was a course in some first-class Kansas City business college."

The letters were swimming before Steavens's eyes. Was it possible that these men did not understand, that the palm on the coffin meant nothing to them? The very name of their town would have remained forever buried in the postal guide had it not been now and again mentioned in the world in connection with Harvey Merrick's. He remembered what his master had said to him on the day of his death, after the congestion of both lungs had shut off any probability of recovery, and the sculptor had asked his pupil to send his body home. "It's not a pleasant place to be lying while the world is moving and doing and bettering," he had said with a feeble smile, "but it rather seems as though we ought to go back to the place we came from in the end. The townspeople will come in for a look at me; and after they have had their say, I shan't have much to fear from the judgment of God. The wings of the Victory, in there"—with a weak gesture toward his studio—"will not shelter me."

The cattleman took up the comment. "Forty's young for a Merrick to cash in; they usually hang on pretty well. Probably he helped it along with whisky."

"His mother's people were not long lived, and Harvey never had a robust constitution," said the minister mildly. He would have liked to say more. He had been the boy's Sunday-school teacher, and had been fond of him; but he felt that he was not in a position to speak. His own sons had turned out badly, and it was not a year since one of them had made his last trip home in the express car, shot in a gambling-house in the Black Hills.

"Nevertheless, there is no disputin' that Harve frequently looked upon the wine when it was red, also variegated, and it shore made an oncommon fool of him," moralized the cattleman.

Just then the door leading into the parlour rattled loudly and every one started involuntarily, looking relieved when only Jim Laird came out. His red face was convulsed with anger, and the Grand Army man ducked his head when he saw the spark in his blue, blood-shot eye. They were all afraid of Jim; he was a drunkard, but he could twist the law to suit his client's needs as no other man in all western Kansas could do; and there were many who tried. The lawyer closed the door gently behind him, leaned back against it and folded his arms, cocking his head a little to one side. When he assumed this attitude in the court-room, ears were always pricked up, as it usually foretold a flood of withering sarcasm.

"I've been with you gentlemen before," he began in a dry, even tone, "when you've sat by the coffins of boys born and raised in this town; and, if I remember rightly, you were never any too well satisfied when you checked them up. What's the matter, anyhow? Why is it that reputable young men are as scarce as millionaires in Sand City? It might almost seem to a stranger that there was some way something the matter with your progressive town. Why did Ruben Sayer, the brightest young lawyer you ever turned out, after

he had come home from the university as straight as a
die, take to drinking and forge a check and shoot
himself? Why did Bill Merrit's son die of the shakes in
a saloon in Omaha? Why was Mr. Thomas's son,
here, shot in a gambling-house? Why did young
Adams burn his mill to beat the insurance companies
and go to the pen?"

The lawyer paused and unfolded his arms, laying
one clenched fist quietly on the table. "I'll tell you
why. Because you drummed nothing but money and
knavery into their ears from the time they wore
knickerbockers; because you carped away at them as
you've been carping here to-night, holding our friends
Phelps and Elder up to them for their models, as our
grandfathers held up George Washington and John
Adams. But the boys, worse luck, were young, and
raw at the business you put them to; and how could
they match coppers with such artists as Phelps and
Elder? You wanted them to be successful rascals; they
were only unsuccessful ones—that's all the difference.
There was only one boy ever raised in this borderland
between ruffianism and civilization who didn't come
to grief, and you hated Harvey Merrick more for win-
ning out than you hated all the other boys who got
under the wheels. Lord, Lord, how you did hate him!
Phelps, here, is fond of saying that he could buy and
sell us all out any time he's a mind to; but he knew
Harve wouldn't have given a tinker's damn for his
bank and all his cattle-farms put together; and a lack
of appreciation, that way, goes hard with Phelps.

"Old Nimrod, here, thinks Harve drank too much;
and this from such as Nimrod and me!

"Brother Elder says Harve was too free with the old
man's money—fell short in filial consideration,
maybe. Well, we can all remember the very tone in

which brother Elder swore his own father was a liar, in the county court; and we all know that the old man came out of that partnership with his son as bare as a sheared lamb. But maybe I'm getting personal, and I'd better be driving ahead at what I want to say."

The lawyer paused a moment, squared his heavy shoulders, and went on: "Harvey Merrick and I went to school together, back East. We were dead in earnest, and we wanted you all to be proud of us some day. We meant to be great men. Even I, and I haven't lost my sense of humour, gentlemen, I meant to be a great man. I came back here to practise, and I found you didn't in the least want me to be a great man. You wanted me to be a shrewd lawyer—oh, yes! Our veteran here wanted me to get him an increase of pension, because he had dyspepsia; Phelps wanted a new county survey that would put the widow Wilson's little bottom farm inside his south line; Elder wanted to lend money at 5 per cent a month, and get it collected; old Stark here wanted to wheedle old women up in Vermont into investing their annuities in real-estate mortgages that are not worth the paper they are written on. Oh, you needed me hard enough, and you'll go on needing me; and that's why I'm not afraid to plug the truth home to you this once.

"Well, I came back here and became the damned shyster you wanted me to be. You pretend to have some sort of respect for me; and yet you'll stand up and throw mud at Harvey Merrick, whose soul you couldn't dirty and whose hands you couldn't tie. Oh, you're a discriminating lot of Christians! There have been times when the sight of Harvey's name in some Eastern paper has made me hang my head like a whipped dog; and, again, times when I liked to think of him off there in the world, away from all this hog-wallow, doing his great work and climbing the big, clean up-grade he'd set for himself.

"And we? Now that we've fought and lied and sweated and stolen, and hated as only the disappointed strugglers in a bitter, dead little Western town know how to do, what have we got to show for it? Harvey Merrick wouldn't have given one sunset over your marshes for all you've got put together, and you know it. It's not for me to say why, in the inscrutable wisdom of God, a genius should ever have been called from this place of hatred and bitter waters; but I want this Boston man to know that the drivel he's been hearing here to-night is the only tribute any truly great man could ever have from such a lot of sick, sidetracked, burnt-dog, land-poor sharks as the herepresent financiers of Sand City—upon which town may God have mercy!"

The lawyer thrust out his hand to Steavens as he passed him, caught up his overcoat in the hall, and had left the house before the Grand Army man had had time to lift his ducked head and crane his long neck about at his fellows.

Next day Jim Laird was drunk and unable to attend the funeral services. Steavens called twice at his office, but was compelled to start East without seeing him. He had a presentiment that he would hear from him again, and left his address on the lawyer's table; but if Laird found it, he never acknowledged it. The thing in him that Harvey Merrick had loved must have gone under ground with Harvey Merrick's coffin; for it never spoke again, and Jim got the cold he died of driving across the Colorado mountains to defend one of Phelps's sons who had got into trouble out there by cutting government timber.

A WAGNER
MATINEE

I received one morning a letter, written in pale ink on glassy, blue-lined note-paper, and bearing the postmark of a little Nebraska village. This communication, worn and rubbed, looking as though it had been carried for some days in a coat pocket that was none too clean, was from my uncle Howard and informed me that his wife had been left a small legacy by a bachelor relative who had recently died, and that it would be necessary for her to go to Boston to attend the settling of the estate. He requested me to meet her at the station and render her whatever services might be necessary. On examining the date indicated as that of her arrival, I found it no later than tomorrow. He had characteristically delayed writing until, had I been away from home for a day, I must have missed the good woman altogether.

The name of my Aunt Georgiana called up not

alone her own figure, at once pathetic and grotesque, but opened before my feet a gulf of recollection so wide and deep that, as the letter dropped from my hand, I felt suddenly a stranger to all the present conditions of my existence, wholly ill at ease and out of place amid the familiar surroundings of my study. I became, in short, the gangling farmer-boy my aunt had known, scourged with chilblains and bashfulness, my hands cracked and sore from the corn husking. I felt the knuckles of my thumb tentatively, as though they were raw again. I sat again before her parlour organ, fumbling the scales with my stiff, red hands, while she, beside me, made canvas mittens for the huskers.

The next morning, after preparing my landlady somewhat, I set out for the station. When the train arrived I had some difficulty in finding my aunt. She was the last of the passengers to alight, and it was not until I got her into the carriage that she seemed really to recognize me. She had come all the way in a day coach; her linen duster had become black with soot and her black bonnet grey with dust during the journey. When we arrived at my boarding-house the landlady put her to bed at once and I did not see her again until the next morning.

Whatever shock Mrs. Springer experienced at my aunt's appearance, she considerately concealed. As for myself, I saw my aunt's misshapen figure with that feeling of awe and respect for which we behold explorers who have left their ears and fingers north of Franz Josef Land, or their health somewhere along the Upper Congo. My Aunt Georgiana had been a music teacher at the Boston Conservatory, somewhere back in the latter sixties. One summer, while visiting the little village among the Green Mountains where her ancestors had dwelt for generations, she had kindled the callow fancy of the most idle and shiftless of all the village lads, and had conceived for this Howard Carpenter one of those extravagant passions which a handsome country boy of twenty-one sometimes inspires in an angular, spectacled woman of thirty. When she returned to her duties in Boston, Howard followed her, and the upshot of this inexplicable infatuation was that she eloped with him, eluding the reproaches of her family and the criticisms of her friends by going with him to the Nebraska frontier. Carpenter, who, of course, had no money, had taken a homestead in Red Willow County, fifty miles from the railroad. There they had measured off their quarter section themselves by driving across the prairie in a wagon, to the wheel of which they had tied a red cotton handkerchief, and counting off its revolutions. They built a dugout in the red hillside, one of those cave dwellings whose inmates so often reverted to primitive conditions. Their water they got from the lagoons where the buffalo drank, and their slender stock of provisions was always at the mercy of bands of roving Indians. For thirty years my aunt had not been farther than fifty miles from the homestead.

But Mrs. Springer knew nothing of all this, and must have been considerably shocked at what was left of my kinswoman. Beneath the soiled linen duster which, on her arrival, was the most conspicuous feature of her costume, she wore a black stuff dress, whose ornamentation showed that she had surrendered herself unquestioningly into the hands of a country dressmaker. My poor aunt's figure, however, would have presented astonishing difficulties to any dressmaker. Originally stooped, her shoulders were now almost bent together over her sunken chest. She wore no stays, and her gown, which trailed unevenly behind, rose in a sort of peak over her abdomen. She wore ill-fitting false teeth, and her skin was as yellow as a Mongolian's from constant exposure to a pitiless wind and to the alkaline water which hardens the most transparent cuticle into a sort of flexible leather.

I owed to this woman most of the good that ever came my way in my boyhood, and had a reverential affection for her. During the years when I was riding herd for my uncle, my aunt, after cooking the three meals—the first of which was ready at six o'clock in the morning—and putting the six children to bed, would often stand until midnight at her ironing-board, with me at the kitchen table beside her, hearing me recite Latin declensions and conjugations, gently shaking me when my drowsy head sank down over a page of irregular verbs. It was to her, at her ironing or mending, that I read my first Shakspere, and her old text-book on mythology was the first that ever came into my empty hands. She taught me my scales and exercises, too—on the little parlour organ which her husband had bought her after fifteen years, during which she had not so much as seen any instrument, but an accordion that belonged to one of the Norwegian farm-hands. She would sit beside me by the hour, darning and counting, while I struggled with the "Joyous Farmer," but she seldom talked to me about music, and I understood why. She was a pious woman; she had the consolations of religion and, to her at least, her martyrdom was not wholly sordid. Once when I had been doggedly beating out some easy passages from an old score of *Euryanthe* I had found among her music books, she came up to me and, putting her hands over my eyes, gently drew my head back upon her shoulder, saying tremulously,

"Don't love it so well, Clark, or it may be taken from you. Oh! dear boy, pray that whatever your sacrifice may be, it be not that."

When my aunt appeared on the morning after her arrival, she was still in a semi-somnambulant state. She seemed not to realize that she was in the city where she had spent her youth, the place longed for hungrily half a lifetime. She had been so wretchedly train-sick throughout the journey that she had no recollection of anything but her discomfort, and, to all intents and purposes, there were but a few hours of nightmare between the farm in Red Willow County and my study on Newbury Street. I had planned a little pleasure for her that afternoon, to repay her for some of the glorious moments she had given me when we used to milk together in the strawthatched cowshed and she, because I was more than usually tired, or because her husband had spoken sharply to me, would tell me of the splendid performance of the *Huguenots* she had seen in Paris, in her youth. At two o'clock the Symphony Orchestra was to give a Wagner programme, and I intended to take my aunt; though, as I conversed with her, I grew doubtful about her enjoyment of it. Indeed, for her own sake, I could only wish her taste for such things quite dead, and the long struggle mercifully ended at last. I suggested our visiting the Conservatory and the Common before lunch, but she seemed altogether too timid to wish to venture out. She questioned me absently about various changes in the city, but she was chiefly concerned that she had forgotten to leave instructions about feeding half-skimmed milk to a certain weakling calf, "old Maggie's calf, you know, Clark," she explained, evidently having forgotten how long I had been away. She was further troubled because she had neglected to tell her daughter about the freshly-opened kit of mackerel in the cellar, which would spoil if it were not used directly.

I asked her whether she had ever heard any of the Wagnerian operas, and found that she had not, though she was perfectly familiar with their respective situations, and had once possessed the piano score of *The Flying Dutchman*. I began to think it would have been best to get her back to Red Willow County without waking her, and regretted having suggested the concert.

From the time we entered the concert hall, however, she was a trifle less passive and inert, and for the first time seemed to perceive her surroundings. I had felt some trepidation lest she might become aware of the absurdities of her attire, or might experience some painful embarrassment at stepping suddenly into the world to which she had been dead for more than a quarter of a century. But, again, I found how superficially I had judged her. She sat looking about her with eyes as impersonal, almost as stony, as those with which the granite Rameses in a museum watches the froth and fret that ebbs and flows about his pedestal —separated from it by the lonely stretch of centuries. I have seen this same aloofness in old miners who drift into the Brown Hotel at Denver, their pockets full of bullion, their linen soiled, their haggard faces unshaven; standing in the thronged corridors as solitary as though they were still in a frozen camp on the Yukon, conscious that certain experiences have isolated them from their fellows by a gulf no haberdasher could bridge.

We sat at the extreme left of the first balcony, facing the arc of our own and the balcony above us, veritable hanging gardens, brilliant as tulip beds. The matinée audience was made up chiefly of women. One lost the contour of faces and figures, indeed any effect of line whatever, and there was only the colour of bodices past counting, the shimmer of fabrics soft and firm, silky and sheer; red, mauve, pink, blue, lilac, purple, ecru, rose, yellow, cream, and white, all the colours that an impressionist finds in a sunlit landscape, with here and there the dead shadow of a frock coat. My Aunt Georgiana regarded them as though they had been so many daubs of tube-paint on a palette.

When the musicians came out and took their places, she gave a little stir of anticipation, and looked with quickening interest down over the rail at that invariable grouping, perhaps the first wholly familiar thing that had greeted her eye since she had left old Maggie and her weakling calf. I could feel how all those details sank into her soul, for I had not forgotten how they had sunk into mine when I came fresh from ploughing forever and forever between green aisles of corn, where, as in a treadmill, one might walk from daybreak to dusk without perceiving a shadow of change. The clean profiles of the musicians, the gloss of their linen, the dull black of their coats, the beloved shapes of the instruments, the patches of yellow light thrown by the green shaded lamps on the smooth, varnished bellies of the 'cellos and the bass viols in the rear, the restless, wind-tossed forest of fiddle necks and bows—I recalled how, in the first orchestra I had ever heard, those long bow strokes seemed to draw the heart out of me, as a conjurer's stick reels out yards of paper ribbon from a hat.

The first number was the *Tannhäuser* overture. When the horns drew out the first strain of the Pilgrim's chorus, my Aunt Georgiana clutched my coat sleeve. Then it was I first realized that for her this broke a silence of thirty years; the inconceivable silence of the plains. With the battle between the two motives, with the frenzy of the Venusberg theme and its ripping of strings, there came to me an overwhelming sense of the waste and wear we are so powerless to combat; and I saw again the tall, naked house on the prairie, black and grim as a wooden fortress; the black pond where I had learned to swim, its margin pitted with sun-dried cattle tracks; the rain gullied clay banks about the naked house, the four dwarf ash seedlings where the dish-cloths were always hung to dry before the kitchen door. The world there was the flat world of the ancients; to the east, a cornfield that stretched to daybreak; to the west, a corral that reached to sunset; between, the conquests of peace, dearer bought than those of war.

The overture closed, my aunt released my coat sleeve, but she said nothing. She sat staring at the orchestra through a dullness of thirty years, through the films made little by little by each of the three hundred and sixty-five days in every one of them. What, I wondered, did she get from it? She had been a good pianist in her day I knew, and her musical education had been broader than that of most music teachers of a quarter of a century ago. She had often told me of Mozart's operas and Meyerbeer's, and I could remember hearing her sing, years ago, certain melodies of Verdi's. When I had fallen ill with a fever in her house she used to sit by my cot in the evening—when the cool, night wind blew in through the faded mosquito netting tacked over the window and I lay watching a certain bright star that burned red above the cornfield—and sing "Home to our mountains, O, let us return!" in a way fit to break the heart of a

Vermont boy near dead of homesickness already.

I watched her closely through the prelude to *Tristan and Isolde,* trying vainly to conjecture what that seething turmoil of strings and winds might mean to her, but she sat mutely staring at the violin bows that drove obliquely downward, like the pelting streaks of rain in a summer shower. Had this music any message for her? Had she enough left to at all comprehend this power which had kindled the world since she had left it? I was in a fever of curiosity, but Aunt Georgiana sat silent upon her peak in Darien. She preserved this utter immobility throughout the number from *The Flying Dutchman,* though her fingers worked mechanically upon her black dress, as though, of themselves, they were recalling the piano score they had once played. Poor old hands! They had been stretched and twisted into mere tentacles to hold and lift and knead with; the palm, unduly swollen, the fingers bent and knotted—on one of them a thin, worn band that had once been a wedding ring. As I pressed and gently quieted one of those groping hands, I remembered with quivering eyelids their services for me in other days.

Soon after the tenor began the "Prize Song," I heard a quick drawn breath and turned to my aunt. Her eyes were closed, but the tears were glistening on her cheeks, and I think, in a moment more, they were in my eyes as well. It never really died, then—the soul that can suffer so excruciatingly and so interminably; it withers to the outward eye only; like that strange moss which can lie on a dusty shelf half a century and yet, if placed in water, grows green again. She wept so throughout the development and elaboration of the melody.

During the intermission before the second half of the concert, I questioned my aunt and found that the "Prize Song" was not new to her. Some years before there had drifted to the farm in Red Willow County a young German, a tramp cow-puncher, who had sung in the chorus at Bayreuth, when he was a boy, along with the other peasant boys and girls. Of a Sunday morning he used to sit on his gingham-sheeted bed in the hands' bedroom which opened off the kitchen, cleaning the leather of his boots and saddle, singing the "Prize Song," while my aunt went about her work in the kitchen. She had hovered about him until she had prevailed upon him to join the country church, though his sole fitness for this step, in so far as I could gather, lay in his boyish face and his possession of this divine melody. Shortly afterward he had gone to town on the Fourth of July, been drunk for several days, lost his money at a faro table, ridden a saddled Texas steer on a bet, and disappeared with a fractured collar-bone. All this my aunt told me huskily, wanderingly, as though she were talking in the weak lapses of illness.

"Well, we have come to better things than the old *Trovatore* at any rate, Aunt Georgie?" I queried, with a well meant effort at jocularity.

Her lip quivered and she hastily put her handkerchief up to her mouth. From behind it she murmured, "And you have been hearing this ever since you left me, Clark?" Her question was the gentlest and saddest of reproaches.

The second half of the programme consisted of four numbers from the *Ring,* and closed with Siegfried's funeral march. My aunt wept quietly, but almost continuously, as a shallow vessel overflows in a rainstorm. From time to time her dim eyes looked up at the lights which studded the ceiling, burning softly under their dull glass globes; doubtless they were stars in truth to her. I was still perplexed as to what measure of musical comprehension was left to her, she who had heard nothing but the singing of Gospel Hymns at Methodist services in the square frame schoolhouse on Section Thirteen for so many years. I was wholly unable to gauge how much of it had been dissolved in soapsuds, or worked into bread, or milked into the bottom of a pail.

The deluge of sound poured on and on; I never knew what she found in the shining current of it; I never knew how far it bore her, or past what happy islands. From the trembling of her face I could well believe that before the last numbers she had been carried out where the myriad graves are, into the grey, nameless burying grounds of the sea; or into some world of death vaster yet, where, from the beginning of the world, hope has lain down with hope and dream with dream and, renouncing, slept.

The concert was over; the people filed out of the hall chattering and laughing, glad to relax and find the living level again, but my kinswoman made no effort to rise. The harpist slipped its green felt cover over his instrument; the flute-players shook the water from their mouthpieces; the men of the orchestra went out one by one, leaving the stage to the chairs and music stands, empty as a winter cornfield.

I spoke to my aunt. She burst into tears and sobbed pleadingly. "I don't want to go, Clark. I don't want to go!"

I understood. For her, just outside the door of the concert hall, lay the black pond with the cattle-tracked bluffs; the tall, unpainted house, with weather-curled boards; naked as a tower, the crook-backed ash seedlings where the dish-cloths hung to dry; the gaunt, moulting turkeys picking up refuse about the kitchen door.

PAUL'S CASE

A Study in Temperament

It was Paul's afternoon to appear before the faculty of the Pittsburgh High School to account for his various misdemeanours. He had been suspended a week ago, and his father had called at the Principal's office and confessed his perplexity about his son. Paul entered the faculty room suave and smiling. His clothes were a trifle out-grown and the tan velvet on the collar of his open overcoat was frayed and worn; but for all that there was something of the dandy about him, and he wore an opal pin in his neatly knotted black four-in-hand, and a red carnation in his button-hole. This latter adornment the faculty somehow felt was not properly significant of the contrite spirit befitting a boy under the ban of suspension.

Paul was tall for his age and very thin, with high, cramped shoulders and a narrow chest. His eyes were remarkable for a certain hysterical brilliancy, and he continually used them in a conscious, theatrical sort of way, peculiarly offensive in a boy. The pupils were abnormally large, as though he were addicted to belladonna, but there was a glassy glitter about them which that drug does not produce.

When questioned by the Principal as to why he was there, Paul stated, politely enough, that he wanted to come back to school. This was a lie, but Paul was quite accustomed to lying; found it, indeed, indispensable for overcoming friction. His teachers were asked to state their respective charges against him, which they did with such a rancour and aggrievedness as evinced that this was not a usual case. Disorder and impertinence were among the offences named, yet each of his instructors felt that it was scarcely possible to put into words the real cause of the trouble, which lay in a sort of hysterically defiant manner of the boy's; in the contempt which they all knew he felt for them, and which he seemingly made not the least effort to conceal. Once, when he had been making a synopsis of a paragraph at the blackboard, his English teacher had stepped to his side and attempted to guide his hand. Paul had started back with a shudder and thrust his hands violently behind him. The astonished woman could scarcely have been more hurt and embarrassed had he struck at her. The insult was so involuntary and definitely personal as to be unforgettable. In one way and another, he had made all his teachers, men and women alike, conscious of the same feeling of physical aversion. In one class he habitually sat with his hand shading his eyes; in another he always looked out of the window during the recitation; in another he made a running commentary on the lecture, with humorous intention.

His teachers felt this afternoon that his whole attitude was symbolized by his shrug and his flippantly red carnation flower, and they fell upon him without mercy, his English teacher leading the pack. He stood through it smiling, his pale lips parted over his white teeth. (His lips were continually twitching, and he had a habit of raising his eyebrows that was contemptuous and irritating to the last degree.) Older boys than Paul had broken down and shed tears under that baptism of fire, but his set smile did not once desert him, and his only sign of discomfort was the nervous trembling of the fingers that toyed with the buttons of his overcoat, and an occasional jerking of the other hand that held his hat. Paul was always smiling, always glancing about him, seeming to feel that people might be watching him and trying to detect something. This conscious expression, since it was as far as possible from boyish mirthfulness, was usually attributed to insolence or "smartness."

As the inquisition proceeded, one of his instructors repeated an impertinent remark of the boy's, and the Principal asked him whether he thought that a courteous speech to have made a woman. Paul shrugged his shoulders slightly and his eyebrows twitched.

"I don't know," he replied. "I didn't mean to be polite or impolite, either. I guess it's a sort of way I have of saying things regardless."

The Principal, who was a sympathetic man, asked him whether he didn't think that a way it would be well to get rid of. Paul grinned and said he guessed so. When he was told that he could go, he bowed gracefully and went out. His bow was but a repetition of the scandalous red carnation.

His teachers were in despair, and his drawing master voiced the feeling of them all when he declared there was something about the boy which none of them understood. He added: "I don't really believe that smile of his comes altogether from insolence; there's something sort of haunted about it. The boy is not strong, for one thing. I happen to know that he was born in Colorado, only a few months before his mother died out there of a long illness. There is something wrong about the fellow."

The drawing master had come to realize that, in looking at Paul, one saw only his white teeth and the forced animation of his eyes. One warm afternoon the boy had gone to sleep at his drawing-board, and his master had noted with amazement what a white, blue-veined face it was; drawn and wrinkled like an old man's about the eyes, the lips twitching even in his sleep, and stiff with a nervous tension that drew them back from his teeth.

His teachers left the building dissatisfied and unhappy; humiliated to have felt so vindictive toward a mere boy, to have uttered this feeling in cutting terms, and to have set each other on, as it were, in the grewsome game of intemperate reproach. Some of them remembered having seen a miserable street cat set at bay by a ring of tormentors.

As for Paul, he ran down the hill whistling the Soldiers' Chorus from *Faust* looking wildly behind him now and then to see whether some of his teachers were not there to writhe under his light-heartedness. As it was now late in the afternoon and Paul was on duty that evening as usher at Carnegie Hall, he decided that he would not go home to supper. When he reached the concert hall the doors were not yet open and, as it was chilly outside, he decided to go up into the picture gallery—always deserted at this hour—where there were some of Raffaelli's gay studies of Paris streets and an airy blue Venetian scene or two that always exhilarated him. He was delighted to find no one in the gallery but the old guard, who sat in one corner, a newspaper on his knee, a black patch over one eye and the other closed. Paul possessed himself of the place and walked confidently up and down, whistling under his breath. After a while he sat down before a blue Rico and lost himself. When he bethought him to look at his watch, it was after seven o'clock, and he rose with a start and ran downstairs, making a face at Augustus, peering out from the castroom, and an evil gesture at the Venus of Milo as he passed her on the stairway.

When Paul reached the ushers' dressing-room half-a-dozen boys were there already, and he began excitedly to tumble into his uniform. It was one of the few that at all approached fitting, and Paul thought it very becoming—though he knew that the tight, straight coat accentuated his narrow chest, about which he was exceedingly sensitive. He was always considerably excited while he dressed, twanging all over to the tuning of the strings and the preliminary flourishes of the horns in the music-room; but tonight he seemed quite beside himself, and he teased and plagued the boys until, telling him that he was crazy, they put him down on the floor and sat on him.

Somewhat calmed by his suppression, Paul dashed out to the front of the house to seat the early comers. He was a model usher; gracious and smiling he ran up and down the aisles; nothing was too much trouble for him; he carried messages and brought programmes as though it were his greatest pleasure in life, and all the people in his section thought him a charming boy, feeling that he remembered and admired them. As the house filled, he grew more and more vivacious and animated, and the colour came to his

cheeks and lips. It was very much as though this were
a great reception and Paul were the host. Just as the
musicians came out to take their places, his English
teacher arrived with checks for the seats which a
prominent manufacturer had taken for the season. She
betrayed some embarrassment when she handed Paul
the tickets, and a *hauteur* which subsequently made
her feel very foolish. Paul was startled for a moment,
and had the feeling of wanting to put her out; what
business had she here among all these fine people and
gay colours? He looked her over and decided that she
was not appropriately dressed and must be a fool to
sit downstairs in such togs. The tickets had probably
been sent her out of kindness, he reflected as he put
down a seat for her, and she had about as much right
to sit there as he had.

When the symphony began Paul sank into one of
the rear seats with a long sigh of relief, and lost himself as he had done before the Rico. It was not that
symphonies, as such, meant anything in particular to
Paul, but the first sigh of the instruments seemed to
free some hilarious and potent spirit within him;
something that struggled there like the Genius in the
bottle found by the Arab fisherman. He felt a sudden
zest for life; the lights danced before his eyes and the
concert hall blazed into unimaginable splendour.
When the soprano soloist came on, Paul forgot even
the nastiness of his teacher's being there and gave
himself up to the peculiar stimulus such personages
always had for him. The soloist chanced to be a German woman, by no means in her first youth, and the
mother of many children; but she wore an elaborate
gown and a tiara, and above all she had that indefin-
able air of achievement, that world-shine upon her,

which, in Paul's eyes, made her a veritable queen of Romance.

After a concert was over Paul was always irritable and wretched until he got to sleep, and tonight he was even more than usually restless. He had the feeling of not being able to let down, of its being impossible to give up this delicious excitement which was the only thing that could be called living at all. During the last number he withdrew and, after hastily changing his clothes in the dressing-room, slipped out to the side door where the soprano's carriage stood. Here he began pacing rapidly up and down the walk, waiting to see her come out.

Over yonder the Schenley, in its vacant stretch, loomed big and square through the fine rain, the windows of its twelve stories glowing like those of a lighted card-board house under a Christmas tree. All the actors and singers of the better class stayed there when they were in the city, and a number of the big manufacturers of the place lived there in the winter. Paul had often hung about the hotel, watching the people go in and out, longing to enter and leave school-masters and dull care behind him forever.

At last the singer came out, accompanied by the conductor, who helped her into her carriage and closed the door with a cordial *auf wiedersehen,* which set Paul to wondering whether she were not an old sweetheart of his. Paul followed the carriage over to the hotel, walking so rapidly as not to be far from the entrance when the singer alighted and disappeared behind the swinging glass doors that were opened by a negro in a tall hat and a long coat. In the moment that the door was ajar, it seemed to Paul that he, too, entered. He seemed to feel himself go after her up the steps, into the warm, lighted building, into an exotic, a tropical world of shiny, glistening surfaces and basking ease. He reflected upon the mysterious dishes that were brought into the dining-room, the green bottles in buckets of ice, as he had seen them in the supper party pictures of the *Sunday World* supplement. A quick gust of wind brought the rain down with sudden vehemence, and Paul was startled to find that he was still outside in the slush of the gravel driveway; that his boots were letting in the water and his scanty overcoat was clinging wet about him; that the lights in front of the concert hall were out, and that the rain was driving in sheets between him and the orange glow of the windows above him. There it was, what he wanted—tangibly before him, like the fairy world of a Christmas pantomime, but mocking spirits stood guard at the doors, and, as the rain beat in his face, Paul wondered whether he were destined always to shiver in the black night outside, looking up at it.

He turned and walked reluctantly toward the car tracks. The end had to come sometime; his father in his night-clothes at the top of the stairs, explanations that did not explain, hastily improvised fictions that were forever tripping him up, his upstairs room and its horrible yellow wall-paper, the creaking bureau with the greasy plush collarbox, and over his painted wooden bed the pictures of George Washington and John Calvin, and the framed motto, "Feed my Lambs," which had been worked in red worsted by his mother.

Half an hour later, Paul alighted from his car and went slowly down one of the side streets off the main thoroughfare. It was a highly respectable street, where all the houses were exactly alike, and where business men of moderate means begot and reared large families of children, all of whom went to Sabbath-school and learned the shorter catechism, and were interested in arithmetic; all of whom were as exactly alike as their homes, and of a piece with the monotony in which they lived. Paul never went up Cordelia Street without a shudder of loathing. His home was next the house of the Cumberland minister. He approached it tonight with the nerveless sense of defeat, the hopeless feeling of sinking back forever into ugliness and commonness that he had always had when he came home. The moment he turned into Cordelia Street he felt the waters close above his head. After each of these orgies of living, he experienced all the physical depression which follows a debauch; the loathing of respectable beds, of common food, of a house permeated by kitchen odours; a shuddering repulsion for the flavourless, colourless mass of every-day existence; a morbid desire for cool things and soft lights and fresh flowers.

The nearer he approached the house, the more absolutely unequal Paul felt to the sight of it all; his ugly sleeping chamber, the cold bathroom with the grimy zinc tub, the cracked mirror, the dripping spiggots; his father, at the top of the stairs, his hairy legs sticking out from his night-shirt, his feet thrust into carpet slippers. He was so much later than usual that there would certainly be inquiries and reproaches. Paul stopped short before the door. He felt that he could not be accosted by his father tonight; that he could not toss again on that miserable bed. He would not go in. He would tell his father that he had no car fare, and it was raining so hard he had gone home with one of the boys and stayed all night.

Meanwhile, he was wet and cold. He went around to the back of the house and tried one of the basement windows, found it open, raised it cautiously, and scrambled down the cellar wall to the floor. There he stood, holding his breath, terrified by the noise he had made, but the floor above him was silent, and there was no creak on the stairs. He found a soap-box, and carried it over to the soft ring of light that streamed from the furnace door, and sat down. He was horribly afraid of rats, so he did not try to sleep, but sat looking distrustfully at the dark, still terrified lest he might have awakened his father. In such reactions, after one of the experiences which made days and nights out of the dreary blanks of the calendar, when his senses were deadened, Paul's head was always singularly clear. Suppose his father had heard him getting in at the window and had come down and shot him for a burglar? Then, again, suppose his father had come down, pistol in hand, and he had cried out in time to save himself, and his father had been horrified to think how nearly he had killed him? Then, again, suppose a day should come when his father would remember that night, and wish there had been no warning cry to stay his hand? With this last supposition Paul entertained himself until daybreak.

The following Sunday was fine; the sodden November chill was broken by the last flash of autumnal summer. In the morning Paul had to go to church and Sabbath-school, as always. On seasonable Sunday afternoons the burghers of Cordelia Street always sat out on their front "stoops," and talked to their neighbours on the next stoop, or called to those across the street in neighbourly fashion. The men usually sat on gay cushions placed upon the steps that led down to the sidewalk, while the women, in their Sunday "waists," sat in rockers on the cramped porches, pretending to be greatly at their ease. The children played in the streets; there were so many of them that the place resembled the recreation grounds of a kindergarten. The men on the steps—all in their shirt sleeves, their vests unbuttoned—sat with their legs well apart, their stomachs comfortably protruding, and talked of the prices of things, or told anecdotes of the sagacity of their various chiefs and overlords. They occasionally looked over the multitude of squabbling children, listened affectionately to their high-pitched, nasal voices, smiling to see their own proclivities reproduced in their offspring, and interspersed their legends of the iron kings with remarks about their sons' progress at school, their grades in arithmetic, and the amounts they had saved in their toy banks.

On this last Sunday of November, Paul sat all the afternoon on the lowest step of his "stoop," staring into the street, while his sisters, in their rockers, were talking to the minister's daughters next door about how many shirt-waists they had made in the last week, and how many waffles some one had eaten at the last church supper. When the weather was warm, and his father was in a particularly jovial frame of mind, the girls made lemonade, which was always brought out in a red-glass pitcher, ornamented with forget-me-nots in blue enamel. This the girls thought very fine, and the neighbours always joked about the suspicious colour of the pitcher.

Today Paul's father sat on the top step, talking to a young man who shifted a restless baby from knee to knee. He happened to be the young man who was daily held up to Paul as a model, and after whom it was his father's dearest hope that he would pattern. This young man was of a ruddy complexion, with a compressed, red mouth, and faded, near-sighted eyes, over which he wore thick spectacles, with gold bows that curved about his ears. He was clerk to one of the magnates of a great steel corporation, and was looked upon in Cordelia Street as a young man with a future. There was a story that, some five years ago—he was now barely twenty-six—he had been a trifle dissipated, but in order to curb his appetites and save the loss of time and strength that a sowing of wild oats might have entailed, he had taken his chief's advice, oft reiterated to his employees, and at twenty-one had married the first woman whom he could persuade to share his fortunes. She happened to be an angular school-mistress, much older than he, who also wore thick glasses, and who had now borne him four children, all near-sighted, like herself.

The young man was relating how his chief, now cruising in the Mediterranean, kept in touch with all the details of the business, arranging his office hours on his yacht just as though he were at home, and "knocking off work enough to keep two stenographers busy." His father told, in turn, the plan his corporation was considering, of putting in an electric railway plant at Cairo. Paul snapped his teeth; he had an awful apprehension that they might spoil it all before he got there. Yet he rather liked to hear these legends of the iron kings, that were told and retold on Sundays and holidays; these stories of palaces in Venice, yachts on the Mediterranean, and high play at Monte Carlo appealed to his fancy, and he was interested in the triumphs of these cash boys who had become famous, though he had no mind for the cash-boy stage.

After supper was over, and he had helped to dry the dishes, Paul nervously asked his father whether he could go to George's to get some help in his geometry, and still more nervously asked for car fare. This latter request he had to repeat, as his father, on principle, did not like to hear requests for money, whether much or little. He asked Paul whether he could not go to some boy who lived nearer, and told him that he ought not to leave his school work until Sunday; but he gave him the dime. He was not a poor man, but he had a worthy ambition to come up in the world. His only reason for allowing Paul to usher was, that he thought a boy ought to be earning a little.

Paul bounded upstairs, scrubbed the greasy odour of the dish-water from his hands with the ill-smelling soap he hated, and then shook over his fingers a few drops of violet water from the bottle he kept hidden in his drawer. He left the house with his geometry conspicuously under his arm, and the moment he got out of Cordelia Street and boarded a downtown car, he shook off the lethargy of two deadening days, and began to live again.

The leading juvenile of the permanent stock company which played at one of the downtown theatres was an acquaintance of Paul's, and the boy had been invited to drop in at the Sunday-night rehearsals whenever he could. For more than a year Paul had spent every available moment loitering about Charley Edwards's dressing-room. He had won a place among Edwards's following not only because the young actor, who could not afford to employ a dresser, often found him useful, but because he recognized in Paul something akin to what churchmen term "vocation."

It was at the theatre and at Carnegie Hall that Paul really lived; the rest was but a sleep and a forgetting. This was Paul's fairy tale, and it had for him all the allurement of a secret love. The moment he inhaled the gassy, painty, dusty odour behind the scenes, he breathed like a prisoner set free, and felt within him the possibility of doing or saying splendid, brilliant, poetic things. The moment the cracked orchestra beat out the overture from *Martha*, or jerked at the serenade from *Rigoletto*, all stupid and ugly things slid from him, and his senses were deliciously, yet delicately fired.

Perhaps it was because, in Paul's world, the natural nearly always wore the guise of ugliness, that a certain element of artificiality seemed to him necessary in beauty. Perhaps it was because his experience of life elsewhere was so full of Sabbath-school picnics, petty economies, wholesome advice as to how to succeed in life, and the unescapable odours of cooking, that he found this existence so alluring, these smartly-clad men and women so attractive, that he was so moved by these starry apple orchards that bloomed perennially under the limelight.

It would be difficult to put it strongly enough how convincingly the stage entrance of that theatre was for Paul the actual portal of Romance. Certainly none of the company ever suspected it, least of all Charley Edwards. It was very like the old stories that used to float about London of fabulously rich Jews, who had subterranean halls there, with palms, and fountains, and soft lamps and richly apparelled women who never saw the disenchanting light of London day. So, in the midst of that smoke-palled city, enamoured of figures and grimy toil, Paul had his secret temple, his wishing carpet, his bit of blue-and-white Mediterranean shore bathed in perpetual sunshine.

Several of Paul's teachers had a theory that his imagination had been perverted by garish fiction, but the truth was that he scarcely ever read at all. The books at home were not such as would either tempt or corrupt a youthful mind, and as for reading the novels that some of his friends urged upon him—well, he got what he wanted much more quickly from music; any sort of music, from an orchestra to a barrel organ. He needed only the spark, the indescribable thrill that made his imagination master of his senses, and he could make plots and pictures enough of his own. It was equally true that he was not stage-struck—not, at any rate, in the usual acceptation of that expression. He had no desire to become an actor, any more than he had to become a musician. He felt no necessity to do any of these things; what he wanted was to see, to be in the atmosphere, float on the wave of it, to be carried out, blue league after blue league, away from everything.

After a night behind the scenes, Paul found the school-room more than ever repulsive; the bare floors and naked walls; the prosy men who never wore frock coats, or violets in their button-holes; the women with their dull gowns, shrill voices, and pitiful seriousness about prepositions that govern the dative. He could not bear to have the other pupils think, for a moment, that he took these people seriously; he must convey to them that he considered it all trivial, and was there only by way of a jest, anyway. He had autograph pictures of all the members of the stock company which he showed his classmates, telling them the most incredible stories of his familiarity with these people, of his acquaintance with the soloists who came to Carnegie Hall, his suppers with them and the flowers he sent them. When these stories lost their effect, and his audience grew listless, he became desperate and would bid all the boys good-bye, announcing that he was going to travel for awhile; going to Naples, to Venice, to Egypt. Then, next Monday, he would slip back, conscious and nervously smiling; his sister was ill, and he should have to defer his voyage until spring.

Matters went steadily worse with Paul at school. In the itch to let his instructors know how heartily he despised them and their homilies, and how thoroughly he was appreciated elsewhere, he mentioned once or twice that he had no time to fool with theorems; adding—with a twitch of the eyebrows and a touch of that nervous bravado which so perplexed them—that he was helping the people down at the stock company; they were old friends of his.

The upshot of the matter was, that the Principal went to Paul's father, and Paul was taken out of school and put to work. The manager at Carnegie Hall was told to get another usher in his stead; the doorkeeper at the theatre was warned not to admit him to the house; and Charley Edwards remorsefully promised the boy's father not to see him again.

The members of the stock company were vastly amused when some of Paul's stories reached them— especially the women. They were hardworking women, most of them supporting indigent husbands or brothers, and they laughed rather bitterly at having stirred the boy to such fervid and florid inventions. They agreed with the faculty and with his father that Paul's was a bad case.

The east-bound train was ploughing through a January snow-storm; the dull dawn was beginning to show grey when the engine whistled a mile out of Newark. Paul started up from the seat where he had lain curled in uneasy slumber, rubbed the breath-misted window glass with his hand, and peered out. The snow was whirling in curling eddies above the white bottom lands, and the drifts lay already deep in the fields and along the fences, while here and there the long dead grass and dried weed stalks protruded black above it. Lights shone from the scattered houses, and a gang of labourers who stood beside the track waved their lanterns.

Paul had slept very little, and he felt grimy and uncomfortable. He had made the all-night journey in a day coach, partly because he was ashamed, dressed as he was, to go into a Pullman, and partly because he was afraid of being seen there by some Pittsburgh business man, who might have noticed him in Denny & Carson's office. When the whistle awoke him, he clutched quickly at his breast pocket, glancing about him with an uncertain smile. But the little, clay-bespattered Italians were still sleeping, the slatternly women across the aisle were in open-mouthed oblivion, and even the crumby, crying babies were for the nonce stilled. Paul settled back to struggle with his impatience as best he could.

When he arrived at the Jersey City station, he hurried through his breakfast, manifestly ill at ease and keeping a sharp eye about him. After he reached the Twenty-third Street station, he consulted a cabman, and had himself driven to a men's furnishing establishment that was just opening for the day. He spent upward of two hours there, buying with endless reconsidering and great care. His new street suit he put on in the fitting-room; the frock coat and dress clothes he had bundled into the cab with his linen. Then he drove to a hatter's and a shoe house. His next errand was at Tiffany's, where he selected his silver and a new scarf-pin. He would not wait to have his silver marked, he said. Lastly, he stopped at a trunk shop on Broadway, and had his purchases packed into various traveling bags.

It was a little after one o'clock when he drove up to the Waldorf, and after settling with the cabman, went into the office. He registered from Washington; said his mother and father had been abroad, and that he had come down to await the arrival of their steamer. He told his story plausibly and had no trouble, since he volunteered to pay for them in advance, in engaging his rooms; a sleeping-room, sitting-room and bath.

Not once, but a hundred times Paul had planned this entry into New York. He had gone over every detail of it with Charley Edwards, and in his scrap book at home there were pages of description about New York hotels, cut from the Sunday papers. When he was shown to his sitting-room on the eighth floor, he saw at a glance that everything was as it should be; there was but one detail in his mental picture that the place did not realize, so he rang for the bell boy and sent him down for flowers. He moved about nervously until the boy returned, putting away his new linen and fingering it delightedly as he did so. When the flowers came, he put them hastily into water, and then tumbled into a hot bath. Presently he came out of his white bathroom, resplendent in his new silk underwear, and playing with the tassels of his red robe. The snow was whirling so fiercely outside his windows that he could scarcely see across the street, but within the air was deliciously soft and fragrant. He put the violets and jonquils on the taboret beside the couch, and threw himself down, with a long sigh, covering himself with a Roman blanket. He was thoroughly tired; he had been in such haste, he had stood up to such a strain, covered so much ground in the last twenty-four hours, that he wanted to think how it had all come about. Lulled by the sound of the wind, the warm air, and the cool fragrance of the flowers, he sank into deep, drowsy retrospection.

It had been wonderfully simple; when they had shut him out of the theatre and concert hall, when they had taken away his bone, the whole thing was virtually determined. The rest was a mere matter of opportunity. The only thing that at all surprised him was his own courage—for he realized well enough that he had always been tormented by fear, a sort of apprehensive dread that, of late years, as the meshes of the lies he had told closed about him, had been pulling the muscles of his body tighter and tighter. Until now, he could not remember the time when he had not been dreading something. Even when he was a little boy, it was always there—behind him, or before, or on either side. There had always been the shadowed corner, the dark place into which he dared not look, but from which something seemed always to be watching him—and Paul had done things that were not pretty to watch, he knew.

But now he had a curious sense of relief, as though he had at last thrown down the gauntlet to the thing in the corner.

Yet it was but a day since he had been sulking in the traces; but yesterday afternoon that he had been sent to the bank with Denny & Carson's deposit, as usual —but this time he was instructed to leave the book to be balanced. There was above two thousand dollars in checks, and nearly a thousand in the bank notes which he had taken from the book and quietly transferred to his pocket. At the bank he had made out a new deposit slip. His nerves had been steady enough to permit of his returning to the office, where he had finished his work and asked for a full day's holiday tomorrow, Saturday, giving a perfectly reasonable pretext. The bank book, he knew, would not be returned before Monday or Tuesday, and his father would be out of town for the next week. From the time he slipped the bank notes into his pocket until he boarded the night train for New York, he had not known a moment's hesitation. It was not the first time Paul had steered through treacherous waters.

How astonishingly easy it had all been; here he was, the thing done; and this time there would be no awakening, no figure at the top of the stairs. He watched the snow flakes whirling by his window until he fell asleep.

When he awoke, it was three o'clock in the afternoon. He bounded up with a start; half of one of his precious days gone already! He spent more than an hour in dressing, watching every stage of his toilet carefully in the mirror. Everything was quite perfect; he was exactly the kind of boy he had always wanted to be.

When he went downstairs, Paul took a carriage and drove up Fifth Avenue toward the Park. The snow had somewhat abated; carriages and tradesmen's wagons were hurrying soundlessly to and fro in the winter twilight; boys in woolen mufflers were shovelling off the doorsteps; the avenue stages made fine spots of colour against the white street. Here and there on the corners were stands, with whole flower gardens blooming under glass cases, against the sides of which the snow flakes stuck and melted; violets, roses, carnations, lilies of the valley—somehow vastly more lovely and alluring that they blossomed thus unnaturally in the snow. The Park itself was a wonderful stage winter-piece.

When he returned, the pause of the twilight had ceased, and the tune of the streets had changed. The snow was falling faster, lights streamed from the hotels that reared their dozen stories fearlessly up into the storm, defying the raging Atlantic winds. A long, black stream of carriages poured down the avenue, intersected here and there by other streams, tending horizontally. There were a score of cabs about the entrance of his hotel, and the driver had to wait. Boys in livery were running in and out of the awning stretched across the sidewalk, up and down the red velvet carpet laid from the door to the street. Above, about, within it all was the rumble and roar, the hurry and toss of thousands of human beings as hot for pleasure as himself, and on every side of him towered the glaring affirmation of the omnipotence of wealth.

The boy set his teeth and drew his shoulders together in a spasm of realization; the plot of all dramas, the text of all romances, the nerve-stuff of all sensations was whirling about him like the snow flakes. He burnt like a faggot in a tempest.

When Paul went down to dinner, the music of the orchestra came floating up the elevator shaft to greet him. His head whirled as he stepped into the thronged corridor, and he sank back into one of the chairs against the wall to get his breath. The lights, the chatter, the perfumes, the bewildering medley of colour— he had, for a moment, the feeling of not being able to stand it. But only for a moment; these were his own people, he told himself. He went slowly about the corridors, through the writing-rooms, smoking-rooms, reception-rooms, as though he were exploring the chambers of an enchanted palace, built and peopled for him alone.

When he reached the dining-room he sat down at a table near a window. The flowers, the white linen, the many-coloured wine glasses, the gay toilettes of the women, the low popping of corks, the undulating repetitions of the *Blue Danube* from the orchestra, all flooded Paul's dream with bewildering radiance. When the roseate tinge of his champagne was added —that cold, precious bubbling stuff that creamed and foamed in his glass—Paul wondered that there were honest men in the world at all. This was what all the world was fighting for, he reflected; this was what all the struggle was about. He doubted the reality of his past. Had he ever known a place called Cordelia Street, a place where fagged-looking business men got on the early car; mere rivets in a machine they seemed to Paul,—sickening men, with combings of children's hair always hanging to their coats, and the smell of cooking in their clothes. Cordelia Street—Ah! that belonged to another time and country; had he not always been thus, had he not sat here night after night, from as far back as he could remember, looking pensively over just such shimmering textures, and slowly twirling the stem of a glass like this one between his thumb and middle finger? He rather thought he had.

He was not in the least abashed or lonely. He had no especial desire to meet or to know any of these people; all he demanded was the right to look on and conjecture, to watch the pageant. The mere stage properties were all he contended for. Nor was he lonely later in the evening, in his loge at the Metropolitan. He was now entirely rid of his nervous misgivings, of his forced aggressiveness, of the imperative desire to show himself different from his surroundings. He felt now that his surroundings explained him. Nobody questioned the purple; he had only to wear it passively. He had only to glance down at his attire to reassure himself that here it would be impossible for any one to humiliate him.

He found it hard to leave his beautiful sitting-room to go to bed that night, and sat long watching the raging storm from his turret window. When he went to sleep, it was with the lights turned on in his bedroom; partly because of his old timidity, and partly so that, if he should wake in the night, there would be no wretched moment of doubt, no horrible suspicion of yellow wall-paper, or of Washington and Calvin above his bed.

Sunday morning the city was practically snowbound. Paul breakfasted late, and in the afternoon he fell in with a wild San Francisco boy, a freshman at Yale, who said he had run down for a "little flyer" over Sunday. The young man offered to show Paul the night side of the town, and the two boys went out together after dinner, not returning to the hotel until seven o'clock the next morning. They had started out in the confiding warmth of a champagne friendship, but their parting in the elevator was singularly cool. The freshman pulled himself together to make his train, and Paul went to bed. He awoke at two o'clock in the afternoon, very thirsty and dizzy, and rang for ice-water, coffee, and the Pittsburgh papers.

On the part of the hotel management, Paul excited no suspicion. There was this to be said for him, that he wore his spoils with dignity and in no way made himself conspicuous. Even under the glow of his wine he was never boisterous, though he found the stuff like a magician's wand for wonder-building. His chief greediness lay in his ears and eyes, and his excesses were not offensive ones. His dearest pleasures were the grey winter twilights in his sitting-room; his quiet enjoyment of his flowers, his clothes, his wide divan, his cigarette and his sense of power. He could not remember a time when he had felt so at peace with himself. The mere release from the necessity of petty lying, lying every day and every day, restored his self-respect. He had never lied for pleasure, even at school; but to be noticed and admired, to assert his difference from other Cordelia Street boys; and he felt a good deal more manly, more honest, even, now that he had no need for boastful pretensions, now that he could, as his actor friends used to say, "dress the part." It was characteristic that remorse did not occur to him. His golden days went by without a shadow, and he made each as perfect as he could.

On the eighth day after his arrival in New York, he found the whole affair exploited in the Pittsburgh papers, exploited with a wealth of detail which indicated that local news of a sensational nature was at a low ebb. The firm of Denny & Carson announced that the boy's father had refunded the full amount of the theft, and that they had no intention of prosecuting. The Cumberland minister had been interviewed, and expressed his hope of yet reclaiming the motherless lad, and his Sabbath-school teacher declared that she would spare no effort to that end. The rumour had reached Pittsburgh that the boy had been seen in a New York hotel, and his father had gone East to find him and bring him home.

Paul had just come in to dress for dinner; he sank into a chair, weak to the knees, and clasped his head in his hands. It was to be worse than jail, even; the tepid waters of Cordelia Street were to close over him finally and forever. The grey monotony stretched before him in hopeless, unrelieved years; Sabbath-school, Young People's Meeting, the yellow-papered room, the damp dish-towels; it all rushed back upon him with a sickening vividness. He had the old feeling that the orchestra had suddenly stopped, the sinking sensation that the play was over. The sweat broke out on his face, and he sprang to his feet, looked about him with his white, conscious smile, and winked at himself in the mirror. With something of the old childish belief in miracles with which he had so often gone to class, all his lessons unlearned, Paul dressed and dashed whistling down the corridor to the elevator.

He had no sooner entered the dining-room and caught the measure of the music than his remembrance was lightened by his old elastic power of claiming the moment, mounting with it, and finding it all sufficient. The glare and glitter about him, the mere scenic accessories had again, and for the last time, their old potency. He would show himself that he was game, he would finish the thing splendidly. He doubted, more than ever, the existence of Cordelia Street, and for the first time he drank his wine recklessly. Was he not, after all, one of those fortunate beings born to the purple, was he not still himself and in his own place? He drummed a nervous accompaniment to the Pagliacci music and looked about him, telling himself over and over that it had paid.

He reflected drowsily, to the swell of the music and the chill sweetness of his wine, that he might have done it more wisely. He might have caught an outbound steamer and been well out of their clutches before now. But the other side of the world had seemed too far away and too uncertain then; he could not have waited for it; his need had been too sharp. If he had to choose over again, he would do the same thing tomorrow. He looked affectionately about the dining-room, now gilded with a soft mist. Ah, it had paid indeed!

Paul was awakened next morning by a painful throbbing in his head and feet. He had thrown himself across the bed without undressing, and had slept with his shoes on. His limbs and hands were lead heavy, and his tongue and throat were parched and burnt. There came upon him one of those fateful attacks of clear-headedness that never occurred except when he was physically exhausted and his nerves hung loose. He lay still and closed his eyes and let the tide of things wash over him.

His father was in New York; "stopping at some joint or other," he told himself. The memory of successive summers on the front stoop fell upon him like a weight of black water. He had not a hundred dollars left; and he knew now, more than ever, that money was everything, the wall that stood between all he loathed and all he wanted. The thing was winding itself up; he had thought of that on his first glorious day in New York, and had even provided a way to snap the thread. It lay on his dressing-table now; he had got it out last night when he came blindly up from dinner, but the shiny metal hurt his eyes, and he disliked the looks of it.

He rose and moved about with a painful effort, succumbing now and again to attacks of nausea. It was the old depression exaggerated; all the world had become Cordelia Street. Yet somehow he was not afraid of anything, was absolutely calm; perhaps because he had looked into the dark corner at last and knew. It was bad enough, what he saw there, but somehow not so bad as his long fear of it had been. He saw everything clearly now. He had a feeling that he had made the best of it, that he had lived the sort of life he was meant to live, and for half an hour he sat staring at the revolver. But he told himself that was not the way, so he went downstairs and took a cab to the ferry.

When Paul arrived at Newark, he got off the train and took another cab, directing the driver to follow the Pennsylvania tracks out of the town. The snow lay heavy on the roadways and had drifted deep in the open fields. Only here and there the dead grass or dried weed stalks projected, singularly black, above it. Once well into the country, Paul dismissed the carriage and walked, floundering along the tracks, his mind a medley of irrelevant things. He seemed to hold in his brain an actual picture of everything he had seen that morning. He remembered every feature of both his drivers, of the toothless old woman from whom he had bought the red flowers in his coat, the agent from whom he had got his ticket, and all of his fellow-passengers on the ferry. His mind, unable to cope with vital matters near at hand, worked feverishly and deftly at sorting and grouping these images. They made for him a part of the ugliness of the world, of the ache in his head, and the bitter burning on his tongue. He stopped and put a handful of snow into his mouth as he walked, but that, too, seemed hot. When he reached a little hillside, where the tracks ran through a cut some twenty feet below him, he stopped and sat down.

The carnations in his coat were drooping with the cold, he noticed; their red glory all over. It occurred to him that all the flowers he had seen in the glass cases that first night must have gone the same way, long before this. It was only one splendid breath they had, in spite of their brave mockery at the winter outside the glass; and it was a losing game in the end, it seemed, this revolt against the homilies by which the world is run. Paul took one of the blossoms carefully from his coat and scooped a little hole in the snow, where he covered it up. Then he dozed a while, from his weak condition, seeming insensible to the cold.

The sound of an approaching train awoke him, and he started to his feet, remembering only his resolution, and afraid lest he should be too late. He stood watching the approaching locomotive, his teeth chattering, his lips drawn away from them in a frightened smile; once or twice he glanced nervously sidewise, as though he were being watched. When the right moment came, he jumped. As he fell, the folly of his haste occurred to him with merciless clearness, the vastness of what he had left undone. There flashed through his brain, clearer than ever before, the blue of Adriatic water, the yellow of Algerian sands.

He felt something strike his chest, and that his body was being thrown swiftly through the air, on and on, immeasurably far and fast, while his limbs were gently relaxed. Then, because the picture making mechanism was crushed, the disturbing visions flashed into black, and Paul dropped back into the immense design of things.

THE ENCHANTED
BLUFF

We had our swim before sundown, and while we were cooking our supper the oblique rays of light made a dazzling glare on the white sand about us. The translucent red ball itself sank behind the brown stretches of cornfield as we sat down to eat, and the warm layer of air that had rested over the water and our clean sand bar grew fresher and smelled of the rank ironweed and sunflowers growing on the flatter shore. The river was brown and sluggish, like any other of the half-dozen streams that water the Nebraska corn lands. On one shore was an irregular line of bald clay bluffs where a few scrub oaks with thick trunks and flat, twisted tops threw light shadows on the long grass. The western shore was low and level, with cornfields that stretched to the skyline, and all along the water's edge were little sandy coves and beaches where slim cottonwoods and willow saplings flickered.

The turbulence of the river in springtime discouraged milling, and, beyond keeping the old red bridge in repair, the busy farmers did not concern themselves with the stream; so the Sandtown boys were left in undisputed possession. In the autumn we hunted quail through the miles of stubble and fodder land along the flat shore, and, after the winter skating season was over and the ice had gone out, the spring freshets and flooded bottoms gave us our great excitement of the year. The channel was never the same for two successive seasons. Every spring the swollen stream undermined a bluff to the east, or bit out a few acres of cornfield to the west and whirled the soil away to deposit it in spumy mud banks somewhere else. When the water fell low in midsummer, new sand bars were thus exposed to dry and whiten in the August sun. Sometimes these were banked so firmly that the fury of the next freshet failed to unseat them; the little willow seedlings emerged triumphantly from the yellow froth, broke into spring leaf, shot up into summer growth, and with their mesh of roots bound together the moist sand beneath them against the batterings of another April. Here and there a cottonwood soon glittered among them, quivering in the low current of air that, even on breathless days when the dust hung like smoke above the wagon road, trembled along the face of the water.

It was on such an island, in the third summer of its yellow green, that we built our watch fire; not in the thicket of dancing willow wands, but on the level terrace of fine sand which had been added that spring; a little new bit of world, beautifully ridged with ripple marks, and strewn with the tiny skeletons of turtles and fish, all as white and dry as if they had been expertly cured. We had been careful not to mar the freshness of the place, although we often swam to it on summer evenings and lay on the sand to rest.

This was our last watch fire of the year, and there were reasons why I should remember it better than any of the others. Next week the other boys were to file back to their old places in the Sandtown High School, but I was to go up to the Divide to teach my first country school in the Norwegian district. I was already homesick at the thought of quitting the boys with whom I had always played; of leaving the river, and going up into a windy plain that was all windmills and cornfields and big pastures; where there was nothing wilful or unmanageable in the landscape, no new islands, and no chance of unfamiliar birds—such as often followed the watercourses.

Other boys came and went and used the river for fishing or skating, but we six were sworn to the spirit of the stream, and we were friends mainly because of the river. There were the two Hassler boys, Fritz and Otto, sons of the little German tailor. They were the youngest of us; ragged boys of ten and twelve, with sunburned hair, weather-stained faces, and pale blue eyes. Otto, the elder, was the best mathematician in school, and clever at his books, but he always dropped out in the spring term as if the river could not get on without him. He and Fritz caught the fat, horned catfish and sold them about the town, and they lived so much in the water that they were as brown and sandy as the river itself.

There was Percy Pound, a fat, freckled boy with chubby cheeks, who took half a dozen boys' story-papers and was always being kept in for reading detective stories behind his desk. There was Tip Smith, destined by his freckles and red hair to be the buffoon in all our games, though he walked like a timid little old man and had a funny, cracked laugh. Tip worked hard in his father's grocery store every afternoon, and swept it out before school in the morning. Even his recreations were laborious. He collected cigarette cards and tin tobacco-tags indefatigably, and would sit for hours humped up over a snarling little scroll-saw which he kept in his attic. His dearest possessions were some little pill bottles that purported to contain grains of wheat from the Holy Land, water from the Jordan and the Dead Sea, and earth from the Mount of Olives. His father had bought these dull things from a Baptist missionary who peddled them, and Tip seemed to derive great satisfaction from their remote origin.

The tall boy was Arthur Adams. He had fine hazel eyes that were almost too reflective and sympathetic for a boy, and such a pleasant voice that we all loved to hear him read aloud. Even when he had to read poetry aloud at school, no one ever thought of laughing. To be sure, he was not at school very much of the time. He was seventeen and should have finished the High School the year before, but he was always off somewhere with his gun. Arthur's mother was dead, and his father, who was feverishly absorbed in promoting schemes, wanted to send the boy away to school and get him off his hands; but Arthur always begged off for another year and promised to study. I remember him as a tall, brown boy with an intelligent face, always lounging among a lot of us little fellows, laughing at us oftener than with us, but such a soft, satisfied laugh that we felt rather flattered when we provoked it. In after-years people said that Arthur had been given to evil ways as a lad, and it is true that we often saw him with the gambler's sons and with old Spanish Fanny's boy, but if he learned anything ugly in their company he never betrayed it to us. We would have followed Arthur anywhere, and I am bound to say that he led us into no worse places than the cattail marshes and the stubble fields. These, then, were the boys who camped with me that summer night upon the sand bar.

After we finished our supper we beat the willow thicket for driftwood. By the time we had collected enough, night had fallen, and the pungent, weedy smell from the shore increased with the coolness. We threw ourselves down about the fire and made another futile effort to show Percy Pound the Little Dipper. We had tried it often before, but he could never be got past the big one.

"You see those three big stars just below the handle, with the bright one in the middle?" said Otto Hassler; "that's Orion's belt, and the bright one is the clasp." I crawled behind Otto's shoulder and sighted up his arm to the star that seemed perched upon the tip of his steady forefinger. The Hassler boys did seine-fishing at night, and they knew a good many stars.

Percy gave up the Little Dipper and lay back on the sand, his hands clasped under his head. "I can see the North Star," he announced, contentedly, pointing toward it with his big toe. "Anyone might get lost and need to know that."

We all looked up at it.

"How do you suppose Columbus felt when his compass didn't point north any more?" Tip asked.

Otto shook his head. "My father says that there was another North Star once, and that maybe this one won't last always. I wonder what would happen to us down here if anything went wrong with it?"

Arthur chuckled. "I wouldn't worry, Ott. Nothing's apt to happen to it in your time. Look at the Milky Way! There must be lots of good dead Indians."

We lay back and looked, meditating, at the dark cover of the world. The gurgle of the water had become heavier. We had often noticed a mutinous, complaining note in it at night, quite different from its cheerful daytime chuckle, and seeming like the voice of a much deeper and more powerful stream. Our water had always these two moods: the one of sunny complaisance, the other of inconsolable, passionate regret.

"Queer how the stars are all in sort of diagrams," remarked Otto. "You could do most any proposition in geometry with 'em. They always look as if they meant something. Some folks say everybody's fortune is all written out in the stars, don't they?"

"They believe so in the old country," Fritz affirmed.

But Arthur only laughed at him. "You're thinking of Napoleon, Fritzey. He had a star that went out when he began to lose battles. I guess the stars don't keep any close tally on Sandtown folks."

We were speculating on how many times we could count a hundred before the evening star went down behind the cornfields, when someone cried, "There comes the moon, and it's as big as a cart wheel!"

We all jumped up to greet it as it swam over the bluffs behind us. It came up like a galleon in full sail; an enormous, barbaric thing, red as an angry heathen god.

"When the moon came up red like that, the Aztecs used to sacrifice their prisoners on the temple top," Percy announced.

"Go on, Perce. You got that out of *Golden Days*. Do you believe that, Arthur?" I appealed.

Arthur answered, quite seriously: "Like as not. The moon was one of their gods. When my father was in Mexico City he saw the stone where they used to sacrifice their prisoners."

As we dropped down by the fire again some one asked whether the Mound-Builders were older than the Aztecs. When we once got upon the Mound-Builders we never willingly got away from them, and we were still conjecturing when we heard a loud splash in the water.

"Must have been a big cat jumping," said Fritz. "They do sometimes. They must see bugs in the dark. Look what a track the moon makes!"

There was a long, silvery streak on the water, and where the current fretted over a big log it boiled up like gold pieces.

"Suppose there ever *was* any gold hid away in this old river?" Fritz asked. He lay like a little brown Indian, close to the fire, his chin on his hand and his bare feet in the air. His brother laughed at him, but Arthur took his suggestion seriously.

"Some of the Spaniards thought there was gold up here somewhere. Seven cities chuck full of gold, they had it, and Coronado and his men came up to hunt it. The Spaniards were all over this country once."

Percy looked interested. "Was that before the Mormons went through?"

We all laughed at this.

"Long enough before. Before the Pilgrim Fathers, Perce. Maybe they came along this very river. They always followed the watercourses."

"I wonder where this river really does begin?" Tip mused. That was an old and a favorite mystery which the map did not clearly explain. On the map the little black line stopped somewhere in western Kansas; but since rivers generally rose in mountains, it was only reasonable to suppose that ours came from the Rockies. Its destination, we knew, was the Missouri, and the Hassler boys always maintained that we could embark at Sandtown in floodtime, follow our noses, and eventually arrive at New Orleans. Now they took up their old argument. "If us boys had grit enough to try it, it wouldn't take no time to get to Kansas City and St. Joe."

We began to talk about the places we wanted to go to. The Hassler boys wanted to see the stockyards in Kansas City, and Percy wanted to see a big store in Chicago. Arthur was interlocutor and did not betray himself.

"Now it's your turn, Tip."

Tip rolled over on his elbow and poked the fire, and his eyes looked shyly out of his queer, tight little face. "My place is awful far away. My Uncle Bill told me about it."

Tip's Uncle Bill was a wanderer, bitten with mining fever, who had drifted into Sandtown with a broken arm, and when it was well had drifted out again.

"Where is it?"

"Aw, it's down in New Mexico somewheres. There aren't no railroads or anything. You have to go on mules, and you run out of water before you get there and have to drink canned tomatoes."

"Well, go on, kid. What's it like when you do get there?"

Tip sat up and excitedly began his story.

"There's a big red rock there that goes right up out of the sand for about nine hundred feet. The country's flat all around it, and this here rock goes up all by itself, like a monument. They call it the Enchanted Bluff down there, because no white man has ever been on top of it. The sides are smooth rock, and straight up, like a wall. The Indians say that hundreds of years ago, before the Spaniards came, there was a village away up there in the air. The tribe that lived there had some sort of steps, made out of wood and bark, hung down over the face of the bluff, and the braves went down to hunt and carried water up in big jars swung on their backs. They kept a big supply of water and dried meat up there, and never went down except to hunt. They were a peaceful tribe that made cloth and pottery, and they went up there to get out of the wars. You see, they could pick off any war party that tried to get up their little steps. The Indians say they were a handsome people, and they had some sort of queer religion. Uncle Bill thinks they were Cliff-Dwellers who had got into trouble and left home. They weren't fighters, anyhow.

"One time the braves were down hunting and an awful storm came up—a kind of waterspout—and when they got back to their rock they found their little staircase had been all broken to pieces, and only a few steps were left hanging away up in the air. While they were camped at the foot of the rock, wondering what to do, a war party from the north came along and massacred 'em to a man, with all the old folks and women looking on from the rock. Then the war party went on south and left the village to get down the best way they could. Of course they never got down. They starved to death up there, and when the war party came back on their way north, they could hear the children crying from the edge of the bluff where they had crawled out, but they didn't see a sign of a grown Indian, and nobody has ever been up there since."

We exclaimed at this dolorous legend and sat up.

"There couldn't have been many people up there," Percy demurred. "How big is the top, Tip?"

"Oh, pretty big. Big enough so that the rock doesn't look nearly as tall as it is. The top's bigger than the base. The bluff is sort of worn away for several hundred feet up. That's one reason it's so hard to climb."

I asked how the Indians got up, in the first place.

"Nobody knows how they got up or when. A hunting party came along once and saw that there was a town up there, and that was all."

Otto rubbed his chin and looked thoughtful. "Of course there must be some way to get up there. Couldn't people get a rope over someway and pull a ladder up?"

Tip's little eyes were shining with excitement. "I know a way. Me and Uncle Bill talked it over. There's a kind of rocket that would take a rope over—life-savers use 'em—and then you could hoist a rope ladder and peg it down at the bottom and make it tight with guy ropes on the other side. I'm going to climb that there bluff, and I've got it all planned out."

Fritz asked what he expected to find when he got up there.

"Bones, maybe, or the ruins of their town, or pottery, or some of their idols. There might be 'most anything up there. Anyhow, I want to see."

"Sure nobody else has been up there, Tip?" Arthur asked.

"Dead sure. Hardly anybody ever goes down there. Some hunters tried to cut steps in the rock once, but they didn't get higher than a man can reach. The Bluff's all red granite, and Uncle Bill thinks it's a boulder the glaciers left. It's a queer place, anyhow.

Nothing but cactus and desert for hundreds of miles, and yet right under the Bluff there's good water and plenty of grass. That's why the bison used to go down there."

Suddenly we heard a scream above our fire, and jumped up to see a dark, slim bird floating southward far above us—a whooping crane, we knew by her cry and her long neck. We ran to the edge of the island, hoping we might see her alight, but she wavered southward along the rivercourse until we lost her. The Hassler boys declared that by the look of the heavens it must be after midnight, so we threw more wood on our fire, put on our jackets, and curled down in the warm sand. Several of us pretended to doze, but I fancy we were really thinking about Tip's Bluff and the extinct people. Over in the wood the ring doves were calling mournfully to one another, and once we heard a dog bark, far away. "Somebody getting into old Tommy's melon patch," Fritz murmured sleepily, but nobody answered him. By and by Percy spoke out of the shadows.

"Say, Tip, when you go down there will you take me with you?"

"Maybe."

"Suppose one of us beats you down there, Tip?"

"Whoever gets to the Bluff first has got to promise to tell the rest of us exactly what he finds," remarked one of the Hassler boys, and to this we all readily assented.

Somewhat reassured, I dropped off to sleep. I must have dreamed about a race for the Bluff, for I awoke in a kind of fear that other people were getting ahead of me and that I was losing my chance. I sat up in my damp clothes and looked at the other boys, who lay tumbled in uneasy attitudes about the dead fire. It was still dark, but the sky was blue with the last wonderful azure of night. The stars glistened like crystal globes, and trembled as if they shone through a depth of clear water. Even as I watched, they began to pale and the sky brightened. Day came suddenly, almost instantaneously. I turned for another look at the blue night, and it was gone. Everywhere the birds began to call, and all manner of little insects began to chirp and hop about in the willows. A breeze sprang up from the west and brought the heavy smell of ripened corn. The boys rolled over and shook themselves. We stripped and plunged into the river just as the sun came up over the windy bluffs.

When I came home to Sandtown at Christmas time, we skated out to our island and talked over the whole project of the Enchanted Bluff, renewing our resolution to find it.

Although that was twenty years ago, none of us have ever climbed the Enchanted Bluff. Percy Pound is a stockbroker in Kansas City and will go nowhere that his red touring car cannot carry him. Otto Hassler went on the railroad and lost his foot braking; after which he and Fritz succeeded their father as the town tailors.

Arthur sat about the sleepy little town all his life— he died before he was twenty-five. The last time I saw him, when I was home on one of my college vacations, he was sitting in a steamer chair under a cottonwood tree in the little yard behind one of the two Sandtown saloons. He was very untidy and his hand was not steady, but when he rose, unabashed, to greet me, his eyes were as clear and warm as ever. When I had talked with him for an hour and heard him laugh again, I wondered how it was that when Nature had taken such pains with a man, from his hands to the arch of his long foot, she had ever lost him in Sandtown. He joked about Tip Smith's Bluff, and declared he was going down there just as soon as the weather got cooler; he thought the Grand Canyon might be worth while, too.

I was perfectly sure when I left him that he would never get beyond the high plank fence and the comfortable shade of the cottonwood. And, indeed, it was under that very tree that he died one summer morning.

Tip Smith still talks about going to New Mexico. He married a slatternly, unthrifty country girl, has been much tied to a perambulator, and has grown stooped and grey from irregular meals and broken sleep. But the worst of his difficulties are now over, and he has, as he says, come into easy water. When I was last in Sandtown I walked home with him late one moonlight night, after he had balanced his cash and shut up his store. We took the long way around and sat down on the schoolhouse steps, and between us we quite revived the romance of the lone red rock and the extinct people. Tip insists that he still means to go down there, but he thinks now he will wait until his boy Bert is old enough to go with him. Bert has been let into the story, and thinks of nothing but the Enchanted Bluff.

THE BOHEMIAN

GIRL

The transcontinental express swung along the wind-ings of the Sand River Valley, and in the rear seat of the observation car a young man sat greatly at his ease, not in the least discomfited by the fierce sunlight which beat in upon his brown face and neck and strong back. There was a look of relaxation and of great passivity about his broad shoulders, which seemed almost too heavy until he stood up and squared them. He wore a pale flannel shirt and a blue silk necktie with loose ends. His trousers were wide and belted at the waist, and his short sack coat hung open. His heavy shoes had seen good service. His red-dish-brown hair, like his clothes, had a foreign cut. He had deep-set, dark blue eyes under heavy reddish eye-brows. His face was kept clean only by close shaving, and even the sharpest razor left a glint of yellow in the smooth brown of his skin. His teeth and the palms of his hands were very white. His head, which looked hard and stubborn, lay indolently in the green cushion of the wicker chair, and as he looked out at the ripe summer country a teasing, not unkindly smile played over his lips. Once, as he basked thus comfortably, a quick light flashed in his eyes, curiously dilating the pupils, and his mouth became a hard, straight line, gradually relaxing into its former smile of rather kindly mockery. He told himself, apparently, that there was no point in getting excited; and he seemed a master hand at taking his ease when he could. Neither the sharp whistle of the locomotive nor the brakeman's call disturbed him. It was not until after the train had stopped that he rose, put on a Panama hat, took from the rack a small valise and a flute case, and stepped deliberately to the station platform. The baggage was already unloaded, and the stranger presented a check for a battered sole-leather steamer trunk.

"Can you keep it here for a day or two?" he asked the agent. "I may send for it, and I may not."

"Depends on whether you like the country, I suppose?" demanded the agent in a challenging tone.

"Just so."

The agent shrugged his shoulders, looked scornfully at the small trunk, which was marked. "N.E.," and handed out a claim check without further comment. The stranger watched him as he caught one end of the trunk and dragged it into the express room. The agent's manner seemed to remind him of something amusing. "Doesn't seem to be a very big place," he remarked, looking about.

"It's big enough for us," snapped the agent, as he banged the trunk into a corner.

That remark, apparently, was what Nils Ericson

had wanted. He chuckled quietly as he took a leather strap from his pocket and swung his valise around his shoulder. Then he settled his Panama securely on his head, turned up his trousers, tucked the flute case under his arm, and started off across the fields. He gave the town, as he would have said, a wide berth, and cut through a great fenced pasture, emerging, when he rolled under the barbed wire at the farther corner, upon a white dusty road which ran straight up from the river valley to the high prairies, where the ripe wheat stood yellow and the tin roofs and weathercocks were twinkling in the fierce sunlight. By the time Nils had done three miles, the sun was sinking and the farm wagons on their way home from town came rattling by, covering him with dust and making him sneeze. When one of the farmers pulled up and offered to give him a lift, he clambered in willingly. The driver was a thin, grizzled old man with a long lean neck and a foolish sort of beard, like a goat's. "How fur ye goin'?" he asked, as he clucked to his horses and started off.

"Do you go by the Ericson place?"

"Which Ericson?" The old man drew in his reins as if he expected to stop again.

"Preacher Ericson's."

"Oh, the Old Lady Ericson's!" He turned and looked at Nils. "La, me! If you're goin' out there you might 'a' rid out in the automobile. That's a pity, now. The Old Lady Ericson was in town with her auto. You might 'a' heard it snortin' anywhere about the post-office er the butcher shop."

"Has she a motor?" asked the stranger absently.

"'Deed an' she has! She runs into town every night about this time for her mail and meat for supper. Some folks say she's afraid her auto won't get exercise enough, but I say that's jealousy."

"Aren't there any other motors about here?"

"Oh, yes! we have fourteen in all. But nobody else gets around like the Old Lady Ericson. She's out, rain er shine, over the whole county, chargin' into town and out amongst her farms, an' up to her sons' places. Sure you ain't goin' to the wrong place?" He craned his neck and looked at Nils' flute case with eager curiosity. "The old woman ain't got any piany that I knows on. Olaf, he has a grand. His wife's musical; took lessons in Chicago."

"I'm going up there tomorrow," said Nils imperturbably. He saw that the driver took him for a piano tuner.

"Oh, I see!" The old man screwed up his eyes mysteriously. He was a little dashed by the stranger's noncommunicativeness, but he soon broke out again.

"I'm one o' Miss Ericson's tenants. Look after one of her places. I did own the place myself oncet, but I lost it a while back, in the bad years just after the World's Fair. Just as well, too, I say. Lets you out o' payin' taxes. The Ericsons do own most of the county now. I remember the old preacher's fav'rite text used to be, 'To them that hath shall be given.' They've spread something wonderful—run over this here country like bindweed. But I ain't one that begretches it to 'em. Folks is entitled to what they kin git; and they're hustlers. Olaf, he's in the Legislature now, and a likely man fur Congress. Listen, if that ain't the old woman comin' now. Want I should stop her?"

Nils shook his head. He heard the deep chug-chug of a motor vibrating steadily in the clear twilight behind them. The pale lights of the car swam over the hill, and the old man slapped his reins and turned clear out of the road, ducking his head at the first of three angry snorts from behind. The motor was running at a hot, even speed, and passed without turning an inch from its course. The driver was a stalwart woman who sat at ease in the front seat and drove her car bareheaded. She left a cloud of dust and a trail of gasoline behind her. Her tenant threw back his head and sneezed.

"Whew! I sometimes say I'd as lief be *before* Mrs. Ericson as behind her. She does beat all! Nearly seventy, and never lets another soul touch that car. Puts it into commission herself every morning, and keeps it tuned up by the hitch-bar all day. I never stop work for a drink o' water that I don't hear her a-churnin' up the road. I reckon her darter-in-laws never sets down easy nowadays. Never know when she'll pop in. Mis' Otto, she says to me: 'We're so afraid that thing'll blow up and do Ma some injury yet, she's so turrible venturesome.' Says I: 'I wouldn't stew, Mis' Otto; the old lady'll drive that car to the funeral of every darter-in-law she's got.' That was after the old woman had jumped a turrible bad culvert."

The stranger heard vaguely what the old man was saying. Just now he was experiencing something very much like homesickness, and he was wondering what had brought it about. The mention of a name or two, perhaps; the rattle of a wagon along a dusty road; the rank, resinous smell of sunflowers and ironweed, which the night damp brought up from the draws and low places; perhaps, more than all, the dancing lights of the motor that had plunged by. He squared his shoulders with a comfortable sense of strength.

The wagon, as it jolted westward, climbed a pretty steady up-grade. The country, receding from the rough river valley, swelled more and more gently, as if it had been smoothed out by the wind. On one of the last of the rugged ridges, at the end of a branch road, stood a grim square house with a tin roof and double porches. Behind the house stretched a row of broken, wind-racked poplars, and down the hill slope to the left straggled the sheds and stables. The old man stopped his horses where the Ericsons' road branched across a dry sand creek that wound about the foot of the hill.

"That's the old lady's place. Want I should drive in?"

"No, thank you. I'll roll out here. Much obliged to you. Good night."

His passenger stepped down over the front wheel, and the old man drove on reluctantly, looking back as if he would like to see how the stranger would be received.

As Nils was crossing the dry creek he heard the restive tramp of a horse coming toward him down the hill. Instantly he flashed out of the road and stood behind a thicket of wild plum bushes that grew in the sandy bed. Peering through the dusk, he saw a light horse, under tight rein, descending the hill at a sharp walk. The rider was a slender woman—barely visible against the dark hillside—wearing an old-fashioned derby hat and a long riding skirt. She sat lightly in the saddle, with her chin high, and seemed to be looking into the distance. As she passed the plum thicket her horse snuffed the air and shied. She struck him, pulling him in sharply, with an angry exclamation, "*Blázne!*" in Bohemian. Once in the main road, she let him out into a lope, and they soon emerged upon the crest of high land, where they moved along the skyline, silhouetted against the band of faint colour that lingered in the west. This horse and rider, with their free, rhythmical gallop, were the only moving things to be seen on the face of the flat country. They seemed, in the last sad light of evening, not to be there accidentally, but as an inevitable detail of the land-scape.

Nils watched them until they had shrunk to a mere moving speck against the sky, then he crossed the sand creek and climbed the hill. When he reached the gate the front of the house was dark, but a light was shining from the side windows. The pigs were squealing in the hog corral, and Nils could see a tall boy, who carried two big wooden buckets, moving about among them. Halfway between the barn and the house, the windmill wheezed lazily. Following the path that ran around to the back porch, Nils stopped to look through the screen door into the lamplit kitchen. The kitchen was the largest room in the house; Nils remembered that his older brothers used to give dances there when he was a boy. Beside the stove stood a little girl with two light yellow braids and a broad, flushed face, peering anxiously into a frying pan. In the dining-room beyond, a large, broad-shouldered woman was moving about the table. She walked with an active, springy step. Her face was heavy and florid, almost without wrinkles, and her hair was black at seventy. Nils felt proud of her as he watched her deliberate activity; never a momentary hesitation, or a movement that did not tell. He waited until she came out into the kitchen and, brushing the child aside, took her place at the stove. Then he tapped on the screen door and entered.

"It's nobody but Nils, Mother. I expect you weren't looking for me."

Mrs. Ericson turned away from the stove and stood staring at him. "Bring the lamp, Hilda, and let me look."

Nils laughed and unslung his valise. "What's the matter, Mother? Don't you know me?"

Mrs. Ericson put down the lamp. "You must be Nils. You don't look very different, anyway."

"Nor you, Mother. You hold your own. Don't you wear glasses yet?"

"Only to read by. Where's your trunk, Nils?"

"Oh, I left that in town. I thought it might not be convenient for you to have company so near thresh-ing-time."

"Don't be foolish, Nils." Mrs. Ericson turned back to the stove. "I don't thresh now. I hitched the wheat land onto the next farm and have a tenant. Hilda, take some hot water up to the company room, and go call little Eric."

The tow-haired child, who had been standing in mute amazement, took up the tea-kettle and with-drew, giving Nils a long, admiring look from the door of the kitchen stairs.

"Who's the youngster?" Nils asked, dropping down on the bench behind the kitchen stove.

"One of your Cousin Henrik's."

"How long has Cousin Henrik been dead?"

"Six years. There are two boys. One stays with Peter and one with Anders. Olaf is their guardeen."

There was a clatter of pails on the porch, and a tall, lanky boy peered wonderingly in through the screen door. He had a fair, gentle face and big grey eyes, and wisps of soft yellow hair hung down under his cap. Nils sprang up and pulled him into the kitchen, hug-ging him and slapping him on the shoulders. "Well, if it isn't my kid! Look at the size of him! Don't you know me, Eric?"

The boy reddened under his sunburn and freckles, and hung his head. "I guess it's Nils," he said shyly.

"You're a good guesser," laughed Nils giving the lad's hand a swing. To himself he was thinking:

"That's why the little girl looked so friendly. He's taught her to like me. He was only six when I went away, and he's remembered for twelve years."

Eric stood fumbling with his cap and smiling. "You look just like I thought you would," he ventured.

"Go wash your hands, Eric," called Mrs. Ericson. "I've got cob corn for supper, Nils. You used to like it. I guess you don't get much of that in the old country. Here's Hilda; she'll take you up to your room. You'll want to get the dust off you before you eat."

Mrs. Ericson went into the dining-room to lay another plate, and the little girl came up and nodded to Nils as if to let him know that his room was ready. He put out his hand and she took it, with a startled glance up at his face. Little Eric dropped his towel, threw an arm about Nils and one about Hilda, gave them a clumsy squeeze, and then stumbled out to the porch.

During supper Nils heard exactly how much land each of his eight grown brothers farmed, how their crops were coming on, and how much livestock they were feeding. His mother watched him narrowly as she talked. "You've got better looking, Nils," she remarked abruptly, whereupon he grinned and the children giggled. Eric, although he was eighteen and as tall as Nils, was always accounted a child, being the last of so many sons. His face seemed childlike, too, Nils thought, and he had the open, wandering eyes of a little boy. All the others had been men at his age.

After supper Nils went out to the front porch and sat down on the step to smoke a pipe. Mrs. Ericson drew a rocking-chair up near him and began to knit busily. It was one of the few Old World customs she had kept up, for she could not bear to sit with idle hands.

"Where's little Eric, Mother?"

"He's helping Hilda with the dishes. He does it of his own will; I don't like a boy to be too handy about the house."

"He seems like a nice kid."

"He's very obedient."

Nils smiled a little in the dark. It was just as well to shift the line of conversation. "What are you knitting there, Mother?"

"Baby stockings. The boys keep me busy." Mrs. Ericson chuckled and clicked her needles.

"How many grandchildren have you?"

"Only thirty-one now. Olaf lost his three. They were sickly, like their mother."

"I supposed he had a second crop by this time!"

"His second wife has no children. She's too proud. She tears about on horseback all the time. But she'll get caught up with, yet. She sets herself very high, though nobody knows what for. They were low enough Bohemians she came of. I never thought much of Bohemians; always drinking."

Nils puffed away at his pipe in silence, and Mrs. Ericson knitted on. In a few moments she added grimly: "She was down here tonight, just before you came. She'd like to quarrel with me and come between me and Olaf, but I don't give her the chance. I suppose you'll be bringing a wife home some day."

"I don't know. I've never thought much about it."

"Well, perhaps it's best as it is," suggested Mrs. Ericson hopefully. "You'd never be contented tied down to the land. There was roving blood in your father's family, and it's come out in you. I expect your own way of life suits you best." Mrs. Ericson had dropped into a blandly agreeable tone which Nils well remembered. It seemed to amuse him a good deal and his white teeth flashed behind his pipe. His mother's strategies had always diverted him, even when he was a boy—they were so flimsy and patent, so illy proportioned to her vigor and force. "They've been waiting to see which way I'd jump," he reflected. He felt that Mrs. Ericson was pondering his case deeply as she sat clicking her needles.

"I don't suppose you've ever got used to steady work," she went on presently. "Men ain't apt to if they roam around too long. It's a pity you didn't come back the year after the World's Fair. Your father picked up a good bit of land cheap then, in the hard times, and I expect maybe he'd have give you a farm. It's too bad you put off comin' back so long, for I always thought he meant to do something by you."

Nils laughed and shook the ashes out of his pipe. "I'd have missed a lot if I had come back then. But I'm sorry I didn't get back to see father."

"Well, I suppose we have to miss things at one end or the other. Perhaps you are as well satisfied with your own doings, now, as you'd have been with a farm," said Mrs. Ericson reassuringly.

"Land's a good thing to have," Nils commented, as he lit another match and sheltered it with his hand.

His mother looked sharply at his face until the match burned out. "Only when you stay on it!" she hastened to say.

Eric came round the house by the path just then, and Nils rose, with a yawn. "Mother, if you don't mind, Eric and I will take a little tramp before bedtime. It will make me sleep."

"Very well; only don't stay long. I'll sit up and wait for you. I like to lock up myself."

Nils put his hand on Eric's shoulder, and the two tramped down the hill and across the sand creek into the dusty highroad beyond. Neither spoke. They swung along at an even gait, Nils puffing at his pipe. There was no moon, and the white road and the wide fields lay faint in the starlight. Over everything was darkness and thick silence, and the smell of dust and sunflowers. The brothers followed the road for a mile or more without finding a place to sit down. Finally, Nils perched on a stile over the wire fence, and Eric sat on the lower step.

"I began to think you never would come back, Nils," said the boy softly.

"Didn't I promise you I would?"

"Yes; but people don't bother about promises they make to babies. Did you really know you were going away for good when you went to Chicago with the cattle that time?"

"I thought it very likely, if I could make my way."

"I don't see how you did it, Nils. Not many fellows could." Eric rubbed his shoulder against his brother's knee.

"The hard thing was leaving home—you and father. It was easy enough, once I got beyond Chicago. Of course I got awful homesick; used to cry myself to sleep. But I'd burned my bridges."

"You had always wanted to go, hadn't you?"

"Always. Do you still sleep in our little room? Is that cottonwood still by the window?"

Eric nodded eagerly and smiled up at his brother in the grey darkness.

"You remember how we always said the leaves were whispering when they rustled at night? Well, they always whispered to me about the sea. Sometimes they said names out of the geography books. In a high wind they had a desperate sound, like someone trying to tear loose."

"How funny, Nils," said Eric dreamily, resting his chin on his hand. "That tree still talks like that, and 'most always it talks to me about you."

They sat a while longer, watching the stars. At last Eric whispered anxiously: "Hadn't we better go back now? Mother will get tired waiting for us." They rose and took a short cut home, through the pasture.

II

The next morning Nils woke with the first flood of light that came with dawn. The white-plastered walls of his room reflected the glare that shone through the thin window shades, and he found it impossible to sleep. He dressed hurriedly and slipped down the hall and up the back stairs to the half-story room which he used to share with his little brother. Eric, in a skimpy nightshirt, was sitting on the edge of the bed, rubbing his eyes, his pale yellow hair standing up in tufts all over his head. When he saw Nils, he murmured something confusedly and hustled his long legs into his trousers. "I didn't expect you'd be up so early, Nils," he said, as his head emerged from his blue shirt.

"Oh, you thought I was a dude, did you?" Nils gave him a playful tap which bent the tall boy up like a clasp knife. "See here; I must teach you to box." Nils thrust his hands into his pockets and walked about. "You haven't changed things much up here. Got most of my old traps, haven't you?"

He took down a bent, withered piece of sapling that hung over the dresser. "If this isn't the stick Lou Sandberg killed himself with!"

The boy looked up from his shoe-lacing.

"Yes; you never used to let me play with that. Just

how did he do it, Nils? You were with father when he found Lou, weren't you?"

"Yes. Father was going off to preach somewhere, and, as we drove along, Lou's place looked sort of forlorn, and we thought we'd stop and cheer him up. When we found him father said he'd been dead a couple days. He'd tied a piece of binding twine round his neck, made a noose in each end, fixed the nooses over the ends of a bent stick, and let the stick spring straight; strangled himself."

"What made him kill himself such a silly way?"

The simplicity of the boy's question set Nils laughing. He clapped little Eric on the shoulder. "What made him such a silly as to kill himself at all, I should say!"

"Oh, well! But his hogs had the cholera, and all up and died on him, didn't they?"

"Sure they did; but he didn't have cholera; and there were plenty of hogs left in the world, weren't there?"

"Well, but, if they weren't his, how could they do him any good?" Eric asked, in astonishment.

"Oh, scat! He could have had lots of fun with other people's hogs. He was a chump, Lou Sandberg. To kill yourself for a pig—think of that, now!" Nils laughed all the way downstairs, and quite embarrassed little Eric, who fell to scrubbing his face and hands at the tin basin. While he was parting his wet hair at the kitchen looking glass, a heavy tread sounded on the stairs. The boy dropped his comb. "Gracious, there's Mother. We must have talked too long." He hurried out to the shed, slipped on his overalls, and disappeared with the milking pails.

Mrs. Ericson came in, wearing a clean white apron,

her black hair shining from the application of a wet brush.

"Good morning, Mother. Can't I make the fire for you?"

"No, thank you, Nils. It's no trouble to make a cob fire, and I like to manage the kitchen stove myself." Mrs. Ericson paused with a shovel full of ashes in her hand. "I expect you will be wanting to see your brothers as soon as possible. I'll take you up to Anders' place this morning. He's threshing, and most of our boys are over there."

"Will Olaf be there?"

Mrs. Ericson went on taking out the ashes, and spoke between shovels. "No; Olaf's wheat is all in, put away in his new barn. He got six thousand bushel this year. He's going to town today to get men to finish roofing his barn."

"So Olaf is building a new barn?" Nils asked absently.

"Biggest one in the county, and almost done. You'll likely be here for the barn-raising. He's going to have a supper and a dance as soon as everybody's done threshing. Says it keeps the voters in good humour. I tell him that's all nonsense; but Olaf has a head for politics."

"Does Olaf farm all Cousin Henrik's land?"

Mrs. Ericson frowned as she blew into the faint smoke curling up about the cobs. "Yes; he holds it in trust for the children, Hilda and her brothers. He keeps strict account of everything he raises on it, and puts the proceeds out at compound interest for them."

Nils smiled as he watched the little flames shoot up. The door of the back stairs opened, and Hilda emerged, her arms behind her, buttoning up her long gingham apron as she came. He nodded to her gaily, and she twinkled at him out of her little blue eyes, set far apart over her wide cheekbones.

"There, Hilda, you grind the coffee—and just put in an extra handful; I expect your Cousin Nils likes his strong," said Mrs. Ericson, as she went out to the shed.

Nils turned to look at the little girl, who gripped the coffee grinder between her knees and ground so hard that her two braids bobbed and her face flushed under its broad spattering of freckles. He noticed on her middle finger something that had not been there last night, and that had evidently been put on for company: a tiny gold ring with a clumsily set garnet stone. As her hand went round and round he touched the ring with the tip of his finger, smiling.

Hilda glanced toward the shed door through which Mrs. Ericson had disappeared. "My Cousin Clara gave me that," she whispered bashfully. "She's Cousin Olaf's wife."

III

Mrs. Olaf Ericson—Clara Vavrika, as many people still called her—was moving restlessly about her big bare house that morning. Her husband had left for the county town before his wife was out of bed—her lateness in rising was one of the many things the Ericson family had against her. Clara seldom came downstairs before eight o'clock, and this morning she was even later, for she had dressed with unusual care. She put on, however, only a tight-fitting black dress, which people thereabouts thought very plain. She was a tall, dark woman of thirty, with a rather sallow complexion and a touch of dull salmon red in her cheeks, where the blood seemed to burn under her brown skin. Her hair, parted evenly above her low forehead, was so black that there were distinctly blue lights in it. Her black eyebrows were delicate half-moons and her lashes were long and heavy. Her eyes slanted a little, as if she had a strain of Tartar or gypsy blood, and were sometimes full of fiery determination and sometimes dull and opaque. Her expression was never altogether amiable; was often, indeed, distinctly sullen, or, when she was animated, sarcastic. She was most attractive in profile, for then one saw to advantage her small, well-shaped head and delicate ears, and felt at once that here was a very positive, if not an altogether pleasing, personality.

The entire management of Mrs. Olaf's household devolved upon her aunt, Johanna Vavrika, a superstitious, doting woman of fifty. When Clara was a little girl her mother died, and Johanna's life had been spent in ungrudging service to her niece. Clara, like many self-willed and discontented persons, was really very apt, without knowing it, to do as other people told her, and to let her destiny be decided for her by intelligences much below her own. It was her Aunt Johanna who had humoured and spoiled her in her girlhood, who had got her off to Chicago to study piano, and who had finally persuaded her to marry Olaf Ericson as the best match she would be likely to make in that part of the country. Johanna Vavrika had been deeply scarred by smallpox in the old country. She was short and fat, homely and jolly and sentimental. She was so broad, and took such short steps when she walked, that her brother, Joe Vavrika, always called her his duck. She adored her niece because of her talent, because of her good looks and masterful ways, but most of all because of her selfishness.

Clara's marriage with Olaf Ericson was Johanna's

particular triumph. She was inordinately proud of Olaf's position, and she found a sufficiently exciting career in managing Clara's house, in keeping it above the criticism of the Ericsons, in pampering Olaf to keep him from finding fault with his wife, and in concealing from every one Clara's domestic infelicities. While Clara slept of a morning, Johanna Vavrika was bustling about, seeing that Olaf and the men had their breakfast, and that the cleaning or the butter-making or the washing was properly begun by the two girls in the kitchen. Then, at about eight o'clock, she would take Clara's coffee up to her, and chat with her while she drank it, telling her what was going on in the house. Old Mrs. Ericson frequently said that her daughter-in-law would not know what day of the week it was if Johanna did not tell her every morning. Mrs. Ericson despised and pitied Johanna, but did not wholly dislike her. The one thing she hated in her daughter-in-law above everything else was the way in which Clara could come it over people. It enraged her that the affairs of her son's big, barnlike house went on as well as they did, and she used to feel that in this world we have to wait overlong to see the guilty punished. "Suppose Johanna Vavrika died or got sick?" the old lady used to say to Olaf. "Your wife wouldn't know where to look for her own dish-cloth." Olaf only shrugged his shoulders. The fact remained that Johanna did not die, and, although Mrs. Ericson often told her she was looking poorly, she was never ill. She seldom left the house, and she slept in a little room off the kitchen. No Ericson, by night or day, could come prying about there to find fault without her knowing it. Her one weakness was that she was an incurable talker, and she sometimes made trouble without meaning to.

This morning Clara was tying a wine-coloured ribbon about her throat when Johanna appeared with her coffee. After putting the tray on a sewing table, she began to make Clara's bed, chattering the while in Bohemian.

"Well, Olaf got off early, and the girls are baking. I'm going down presently to make some poppy-seed bread for Olaf. He asked for prune preserves at breakfast, and I told him I was out of them, and to bring some prunes and honey and cloves from town."

Clara poured her coffee. "Ugh! I don't see how men can eat so much sweet stuff. In the morning, too!"

Her aunt chuckled knowingly. "Bait a bear with honey, as we say in the old country."

"Was he cross?" her niece asked indifferently.

"Olaf? Oh, no! He was in fine spirits. He's never cross if you know how to take him. I never knew a man to make so little fuss about bills. I gave him a list of things to get a yard long, and he didn't say a word; just folded it up and put it in his pocket."

"I can well believe he didn't say a word," Clara remarked with a shrug. "Some day he'll forget how to talk."

"Oh, but they say he's a grand speaker in the Legislature. He knows when to keep quiet. That's why he's got such influence in politics. The people have confidence in him." Johanna beat up a pillow and held it under her fat chin while she slipped on the case. Her niece laughed.

"Maybe we could make people believe we were wise, Aunty, if we held our tongues. Why did you tell Mrs. Ericson that Norman threw me again last Saturday and turned my foot? She's been talking to Olaf."

Johanna fell into great confusion. "Oh, but, my precious, the old lady asked for you, and she's always so angry if I can't give an excuse. Anyhow, she needn't talk; she's always tearing up something with that motor of hers."

When her aunt clattered down to the kitchen, Clara went to dust the parlour. Since there was not much there to dust, this did not take very long. Olaf had built the house new for her before their marriage, but her interest in furnishing it had been short-lived. It went, indeed, little beyond a bathtub and her piano. They had disagreed about almost every other article of furniture, and Clara had said she would rather have her house empty than full of things she didn't want. The house was set in a hillside, and the west windows of the parlour looked out above the kitchen yard thirty feet below. The east windows opened directly into the front yard. At one of the latter, Clara, while she was dusting, heard a low whistle. She did not turn at once, but listened intently as she drew her cloth slowly along the round of a chair. Yes, there it was:

I dreamt that I dwelt in ma-a-arble halls.

She turned and saw Nils Ericson laughing in the sunlight, his hat in his hand, just outside the window. As she crossed the room he leaned against the wire screen. "Aren't you at all surprised to see me, Clara Vavrika?"

"No; I was expecting to see you. Mother Ericson telephoned Olaf last night that you were here."

Nils squinted and gave a long whistle. "Telephoned? That must have been while Eric and I were out walking. Isn't she enterprising? Lift this screen, won't you?"

Clara lifted the screen, and Nils swung his leg across the window-sill. As he stepped into the room she said: "You didn't think you were going to get ahead of your mother, did you?"

He threw his hat on the piano. "Oh, I do sometimes. You see, I'm ahead of her now. I'm supposed to be in Anders' wheat-field. But, as we were leaving, Mother ran her car into a soft place beside the road and sank up to the hubs. While they were going for the horses to pull her out, I cut away behind the stacks and escaped." Nils chuckled. Clara's dull eyes lit up as she looked at him admiringly.

"You've got them guessing already. I don't know what your mother said to Olaf over the telephone, but he came back looking as if he'd seen a ghost, and he didn't go to bed until a dreadful hour—ten o'clock, I should think. He sat out on the porch in the dark like a graven image. It had been one of his talkative days, too." They both laughed, easily and lightly, like people who have laughed a great deal together; but they remained standing.

"Anders and Otto and Peter looked as if they had seen ghosts, too, over in the threshing field. What's the matter with them all?"

Clara gave him a quick, searching look. "Well, for one thing, they've always been afraid you have the other will."

Nils looked interested. "The other will?"

"Yes. A later one. They knew your father made another, but they never knew what he did with it. They almost tore the old house to pieces looking for it. They always suspected that he carried on a clandestine correspondence with you, for the one thing he would do was to get his own mail himself. So they thought he might have sent the new will to you for safekeeping. The old one, leaving everything to your mother, was made long before you went away, and it's understood among them that it cuts you out—that she will leave all the property to the others. Your father made the second will to prevent that. I've been hoping you had it. It would be such fun to spring it on them." Clara laughed mirthfully, a thing she did not often do now.

Nils shook his head reprovingly. "Come, now, you're malicious."

"No, I'm not. But I'd like something to happen to stir them all up, just for once. There never was such a family for having nothing ever happen to them but dinner and threshing. I'd almost be willing to die, just to have a funeral. *You* wouldn't stand it for three weeks."

Nils bent over the piano and began pecking at the keys with the finger of one hand. "I wouldn't? My dear young lady, how do you know what I can stand? *You* wouldn't wait to find out."

Clara flushed darkly and frowned. "I didn't believe you would ever come back—" she said defiantly.

"Eric believed I would, and he was only a baby when I went away. However, all's well that ends well, and I haven't come back to be a skeleton at the feast. We mustn't quarrel. Mother will be here with a search warrant pretty soon." He swung round and faced her, thrusting his hands into his coat pockets. "Come, you ought to be glad to see me, if you want something to happen. I'm something, even without a will. We can have a little fun, can't we? I think we can!"

She echoed him, "I think we can!" They both laughed and their eyes sparkled. Clara Vavrika looked ten years younger than when she had put the velvet ribbon about her throat that morning.

"You know, I'm so tickled to see mother," Nils went on. "I didn't know I was so proud of her. A regular pile driver. How about little pigtails, down at the house? Is Olaf doing the square thing by those children?"

Clara frowned pensively. "Olaf has to do something that looks like the square thing, now that he's a public man!" She glanced drolly at Nils. "But he makes a good commission out of it. On Sundays they all get together here and figure. He lets Peter and Anders put in big bills for the keep of the two boys, and he pays them out of the estate. They are always having what they call accountings. Olaf gets something out of it, too. I don't know just how they do it, but it's entirely a family matter, as they say. And when the Ericsons say that—" Clara lifted her eyebrows.

Just then the angry *honk-honk* of an approaching motor sounded from down the road. Their eyes met and they began to laugh. They laughed as children do when they can not contain themselves, and can not explain the cause of their mirth to grown people, but share it perfectly together. When Clara Vavrika sat down at the piano after he was gone, she felt that she had laughed away a dozen years. She practised as if the house were burning over her head.

When Nils greeted his mother and climbed into the front seat of the motor beside her, Mrs. Ericson looked grim, but she made no comment upon his truancy until she had turned her car and was retracing her revolutions along the road that ran by Olaf's big pasture. Then she remarked dryly:

"If I were you I wouldn't see too much of Olaf's wife while you are here. She's the kind of woman who can't see much of men without getting herself talked about. She was a good deal talked about before he married her."

"Hasn't Olaf tamed her?" Nils asked indifferently.

Mrs. Ericson shrugged her massive shoulders. "Olaf don't seem to have much luck, when it comes to wives. The first one was meek enough, but she was always ailing. And this one has her own way. He says if he quarreled with her she'd go back to her father, and then he'd lose the Bohemian vote. There are a great many Bohunks in this district. But when you find a man under his wife's thumb you can always be sure there's a soft spot in him somewhere."

Nils thought of his own father, and smiled. "She brought him a good deal of money, didn't she, besides the Bohemian vote?"

Mrs. Ericson sniffed. "Well, she has a fair half section in her own name, but I can't see as that does Olaf much good. She will have a good deal of property some day, if old Vavrika don't marry again. But I don't consider a saloonkeeper's money as good as other people's money."

Nils laughed outright. "Come, Mother, don't let your prejudices carry you that far. Money's money. Old Vavrika's a mighty decent sort of saloonkeeper. Nothing rowdy about him."

Mrs. Ericson spoke up angrily. "Oh, I know you always stood up for them! But hanging around there when you were a boy never did you any good, Nils, nor any of the other boys who went there. There weren't so many after her when she married Olaf, let me tell you. She knew enough to grab her chance."

Nils settled back in his seat. "Of course I liked to go there, Mother, and you were always cross about it. You never took the trouble to find out that it was the one jolly house in this country for a boy to go to. All the rest of you were working yourselves to death, and the houses were mostly a mess, full of babies and washing and flies. Oh, it was all right—I understand that; but you are young only once, and I happened to be young then. Now, Vavrika's was always jolly. He played the violin, and I used to take my flute, and Clara played the piano, and Johanna used to sing Bohemian songs. She always had a big supper for us— herrings and pickles and poppy-seed bread, and lots of cake and preserves. Old Joe had been in the army in the old country, and he could tell lots of good stories. I can see him cutting bread, at the head of the table, now. I don't know what I'd have done when I was a kid if it hadn't been for the Vavrikas, really."

"And all the time he was taking money that other people had worked hard in the fields for," Mrs. Ericson observed.

"So do the circuses, Mother, and they're a good thing. People ought to get fun for some of their money. Even father liked old Joe."

"Your father," Mrs. Ericson said grimly, "liked everybody."

As they crossed the sand creek and turned into her own place, Mrs. Ericson observed, "There's Olaf's buggy. He's stopped on his way from town." Nils shook himself and prepared to greet his brother, who was waiting on the porch.

Olaf was a big, heavy Norwegian, slow of speech and movement. His head was large and square, like a block of wood. When Nils, at a distance, tried to remember what his brother looked like, he could recall only his heavy head, high forehead, large nostrils, and pale blue eyes, set far apart. Olaf's features were rudimentary: the thing one noticed was the face itself, wide and flat and pale; devoid of any expression, betraying his fifty years as little as it betrayed anything else, and powerful by reason of its very stolidness. When Olaf shook hands with Nils he looked at him from under his light eyebrows, but Nils felt that no one could ever say what that pale look might mean. The one thing he had always felt in Olaf was a heavy stubbornness, like the unyielding stickiness of wet loam against the plow. He had always found Olaf the most difficult of his brothers.

"How do you do, Nils? Expect to stay with us long?"

"Oh, I may stay forever," Nils answered gaily. "I like this country better than I used to."

"There's been some work put into it since you left," Olaf remarked.

"Exactly. I think it's about ready to live in now— and I'm about ready to settle down." Nils saw his brother lower his big head ("Exactly like a bull," he thought.) "Mother's been persuading me to slow down now, and go in for farming," he went on lightly.

Olaf made a deep sound in his throat. "Farming ain't learned in a day," he brought out, still looking at the ground.

"Oh, I know! But I pick things up quickly." Nils had not meant to antagonize his brother, and he did not know now why he was doing it. "Of course," he went on, "I shouldn't expect to make a big success, as you fellows have done. But then, I'm not ambitious. I won't want much. A little land, and some cattle, maybe."

Olaf still stared at the ground, his head down. He wanted to ask Nils what he had been doing all these years, that he didn't have a business somewhere he couldn't afford to leave; why he hadn't more pride than to come back with only a little sole-leather trunk to show for himself, and to present himself as the only failure in the family. He did not ask one of these questions, but he made them all felt distinctly.

"Humph!" Nils thought. "No wonder the man never talks, when he can butt his ideas into you like that without ever saying a word. I suppose he uses that kind of smokeless powder on his wife all the time. But I guess she has her innings." He chuckled, and Olaf looked up. "Never mind me, Olaf. I laugh without knowing why, like little Eric. He's another cheerful dog."

"Eric," said Olaf slowly, "is a spoiled kid. He's just let his mother's best cow go dry because he don't milk her right. I was hoping you'd take him away somewhere and put him into business. If he don't do any good among strangers, he never will." This was a long speech for Olaf, and as he finished it he climbed into his buggy.

Nils shrugged his shoulders. "Same old tricks," he thought. "Hits from behind you every time. What a whale of a man!" He turned and went round to the kitchen, where his mother was scolding little Eric for letting the gasoline get low.

IV

Joe Vavrika's saloon was not in the county seat, where Olaf and Mrs. Ericson did their trading, but in a cheerfuller place, a little Bohemian settlement which lay at the other end of the county, ten level miles north of Olaf's farm. Clara rode up to see her father almost every day. Vavrika's house was, so to speak, in the back yard of his saloon. The garden between the two buildings was inclosed by a high board fence as tight as a partition, and in summer Joe kept beer tables and wooden benches among the gooseberry bushes under his little cherry tree. At one of these tables Nils Ericson was seated in the late afternoon, three days after his return home. Joe had gone in to serve a customer, and Nils was lounging on his elbows, looking rather mournfully into his half-emptied pitcher, when he heard a laugh across the little garden. Clara, in her riding habit, was standing at the back door of the house, under the grapevine trellis that old Joe had grown there long ago. Nils rose.

"Come out and keep your father and me company. We've been gossiping all afternoon. Nobody to bother us but the flies."

She shook her head. "No, I never come out here any more. Olaf doesn't like it. I must live up to my position, you know."

"You mean to tell me you never come out and chat with the boys, as you used to? He *has* tamed you! Who keeps up these flower-beds?"

"I come out on Sundays, when father is alone, and read the Bohemian papers to him. But I am never here when the bar is open. What have you two been doing?"

"Talking, as I told you. I've been telling him about my travels. I find I can't talk much at home, not even to Eric."

Clara reached up and poked with her riding-whip at a white moth that was fluttering in the sunlight among the vine leaves. "I suppose you will never tell me about all those things."

"Where can I tell them? Not in Olaf's house, certainly. What's the matter with our talking here?" He pointed persuasively with his hat to the bushes and the green table, where the flies were singing lazily above the empty beer glasses.

Clara shook her head weakly. "No, it wouldn't do. Besides, I am going now."

"I'm on Eric's mare. Would you be angry if I overtook you?"

Clara looked back and laughed. "You might try and see. I can leave you if I don't want you. Eric's mare can't keep up with Norman."

Nils went into the bar and attempted to pay his score. Big Joe, six feet four, with curly yellow hair and mustache, clapped him on the shoulder. "Not a Goddamn a your money go in my drawer, you hear? Only next time you bring your flute, te-te-te-te-te-ty." Joe wagged his fingers in imitation of the flute player's position. "My Clara, she come all-a-time Sundays an' play for me. She not like to play at Ericson's place." He shook his yellow curls and laughed. "Not a Goddamn a fun at Ericson's. You come a Sunday. You like-a fun. No forget de flute." Joe talked very rapidly and always tumbled over his English. He seldom spoke it to his customers, and had never learned much.

Nils swung himself into the saddle and trotted to the west of the village, where the houses and gardens scattered into prairie land and the road turned south. Far ahead of him, in the declining light, he saw Clara Vavrika's slender figure, loitering on horseback. He touched his mare with the whip, and shot along the white, level road, under the reddening sky. When he overtook Olaf's wife he saw that she had been crying. "What's the matter, Clara Vavrika?" he asked kindly.

"Oh, I get blue sometimes. It was awfully jolly living there with father. I wonder why I ever went away."

Nils spoke in a low, kind tone that he sometimes used with women: "That's what I've been wondering these many years. You were the last girl in the country

I'd have picked for a wife for Olaf. What made you do it, Clara?"

"I suppose I really did it to oblige the neighbours" —Clara tossed her head. "People were beginning to wonder."

"To wonder?"

"Yes—why I didn't get married. I suppose I didn't like to keep them in suspense. I've discovered that most girls marry out of consideration for the neighbourhood."

Nils bent his head toward her and his white teeth flashed. "I'd have gambled that one girl I knew would say, 'Let the neighbourhood be damned.'"

Clara shook her head mournfully. "You see, they have it on you, Nils; that is, if you're a woman. They say you're beginning to go off. That's what makes us get married: we can't stand the laugh."

Nils looked sidewise at her. He had never seen her head droop before. Resignation was the last thing he would have expected of her. "In your case, there wasn't something else?"

"Something else?"

"I mean, you didn't do it to spite somebody? Somebody who didn't come back?"

Clara drew herself up. "Oh, I never thought you'd come back. Not after I stopped writing to you, at least. *That* was all over, long before I married Olaf."

"It never occurred to you, then, that the meanest thing you could do to me was to marry Olaf?"

Clara laughed. "No; I didn't know you were so fond of Olaf."

Nils smoothed his horse's mane with his glove. "You know, Clara Vavrika, you are never going to stick it out. You'll cut away some day, and I've been thinking you might as well cut away with me."

Clara threw up her chin. "Oh, you don't know me as well as you think. I won't cut away. Sometimes, when I'm with father, I feel like it. But I can hold out as long as the Ericsons can. They've never got the best of me yet, and one can live, so long as one isn't beaten. If I go back to father, it's all up with Olaf in politics. He knows that, and he never goes much beyond sulking. I've as much wit as the Ericsons. I'll never leave them unless I can show them a thing or two."

"You mean unless you can come it over them?"

"Yes—unless I go away with a man who is cleverer than they are, and who has more money."

Nils whistled. "Dear me, you are demanding a good deal. The Ericsons, take the lot of them, are a bunch to beat. But I should think the excitement of tormenting them would have worn off by this time."

"It has, I'm afraid," Clara admitted mournfully.

"Then why don't you cut away? There are more amusing games than this in the world. When I came home I thought it might amuse me to bully a few quarter sections out of the Ericsons; but I've almost decided I can get more fun for my money somewhere else."

Clara took in her breath sharply. "Ah, you have got the other will! That was why you came home!"

"No, it wasn't. I came home to see how you were getting on with Olaf."

Clara struck her horse with the whip, and in a bound she was far ahead of him. Nils dropped one word, "Damn!" and whipped after her; but she leaned forward in her saddle and fairly cut the wind. Her long riding skirt rippled in the still air behind her. The sun was just sinking behind the stubble in a vast, clear sky, and the shadows drew across the fields so rapidly that Nils could scarcely keep in sight the dark figure on the road. When he overtook her he caught her horse by the bridle. Norman reared, and Nils was frightened for her; but Clara kept her seat.

"Let me go, Nils Ericson!" she cried. "I hate you more than any of them. You were created to torture me, the whole tribe of you—to make me suffer in every possible way."

She struck her horse again and galloped away from him. Nils set his teeth and looked thoughtful. He rode slowly home along the deserted road, watching the stars come out in the clear violet sky. They flashed softly into the limpid heavens, like jewels let fall into clear water. They were a reproach, he felt, to a sordid world. As he turned across the sand creek, he looked up at the North Star and smiled, as if there were an understanding between them. His mother scolded him for being late for supper.

V

On Sunday afternoon Joe Vavrika, in his shirt sleeves and carpet slippers, was sitting in his garden, smoking a long-tasseled porcelain pipe with a hunting scene painted on the bowl. Clara sat under the cherry tree, reading aloud to him from the weekly Bohemian papers. She had worn a white muslin dress under her riding habit, and the leaves of the cherry tree threw a pattern of sharp shadows over her skirt. The black cat was dozing in the sunlight at her feet, and Joe's dachshund was scratching a hole under the scarlet geraniums and dreaming of badgers. Joe was filling his pipe for the third time since dinner, when he heard a knocking on the fence. He broke into a loud guffaw and unlatched the little door that led into the street.

He did not call Nils by name, but caught him by the hand and dragged him in. Clara stiffened and the colour deepened under her dark skin. Nils, too, felt a little awkward. He had not seen her since the night when she rode away from him and left him alone on the level road between the fields. Joe dragged him to the wooden bench beside the green table.

"You bring de flute," he cried, tapping the leather case under Nils' arm. "Ah, das-a good! Now we have some liddle fun like old times. I got somet'ing good for you." Joe shook his finger at Nils and winked his blue eye, a bright clear eye, full of fire, though the tiny bloodvessels on the ball were always a little distended. "I got somet'ing for you from"—he paused and waved his hand—"Hongarie. You know Hongarie? You wait!" He pushed Nils down on the bench, and went through the back door of his saloon.

Nils looked at Clara, who sat frigidly with her white skirts drawn tight about her. "He didn't tell you he had asked me to come, did he? He wanted a party and proceeded to arrange it. Isn't he fun? Don't be cross; let's give him a good time."

Clara smiled and shook out her skirt. "Isn't that like father? And he has sat here so meekly all day. Well, I won't pout. I'm glad you came. He doesn't have very many good times now any more. There are so few of his kind left. The second generation are a tame lot."

Joe came back with a flask in one hand and three wine glasses caught by the stems between the fingers of the other. These he placed on the table with an air of ceremony, and, going behind Nils, held the flask between him and the sun, squinting into it admiringly. "You know dis, Tokai? A great friend of mine, he bring dis to me, a present out of Hongarie. You know how much it cost, dis wine? Chust so much what it weigh in gold. Nobody but de nobles drink him in Bohemie. Many, many years I save him up, dis Tokai." Joe whipped out his official corkscrew and delicately removed the cork. "De old man die what bring him to me, an' dis wine he lay on his belly in my cellar an' sleep. An' now," carefully pouring out the heavy yellow wine, "an' now he wake up; and maybe he wake us up, too!" He carried one of the glasses to his daughter and presented it with great gallantry.

Clara shook her head, but, seeing her father's disappointment, relented. "You taste it first. I don't want so much."

Joe sampled it with a beatific expression, and turned to Nils. "You drink him slow, dis wine. He very soft, but he go down hot. You see!"

After a second glass Nils declared that he couldn't take any more without getting sleepy. "Now get your fiddle, Vavrika," he said as he opened his flute case.

But Joe settled back in his wooden rocker and wagged his big carpet slipper. "No-no-no-no-no-no-no! No play fiddle now any more: too much ache in de finger," waving them, "all-a-time rheumatiz. You play de flute, te-tety-te-tety-te. Bohemie songs."

"I've forgotten all the Bohemian songs I used to play with you and Johanna. But here's one that will make Clara pout. You remember how her eyes used to snap when we called her the Bohemian Girl?" Nils lifted his flute and began "When Other Lips and Other Hearts," and Joe hummed the air in a husky baritone, waving his carpet slipper. "Oh-h-h, das-a fine music," he cried, clapping his hands as Nils finished. "Now 'Marble Halls, Marble Halls'! Clara, you sing him."

Clara smiled and leaned back in her chair, beginning softly:

> "I dreamt that I dwelt in ma-a-arble halls,
>   With vassals and serfs at my knee,"

and Joe hummed like a big bumblebee.

"There's one more you always played," Clara said quietly, "I remember that best." She locked her hands over her knee and began "The Heart Bowed Down," and sang it through without groping for the words. She was singing with a good deal of warmth when she came to the end of the old song:

> "For memory is the only friend
>   That grief can call its own."

Joe flashed out his red silk handkerchief and blew his nose, shaking his head. "No-no-no-no-no-no-no! Too sad, too sad! I not like-a dat. Play quick somet'ing gay now."

Nils put his lips to the instrument, and Joe lay back in his chair, laughing and singing, "Oh, Evelina, Sweet Evelina!" Clara laughed, too. Long ago, when she and Nils went to high school, the model student of their class was a very homely girl in thick spectacles. Her name was Evelina Oleson; she had a long, swinging walk which somehow suggested the measure of that song, and they used mercilessly to sing it at her.

"Dat ugly Oleson girl, she teach in de school," Joe gasped, "an' she still walks chust like dat, yup-a, yup-a, yup-a, chust like a camel she go! Now, Nils, we have some more li'l drink. Oh, yes-yes-yes-yes-yes-yes-yes! Dis time you haf to drink, and Clara she haf to, so she show she not jealous. So, we all drink to your girl. You not tell her name, eh? No-no-no, I no make you tell. She pretty, eh? She make good sweetheart? I bet!" Joe winked and lifted his glass. "How soon you get married?"

Nils screwed up his eyes. "That I don't know. When she says."

Joe threw out his chest. "Das-a way boys talks. No way for mans. Mans say, 'You come to de church, an' get a hurry on you.' Das-a way mans talks."

"Maybe Nils hasn't got enough to keep a wife," put in Clara ironically. "How about that, Nils?" she asked him frankly, as if she wanted to know.

Nils looked at her coolly, raising one eyebrow. "Oh, I can keep her, all right."

"The way she wants to be kept?"

"With my wife, I'll decide that," replied Nils calmly. "I'll give her what's good for her."

Clara made a wry face. "You'll give her the strap, I expect, like old Peter Oleson gave his wife."

"When she needs it," said Nils lazily, locking his hands behind his head and squinting up through the leaves of the cherry tree. "Do you remember the time I squeezed the cherries all over your clean dress, and Aunt Johanna boxed my ears for me? My gracious, weren't you mad! You had both hands full of cherries, and I squeezed 'em and made the juice fly all over you. I liked to have fun with you; you'd get so mad."

"We *did* have fun, didn't we? None of the other kids ever had so much fun. We knew how to play."

Nils dropped his elbows on the table and looked steadily across at her. "I've played with lots of girls since, but I haven't found one who was such good fun."

Clara laughed. The late afternoon sun was shining full in her face, and deep in the back of her eyes there shone something fiery, like the yellow drops of Tokai in the brown glass bottle. "Can you still play, or are you only pretending?"

"I can play better than I used to, and harder."

"Don't you ever work, then?" She had not intended to say it. It slipped out because she was confused enough to say just the wrong thing.

"I work between times." Nils' steady gaze still beat upon her. "Don't you worry about my working, Mrs. Ericson. You're getting like all the rest of them." He reached his brown, warm hand across the table and dropped it on Clara's, which was cold as an icicle. "Last call for play, Mrs. Ericson!" Clara shivered, and suddenly her hands and cheeks grew warm. Her fingers lingered in his a moment, and they looked at each other earnestly. Joe Vavrika had put the mouth of the bottle to his lips and was swallowing the last drops of the Tokai, standing. The sun, just about to sink behind his shop, glistened on the bright glass, on his flushed face and curly yellow hair. "Look," Clara whispered, "that's the way I want to grow old."

VI

On the day of Olaf Ericson's barn-raising, his wife, for once in a way, rose early. Johanna Vavrika had been baking cakes and frying and boiling and spicing meats for a week beforehand, but it was not until the day before the party was to take place that Clara showed any interest in it. Then she was seized with one of her fitful spasms of energy, and took the wagon and little Eric and spent the day on Plum Creek, gathering vines and swamp goldenrod to decorate the barn.

By four o'clock in the afternoon buggies and wagons began to arrive at the big unpainted building in front of Olaf's house. When Nils and his mother came at five, there were more than fifty people in the barn, and a great drove of children. On the ground floor stood six long tables, set with the crockery of seven flourishing Ericson families, lent for the occasion. In the middle of each table was a big yellow pumpkin, hollowed out and filled with woodbine. In one corner of the barn, behind a pile of green-and-white striped watermelons, was a circle of chairs for the old people; the younger guests sat on bushel measures or barbed-wire spools, and the children tumbled about in the haymow. The box stalls Clara had converted into booths. The framework was hidden by goldenrod and sheaves of wheat, and the partitions were covered with wild grapevines full of fruit. At one of these Johanna Vavrika watched over her cooked meats, enough to provision an army; and at the next her kitchen girls had ranged the ice-cream freezers, and Clara was already cutting pies and cakes against the hour of serving. At the third stall, little Hilda, in a bright pink lawn dress, dispensed lemonade throughout the afternoon. Olaf, as a public man, had thought it inadvisable to serve beer in his barn; but Joe Vavrika had come over with two demijohns concealed in his buggy, and after his arrival the wagon shed was much frequented by the men.

"Hasn't Cousin Clara fixed things lovely?" little Hilda whispered, when Nils went up to her stall and asked for lemonade.

Nils leaned against the booth, talking to the excited little girl and watching the people. The barn faced the west, and the sun, pouring in at the big doors, filled the whole interior with a golden light, through which filtered fine particles of dust from the haymow, where the children were romping. There was a great chattering from the stall where Johanna Vavrika exhibited to the admiring women her platters heaped with fried chicken, her roasts of beef, boiled tongues, and baked hams with cloves stuck in the crisp brown fat and garnished with tansy and parsley. The older women, having assured themselves that there were twenty kinds of cake, not counting cookies, and three dozen fat pies, repaired to the corner behind the pile of watermelons, put on their white aprons, and fell to their knitting and fancywork. They were a fine company of old women, and a Dutch painter would have loved to find them there together, where the sun made bright patches on the floor and sent long, quivering shafts of gold through the dusky shade up among the rafters. There were fat, rosy old women who looked hot in their best black dresses; spare, alert old women with brown, dark-veined hands; and several of almost heroic frame, not less massive than old Mrs. Ericson herself. Few of them wore glasses, and old Mrs. Svendsen, a Danish woman, who was quite bald, wore the only cap among them. Mrs. Oleson, who had twelve big grandchildren, could still show two braids of yellow hair as thick as her own wrists. Among all these grandmothers there were more brown heads than white. They all had a pleased, prosperous air, as if they were more than satisfied with themselves and with life. Nils, leaning against Hilda's lemonade stand, watched them as they sat chattering in four languages, their fingers never lagging behind their tongues.

"Look at them over there," he whispered, detaining Clara as she passed him. "Aren't they the Old Guard? I've just counted thirty hands. I guess they've wrung many a chicken's neck and warmed many a boy's jacket for him in their time."

In reality he fell into amazement when he thought of the Herculean labours those fifteen pairs of hands had performed: of the cows they had milked, the butter they had made, the gardens they had planted, the children and grandchildren they had tended, the brooms they had worn out, the mountains of food they had cooked. It made him dizzy. Clara Vavrika smiled a hard, enigmatical smile at him and walked rapidly away. Nils' eyes followed her white figure as she went toward the house. He watched her walking alone in the sunlight, looked at her slender, defiant shoulders and her little hard-set head with its coils of blue-black hair. "No," he reflected; "she'd never be like them, not if she lived here a hundred years. She'd only grow more bitter. You can't tame a wild thing; you can only chain it. People aren't all alike. I mustn't lose my nerve." He gave Hilda's pigtail a parting tweak and set out after Clara. "Where to?" he asked, as he came upon her in the kitchen.

"I'm going to the cellar for preserves."

"Let me go with you. I never get a moment alone with you. Why do you keep out of my way?"

Clara laughed. "I don't usually get in anybody's way."

Nils followed her down the stairs and to the far corner of the cellar, where a basement window let in a stream of light. From a swinging shelf Clara selected several glass jars, each labeled in Johanna's careful hand. Nils took up a brown flask. "What's this? It looks good."

"It is. It's some French brandy father gave me when I was married. Would you like some? Have you a corkscrew? I'll get glasses."

When she brought them, Nils took them from her and put them down on the window-sill. "Clara

Vavrika, do you remember how crazy I used to be about you?"

Clara shrugged her shoulders. "Boys are always crazy about somebody or another. I dare say some silly has been crazy about Evelina Oleson. You got over it in a hurry."

"Because I didn't come back, you mean? I had to get on, you know, and it was hard sledding at first. Then I heard you'd married Olaf."

"And then you stayed away from a broken heart," Clara laughed.

"And then I began to think about you more than I had since I first went away. I began to wonder if you were really as you had seemed to me when I was a boy. I thought I'd like to see. I've had lots of girls, but no one ever pulled me the same way. The more I thought about you, the more I remembered how it used to be—like hearing a wild tune you can't resist, calling you out at night. It had been a long while since anything had pulled me out of my boots, and I wondered whether anything ever could again." Nils thrust his hands into his coat pockets and squared his shoulders, as his mother sometimes squared hers, as Olaf, in a clumsier manner, squared his. "So I thought I'd come back and see. Of course the family have tried to do me, and I rather thought I'd bring out father's will and make a fuss. But they can have their old land; they've put enough sweat into it." He took the flask and filled the two glasses carefully to the brim. "I've found out what I want from the Ericsons. Drink *skoal*, Clara." He lifted his glass, and Clara took hers with downcast eyes. "Look at me, Clara Vavrika. *Skoal!*"

She raised her burning eyes and answered fiercely: "*Skoal!*"

The barn supper began at six o'clock and lasted for two hilarious hours. Yense Nelson had made a wager that he could eat two whole fried chickens, and he did. Eli Swanson stowed away two whole custard pies, and Nick Hermanson ate a chocolate layer cake to the last crumb. There was even a cooky contest among the children, and one thin, slablike Bohemian boy consumed sixteen and won the prize, a gingerbread pig which Johanna Vavrika had carefully decorated with red candies and burnt sugar. Fritz Sweiheart, the German carpenter, won in the pickle contest, but he disappeared soon after supper and was not seen for the rest of the evening. Joe Vavrika said that Fritz could have managed the pickles all right, but he had sampled the demijohn in his buggy too often before sitting down to the table.

While the supper was being cleared away the two fiddlers began to tune up for the dance. Clara was to accompany them on her old upright piano, which had been brought down from her father's. By this time Nils had renewed old acquaintances. Since his interview with Clara in the cellar, he had been busy telling all the old women how young they looked, and all the young ones how pretty they were, and assuring the men that they had here the best farmland in the world. He had made himself so agreeable that old Mrs. Ericson's friends began to come up to her and tell how lucky she was to get her smart son back again, and please to get him to play his flute. Joe Vavrika, who could still play very well when he forgot that he had rheumatism, caught up a fiddle from

Johnny Oleson and played a crazy Bohemian dance tune that set the wheels going. When he dropped the bow every one was ready to dance.

Olaf, in a frock coat and a solemn made-up necktie, led the grand march with his mother. Clara had kept well out of *that* by sticking to the piano. She played the march with a pompous solemnity which greatly amused the prodigal son, who went over and stood behind her.

"Oh, aren't you rubbing it into them, Clara Vavrika? And aren't you lucky to have me here, or all your wit would be thrown away."

"I'm used to being witty for myself. It saves my life."

The fiddles struck up a polka, and Nils convulsed Joe Vavrika by leading out Evelina Oleson, the homely schoolteacher. His next partner was a very fat Swedish girl, who, although she was an heiress, had not been asked for the first dance, but had stood against the wall in her tight, high-heeled shoes, nervously fingering a lace handkerchief. She was soon out of breath, so Nils led her, pleased and panting, to her seat, and went over to the piano, from which Clara had been watching his gallantry. "Ask Olena Yenson," she whispered. "She waltzes beautifully."

Olena, too, was rather inconveniently plump, handsome in a smooth, heavy way, with a fine colour and good-natured, sleepy eyes. She was redolent of violet sachet powder, and had warm, soft, white hands, but she danced divinely, moving as smoothly as the tide coming in. "There, that's something like," Nils said as he released her. "You'll give me the next waltz, won't you? Now I must go and dance with my little cousin."

Hilda was greatly excited when Nils went up to her stall and held out his arm. Her little eyes sparkled, but she declared that she could not leave her lemonade. Old Mrs. Ericson, who happened along at this moment, said she would attend to that, and Hilda came out, as pink as her pink dress. The dance was a schottische, and in a moment her yellow braids were fairly standing on end. "Bravo!" Nils cried encouragingly. "Where did you learn to dance so nicely?"

"My Cousin Clara taught me," the little girl panted.

Nils found Eric sitting with a group of boys who were too awkward or too shy to dance, and told him that he must dance the next waltz with Hilda.

The boy screwed up his shoulders. "Aw, Nils, I can't dance. My feet are too big; I look silly."

"Don't be thinking about yourself. It doesn't matter how boys look."

Nils had never spoken to him so sharply before, and Eric made haste to scramble out of his corner and brush the straw from his coat.

Clara nodded approvingly. "Good for you, Nils. I've been trying to get hold of him. They dance very nicely together; I sometimes play for them."

"I'm obliged to you for teaching him. There's no reason why he should grow up to be a lout."

"He'll never be that. He's more like you than any of them. Only he hasn't your courage." From her slanting eyes Clara shot forth one of those keen glances, admiring and at the same time challenging, which she seldom bestowed on any one, and which seemed to say, "Yes, I admire you, but I am your equal."

Clara was proving a much better host than Olaf, who, once the supper was over, seemed to feel no interest in anything but the lanterns. He had brought a locomotive headlight from town to light the revels, and he kept skulking about as if he feared the mere light from it might set his new barn on fire. His wife, on the contrary, was cordial to every one, was animated and even gay. The deep salmon colour in her cheeks burned vividly, and her eyes were full of life. She gave the piano over to the fat Swedish heiress, pulled her father away from the corner where he sat gossiping with his cronies, and made him dance a Bohemian dance with her. In his youth Joe had been a famous dancer, and his daughter got him so limbered up that every one sat around and applauded them. The old ladies were particularly delighted, and made them go through the dance again. From their corner where they watched and commented, the old women kept time with their feet and hands, and whenever the fiddles struck up a new air old Mrs. Svendsen's white cap would begin to bob.

Clara was waltzing with little Eric when Nils came up to them, brushed his brother aside, and swung her out among the dancers. "Remember how we used to waltz on rollers at the old skating rink in town? I suppose people don't do that any more. We used to keep it up for hours. You know, we never did moon around as other boys and girls did. It was dead serious with us from the beginning. When we were most in love with each other, we used to fight. You were always pinching people; your fingers were like little nippers. A regular snapping turtle, you were. Lord, how you'd like Stockholm! Sit out in the streets in front of cafés and talk all night in summer. Just like a reception—officers and ladies and funny English people. Jolliest people in the world, the Swedes, once you get them going. Always drinking things—champagne and stout mixed, half-and-half; serve it out of big pitchers, and serve plenty. Slow pulse, you know; they can stand a lot. Once they light up, they're glow-worms, I can tell you."

"All the same, you don't really like gay people."

"*I* don't?"

"No; I could tell that when you were looking at the old women there this afternoon. They're the kind you really admire, after all; women like your mother. And that's the kind you'll marry."

"Is it, Miss Wisdom? You'll see who I'll marry, and she won't have a domestic virtue to bless herself with. She'll be a snapping turtle, and she'll be a match for me. All the same, they're a fine bunch of old dames over there. You admire them yourself."

"No, I don't; I detest them."

"You won't, when you look back on them from Stockholm or Budapest. Freedom settles all that. Oh, but you're the real Bohemian Girl, Clara Vavrika!" Nils laughed down at her sullen frown and began mockingly to sing:

"Oh, how could a poor gypsy maiden like me
   Expect the proud bride of a baron to be?"

Clara clutched his shoulder. "Hush, Nils; every one is looking at you."

"I don't care. They can't gossip. It's all in the family, as the Ericsons say when they divide up little Hilda's patrimony amongst them. Besides, we'll give them something to talk about when we hit the trail. Lord, it will be a godsend to them! They haven't had anything so interesting to chatter about since the grasshopper year. It'll give them a new lease of life. And Olaf won't lose the Bohemian vote, either. They'll have the laugh on him so that they'll vote two apiece. They'll send him to Congress. They'll never forget his barn party, or us. They'll always remember us as we're dancing together now. We're making a legend. Where's my waltz, boys?" he called as they whirled past the fiddlers.

The musicians grinned, looked at each other, hesitated, and began a new air; and Nils sang with them, as the couples fell from a quick waltz to a long, slow glide:

> "When other lips and other hearts
> Their tale of love shall tell,
> In language whose excess imparts
> The power they feel so well."

The old women applauded vigorously. "What a gay one he is, that Nils!" And old Mrs. Svendsen's cap lurched dreamily from side to side to the flowing measure of the dance.

> "Of days that have as ha-a-p-py been,
> And you'll remember me."

VII

The moonlight flooded that great, silent land. The reaped fields lay yellow in it. The straw stacks and poplar windbreaks threw sharp black shadows. The roads were white rivers of dust. The sky was a deep, crystalline blue, and the stars were few and faint. Everything seemed to have succumbed, to have sunk to sleep, under the great, golden, tender, midsummer moon. The splendour of it seemed to transcend human life and human fate. The senses were too feeble to take it in, and every time one looked up at the sky one felt unequal to it, as if one were sitting deaf under the waves of a great river of melody. Near the road, Nils Ericson was lying against a straw stack in Olaf's wheat field. His own life seemed strange and unfamiliar to him, as if it were something he had read about, or dreamed, and forgotten. He lay very still, watching the white road that ran in front of him, lost itself among the fields, and then, at a distance, reappeared over a little hill. At last, against this white band he saw something moving rapidly, and he got up and walked to the edge of the field. "She is passing the row of poplars now," he thought. He heard the padded beat of hoofs along the dusty road, and as she came into sight he stepped out and waved his arms. Then, for fear of frightening the horse, he drew back and waited. Clara had seen him, and she came up at a walk. Nils took the horse by the bit and stroked his neck.

"What are you doing out so late, Clara Vavrika? I went to the house, but Johanna told me you had gone to your father's."

"Who can stay in the house on a night like this? Aren't you out yourself?"

"Ah, but that's another matter."

Nils turned the horse into the field.

"What are you doing? Where are you taking Norman?"

"Not far, but I want to talk to you tonight; I have something to say to you. I can't talk to you at the house, with Olaf sitting there on the porch, weighing a thousand tons."

Clara laughed. "He won't be sitting there now. He's in bed by this time, and asleep—weighing a thousand tons."

Nils plodded on across the stubble. "Are you really going to spend the rest of your life like this, night after night, summer after summer? Haven't you anything better to do on a night like this than to wear yourself and Norman out tearing across the country to your father's and back? Besides, your father won't live forever, you know. His little place will be shut up or sold, and then you'll have nobody but the Ericsons. You'll have to fasten down the hatches for the winter then."

Clara moved her head restlessly. "Don't talk about that. I try never to think of it. If I lost father I'd lose everything, even my hold over the Ericsons."

"Bah! You'd lose a good deal more than that. You'd lose your race, everything that makes you yourself. You've lost a good deal of it now."

"Of what?"

"Of your love of life, your capacity for delight."

Clara put her hands up to her face. "I haven't, Nils Ericson, I haven't! Say anything to me but that. I won't have it!" she declared vehemently.

Nils led the horse up to a straw stack, and turned to Clara, looking at her intently, as he had looked at her that Sunday afternoon at Vavrika's. "But why do you fight for that so? What good is the power to enjoy, if you never enjoy? Your hands are cold again; what are you afraid of all the time? Ah, you're afraid of losing it; that's what's the matter with you! And you will, Clara Vavrika, you will! When I used to know you— listen; you've caught a wild bird in your hand, haven't you, and felt its heart beat so hard that you were afraid it would shatter its little body to pieces? Well, you used to be just like that, a slender, eager thing with a wild delight inside you. That is how I remembered you. And I come back and find you— a bitter woman. This is a perfect ferret fight here; you live by biting and being bitten. Can't you remember what life used to be? Can't you remember that old delight? I've never forgotten it, or known its like, on land or sea."

He drew the horse under the shadow of the straw stack. Clara felt him take her foot out of the stirrup, and she slid softly down into his arms. He kissed her slowly. He was a deliberate man, but his nerves were steel when he wanted anything. Something flashed out from him like a knife out of a sheath. Clara felt everything slipping away from her; she was flooded by the summer night. He thrust his hand into his pocket, and then held it out at arm's length. "Look," he said. The shadow of the straw stack fell sharp across his wrist, and in the palm of his hand she saw a silver dollar shining. "That's my pile," he muttered; "will you go with me?"

Clara nodded, and dropped her forehead on his shoulder.

Nils took a deep breath. "Will you go with me to-night?"

"Where?" she whispered softly.

"To town, to catch the midnight flyer."

Clara lifted her head and pulled herself together. "Are you crazy, Nils? We couldn't go away like that."

"That's the only way we ever will go. You can't sit on the bank and think about it. You have to plunge. That's the way I've always done, and it's the right way for people like you and me. There's nothing so dangerous as sitting still. You've only got one life, one youth, and you can let it slip through your fingers if you want to; nothing easier. Most people do that. You'd be better off tramping the roads with me than you are here." Nils held back her head and looked into her eyes. "But I'm not that kind of a tramp, Clara. You won't have to take in sewing. I'm with a Norwegian shipping line; came over on business with the New York offices, but now I'm going straight back to Bergen. I expect I've got as much money as the

Ericsons. Father sent me a little to get started. They never knew about that. There, I hadn't meant to tell you; I wanted you to come on your own nerve."

Clara looked off across the fields. "It isn't that, Nils, but something seems to hold me. I'm afraid to pull against it. It comes out of the ground, I think."

"I know all about that. One has to tear loose. You're not needed here. Your father will understand; he's made like us. As for Olaf, Johanna will take better care of him than ever you could. It's now or never, Clara Vavrika. My bag's at the station; I smuggled it there yesterday."

Clara clung to him and hid her face against his shoulder. "Not tonight," she whispered. "Sit here and talk to me tonight. I don't want to go anywhere tonight. I may never love you like this again."

Nils laughed through his teeth. "You can't come that on me. That's not my way, Clara Vavrika. Eric's mare is over there behind the stacks, and I'm off on the midnight. It's goodbye, or off across the world with me. My carriage won't wait. I've written a letter to Olaf; I'll mail it in town. When he reads it he won't bother us—not if I know him. He'd rather have the land. Besides, I could demand an investigation of his administration of Cousin Henrik's estate, and that would be bad for a public man. You've no clothes, I know; but you can sit up tonight, and we can get everything on the way. Where's your old dash, Clara Vavrika? What's become of your Bohemian blood? I used to think you had courage enough for anything. Where's your nerve—what are you waiting for?"

Clara drew back her head, and he saw the slumberous fire in her eyes. "For you to say one thing, Nils Ericson."

"I never say that thing to any woman, Clara

Vavrika." He leaned back, lifted her gently from the ground, and whispered through his teeth: "But I'll never, never let you go, not to any man on earth but me! Do you understand me? Now, wait here."

Clara sank down on a sheaf of wheat and covered her face with her hands. She did not know what she was going to do—whether she would go or stay. The great, silent country seemed to lay a spell upon her. The ground seemed to hold her as if by roots. Her knees were soft under her. She felt as if she could not bear separation from her old sorrows, from her old discontent. They were dear to her, they had kept her alive, they were a part of her. There would be nothing left of her if she were wrenched away from them. Never could she pass beyond that skyline against which her restlessness had beat so many times. She felt as if her soul had built itself a nest there on that horizon at which she looked every morning and every evening, and it was dear to her, inexpressibly dear. She pressed her fingers against her eyeballs to shut it out. Beside her she heard the tramping of horses in the soft earth. Nils said nothing to her. He put his hands under her arms and lifted her lightly to her saddle. Then he swung himself into his own.

"We shall have to ride fast to catch the midnight train. A last gallop, Clara Vavrika. Forward!"

There was a start, a thud of hoofs along the moonlit road, two dark shadows going over the hill; and then the great, still land stretched untroubled under the azure night. Two shadows had passed.

VII

A year after the flight of Olaf Ericson's wife, the night train was steaming across the plains of Iowa. The conductor was hurrying through one of the day coaches, his lantern on his arm, when a lank, fair-haired boy sat up in one of the plush seats and tweaked him by the coat.

"What is the next step, please, sir?"

"Red Oak, Iowa. But you go through to Chicago, don't you?" He looked down, and noticed that the boy's eyes were red and his face was drawn, as if he were in trouble.

"Yes. But I was wondering whether I could get off at the next place and get a train back to Omaha."

"Well, I suppose you could. Live in Omaha?"

"No. In the western part of the State. How soon do we get to Red Oak?"

"Forty minutes. You'd better make up your mind, so I can tell the baggageman to put your trunk off."

"Oh, never mind about that! I mean, I haven't got any," the boy added, blushing.

"Run away," the conductor thought, as he slammed the coach door behind him.

Eric Ericson crumpled down in his seat and put his brown hand to his forehead. He had been crying, an he had had no supper, and his head was aching vio lently. "Oh, what shall I do?" he thought, as he looked dully down at his big shoes. "Nils will be ashamed of me; I haven't got any spunk."

Ever since Nils had run away with his brother's wife, life at home had been hard for little Eric. His mother and Olaf both suspected him of complicity. Mrs. Ericson was harsh and faultfinding, constantly wounding the boy's pride; and Olaf was always setting her against him.

Joe Vavrika heard often from his daughter. Clara had always been fond of her father, and happiness made her kinder. She wrote him long accounts of the voyage to Bergen, and of the trip she and Nils took through Bohemia to the little town where her father had grown up and where she herself was born. She visited all her kinsmen there, and sent her father news of his brother, who was a priest; of his sister, who had married a horse-breeder—of their big farm and their many children. These letters Joe always managed to read to little Eric. They contained messages for Eric and Hilda. Clara sent presents, too, which Eric never dared to take home and which poor little Hilda never even saw, though she loved to hear Eric tell about them when they were out getting the eggs together. But Olaf once saw Eric coming out of Vavrika's house —the old man had never asked the boy to come into his saloon—and Olaf went straight to his mother and told her. That night Mrs. Ericson came to Eric's room after he was in bed and made a terrible scene. She could be very terrifying when she was really angry. She forbade him ever to speak to Vavrika again, and after that night she would not allow him to go to town alone. So it was a long while before Eric got any more news of his brother. But old Joe suspected what was going on, and he carried Clara's letters about in his pocket. One Sunday he drove out to see a German friend of his, and chanced to catch sight of Eric, sitting by the cattle pond in the big pasture. They went together into Fritz Oberlies' barn, and read the letters and talked things over. Eric admitted that things were getting hard for him at home. That very night old Joe sat down and laboriously penned a statement of the case to his daughter.

Things got no better for Eric. His mother and Olaf felt that, however closely he was watched, he still, as they said, "heard." Mrs. Ericson could not admit neutrality. She had sent Johanna Vavrika packing back to her brother's, though Olaf would much rather have kept her than Anders' eldest daughter, whom Mrs. Ericson installed in her place. He was not so highhanded as his mother, and he once sulkily told her that she might better have taught her granddaughter to cook before she sent Johanna away. Olaf could have borne a good deal for the sake of prunes spiced in honey, the secret of which Johanna had taken away with her.

At last two letters came to Joe Vavrika: one from Nils, inclosing a postal order for money to pay Eric's passage to Bergen, and one from Clara, saying that Nils had a place for Eric in the offices of his company, that he was to live with them, and that they were only waiting for him to come. He was to leave New York on one of the boats of Nils' own line; the captain was one of their friends, and Eric was to make himself known at once.

Nils' directions were so explicit that a baby could have followed them, Eric felt. And here he was, nearing Red Oak, Iowa, and rocking backward and forward in despair. Never had he loved his brother so much, and never had the big world called to him so hard. But there was a lump in his throat which would not go down. Ever since nightfall he had been tormented by the thought of his mother, alone in that big house that had sent forth so many men. Her unkindness now seemed so little, and her loneliness so great. He remembered everything she had ever done for him: how frightened she had been when he tore his hand in the corn-sheller, and how she wouldn't let Olaf scold him. When Nils went away he didn't leave his mother all alone, or he would never have gone. Eric felt sure of that.

The train whistled. The conductor came in, smiling not unkindly. "Well, young man, what are you going to do? We stop at Red Oak in three minutes."

"Yes, thank you. I'll let you know." The conductor went out, and the boy doubled up with misery. He couldn't let his one chance go like this. He felt for his breast pocket and crackled Nils' letter to give him courage. He didn't want Nils to be ashamed of him. The train stopped. Suddenly he remembered his brother's kind, twinkling eyes, that always looked at you as if from far away. The lump in his throat softened. "Ah, but Nils, Nils would *understand*!" he thought. "That's just it about Nils; he always understands."

A lank, pale boy with a canvas telescope stumbled off the train to the Red Oak siding, just as the conductor called, "All aboard!"

The next night Mrs. Ericson was sitting alone in her wooden rocking-chair on the front porch. Little Hilda had been sent to bed and had cried herself to sleep. The old woman's knitting was on her lap, but her hands lay motionless on top of it. For more than an hour she had not moved a muscle. She simply sat, as only the Ericsons and the mountains can sit. The house was dark, and there was no sound but the croaking of the frogs down in the pond of the little pasture.

Eric did not come home by the road, but across the fields, where no one could see him. He set his telescope down softly in the kitchen shed, and slipped noiselessly along the path to the front porch. He sat down on the step without saying anything. Mrs. Ericson made no sign, and the frogs croaked on. At last the boy spoke timidly.

"I've come back, Mother."

"Very well," said Mrs. Ericson.

Eric leaned over and picked up a little stick out of the grass.

"How about the milking?" he faltered.

"That's been done, hours ago."

"Who did you get?"

"Get? I did it myself. I can milk as good as any of you."

Eric slid along the step nearer to her. "Oh, Mother, why did you?" he asked sorrowfully. "Why didn't you get one of Otto's boys?"

"I didn't want anybody to know I was in need of a boy," said Mrs. Ericson bitterly. She looked straight in front of her and her mouth tightened. "I always meant to give you the home farm," she added.

The boy stared and slid closer. "Oh, Mother," he faltered, "I don't care about the farm. I came back because I thought you might be needing me, maybe." He hung his head and got no further.

"Very well," said Mrs. Ericson. Her hand went out from her suddenly and rested on his head. Her fingers twined themselves in his soft, pale hair. His tears splashed down on the boards; happiness filled his heart.

UNCLE VALENTINE

(Adagio non troppo)

One morning not long ago I heard Louise Ireland give a singing lesson to a young countrywoman of mine, in her studio in Paris. Ireland must be quite sixty now, but there is not a break in the proud profile; she is still beautiful, still the joy of men, young and old. To hear her give a lesson is to hear a fine performance. The pupil was a girl of exceptional talent, handsome and intelligent, but she had the characteristic deficiency of her generation—she found nothing remarkable. She realized that she was fortunate to get in a few lessons with Ireland, but good fortune was what she expected, and she probably thought Ireland didn't every day find such good material to work with.

When the vocal lesson was over the girl said, "May I try that song you told me to look at?"

"If you wish. Have you done anything with it?"

"I've worked on it a little." The young woman unstrapped a roll of music. "I've tried over most of the songs in this book. I'm crazy about them. I never heard of Valentine Ramsay before."

"Sad for him," murmured the teacher.

"Was he English?"

"No, American, like you," sarcastically.

"I went back to the shop for more of his things, but they had only this one collection. Didn't he do any others?"

"A few. But these are the best."

"But I don't understand. If he could do things like these, why didn't he keep it up? What prevented him?"

"Oh, the things that always prevent one: marriage, money, friends, the general social order. Finally a motor truck prevented him, one of the first in Paris. He was struck and killed one night, just out of the window there, as he was going on to the Pont Royal. He was barely thirty."

The girl said, "Oh!" in a subdued voice, and actually crossed the room to look out of the window.

"If you wish to know anything further about him, this American lady can tell you. She knew him in his own country. Now I'll see what you've done with that." Ireland shook her loose sleeves back from her white arms and began to play the song:

I know a wall where red roses grow. . . .

I

Yes, I had known Valentine Ramsay. I knew him in a lovely place, at a lovely time, in a bygone period of American life; just at the incoming of this century which has made all the world so different.

I was a girl of sixteen, living with my aunt and uncle at Fox Hill, in Greenacre. My mother and father had died young, leaving me and my little sister, Betty Jane, with scant provision for our future. Aunt Charlotte and Uncle Harry Waterford took us to live with them, and brought us up with their own four little daughters. Harriet, their oldest girl, was two years younger than I, and Elizabeth, the youngest, was just the age of Betty Jane. When cousins agree at all, they agree better than sisters, and we were all extraordinarily happy. The Ramsays were our nearest neighbours; their place, Bonnie Brae, sat on the same hilltop as ours—a houseful of lonely men (and such strange ones!) tyrannized over by a Swedish woman who was housekeeper.

Greenacre was a little railway station where every evening dogcarts and carriages drew up and waited for the express that brought the business men down from the City, and then rolled them along smooth roads to their dwellings, scattered about on the fine line of hills, clad with forest, that rose above a historic American river.

The City up the river it is scarcely necessary to name; a big inland American manufacturing city, older and richer and gloomier than most, also more powerful and important. Greenacre was not a suburb in the modern sense. It was as old as the City, and there were no small holdings. The people who lived there had been born there, and inherited their land from fathers and grandfathers. Every householder had his own stables and pasture land, and hay meadows and orchard. There were plenty of servants in those days.

My Aunt Charlotte lived in the house where she was born, and ever since her marriage she had been playing with it and enlarging it, as if she had foreseen that she was one day to have a large family on her hands. She loved that house and she loved to work on it, making it always more and more just as she wanted it to be, and yet keeping it what it always had been—a big, rambling, hospitable old country house. As one drove up the hill from the station, Fox Hill, under its tall oaks and sycamores, looked like several old farmhouses pieced together; uneven roofs with odd gables and dormer windows sticking out, porches on different levels connected by sagging steps. It was all in the dull tone of scaling brown paint and old brown wood—though often, as we came up the hill in the late afternoon, the sunset flamed wonderfully on the diamond-paned windows that were so grey and inconspicuous by day.

The house kept its rusty outer shell, like an old turtle's, all the while that it was growing richer in colour and deeper in comfort within. These changes were made very cautiously, very delicately. Though my aunt was constantly making changes, she was terribly afraid of them. When she brought things back from Spain or Italy for her house, they used to stay in the barn, in their packing cases, for months before she would even try them. Then some day, when we children were all at school and she was alone, they would be smuggled in one at a time—sometimes to vanish forever after a day or two. There was something she wanted to get, in this corner or that, but there was something she was even more afraid of losing. The boldest enterprise she ever undertook was the construction of the new music-room, on the north side of the house, toward the Ramsays'. Even that was done very quietly, by the village workmen. The piano was moved out into the big square hall, and the door between the hall and the scene of the carpenters' activities was closed up. When, after a month or so, it was opened again, there was the new music-room, a proper room for chamber music, such as the petty kings and grand dukes of old Germany had in their castles; finished and empty, as it was to remain; nothing to be seen but a long room of satisfying proportions, with many wax candles flickering in the polish of the dark wooden walls and floor.

It was into this music-room that Aunt Charlotte called Harriet and me one November afternoon to tell us that Valentine Ramsay was coming home. She was sitting at the piano with a book of Debussy's piano pieces open before her. His music was little known in America then, but when she was alone she played it a great deal. She took a letter from between the leaves of the book. There was a flutter of excitement in her voice and in her features as she told us: "He says he will take the next fast steamer after his letter. He must be on the water now."

"Oh, aren't you happy, Aunt Charlotte!" I cried, knowing well how fond she was of him.

"Very, Marjorie. And a little troubled too. I'm not quite sure that people will be nice to him. The Oglethorpes are very influential, and now that Janet is living here—"

"But she's married again."

"Nevertheless, people feel that Valentine behaved very badly. He'll be here for Christmas, and I've been thinking what we can do for him. We must work very hard on our part songs. Good singing pleases him more than anything. I've been hoping he may fall into the way of composing again while he's with us. His life has been so distracted for the last few years that he's almost given up writing songs. Go to the play-room, Harriet, and tell the little girls to get their school work done early. We'll have a long rehearsal tonight. I suppose they scarcely remember him."

Three years before Valentine Ramsay had been at home for several weeks before his brother Horace died. Even at that sad time his being there was like a holiday for us children, and all the Greenacre people seemed glad to have him back again. But much had happened since then. Valentine had deserted his wife for a singer, notorious for her beauty and misconduct; had, as my friends at school often told me, utterly disgraced himself. His wife, Janet Oglethorpe, was now living in her house in the City. I had seen her twice at Saturday matinées, and I didn't wonder that Valentine had run away with a beautiful woman. The second time I saw her very well—it was a charity performance, and she was sitting in a box with her new husband, a young man who was the perfection of good tailoring, who was reputed handsome, who appeared so, indeed, until you looked closely into his vain, apprehensive face. He was immensely conceited, but not sure of himself, and kept arranging his features as he talked to the women in the box. As for Janet, I thought her an unattractive, red-faced woman, very ordinary, as we said. Aunt Charlotte murmured in my ear that she had once been better looking, but that after her marriage with Valentine she had grown stouter and "coarsened"—my aunt hurried over the word.

Aunt Charlotte had never, I knew, approved of the marriage. When he was a little boy Valentine had been her squire and had loved her devotedly. After his mother died, leaving him in a houseful of grown men, she had looked out for him and tried to direct his studies. She was ten years older than Valentine, and, in the years when Uncle Harry came a-courting, the spoiled neighbour boy was always hanging about and demanding attention. He had a pretty talent for the piano, and for composition; but he wouldn't work regularly at anything, and there was no one to make him. He drifted along until he was a young fellow of twenty, and then he met Janet Oglethorpe.

Valentine had a habit of running up to the City to dawdle about the Steinerts' music store and practise on their pianos. The two young Steinert lads were musical and were great friends of his. It was there, when she went in to buy tickets for a concert, that Janet Oglethorpe first saw Valentine and heard him play. He was a strikingly handsome boy, and picturesque—certainly very different from the canny Oglethorpe men and their friends. Janet took to him at once, began inviting him to the house and asking musicians there to meet him. The Ramsays were greatly pleased; the Oglethorpes were the richest family in a whole cityful of rich people. They owned mines and mills and oil wells and gas works and farms and banks. Unlike some of our great Scotch families, they didn't become idlers and coupon-clippers in the third generation. They held their edge—kept their keenness for money as if they were just beginning, must sink or swim, and hadn't millions behind them. Janet was one of the third generation, and it was well known that she was as shrewd in business as old Duncan himself, the founder of the Oglethorpe fortune, who was still living, having buried three wives, and spry enough to attend directors' meetings and make plenty of trouble for the young men.

Janet was older than Valentine in years, and much older in experience and judgment. Even after she had announced her engagement to him, Aunt Charlotte prevailed upon him to go abroad to study for a little. He was happily settled in Paris, under Saint-Saëns, but before the year was out Janet followed him up and married him. They lived abroad. Aunt Charlotte had visited them in Rome, but she never said much about them.

Later, when the scandal came, and everyone in the City, and in Greenacre as well, fell upon Valentine for a worthless scamp, Uncle Harry and Aunt Charlotte always stood up for him, and said that when Janet married a flighty student she took the chance with her eyes open. Some of our friends insisted that he had shattered himself with drink, like so many of the Ramsay men; others hinted that he must "take something," meaning drugs. No one could believe that a man entirely in his right mind would run away from so much money—toss it overboard, mills and mines, stocks and bonds, and that when he had none himself, and Bonnie Brae was plastered with mortgages, and old Uncle Jonathan had already two helpless men to take care of.

II

For ten days after his letter came we waited and waited for Valentine. Everyone was restless—except Uncle Jonathan, who often told us that he enjoyed anticipation as much as realization. Uncle Morton, Valentine's much older brother, used to stumble in of an evening, when we were all gathered in the big hall after dinner, to announce the same news about boats that he had given us the evening before, wave his long thin hands a little, and boast in a husky voice about his gifted brother. Aunt Charlotte put her impatience to some account by rehearsing us industriously in the part songs we were working up for Valentine. She called us her sextette, and she trained us very well. Several of us were said to have good voices. My aunt used to declare that she liked us better when we were singing than at any other time, and that drilling us was the chief pleasure she got out of having such a large family.

Aunt Charlotte was the person who felt all that went on about her—and all that did not go on—and understood it. I find that I did not know her very well then. It was not until years afterward, not until after her death, indeed, that I began really to know her. Recalling her quickly, I see a dark, full-figured woman, dressed in dark, rich materials; I remember certain velvet dresses, brown, claret-coloured, deep violet, which especially became her, and certain fur hats and capes and coats. Though she was a little overweight, she seemed often to be withdrawing into her clothes, not shrinking, but retiring behind the folds of her heavy cloaks and gowns and soft barricades of fur. She had to do with people constantly, and her house was often overflowing with guests, but she was by nature very shy. I now believe that she suffered all her life from a really painful timidity, and had to keep taking herself in hand. I have said that she was dark; her skin and hair and eyes were all brown. Even when she was out in the garden her face seemed always in shadow.

As a child I understood that my aunt had what we call a strong nature; still, deep and, on the whole, happy. Whatever it is that enables us to make our peace with life, she had found it. She cared more for music than for anything else in the world, and after that for her family and her house and her friends. She was very intelligent, but she had entirely too much respect for the opinions of others. Even in music she was often dominated by people who were much less discerning than she, but more aggressive. If her preference was disputed or challenged, she easily gave up. She knew what she liked, but she was apt to be apologetic about it. When she mentioned a composition or an artist she admired, or spoke the name of a person or place she loved, I remember a dark, rich colour used to come into her voice, and sometimes she uttered the name with a curious little intake of the breath.

Aunt Charlotte's real life went on very deep within her, I suspect, though she seemed so open and cordial, and not especially profound. No one ever thought of her as intellectual, though people often spoke of her wonderful taste; of how, without effort, she was able to make her garden and house exactly right. Our old friends considered taste as something quite apart from intelligence, instead of the flower of it. She read little, it is true; what other people learned from books she learned from music,—all she needed to give her a rich enjoyment of art and life. She played the piano extremely well; it was not an accomplishment with her, but a way of living. The rearing of six little girls did not seem to strain her patience much. She allowed us a great deal of liberty and demanded her own in return. We were permitted to have our own thoughts and feelings, and even Elizabeth and Betty Jane understood that it is a great happiness to be permitted to be glad or sorry in one's own way.

III

On the night of Valentine's return, our household went in a body over to Bonnie Brae to make a short call. It was delightful to see the old house looking so festive, with lights streaming from all the windows. We found the family in the long, pale parlour; the men of the house, and half a dozen Ramsay cousins with their wives and children.

Valentine was standing near the fireplace when we entered, beside his father's armchair. The little girls at once tripped down the long room toward him, Uncle Harry following. But Aunt Charlotte stopped short in the doorway and stood there in the shadow of the curtains, watching Valentine across the heads of the company, as if she wished to remain an outsider. Through the buzz and flutter of greetings, his eyes found her there. He left the others, crossed the room in a flash, and, giving her a quick, sidewise look, put down his head to be kissed, like a little boy. As he stood there for a moment, so close to us, he struck me at once as altogether too young to have had so much history, as very hardy and high-coloured and unsubdued. His thick, seal-brown hair grew on his head exactly like fur, there was no part in it anywhere. His short mustache and eyebrows had the same furry look. His red lips and white teeth gave him a striking freshness—there was something very roguish and wayward, very individual about his mouth. He seldom looked at one when he talked to one—he had a habit of frowning at the floor or looking fixedly at some object when he was speaking, but one felt his eyes through the lowered lids—felt his pleasure or his annoyance, his affection or impatience.

Since gay Uncle Horace died the Ramsay men did not often give parties, and that night they roamed about somewhat uneasily, all but Uncle Jonathan, who was always superbly at his ease. He kept his armchair, with a cape about his shoulders to protect him from drafts. The old man's hair and beard were just the colour of dirty white snow, and he was averse to having them trimmed. He was a gracious host, having the air of one to whom many congratulations are due. Roland had put on a frock coat and was doing his duty, making himself quietly agreeable to everyone. His handsome silver-grey head and fine physique would have added to the distinction of any company. Uncle Morton was wandering about from group to group, jerking his hands this way and that— a curiously individual gesture from the wrist, as if he were making signals from a world too remote for speech. He fastened himself upon me, as he was very likely to do (finding me out in the little corner sofa to which I had retreated), sat down beside me and began talking about his brother in disconnected sentences, trying to focus his almost insensible eyes upon me.

"My brother is very devoted to your aunt. She must help me with his studio. We are going to make a studio for him off in the wing, for the quiet. Something very nice. I think I shall have the walls upholstered, like cushions, to keep the noise out. It will be handsome, you understand. We can give parties there—receptions. My brother is a fine musician. Could play anything when he was eleven—classical music—the most difficult compositions." In the same expansive spirit Uncle Morton had once planned a sunken garden for my aunt, and a ballroom for Harriet and me.

Molla Carlsen brought in cake and port and sherry. She had been at the door to admit us, and had since been intermittently in the background, disappearing and reappearing as if she were much occupied. She had always this air of moving quietly and efficiently in her own province. Molla was very correct in her deportment, was there and not too much there. She was fair, and good looking, very. The only fault Aunt

Charlotte had to find with her appearance was the way she wore her hair. It was yellow enough to be showy in any case, and she made it more so by parting it very low on one side, just over her left ear, indeed, so that it lay across her head on a long curly wave, making her low forehead lower still and giving her an air that, as some of our neighbours declared, was little short of "tough."

After we had sipped our wine the cousins began to gather up their babies for departure, and we younger ones had all to go up to Uncle Jonathan and kiss him good night. It was a rite we shrank from, he was always so strong of tobacco and snuff, but he liked to kiss us, and there was no escape.

When we left, Uncle Valentine put his arm through Aunt Charlotte's and walked with us as far as the summerhouse, looking about him and up overhead through the trees. I heard him say suddenly, as if it had just struck him:

"Isn't it funny, Charlotte; no matter how much things or people ought to be different, what we love them for is for being just the same!"

IV

The next afternoon when Harriet and I got home from Miss Demming's school, we heard two pianos going, and knew that Uncle Valentine was there. The door between the big hall and the music-room was open, and Aunt Charlotte called to us:

"Harriet and Marjorie? Run upstairs and make yourselves neat. You may have tea with us presently."

When we came down, the music had ceased, and the hall was empty. Black John, coming through with a plate of toast, told us he had taken tea into the study.

My uncle's study was my favourite spot in that house full of lovely places. It was a little room just off the library, very quiet, like a little pond off the main currents of the house. There was but one door, and no one ever passed through it on the way to another room. As it had formerly been a conservatory for winter flowers, it was all glass on two sides, with heavy curtains one could draw at night to shut out the chill. There was always a little coal fire in the grate, Uncle Harry's favourite books on the shelves, and the new ones he was reading arranged on the table, along with his pipes and tobacco jars. Sitting beside the red coals one could look out into the great forking syca-more limbs, with their mottled bark of white and olive green, and off across the bare tops of the winter trees that grew down the hill slopes—until finally one looked into nothingness, into the great stretch of open sky above the river, where the early sunsets burned or brooded over our valley. It was with delight I heard we were to have our tea there.

We found my aunt and Valentine before the grate, the steaming samovar between them, the glass room full of grey light, a little warmed by the glowing coals.

"Aren't you surprised to find us here?" There was just a shade of embarrassment in my aunt's voice. "This was Uncle Valentine's choice." Curious; though she always looked so at ease, so calm in her matronly figure, a little thing like having tea in an unusual room could make her a trifle self-conscious and apologetic.

Valentine, in brown corduroys with a soft shirt and a Chinese-red necktie, was sitting in Uncle Harry's big chair, one foot tucked under him. He told us he had been all over the hills that morning, clear up to Flint

Ridge. "I came home by the near side of Blinker's Hill, past the Wakeley place. I wish Belle wouldn't stay abroad so long; it's a shame to keep that jolly old house shut up." He said he liked having tea in the study because the outlook was the same as from his upstairs room at home. "I was always supposed to be doing lessons there as evening came on. I'm sure I don't know what I was doing—writing serenades for you, probably, Charlotte."

Aunt Charlotte was nursing the samovar along—it never worked very well. "I've been hoping," she murmured, "that you would bring me home some new serenades—or songs of some kind."

"Songs? Oh, hell, Charlotte!" He jerked his foot from under him and sat up straight. "Sorry I swore, but you evidently don't know what I've been up against these last four years. You'll have to know, and so will your maidens fair. Anyhow, if you're to have a rake next door to a houseful of daughters, you'd better look into it."

Aunt Charlotte caught her breath painfully, glanced at Harriet and me and then at the door. Valentine sprang up, went to the door and closed it. "Oh, don't look so frightened!" he exclaimed irritably, "and don't send the girls away. Do you suppose they've heard nothing? What do you think girls whisper about at school, anyway? You'd better let me explain a little."

"I think it unnecessary," she murmured entreatingly.

"It isn't unnecessary!" he stamped his foot down upon the rug. "You mean they'll think what you tell them to—stay where you put them, like china shepherdesses. Well, they won't!"

We were almost as much frightened as Aunt Charlotte. He was standing before us, his brow wrinkled in a heavy frown, his shoulders lowered, his red lips thrust out petulantly. I am sure I was hoping that he wouldn't quite explain away the legend of his awful wickedness. As he addressed us he looked not at us but at the floor.

"You've heard, haven't you, Harriet and Marjorie, that I deserted a noble wife and ran away with a wicked woman? Well, she wasn't a wicked woman. She is kind and generous, and she ran away with me out of charity, to get me out of the awful mess I was in. The mess, you understand, was just being married to this noble wife. Janey is all right for her own kind, for Oglethorpes in general, but she was all wrong for me."

Here he stopped and made a wry face, as if his pedagogical tone put a bad taste in his mouth. He glanced at my aunt for help, but she was looking steadfastly at the samovar.

"Hang it, Charlotte," he broke out, "these girls are not in the nursery! They must hear what they hear and think what they think. It's got to come out. You know well enough what dear Janey is; you've known ever since you stayed with us in Rome. She's a common, energetic, close-fisted little tradeswoman, who ought to be keeping a shop and doing people out of their eyeteeth. She thinks, day and night, about common, trivial, worthless things. And what's worse, she talks about them day and night. She bargains in her sleep. It's what she can get out of this dressmaker or that porter; it's getting the royal suite in a hotel for the price of some other suite. We left you in Rome and dashed off to Venice that fall because she could get a palazzo at a bargain. Some English people had to go home on account of a grandmother dying and had to sub-let in a hurry. That was her only reason for going to Venice. And when we got there she did nothing but beat the house servants down to lower wages, and get herself burned red as a lobster staying out in boats all day to get her money's worth. I was dragged about the world for five years in an atmosphere of commonness and meanness and coarseness. I tell you I was paralyzed by the flood of trivial, vulgar nagging that poured over me and never stopped. Even Dickie—I might have had some fun with the little chap, but she never let me. She never let me have any but the most painful relations with him. With two nurses sitting idle, she'd make me chase off in a cab to demand his linen from special laundresses, or scurry around a whole day to find some silly kind of milk—all utter nonsense. The child was never sick and could take any decent milk. But she likes to make a fuss; calls it 'managing.'

"Sometimes I used to try to get off by myself long enough to return to consciousness, to find whether I had any consciousness left to return to—but she always came pelting after. I got off for Bayreuth one time. Thought I'd covered my tracks so well. She arrived in the middle of the Ring. My God, the agony of having to sit through music with that woman!" Valentine sat down and wiped his forehead. It glistened with perspiration; the roots of his furry hair were quite wet.

After a moment he said doggedly, "I give you my word, Charlotte, there was nothing for it but to make a scandal; to hurt her pride so openly that she'd have to take action. I don't know that she'd have done it then, if Seymour Towne hadn't turned up to sympathize with her. You can't hurt anybody as beefy as that without being a butcher!" He shuddered.

"Louise Ireland offered to be the sacrifice. She hadn't much to lose in the way of—well, of the proprieties, of course. But she's a glorious creature. I couldn't have done it with a horrid woman. Don't think anything nasty of her, any of you, I won't have it. Everything she does is lovely, somehow or other, just as every song she sings is more beautiful than it ever was before. She's been more or less irregular in behavior—as you've doubtless heard with augmentation. She had certainly run away with desperate men before. But behavior, I find, is more or less accidental, Charlotte. Oh, don't look so scared! Your dovelets will have to face facts some day. Æsthetics come back to predestination, if theology doesn't. A woman's behavior may be irreproachable and she herself may be gross—just gross. She may do her duty, and defile everything she touches. And another woman may be erratic, imprudent, self-indulgent if you like, and all the while be—what is it the Bible says? Pure in heart. People are as they are, and that's all there is to life. And now—" Valentine got up and went toward the door to open it.

Aunt Charlotte came out of her lethargy and held up her finger. "Valentine," she said with a deep breath, "I wasn't afraid of letting the girls hear what you had to say—not exactly afraid. But I thought it unnecessary. I understood everything as soon as I looked at you last night. One hasn't watched people from their childhood for nothing."

He wheeled round to her. "Of course you would know! But these girls aren't you, my dear! I doubt if they ever will be, even with luck!" The tone in which he said this, the proud, sidelong glance he flashed upon her, made this a rich and beautiful compliment

—so violent a one that it seemed almost to hurt that timid woman. Slowly, slowly, the red burned up in her dark cheeks, and it was a long while dying down.

"Now we've finished with this—what a relief!" Valentine knelt down on the window seat between Harriet and me and put an arm lightly around each of us. "There's a fine sunset coming on, come and look at it, Charlotte."

We huddled together, looking out over the descending knolls of bare tree tops into the open space over the river, where the smoky grey atmosphere was taking on a purple tinge, like some thick liquid changing colour. The sun, which had all day been a shallow white ring, emerged and swelled into an orange-red globe. It hung there without changing, as if the density of the atmosphere supported it and would not let it sink. We sat hushed and still, living in some strong wave of feeling or memory that came up in our visitor. Valentine had that power of throwing a mood over people. There was nothing imaginary about it; it was as real as any form of pain or pleasure. One had only to look at Aunt Charlotte's face, which had become beautiful, to know that.

It was Uncle Harry who brought us back into the present again. He had caught an early train down from the City, hoping to come upon us just like this, he said. He was almost pathetically eager for anything of this sort he could get, and was glad to come in for cold toast and tea.

"Awfully happy I got here before Valentine got away," he said, as he turned on the light. "And, Charlotte, how rosy you are! It takes you to do that to her, Val." She still had the dusky colour which had been her unwilling response to Valentine's compliment.

V

Within a few days Uncle Valentine ran over to beg my aunt to go shopping with him. Something had reminded him that Christmas was very near.

"It's awfully embarrassing," he said. "Nobody in Paris was saying anything about Christmas before I sailed. Here I've come home with empty trunks, and Paris full of things that everybody wants."

Aunt Charlotte laughed at him and said she thought they would find plenty of things from Paris up in the City.

The next morning Valentine appeared before we left for school. He was in a very businesslike mood, and his check book was sticking out from the breast pocket of his fur coat. They were to catch the eight-thirty train. The day was dark and grey, I remember, though our valley was white, for there had been a snowfall the day before. Standing on the porch with my school satchel, I watched them get into the carriage and go down the hill as the train whistled for the station below ours—they would just have time to catch it. Aunt Charlotte looked so happy. She didn't often have Valentine to herself for a whole day. Well, she deserved it.

I could follow them in my mind: Valentine with his brilliant necktie and foreign-cut clothes, hurrying about the shops, so lightning-quick, when all the men they passed in the street were so slow and ponderous or, when they weren't ponderous, stiff—stiff because they were wooden, or because they weren't wooden and were in constant dread of betraying it. Everybody would be trying not to look at bright-coloured, foreign-living, disgracefully divorced Valentine Ramsay;

some in contempt—some in secret envy, because everything about him told how free he was. And up there, nobody was free. They were imprisoned in their harsh Calvinism, or in their merciless business grind, or in mere apathy—a mortal dullness.

Oh, I could see those two, walking about the narrow streets of the grim, raw, dark grey old city, cold with its river damp, and severe by reason of the brooding frown of huge stone churches that loomed up even in the most congested part of the shopping district. There were old graveyards round those churches, with gravestones sunken and tilted and blackened—covered this morning with dirty snow— and jangling car lines all about them. The street lamps would be burning all day, on account of the fog, full of black smoke from the furnace chimneys. Hidden away in the grim and damp and noise were the half dozen special shops which imported splendours for the owners of those mills that made the city so dark and so powerful.

Their shopping over, Valentine was going to take Aunt Charlotte to lunch at a hotel where they could get a very fine French wine she loved. What a day they would have! There was only one thing to be feared. They might easily chance to meet one of the Oglethorpe men, there were so many of them, or Janet herself, face to face, or her new husband, Seymour Towne, who had been the idle son of an industrious family, and by idling abroad had stepped into such a good thing that now his hard-working brothers found life bitter in their mouths.

But they didn't meet with anything disagreeable. They came home on the four-thirty train, before the rush, bringing their spoils with them (no motor truck deliveries down the valley in those days), and their faces shone like the righteous in his Heavenly Father's house. Aunt Charlotte admitted that she was tired and went upstairs to lie down directly after tea. Valentine took me down into the music-room to show me where to put the blossoming mimosa tree he had found for Aunt Charlotte, when it came down on the express tomorrow. The little girls followed us, and when he told them to be still they crept into the corners.

Valentine sat down at the piano and began to play very softly; something dark and rich and shadowy, but not somber, with a silvery air flowing through its mysteriousness. It might, I thought, be something of Debussy's that I had never heard... but no, I was sure it was not.

Presently he rose abruptly to go without taking leave, but one of the little girls ran up to him—Helen, probably, she was the most musical—and asked him what he had been playing, please.

"Oh, some old thing, I guess. I wasn't thinking," he muttered vaguely, and escaped through the glass doors that led directly into the garden between our house and his. I felt very sure that it was nothing old, but something new—just beginning, indeed. That would be a pleasant thing to tell Aunt Charlotte. I ran upstairs; the door of her room was ajar, but all was dark within. I entered on tiptoe and listened, she was sound asleep. What a day she had had!

VI

Aunt Charlotte planned a musical party for Christmas eve and invited a dozen or more of her old friends. They were coming home with her after the evening church service; we were to sing carols, and Uncle Valentine was to play. She telephoned the invitations, and made it very clear that Valentine Ramsay was going to be there. Whoever didn't want to meet him could decline. Nobody declined; some even said it would be a pleasure to hear him play again.

On Christmas eve, after dinner, Uncle Harry and I were left alone in the house. All the children went to the church with Aunt Charlotte; she left me to help Black John arrange the table for a late supper after the music. After I had seen to everything, I had an hour or so alone upstairs in my own room.

I well remember how beautiful our valley looked from my window that winter night. Through the creaking, shaggy limbs of the great sycamores I could look off at the white, white landscape; the deep folds of the snow-covered hills, the high drifts over the bushes, the gleaming ice on the broken road, and the thin, gauzy clouds driving across the crystal-clear, star-spangled sky.

Across the garden was Bonnie Brae, with so many windows lighted; the parlour, the library, Uncle Jonathan's room, Morton's room, a yellow patch on the snow from Roland's window, which I could not see; off there, at the end of the long, dark, sagging wing, Valentine's study, lit up like a lantern. I often looked over at our neighbours' house and thought about how much life had gone on in it, and about the muted, mysterious lives that still went on there. In the garret were chests full of old letters; all the highly descriptive letters that Uncle Jonathan had written his wife when he was travelling abroad; family letters, love letters, every letter the boys had written home when they were away at school. And in all these letters were tender references to the garden, the old trees, the house itself. And now so many of those who had loved the old place and danced in the long parlour were dead. I wondered, as young people often do, how my elders had managed to bear life at all, either its killing happiness or its despair.

I heard wheels on the drive, and laughter. Looking out I saw guests alighting on one side of the house, and on the other side Uncle Valentine running across the garden, bareheaded in the snow. I started downstairs with a little faintness at heart—I knew how much my aunt had counted on bringing Valentine again into the circle of her friends, under her own roof. I found him in the big hall, surrounded by the ladies—they hadn't yet taken off their wraps—and I surveyed them from the second landing where the stairway turned. They were doing their best, I thought. Some of the younger women kept timidly at the outer edge of the group, but all the ones who counted most were emphatic in their cordiality. Deaf old Mrs. Hungerford, who rather directed public opinion in Greenacre, patted him on the back, shouted that now the naughty boy had come home to be good, and thrust out her ear trumpet at him. Julia Knewstubb, who for some reason, I never discovered why, was an important person, stood beside him in a brassy, patronizing way, and Ida Milholland, the intellectual light of the valley, began speaking slow, crusty French at him. In short, all was well.

Salutations over, Aunt Charlotte led the way to the music-room and signaled to her six girls. We sang one carol after another, and a fragment of John Bennett's we had especially practised for Uncle Valentine—a song about a bluebird flying over a grey landscape and making it all blue; a pretty thing for high voices. But when we finished this and looked about to see whether it had pleased him, Valentine was nowhere to be found. Aunt Charlotte drew me aside while the others went out to supper and told me I must search all through the house, go to Bonnie Brae if necessary, and fetch him. It would never do for him to behave thus, when they had unbent so far as to come and greet him.

I looked out of the window and saw a light in his study at the end of the wing. The rooms between his study and the main house were unused, filled with old furniture. He avoided that chain of dusty, echoing chambers and came and went by a back door that opened into the old apple orchard. I dashed across the garden and ran in upon him without knocking.

There he was, lounging before the fire in his slippers and wine-coloured velvet jacket, a pipe in his mouth and a yellow French book on his knee. I gasped and explained to him that he must come at once; the company was waiting for him.

He shrugged and waved his pipe. "I'm not going back at all. Pouf, what's the use? I'd only behave badly if I did. I don't want to lose my temper on Christmas eve."

"But you promised Aunt Charlotte, and she's told them you'd play," I pleaded.

He flung down his book wrathfully. "Oh, I can't stand them! I didn't know who Charlotte was going to ask...seems to me she's got together all the most objectionable old birds in the valley. There's Julia Knewstubb, with her nippers hanging on her nose, looking more like a horse than ever. Old Mrs. Hungerford, poking her ear trumpet at me and stroking me on the back—I can't talk into an ear trumpet— can't think of anything important enough to say! And that bump of intellect, Ida Milholland, creaking at every joint and practising her French grammar on me. Charlotte knows I hate ugly women—what did she get such a bunch together for? Not much, I'm not going back. Sit down and I'll read you something. I've got a new collection of all the legends about Tristan and Iseult. You can understand French?"

I said I would be dreadfully scolded if I did such a thing. "And you will hurt Aunt Charlotte's feelings, terribly!"

He laughed and poked out his red lower lip at me. "Shall I? Oh, but I can mend them again! Listen, I've got a new song for her, a good one. You sit down, and we'll work a spell on her; we'll wish and wish, and she'll come running over. While we wait I'll play it for you."

He put his pipe on the mantel, went to the piano, and commenced to play the Ballad of the Young Knight, which begins:

> "From the Ancient Kingdoms,
>   Through the wood of dreaming, . . ."

It was the same thing I had heard him trying out the afternoon he and Aunt Charlotte got home from the City.

"Now, you try it over with me, Margie. It's meant for high voice, you see. By the time she comes, we can give her a good performance."

"But she won't come, Uncle Valentine! She can't leave her guests."

"Oh, they'll soon be gone! Old tabbies always get sleepy after supper—you said they were at supper. She'll come."

I was so excited, so distressed and delighted, that I made a poor showing at reading the manuscript, and was well scolded. Valentine always wrote the words of his songs, as well as the music, like the old troubadours, and the words of this one were beautiful. "And what wood do you suppose it is?" He played the dark music with his left hand.

I said it made me think of the wood on the other side of Blinker's Hill.

"I guess so," he muttered. "But of course it will be different woods to different people. Don't tell Charlotte, but I'm doing a lot of songs. I think of a new one almost every morning, when I waken up. Our woods are full of them, but they're terribly, terribly coy. You can't trap them, they're too wild.... No, you can't catch them...sometimes one comes and lights on your shoulder; I always wonder why."

It did not seem very long until Aunt Charlotte entered, bareheaded, her long black cape over her shoulders, a look of distress and anxiety on her face. Valentine sprang up and caught her hand.

"Not a word, Charlotte, don't scold, look before you leap! I kept Margie because I knew you'd come to hunt her, and I didn't just know any other way of getting you here. Now don't be angry, because when you get angry your face puffs up just a little, and I have reason to hate women whose faces swell. Sit down by the fire. We've had a rehearsal, and now we'll sing my new song for you. Don't glare at the child, or she can't sing. Why haven't you taught her to follow manuscript better?"

Aunt Charlotte didn't have a chance to speak until we had gone through with the song. But though my eyes were glued to the page, I knew her face was going through many changes.

"Now," he said exultantly as we finished, "with a song like that under my shirt, did I have to sit over there and let old Ida wise-bump practise her French on me—period of Bossuet, I guess!"

Aunt Charlotte laughed softly and asked us to sing it again. The second time we did better; Valentine hadn't much voice, but of course he knew how. As we finished we heard a queer sound, something like a snore and something like a groan, in the wall behind us. Valentine held up his finger sharply, tiptoed to the door behind the fireplace that led into the old wing, put down his head and listened for a moment. Then he wrenched open the door.

There stood Roland, holding himself steady by an old chest of drawers, his eyes looking blind, tears shining on his white face. He did not say a word; put his hands to his forehead as if to collect himself, and went away through the dark rooms, swaying slightly and groping along the floor with his feet.

"Poor old chap, perfectly soaked! I thought it was Molla Carlsen, spooking round." Valentine threw himself into a chair. "Do you suppose that's the way I'll be keeping Christmas ten years from now, Charlotte? What else is there for us to do, I ask you? Sons of an easy-going, self-satisfied American family, never taught anything until we are too old to learn. What could Roland do when he came home from Germany fifteen years ago?... Lord, it's more than that now... it's nineteen! Nineteen years!" Valentine dropped his head into his hands and rumpled his hair as if he were washing it, which was a sign with him that a situation was too hopeless for discussion. "Well, what could he have done, Charlotte? What could he do now? Teach piano, take the bread out of somebody's mouth? My son Dickie, he'll be an Oglethorpe! He'll get on, and won't carry this damned business any further."

On Christmas morning Molla Carlsen came over and reported with evident satisfaction that Roland and Valentine had made a night of it, and were both keeping their rooms in consequence. Aunt Charlotte was sad and downcast all day long.

VII

Molla Carlsen loved to give my aunt the worst possible account of the men she kept house for, though in talking to outsiders I think she was discreet and loyal. She was a strange woman, then about forty years old, and she had been in the Ramsay household for more than twelve years. She managed everything over there, and was paid very high wages. She was grasping, but as honest as she was heartless. The house was well conducted, though it was managed, as Valentine said, somewhat like an institution. No matter how many thousand roses were blooming in the garden, it never occurred to Molla to cut any and put them in the bare, faded parlour. The men who lived there got no coddling; they were terribly afraid of her. When a wave of red went over Molla's white skin, poor Uncle Morton's shaky hands trembled more than ever, and his faraway eyes shrank to mere pin-points. He was the one who most often angered her, because he dropped things. Once when Aunt Charlotte remonstrated with her about her severity, she replied that a woman who managed a houseful of alcoholics must be a tyrant, or the place would be a sty.

This made us all indignant. Morton, we thought, was the only one who could justly be thus defined. He was the oldest of Uncle Jonathan's sons; tall, narrow, utterly spare, with a long, thin face, a shriveled scalp with a little dry hair on it, parted in the middle, eyes that never looked at you because the pupils were always shrunk so small. Morton was awfully proud of the fact that he was a business man; he alone of that household went up on the business men's train in the morning. He went to an office in the City, climbed upon a high stool, and fastened his distant eyes upon a ledger. (It was a coal business, in which his father owned a good deal of stock, and every night an accountant went over Morton's books and corrected his mistakes.) On his way to the office, he stopped at the bar of a most respectable hotel. He stopped there again before lunch at noon, and on his way to the station in the late afternoon. He often told Uncle Harry that he never took anything during business hours. Nobody ever saw Morton thoroughly intoxicated, but nobody ever saw him quite himself. He had good manners, a kind voice, though husky, and he was usually very quiet.

Uncle Jonathan, to be sure, took a good deal of whisky during the day—but then he ate almost nothing. Whisky and tobacco were his nourishment. He was frail, but he had been so even as a young man, and he outlived all his sons except Morton—lived on until the six little girls at Fox Hill were all grown women. No, I don't think it was alcohol that preserved him; I think it was his fortunate nature, his happy form of self-esteem. He was perfectly satisfied with himself and his family—with whatever they had done and whatever they had not done. He was glad that Roland had declined the nervous strain of an artistic career, and that Morton was in business; in each generation some of the Ramsays had been business men. Uncle Jonathan had loved his wife dearly and he must have missed her, but he was pleased with the verses he had written about her since her death, verses in the manner of Tom Moore, whom he considered an absolutely satisfactory poet. He had, of course, been proud of Valentine's brilliant marriage. The divorce he certainly regretted. But whatever pill life handed out to him he managed to swallow with equanimity.

Uncle Jonathan spent his days in the library, across the hall from the parlour, where he was writing a romance of the French and Indian wars. The room was lined with his father's old brown theological books, and everything one touched there felt dusty. There was always a scattering of tobacco crumbs over the hearth, the floor, the desk, and over Uncle Jonathan's waistcoat and whiskers. It wasn't in Molla Carlsen's contract to keep the tobacco dust off her master.

Roland Ramsay was Uncle Jonathan's much younger brother. When he was a boy of twelve and fourteen, he had been a musical prodigy, had played to large and astonished audiences in New York and Boston and Philadelphia. Later he was sent to Germany to study under Liszt and D'Albert. At twenty-eight he returned to Bonnie Brae—and he had been there ever since. He was a big, handsome man, never ill, but something had happened to his nervous system. He could not play in public, not even in his own city. Ever since Valentine was a little boy, Uncle Roland and his piano had lived upstairs at Bonnie Brae. There were several stories: that he had been broken by a love affair with a German singer; that Wagner had hurt his feelings so cruelly he could never get over it; that at his début in Paris he had forgotten in the middle of his sonata in what key the next movement was written, and had laboured through the rest of his program like a man stupefied by drugs.

At any rate, Roland had broken nerves, just as some people have a weak heart, and he lived in solitude and silence. Occasionally when some fine orchestra or a new artist played in the City up the river, Roland's waxy, frozen face was to be seen in the audience; but not often. Five or six times a year he went on a long spree. Then he would shut himself up in his room and play the piano—it couldn't be called practising—for eight or ten hours a day. Sometimes in the evening Aunt Charlotte would put on a cloak and go out into the garden to listen to him. "Harry," she said once when she came back into the house, "I was walking under Roland's window. Really, he is playing like a god tonight."

Inert and inactive as he was, Roland kept his good physique. He used to sit all afternoon beside his window with a book; as we came up the hill we could see his fine head and shoulders there, motionless as if in a frame. I never liked to look at his face, for his strong, well-cut features never moved. His eyes were large and uncomfortable-looking, under heavy lids with deep hollows beneath—curiously like the eyes of the tired American business men whose pictures appear in the papers when they are getting a divorce.

I had heard it whispered at school that Uncle Jonathan was "in Molla Carlsen's power," because Horace, the wild son, had made vehement advances to her long ago when she first came into the house, and that his bad behavior had hastened his mother's end. However it came about, in her power the lonely men at Bonnie Brae certainly were. When Molla was dressed to go up to the City, she walked down the front steps and got into the carriage with the air of mistress of the place. And her furs, we knew, had cost more than Aunt Charlotte's.

VIII

All that winter Valentine was tremendously busy. He was not only writing ever so many new songs, but was hunting up beautiful old ones for our sextette, and he trained us so industriously that the little girls fell behind in their lessons, and Aunt Charlotte had to limit rehearsals to three nights a week. I remember he made us an arrangement for voices of the minuet in the third movement of Brahms' second symphony, and wrote words to it.

We were not allowed to sing any of Valentine's songs in company, not even for Aunt Charlotte's old friends. He was rather proud and sulky with most of the neighbours, and wouldn't have it. When we tried out his new songs for the home circle, as he said, Uncle Morton was allowed to come over, and Uncle Jonathan in his black cape. Roland came too, and sat off in a corner by himself. Uncle Jonathan thought very well of his own judgment in music. He liked all Valentine's songs, but warned him against writing things without a sufficient "climax," mildly bidding him beware of a too modern manner.

I remember he used to repeat for his son's guidance two lines from one of his favorite poets, accenting the measure with the stogie he held in his fingers—a particularly noxious kind of cigar which he not only smoked but, on occasion, ate!

"Avoid eccentricity, Val," he would say, beaming softly at his son. "Remember this admirable rule for poets and composers:

> Be not the first by whom the new is tried,
> Nor yet the last to lay the old aside."

That year the spring began early. I remember March and April as a succession of long walks and climbs with Valentine. Sometimes Aunt Charlotte went with us, but she was not a nimble walker, and Valentine liked climb and dash and short-cut. We would plunge into the wooded course of Blue Run or Powhatan Creek, and get to the top of Flint Ridge by a quicker route than any path. That long, windy ridge lay behind Blinker's Hill; the top was a bare expanse, except for a few bleached boulders and twisted oaks. From there we could look off over all the great wrinkles of hills, catch glimpses of the river, and see the black pillar of cloud to the north where the City lay. This dark cloud, as evening came on, took deep rich colours from the sunset; and after the sun was gone it sent out all night an orange glow from the furnace fires that burned there. But that smoke did not come down to us; our evenings were pure and silvery—soft blue skies seen through the budding trees above us, or over the folds of lavender forest below us.

One Saturday afternoon we took Aunt Charlotte along and got to the top of Flint Ridge by the winding roadway. As we were walking upon the crest, curtains of mist began to rise from the river and from between the lines of hills. Soon the darkening sky was full of fleecy clouds, and the countryside below us disappeared into nothingness.

Suddenly, in the low cut between the hills across the river, we saw a luminousness, throbbing and phosphorescent, a ghostly brightness with mists streaming about it and enfolding it, struggling to quench it. We knew it was the moon, but we could see no form, no solid image; it was a flowing, surging, liquid gleaming; now stronger, now softer.

"The Rhinegold!" murmured Valentine and Aunt Charlotte in one breath. The little girls were silent; Betty Jane felt for my hand. They were awed, not so much by the light, as by something in the two voices that had spoken together. Presently we dropped into the dark winding road along Blue Run and got home late for dinner.

While we were at dessert, Uncle Valentine went into the music-room and began to play the Rhine music. He played on as if he would never stop; Siegmund's love song and the Valhalla music and back to the Rhine journey and the Rhine maidens. The cycle was like a plaything in his hands. Presently a shadow fell in the patch of moonlight on the floor, and looking out I saw Roland, without a hat, standing just outside the open window. He often appeared at the window or the doorway when we were singing with Valentine, but if we noticed him, or addressed him, he faded quickly away.

As Valentine stopped for a moment, his uncle tapped on the window glass.

"Going over now, Valentine? It's getting late."

"Yes, I suppose it is. I say, Charlotte, do you remember how we used to play the Ring to each other hours on end, long ago, when Damrosch first brought the German opera over? Why can't people stay young forever?"

"Maybe you will, Val," said Aunt Charlotte, musing. "What a difference Wagner made in the world, after all!"

"It's not a good thing to play Wagner at night," said the grey voice outside the window. "It brings on sleeplessness."

"I'll come along presently, Roland," the nephew called. "I'm warm now; I'll take cold if I go out."

The large figure went slowly away.

"Poor old Roland, isn't he just a coffin of a man!" Valentine got up and lit the fagots in the fireplace. "I feel shivery. I've had him on my hands a good deal this winter. He'll come drifting in through the wing and settle himself in my study and sit there half the night without opening his head."

"Doesn't he talk to you, even?" I asked.

"Hardly, though I get fidgety and talk to him. Sometimes he plays. He's always interesting at the piano. It's remarkable that he plays as well as he does, when he's so irregular."

"Does he really read? We so often see him sitting by his upstairs window with a book."

"He reads too much, German philosophy and things that aren't good for him. Did you know, Charlotte, that he keeps a diary. At least he writes often in a big ledger Morton brought him from town. Sometimes he's at it for hours. Lord, I'd like to know what he puts down in it!" Valentine plunged his head in his hands and began rumpling his hair. "Can you remember him much before he went abroad, Charlotte?"

"When I was little I was taken to hear him play in Steinway Hall, just before he went to Germany. From what I can remember, it was very brilliant. He had splendid hands, and a wonderful memory. When he came back he was much more musical, but he couldn't play in public."

"Queer! How he supports the years as they come and go.... Of course, he loves the place, just as I do; that's something. By the way, when I was home three years ago I was let into a family secret; it was Roland who was Molla Carlsen's suitor and made all the row, not poor Horace at all! Oh, shouldn't I have said that before the sextette? They'll forget it. They forget most things. What haunts me about Roland is the feeling of kinship. So often it flashes into my mind: 'Yes, I might be struck dumb some day, just like that.' Oh, don't laugh! It *was* like that, for months and months, while

I was trying to live with Janet. My skin would get yellow, and I'd feel a perfect loathing of speech. My jaws would set together so that I couldn't open them. I'd walk along the quais in Paris and go without a newspaper because I couldn't bring myself to say good-morning to the old woman and buy one. I'd wander about awfully hungry because I couldn't bear the sound of talk in a restaurant. I dodged everybody I knew, or cut them."

There was something funny about his self-commiseration, and I wanted to hear more; but just at this point we were told that we must go instantly to bed.

"And I?" Valentine asked, "must I go too?"

"No. You may stay a little longer."

Aunt Charlotte must have thought he needed a serious talking-to, for she almost never saw him alone. Her life was hedged about by very subtle but sure conventionalities, and that was only one of many things she did not permit herself.

IX

Fox Hill was soon besieged on all sides by spring. The first attack came by way of the old apple orchard that ran irregularly behind our carriage house and Uncle Valentine's studio. The foaming, flowery trees were a beautiful sight from his doorstep. Aunt Charlotte and Morton were carrying on a hot rivalry in tulips. Uncle Jonathan now came out to sun himself on the front porch, in a broad-rimmed felt hat and a green plaid shawl which his father used to wear on horseback trips over the hills.

Though spring first attacked us through the orchard, the great assault, for which we children waited, came on the side of the hill next the river; it was violent, blood-red, long drawn-out, and when it was over, our hill belonged to summer. The vivid event of our year was the blooming of the wall.

Along the front of Fox Hill, where the lawn ended in a steep descent, Uncle Harry had put in a stone retaining wall to keep the ground from washing out. This wall, he said, he intended to manage himself, and when he first announced that he was going to cover it with red rambler roses, his wife laughed at him and told him he would spoil the whole hill. But in the event she was converted. Nowhere in the valley did ramblers thrive so well and bloom so gorgeously. From the railway station our home-coming business men could see that crimson wall, running along high on the green hillside.

One Sunday morning when the ramblers were at their height, we all went with Uncle Harry and Valentine down the driveway to admire them. Aunt Charlotte admitted that they were very showy, very decorative, but she added under her breath that she couldn't feel much enthusiasm for scentless roses.

"But they are quite another sort of thing," Uncle Harry expostulated. "They go right about their business and bloom. I like their being without an odour; it gives them a kind of frankness and innocence."

In the bright sunlight I could see her dark skin flush a little. "Innocence?" she murmured, "I shouldn't call it just that."

I was wondering what she would call it, when our stableman Bill came up from the post-office with his leather bag and emptied the contents on the grass. He always brought the Ramsays' mail with ours, and we often teased Uncle Valentine about certain bright purple letters from Paris, addressed to him in a woman's hand. Because of the curious ways of mail steamers they sometimes came in pairs, and that morning there were actually five of these purple punctuations in the pile of white letters. The children laughed immoderately. Betty Jane and Elizabeth shouted for joy as they fished them out. "Poor Uncle Val! When will you ever get time to answer them all?"

"Ah, that's it!" he said as he began stuffing them away in his pockets.

The next afternoon Aunt Charlotte and I were sewing, seated in the little covered balcony out of her room, with honeysuckle vines all about us. We saw Valentine, hatless, in his striped blazer, come around the corner of the house and seat himself at the tea-table under one of the big sycamores, just below us. We were about to call to him, when he took out those five purple envelopes and spread them on the table before him as if he were going to play a game with them. My aunt looked at me with a sparkle in her eye and put her finger to her lips to keep me quiet. Elizabeth came running across from the summerhouse with her kitten. He called to her.

"Just a moment, Elizabeth. I want you to choose one of these."

"But how? What for?" she asked, much astonished.

"Oh, just choose one, any one," he said carelessly. "Put your finger down." He took out a lead pencil. "Now, we'll mark that 1. Choose again; very well, that's number 2; another, another. Thank you. Now the one that's left will necessarily be 5, won't it?"

"But, Uncle Val, aren't these the ones that came yesterday? And you haven't read them yet?"

"Hush, not so loud, dear." He took up his half-burned cigarette. "You see, when so many come at once, it's not easy to know which should be read first. But you've settled that difficulty for me." He swept them lightly into the two side pockets of his blazer and sprang up. "Where are the others? Can't we go off for a tramp somewhere? Up Blue Run, to see the wild azaleas?"

Elizabeth came into the house calling for us, and Aunt Charlotte and I went down to him.

"We're going up Blue Run to see the azaleas, Charlotte, won't you come?"

She looked wistful. "It's very hot. I'm afraid I ought not to climb, and you'll want to go the steep way."

She waited, hoping to be urged, but he said no more about it. He was sometimes quite heartless.

That evening we came home tired, and the little girls were sent to bed soon after dinner. It was the most glorious of summer nights; I couldn't think of giving it up and going to sleep. Our valley was still, breathlessly still, and full of white moonlight. The garden gave off a heavy perfume, the lawn and house were mottled with intense black and intense white, a mosaic so perplexing that I could hardly find my way along the familiar paths. There was a languorous spirit of beauty abroad—warm, sensuous, oppressive, like the pressure of a warm, clinging body. I felt vaguely afraid to be alone.

I looked for Aunt Charlotte, and found her in the little balcony off her bedroom, where we had been sitting that morning. She spoke to me impatiently, in a way that quite hurt my feelings.

"You must go to bed, Marjorie. I have a headache and I can't be with anyone tonight."

I could feel that she did not want me near her, that my intrusion was most unwelcome. I went downstairs. Uncle Harry was in his study, doing accounts.

"Fine night, isn't it?" he said cheerfully. "I'm going out to see a little of it presently. Almost done my figures." His accounts must have troubled him sometimes; his household cost a great deal of money.

I retreated to the apple orchard. Seeing that the door of Valentine's study was open, I approached cautiously and looked in. He was on his divan, which he had pulled up into the moonlight, lying on his back with his arms under his head.

"Run away, Margie, I'm busy," he muttered, not looking at me but staring past me.

I walked alone about the garden, smelling the stocks until I could smell them no more. I noticed how many moonflowers had come out on the Japanese summerhouse that stood on the line between our ground and the Ramsays'. As I drew near it I heard a groan, not loud, but long, long, as if the unhappiness of a whole lifetime were coming out in one despairing breath. I looked in through the vines. There sat Roland, his head in his hands, the moonlight on his silver hair. I stole softly away through the grass. It seemed that tonight everyone wanted to be alone with his ghost.

Going home through the garden I heard a low call; "Wait, wait a minute!" Uncle Morton came out of the darkness of the vine-covered side porch and beckoned me to follow him. He led me to the plot where his finest roses were in bloom and stopped before a bush that had a great many buds on it, but only one open flower—a great white rose, almost as big as a moonflower, its petals beautifully curled.

"Wait a minute," he whispered again. He took out his pocket-knife, and with great care and considerable difficulty managed to cut the rose with a long stem. He held it out to me in his shaking hand. "There," he said proudly. "That's my best one, the Queen of Savoy. I've been waiting for someone to give it to!"

This was a bold adventure for Morton. I saw that he meant it as a high compliment, and that he was greatly pleased with himself as he wavered back along the white path and disappeared into the darkness under the honeysuckle vines.

X

The next morning Valentine went up to town with Morton on the early train, and at six o'clock that evening Morton came back without him. Aunt Charlotte, who was watching in the garden, went quickly across the Ramsays' lawn.

"Morton, where is Valentine?"

Morton stood holding his straw hat before him in both hands, telling her vaguely that Valentine was going to spend the night in town, at a hotel. "He has to be near the cable office—been sending messages all day—something very important."

Valentine remained in the City for several days. We did not see him again until he joined us one afternoon when we were having tea in the garden. He looked fresh and happy, in new white flannels and one of his gayest neckties.

"Oh, it's delightful to be back, Charlotte!" he exclaimed as he sank into a chair near her.

"We've missed you, Valentine." She, too, looked radiantly happy.

"I should hope so! Because you're probably going to have a great deal of me. Likely I'm here forever, like Roland and the oak trees. I've been staying up in the City, on neutral ground for a few days, to find out what I really want. Do you know, Betty Jane and Elizabeth, that's a sure test; the place you wish for the first moment you're awake in the morning, is the place where you most want to be. I often want to do two things at once, be in two places at once, but this time I don't think I had a moment's indecision." He did not say about what, but presently he drew off a seal ring he wore on his little finger and began playing with it. I knew it was Louise Ireland's ring, he had told me so once. It was an intaglio, a three-masted ship under full sail, and over it, in old English letters. *Telle est la Vie.*

He sat playing with the ring, tossing it up into the sunlight and catching it in his palm, while he addressed my aunt.

"Ireland's leaving Paris. Off for a long tour in South Africa and Australia. She's like a sea gull or a swallow, that woman, forever crossing water. I'm sorry I can't be with her. She's the best friend I've ever had—except you, Charlotte." He did not look at my aunt, but the drop in his voice was a look. "I do seem to be tied to you."

"It's the valley you're tied to. The place is necessary to you, Valentine."

"Yes, it's the place, and it's you and the children—it's even Morton and Roland, God knows why!"

Aunt Charlotte was right. It was the place. The people were secondary. Indeed, I have often wondered, had he been left to his own will, how long he would have been content there. A man under thirty does not settle down to live with old men and children. But the place was vocal to him. During the year that he was with us he wrote all of the thirty-odd songs by which he lives. Some artists profit by exile. He was one of those who do not. And his country was not a continent, but a few wooded hills in a river valley, a few old houses and gardens that were home.

XI

The summer passed joyously. Valentine went on making new songs for us and we went on singing them. I expected life to be like that forever. The golden year, Aunt Charlotte called it, when I visited her at Fox Hill years afterward. September came and went, and then a cold wind blew down upon us.

Uncle Harry and Morton came home one night with disturbing news. It was said in the City that the old Wakeley estate had been sold. Miss Belle Wakeley, the sole heir, had lived in Italy for several years; her big house on the unwooded side of Blinker's Hill had been shut up, her many acres rented out or lying idle.

Very soon after Uncle Harry startled us with this news, Valentine came over to ask whether such a thing were possible. No large tract of land had changed hands in Greenacre for many years.

"I rather think it's true," said Uncle Harry. "I'm going to the agent tomorrow to find out any particulars I can. It seems to be a very guarded transaction. I suppose this means that Belle has decided to live abroad for good. I'm sorry."

"It's very wrong of her," said Aunt Charlotte, "and I think she'll regret it. If she hasn't any feeling for her property now, she will have some day. Why, her grandfather was born there!"

"Yes, I'm disappointed. I thought Belle had a great deal of sentiment underneath." Uncle Harry had always been Miss Wakeley's champion, liked her independent ways, and was amused by her brusque manners.

Valentine was standing by the fireplace, abstracted and deeply concerned.

"Just how much does the Wakeley property take in, Harry? I've never known exactly."

"A great deal. It covers the courses of both creeks, Blue Run and Powhatan Creek, and runs clear back to the top of Flint Ridge. It's our biggest estate, by long odds."

Valentine began pacing the floor. "Did you know she wanted to sell? Couldn't the neighbours have clubbed together and bought it, rather than let strangers in?"

Uncle Harry laughed and shook his head. "I'm afraid we're not rich enough, Val. It's worth a tremendous lot of money. Most of us have all the land we can take care of."

"I suppose so," he muttered. "Father's pretty well mortgaged up, isn't he?"

"Pretty well," Uncle Harry admitted. "Don't worry. I'll see what I can find out tomorrow. I can't think Belle would sell to a speculator, and let her estate be parceled out. She'd have too much consideration for the rest of us. She was the finest kind of neighbour. I wish we had her back."

"It never occurred to me, Harry, that the actual countryside could be sold; the creeks and woods and hills. That shouldn't be permitted. They ought to be kept just as they are, since they give the place its character."

Uncle Harry said he was afraid the only way of keeping a place the same, in this country, was to own it.

"But there are some things one doesn't think of in terms of money," Valentine persisted. "If I'd had bushels of money when I came home last winter, it would never have occurred to me to try to buy Blinker's Hill, any more than the sky over it. I didn't know that the Wakeleys or anybody else owned the creeks, and the forest up toward the Ridge."

Aunt Charlotte rose and went up to Uncle Harry's chair. "Is it really too late to do anything? Too late to cable Belle and ask her to give her neighbours a chance to buy it in first?"

"My dear, you never do realize much about the cost of things. But remember, Belle is a shrewd business woman. She knows well enough that no dozen of her neighbours could raise so much ready money. I understand it's a cash transaction."

Aunt Charlotte looked hurt. "Well, I can only say it was faithless of her. People have some responsibility toward their old friends."

Dinner was announced, and Valentine was urged to stay, but he refused.

"I don't want any dinner, I'm too nervous. I'm awfully fussed by this affair, Charlotte." He stood beside my aunt at the door for a moment, hanging his head despondently, and went away.

That evening my aunt and uncle could talk of nothing but the sale of the Wakeley property. Uncle Harry said sadly that he had never before so wished that he were a rich man. "Though even if I were, I don't know that I'd have thought of making Belle an offer. I'm as impractical as Valentine. But if I'd had money, I do believe Belle would have given me the first chance. We're her nearest neighbours, and whoever buys Blinker's Hill has to be a part of our landscape, and to come into our life more or less."

"Have you any suspicion who it may be?" She spoke very low.

Uncle Harry was standing beside her, his back to the hall fire, smoking his church-warden pipe. "The purchaser? Not the slightest. Have you?"

"Yes." She spoke lower still. "A suspicion that tortures me. It flashed into my mind the moment you told us. I don't know why."

"Then keep it to yourself, my dear," he said resolutely, as if he had all he cared to shoulder. I heard a snap, and saw that he had broken the long stem of his pipe. "There," he said, throwing it into the fire, "you and Valentine have got me worked up with your fussing. I'm as shaky as poor Morton tonight."

XII

The next day Uncle Harry telephoned my aunt from his office in town; Miss Wakeley's agent was not at liberty to disclose the purchaser's name, but assured him that the estate was not sold to a speculator, but an old resident of the City who would preserve the property very much as it was and would respect the feelings of the community.

I was sent over to Bonnie Brae with the good tidings. We all felt so much encouraged that we decided to spend the afternoon in the woods that had been restored to us. It was a yellow October day, and our country had never looked more beautiful. We had tea beside Powhatan Creek, where it curved wide and shallow through green bottom land. A plantation of sycamores grew there, their old white roots bursting out of the low banks and forking into the stream itself. The bark of those sycamores was always peculiarly white, and the sunlight played on the silvery interlacing of the great boughs. Dry ledges of slate rock stood out of the cold green water here and there, and on the up-stream side of each ledge lay a little trembling island of yellow leaves, unable to pass the barrier. The meadow in which we lingered was

smooth turf, of that intense green of autumn grass
that has been already a little touched by frost.

As we sat on the warm slate rocks, we looked up at
the wooded side of Blinker's Hill—like a mellow old
tapestry. The fiercest autumn colours had burned
themselves out; the gold on the smoke-coloured
beeches was thin and pale, so that through their hori-
zontal branches one could see the coloured carpet of
leaves on the ground. Only the young oaks held all
their ruby leaves, the deepest tone in the whole scale
of reds—and they would still be there, a little duller,
when the snow was flying.

I remember my aunt's voice, a tone not quite natural, when she said suddenly, "Valentine, how beautiful
the Tuileries gardens are on an afternoon like this—
down about the second fountain. The colour lasts in
the sky so long after dusk comes on,—behind the Eif-
fel tower."

He was lying on his back. He sat up and looked at
her sharply. "Oh, yes!"

"Aren't you beginning to be a little homesick for
it?" she asked bashfully.

"A little. But it's rather nice to sit safe and lazy on
Fox Hill and be a trifle homesick for far-away places.
Even Roland gets homesick for Bavaria in the spring,
he tells me. He takes a drink or two and recovers. Are
you trying to shove me off somewhere?"

She sighed. "Oh, no! No, indeed, I'm not."

But she had, in some way, broken the magical con-
tentment of the afternoon. The little girls began to
seem restless, so we gathered them up and started
home.

We followed the road round the foot of Blinker's
Hill, to the cleared side on which stood the old Wakeley house. There we saw a man and woman coming

down the driveway from the house itself. The man stopped and hesitated, but the woman quickened her pace and came toward us. Aunt Charlotte became very pale. She had recognized them at a distance, and so had I; Janet Oglethorpe and her second husband. I remember exactly how she looked. She was wearing a black and white check out-of-door coat and a hard black turban. Her face, always high-coloured, was red and shiny from exercise. She waved to us cordially as she came up, but did not offer to shake hands. Her husband took off his hat and smiled scornfully. He stood well behind her, looking very ill at ease, with his elbows out and his chin high, and as the conversation went on his haughty smile became a nervous grin.

"How do you do, Mrs. Waterford, and how do you do, Valentine," Mrs. Towne began effusively. She spoke very fast, and her lips seemed not to keep up with her enunciation; they were heavy and soft, and made her speech slushy. Her mouth was her bad feature—her teeth were too far apart, there was something crude and inelegant about them. "We are going to be neighbours, Mrs. Waterford. I don't want it noised abroad yet, but I've just bought the Wakeley place. I'm going to do the house over and live down here. I hope you won't mind our coming."

Aunt Charlotte made some reply. Valentine did not utter a sound. He took off his hat, replaced it, and stood with his hands in his jacket pockets, looking at the ground.

"I've always had my eye on this property," Mrs. Towne went on, "but it took Belle a long while to make up her mind. It's too fine a place to be left going to waste. It will be nice for Valentine's boy to grow up here where he did, and to be near his Grandfather Ramsay. I want him to know his Ramsay kin."

Valentine behaved very badly. He addressed her without lifting his eyes from the ground or taking his hands out of his pockets; merely kicked a dead leaf out of the road and said: "He's not my boy, and the less he sees of the Ramsays, the better. You've got him, it's your affair to make an Oglethorpe of him and see that he stays one. What do you want to make the kid miserable for?"

Mrs. Towne grew as much redder as it was possible to be, but she spoke indulgently. "Now, Valentine, why can't you be sensible? Certainly, on Mrs. Waterford's account—"

"Oh, yes!" he muttered. "That's the Oglethorpe notion of good manners, before people!"

"I'm sorry, Mrs. Waterford. I had no idea he would be so naughty, or I wouldn't have stopped you. But I did want you to be the first person to know." Mrs. Towne turned to my aunt with great self-command and a ready flow of speech. Her alarmingly high colour and a slight swelling of the face, a puffing-up about her eyes and nose, betrayed her state of feeling.

The women talked politely for a few moments, while the two men stood sulking, each in his own way. When the conference was over, Mrs. Towne crossed the road resolutely and took the path to the station. Towne again took off his hat, looking nowhere, and followed her. Valentine did not return the salute.

As our meek band went on around the foot of the hill, he merely pulled his hat lower over his eyes and said, "She's Scotch; she couldn't let anything get away—not even me. All damned bunk about wanting to get Dickie down here. Everything about her's bunk, except her damned money. That's a fact, and it's got me—it's got me."

Aunt Charlotte's breathing was so irregular that she could scarcely speak. "Valentine, I've had a presentiment of that, from the beginning. I scarcely slept at all last night. I can't have it so. Harry must find some way out."

"No way out, Charlotte," he went along swinging his shoulders and speaking in a dull sing-song voice. "That was her creek we were playing along this afternoon; Blue Run, Powhatan Creek, the big woods, Flint Ridge, Blinker's Hill. I can't get in or out. What does it say on the rat-bane bottle; *put the poison along all his runways*. That's the right idea!"

He did not stop with us, but cut back through the orchard to his study. After dinner we waited for him, sitting solemnly about the fire. At last Aunt Charlotte started up as if she could bear it no longer.

"Come on, Harry," she said firmly. "We must see about Valentine."

He looked up at her pathetically. "Take Marjorie, won't you? I really don't want to see the poor chap tonight, Charlotte."

We hurried across the garden. The studio was dark, the fire had gone out. He was lying on the couch, but he did not answer us. I found a box of matches and lit a candle.

One of Uncle Jonathan's rye bottles stood half empty on the mantel-piece. He had had no dinner, had drunk off nearly a pint of whisky and dropped on the couch. He was deathly white, and his eyes were rolled up in his head.

Aunt Charlotte knelt down beside him and covered him with her cloak. "Run for your Uncle Harry, as fast as you can," she said.

XIII

The end? That was the end for us. Within the week workmen were pulling down the wing of the Wakeley house, in order to get as much work as possible done before the cold weather came on. The sound of the stone masons' tools rang out clear across the cut between the two hills; even in Valentine's study one could not escape it. We wished that Morton had carried out his happy idea of making a padded cell of it!

Valentine lingered on at Bonnie Brae for a month, though he never went off his father's place again. He did not sail until the end of November, stayed out his year with us, but he had become a different man. All of us, except Aunt Charlotte, were eager to have him go. He had tonsillitis, I remember, and lay on the couch in his study ill and feverish for two weeks. He seemed not to be working, yet he must have been, for when he went away he left between the leaves of one of my aunt's music books the manuscript of the most beautiful and heart-breaking of all his songs:

I know a wall where red roses grow...

He deferred his departure from date to date, changed his passage several times. The night before he went we were sitting by the hall fire, and he said he wished that all the trains and all the boats in the world would stop moving, stop forever.

When his trunks had gone, and his bags were piled up ready to be put into the carriage, he took a latch-key from his pocket and gave it to Aunt Charlotte.

"That's the key to my study. Keep it for me. I don't

know that I'll ever need it again, but I'd like to think that you have it."

Less than two years afterward, Valentine was accidentally killed, struck by a motor truck one night at the Pont Royal, just as he was leaving Louise Ireland's apartment on the quai.

Aunt Charlotte survived him by eleven years, but after her death we found his latchkey in her jewel box. I have it still. There is now no door for it to open. Bonnie Brae was pulled down during the war. The wave of industrial expansion swept down that valley, and roaring mills belch their black smoke up to the heights where those lovely houses used to stand. Fox Hill is gone, and our wall is gone. *I know a wall where red roses grow;* youngsters sing it still. The roses of song and the roses of memory, they are the only ones that last.

NEIGHBOUR ROSICKY

I

When Doctor Burleigh told neighbour Rosicky he had a bad heart, Rosicky protested.

"So? No, I guess my heart was always pretty good. I got a little asthma, maybe. Just a awful short breath when I was pitchin' hay last summer, dat's all."

"Well now, Rosicky, if you know more about it than I do, what did you come to me for? It's your heart that makes you short of breath, I tell you. You're sixty-five years old, and you've always worked hard, and your heart's tired. You've got to be careful from now on, and you can't do heavy work any more. You've got five boys at home to do it for you."

The old farmer looked up at the Doctor with a gleam of amusement in his queer triangular-shaped eyes. His eyes were large and lively, but the lids were caught up in the middle in a curious way, so that they formed a triangle. He did not look like a sick man. His brown face was creased but not wrinkled, he had a ruddy colour in his smooth-shaven cheeks and in his lips, under his long brown moustache. His hair was thin and ragged around his ears, but very little grey. His forehead, naturally high and crossed by deep parallel lines, now ran all the way up to his pointed crown. Rosicky's face had the habit of looking interested,—suggested a contented disposition and a reflective quality that was gay rather than grave. This gave him a certain detachment, the easy manner of an onlooker and observer.

"Well, I guess you ain't got no pills fur a bad heart, Doctor Ed. I guess the only thing is fur me to git me a new one."

Doctor Burleigh swung round in his desk-chair and frowned at the old farmer. "I think if I were you I'd take a little care of the old one, Rosicky."

Rosicky shrugged. "Maybe I don't know how. I expect you mean fur me not to drink my coffee no more."

"I wouldn't, in your place. But you'll do as you choose about that. I've never yet been able to separate a Bohemian from his coffee or his pipe. I've quit trying. But the sure thing is you've got to cut out farm work. You can feed the stock and do chores about the barn, but you can't do anything in the fields that makes you short of breath."

"How about shelling corn?"

"Of course not!"

Rosicky considered with puckered brows.

"I can't make my heart go no longer'n it wants to, can I, Doctor Ed?"

"I think it's good for five or six years yet, maybe more, if you'll take the strain off it. Sit around the house and help Mary. If I had a good wife like yours, I'd want to stay around the house."

His patient chuckled. "It ain't no place fur a man. I don't like no old man hanging round the kitchen too much. An' my wife, she's a awful hard worker her own self."

"That's it; you can help her a little. My Lord, Rosicky, you are one of the few men I know who has a family he can get some comfort out of; happy dispositions, never quarrel among themselves, and they treat you right. I want to see you live a few years and enjoy them."

"Oh, they're good kids, all right," Rosicky assented.

The Doctor wrote him a prescription and asked him how his oldest son, Rudolph, who had married in the spring, was getting on. Rudolph had struck out for himself, on rented land. "And how's Polly? I was afraid Mary mightn't like an American daughter-in-law, but it seems to be working out all right."

"Yes, she's a fine girl. Dat widder woman bring her daughters up very nice. Polly got lots of spunk, an' she got some style, too. Da's nice, for young folks to have some style." Rosicky inclined his head gallantly. His voice and his twinkly smile were an affectionate compliment to his daughter-in-law.

"It looks like a storm, and you'd better be getting home before it comes. In town in the car?" Doctor Burleigh rose.

"No, I'm in de wagon. When you got five boys, you ain't got much chance to ride round in de Ford. I ain't much for cars, noway."

"Well, it's a good road out to your place; but I don't want you bumping around in a wagon much. And never again on a hay-rake, remember!"

Rosicky placed the Doctor's fee delicately behind the desk-telephone, looking the other way, as if this were an absent-minded gesture. He put on his plush cap and his corduroy jacket with a sheepskin collar, and went out.

The Doctor picked up his stethoscope and frowned at it as if he were seriously annoyed with the instrument. He wished he had been telling tales about some other man's heart, some old man who didn't look the Doctor in the eye so knowingly, or hold out such a warm brown hand when he said good-bye. Doctor Burleigh had been a poor boy in the country before he went away to medical school; he had known Rosicky almost ever since he could remember, and he had a deep affection for Mrs. Rosicky.

Only last winter he had had such a good breakfast at Rosicky's, and that when he needed it. He had been out all night on a long, hard confinement case at Tom Marshall's,—a big rich farm where there was plenty of stock and plenty of feed and a great deal of expensive farm machinery of the newest model, and no comfort whatever. The woman had too many children and too much work, and she was no manager. When the baby was born at last, and handed over to the assisting neighbour woman, and the mother was properly attended to, Burleigh refused any breakfast in that slovenly house, and drove his buggy—the snow was too deep for a car—eight miles to Anton Rosicky's place. He didn't know another farm-house where a man could get such a warm welcome, and such good strong coffee with rich cream. No wonder the old chap didn't want to give up his coffee!

He had driven in just when the boys had come back from the barn and were washing up for breakfast. The long table, covered with a bright oilcloth, was set out with dishes waiting for them, and the warm kitchen was full of the smell of coffee and hot biscuit and sausage. Five big handsome boys, running from twenty to twelve, all with what Burleigh called natural good manners,—they hadn't a bit of the painful self-consciousness he himself had to struggle with when he was a lad. One ran to put his horse away, another helped him off with his fur coat and hung it up, and Josephine, the youngest child and the only daughter, quickly set another place under her mother's direction.

With Mary, to feed creatures was the natural expression of affection,—her chickens, the calves, her big hungry boys. It was a rare pleasure to feed a young man whom she seldom saw and of whom she was as proud as if he belonged to her. Some country housekeepers would have stopped to spread a white cloth over the oilcloth, to change the thick cups and plates for their best china, and the wooden-handled knives for plated ones. But not Mary.

"You must take us as you find us, Doctor Ed. I'd be glad to put out my good things for you if you was expected, but I'm glad to get you any way at all."

He knew she was glad,—she threw back her head and spoke out as if she were announcing him to the whole prairie. Rosicky hadn't said anything at all; he merely smiled his twinkling smile, put some more coal on the fire, and went into his own room to pour the Doctor a little drink in a medicine glass. When they were all seated, he watched his wife's face from his end of the table and spoke to her in Czech. Then, with the instinct of politeness which seldom failed him, he turned to the Doctor and said slyly; "I was just tellin' her not to ask you no questions about Mrs. Marshall till you eat some breakfast. My wife, she's terrible fur to ask questions."

The boys laughed, and so did Mary. She watched

the Doctor devour her biscuit and sausage, too much excited to eat anything herself. She drank her coffee and sat taking in everything about her visitor. She had known him when he was a poor country boy, and was boastfully proud of his success, always saying: "What do people go to Omaha for, to see a doctor, when we got the best one in the State right here?" If Mary liked people at all, she felt physical pleasure in the sight of them, personal exultation in any good fortune that came to them. Burleigh didn't know many women like that, but he knew she was like that.

When his hunger was satisfied, he did, of course, have to tell them about Mrs. Marshall, and he noticed what a friendly interest the boys took in the matter.

Rudolph, the oldest one (he was still living at home then), said: "The last time I was over there, she was lifting them big heavy milk-cans, and I knew she oughtn't to be doing it."

"Yes, Rudolph told me about that when he come home, and I said it wasn't right," Mary put in warmly. "It was all right for me to do them things up to the last, for I was terrible strong, but that woman's weakly. And do you think she'll be able to nurse it, Ed?" She sometimes forgot to give him the title she was so proud of. "And to think of your being up all night and then not able to get a decent breakfast! I don't know what's the matter with such people."

"Why, Mother," said one of the boys, "if Doctor Ed had got breakfast there, we wouldn't have him here. So you ought to be glad."

"He knows I'm glad to have him, John, any time. But I'm sorry for that poor woman, how bad she'll feel the Doctor had to go away in the cold without his breakfast."

"I wish I'd been in practice when these were getting

born." The doctor looked down the row of close-clipped heads. "I missed some good breakfasts by not being."

The boys began to laugh at their mother because she flushed so red, but she stood her ground and threw up her head. "I don't care, you wouldn't have got away from this house without breakfast. No doctor ever did. I'd have had something ready fixed that Anton could warm up for you."

They boys laughed harder than ever, and exclaimed at her: "I'll bet you would!" "She would, that!"

"Father, did you get breakfast for the doctor when we were born?"

"Yes, and he used to bring me my breakfast, too, mighty nice. I was always awful hungry!" Mary admitted with a guilty laugh.

While the boys were getting the Doctor's horse, he went to the window to examine the house plants. "What do you do to your geraniums to keep them blooming all winter, Mary? I never pass this house that from the road I don't see your windows full of flowers."

She snapped off a dark red one, and a ruffled new green leaf, and put them in his buttonhole. "There, that looks better. You look too solemn for a young man, Ed. Why don't you git married? I'm worried about you. Settin' at breakfast, I looked at you real hard, and I seen you've got some grey hairs already."

"Oh, yes! They're coming. Maybe they'd come faster if I married."

"Don't talk so. You'll ruin your health eating at the hotel. I could send your wife a nice loaf of nut bread, if you only had one. I don't like to see a young man getting grey. I'll tell you something, Ed; you make some strong black tea and keep it handy in a bowl, and every morning just brush it into your hair, an' it'll keep the grey from showin' much. That's the way I do!"

Sometimes the Doctor heard the gossipers in the drug-store wondering why Rosicky didn't get on faster. He was industrious, and so were his boys, but they were rather free and easy, weren't pushers, and they didn't always show good judgment. They were comfortable, they were out of debt, but they didn't get much ahead. Maybe, Doctor Burleigh reflected, people as generous and warm-hearted and affectionate as the Rosickys never got ahead much; maybe you couldn't enjoy your life and put it into the bank, too.

II

When Rosicky left Doctor Burleigh's office he went into the farm-implement store to light his pipe and put on his glasses and read over the list Mary had given him. Then he went into the general merchandise place next door and stood about until the pretty girl with the plucked eyebrows, who always waited on him, was free. Those eyebrows, two thin India-ink strokes, amused him, because he remembered how they used to be. Rosicky always prolonged his shopping by a little joking; the girl knew the old fellow admired her, and she liked to chaff with him.

"Seems to me about every other week you buy tick-ing, Mr. Rosicky, and always the best quality," she remarked as she measured off the heavy bolt with red stripes.

"You see, my wife is always makin' goose-fedder pillows, an' de thin stuff don't hold in dem little down-fedders."

"You must have lots of pillows at your house."

"Sure. She makes quilts of dem, too. We sleeps easy. Now she's makin' a fedder quilt for my son's wife. You know Polly, that married my Rudolph. How much my bill, Miss Pearl?"

"Eight eighty-five."

"Chust make it nine, and put in some candy fur de women."

"As usual. I never did see a man buy so much candy for his wife. First thing you know, she'll be getting too fat."

"I'd like dat. I ain't much fur all dem slim women like what de style is now."

"That's one for me, I suppose, Mr. Bohunk!" Pearl sniffed and elevated her India-ink strokes.

When Rosicky went out to his wagon, it was beginning to snow,—the first snow of the season, and he was glad to see it. He rattled out of town and along the highway through a wonderfully rich stretch of country, the finest farms in the county. He admired this High Prairie, as it was called, and always liked to drive through it. His own place lay in a rougher territory, where there was some clay in the soil and it was not so productive. When he bought his land, he hadn't the money to buy on High Prairie; so he told his boys, when they grumbled, that if their land hadn't some clay in it, they wouldn't own it at all. All the same, he enjoyed looking at these fine farms, as he enjoyed looking at a prize bull.

After he had gone eight miles, he came to the graveyard, which lay just at the edge of his own hay-land. There he stopped his horses and sat still on his wagon seat, looking about at the snowfall. Over yonder on the hill he could see his own house, crouching low, with the clump of orchard behind and the windmill before, and all down the gentle hill-slope the rows of pale gold cornstalks stood out against the white field. The snow was falling over the cornfield and the pasture and the hay-land, steadily, with very little wind, —a nice dry snow. The graveyard had only a light wire fence about it and was all overgrown with long red grass. The fine snow, settling into this red grass and upon the few little evergreens and the headstones, looked very pretty.

It was a nice graveyard, Rosicky reflected, sort of snug and homelike, not cramped or mournful,—a big sweep all round it. A man could lie down in the long grass and see the complete arch of the sky over him, hear the wagons go by; in summer the mowing-machine rattled right up to the wire fence. And it was so near home. Over there across the cornstalks his own roof and windmill looked so good to him that he promised himself to mind the Doctor and take care of himself. He was awful fond of his place, he admitted. He wasn't anxious to leave it. And it was a comfort to think that he would never have to go farther than the edge of his own hayfield. The snow, falling over his barnyard and the graveyard, seemed to draw things together like. And they were all old neighbours in the graveyard, most of them friends; there was nothing to feel awkward or embarrassed about. Embarrassment was the most disagreeable feeling Rosicky knew. He didn't often have it,—only with certain people whom he didn't understand at all.

Well, it was a nice snowstorm; a fine sight to see the snow falling so quietly and graciously over so much open country. On his cap and shoulders, on the horses' backs and manes, light, delicate, mysterious it fell; and with it a dry cool fragrance was released into the air. It meant rest for vegetation and men and beasts, for the ground itself; a season of long nights for sleep, leisurely breakfasts, peace by the fire. This and much more went through Rosicky's mind, but he merely told himself that winter was coming, clucked to his horses, and drove on.

When he reached home, John, the youngest boy, ran out to put away his team for him, and he met Mary coming up from the outside cellar with her apron full of carrots. They went into the house together. On the table, covered with oilcloth figured with clusters of blue grapes, a place was set, and he smelled hot coffee-cake of some kind. Anton never lunched in town; he thought that extravagant, and anyhow he didn't like the food. So Mary always had something ready for him when he got home.

After he was settled in his chair, stirring his coffee in a big cup, Mary took out of the oven a pan of *kolache* stuffed with apricots, examined them anxiously to see whether they had got too dry, put them beside his plate, and then sat down opposite him.

Rosicky asked her in Czech if she wasn't going to have any coffee.

She replied in English, as being somehow the right language for transacting business: "Now what did Doctor Ed say, Anton? You tell me just what."

"He said I was to tell you some compliments, but I forgot 'em." Rosicky's eyes twinkled.

"About you, I mean. What did he say about your asthma?"

"He says I ain't got no asthma." Rosicky took one of the little rolls in his broad brown fingers. The thickened nail of his right thumb told the story of his past.

"Well, what is the matter? And don't try to put me off."

"He don't say nothing much, only I'm a little older, and my heart ain't so good like it used to be."

Mary started and brushed her hair back from her temples with both hands as if she were a little out of her mind. From the way she glared, she might have been in a rage with him.

"He says there's something the matter with your heart? Doctor Ed says so?"

"Now don't yell at me like I was a hog in de garden, Mary. You know I always did like to hear a woman talk soft. He didn't say anything de matter wid my heart, only it ain't so young like it used to be, an' he tell me not to pitch hay or run de corn-sheller."

Mary wanted to jump up, but she sat still. She admired the way he never under any circumstances raised his voice or spoke roughly. He was city-bred, and she was country-bred; she often said she wanted her boys to have their papa's nice ways.

"You never have no pain there, do you? It's your breathing and your stomach that's been wrong. I wouldn't believe nobody but Doctor Ed about it. I guess I'll go see him myself. Didn't he give you no advice?"

"Chust to take it easy like, an' stay round de house dis winter. I guess you got some carpenter work for me to do. I kin make some new shelves for you, and I want dis long time to build a closet in de boys' room and make dem two little fellers keep dere clo'es hung up."

Rosicky drank his coffee from time to time, while he considered. His moustache was of the soft long variety and came down over his mouth like the teeth of a buggy-rake over a bundle of hay. Each time he put down his cup, he ran his blue handkerchief over his lips. When he took a drink of water, he managed very neatly with the back of his hand.

Mary sat watching him intently, trying to find any change in his face. It is hard to see anyone who has become like your own body to you. Yes, his hair had got thin, and his high forehead had deep lines running from left to right. But his neck, always clean shaved except in the busiest seasons, was not loose or baggy. It was burned a dark reddish brown, and there were deep creases in it, but it looked firm and full of blood. His cheeks had a good colour. On either side of his mouth there was a half-moon down the length of his cheek, not wrinkles, but two lines that had come there from his habitual expression. He was shorter and broader than when she married him; his back had grown broad and curved, a good deal like the shell of an old turtle, and his arms and legs were short.

He was fifteen years older than Mary, but she had hardly ever thought about it before. He was her man, and the kind of man she liked. She was rough, and he was gentle,—city-bred, as she always said. They had been shipmates on a rough voyage and had stood by each other in trying times. Life had gone well with them because, at bottom, they had the same ideas about life. They agreed, without discussion, as to what was most important and what was secondary. They didn't often exchange opinions, even in Czech, —it was as if they had thought the same thought together. A good deal had to be sacrificed and thrown overboard in a hard life like theirs, and they had never disagreed as to the things that could go. It had been a hard life, and a soft life, too. There wasn't anything brutal in the short, broad-backed man with the three-cornered eyes and the forehead that went on to the top of his skull. He was a city man, a gentle man, and though he had married a rough farm girl, he had never touched her without gentleness.

They had been at one accord not to hurry through life, not to be always skimping and saving. They saw their neighbours buy more land and feed more stock than they did, without discontent. Once when the creamery agent came to the Rosickys to persuade them to sell him their cream, he told them how much money the Fasslers, their nearest neighbours, had made on their cream last year.

"Yes," said Mary, "and look at them Fassler children! Pale, pinched little things, they look like skimmed milk. I'd rather put some colour into my children's faces than put money into the bank."

The agent shrugged and turned to Anton.

"I guess we'll do like she says," said Rosicky.

III

Mary very soon got into town to see Doctor Ed, and then she had a talk with her boys and set a guard over Rosicky. Even John, the youngest, had his father on his mind. If Rosicky went to throw hay down from the loft, one of the boys ran up the ladder and took the fork from him. He sometimes complained that though he was getting to be an old man, he wasn't an old woman yet.

That winter he stayed in the house in the afternoons and carpentered, or sat in the chair between the window full of plants and the wooden bench where the two pails of drinking-water stood. This spot was called "Father's corner," though it was not a corner at all. He had a shelf there, where he kept his Bohemian papers and his pipes and tobacco, and his shears and needles and thread and tailor's thimble. Having been a tailor in his youth, he couldn't bear to see a woman

patching at his clothes, or at the boys'. He liked tailoring, and always patched all the overalls and jackets
and work shirts. Occasionally he made over a pair of
pants one of the older boys had outgrown, for the
little fellow.

While he sewed, he let his mind run back over his
life. He had a good deal to remember, really; life in
three countries. The only part of his youth he didn't
like to remember was the two years he had spent in
London, in Cheapside, working for a German tailor
who was wretchedly poor. Those days, when he was
nearly always hungry, when his clothes were dropping
off him for dirt, and the sound of a strange language
kept him in continual bewilderment, had left a sore
spot in his mind that wouldn't bear touching.

He was twenty when he landed at Castle Garden in
New York, and he had a protector who got him work
in a tailor shop in Vesey Street, down near the Washington Market. He looked upon that part of his life as
very happy. He became a good workman, he was industrious, and his wages were increased from time to
time. He minded his own business and envied nobody's good fortune. He went to night school and
learned to read English. He often did overtime work
and was well paid for it, but somehow he never saved
anything. He couldn't refuse a loan to a friend, and he
was self-indulgent. He liked a good dinner, and a little
went for beer, a little for tobacco; a good deal went to
the girls. He often stood through an opera on Saturday nights; he could get standing-room for a dollar.
Those were the great days of opera in New York, and
it gave a fellow something to think about for the rest
of the week. Rosicky had a quick ear, and a childish
love of all the stage splendour; the scenery, the cos-
tumes, the ballet. He usually went with a chum, and

after the performance they had beer and maybe some oysters somewhere. It was a fine life; for the first five years or so it satisfied him completely. He was never hungry or cold or dirty, and everything amused him: a fire, a dog fight, a parade, a storm, a ferry ride. He thought New York the finest, richest, friendliest city in the world.

Moreover, he had what he called a happy home life. Very near the tailor shop was a small furniture-factory, where an old Austrian, Loeffler, employed a few skilled men and made unusual furniture, most of it to order, for the rich German housewives up-town. The top floor of Loeffler's five-storey factory was a loft, where he kept his choice lumber and stored the odd pieces of furniture left on his hands. One of the young workmen he employed was a Czech, and he and Rosicky became fast friends. They persuaded Loeffler to let them have a sleeping-room in one corner of the loft. They bought good beds and bedding and had their pick of the furniture kept up there. The loft was low-pitched, but light and airy, full of windows, and good-smelling by reason of the fine lumber put up there to season. Old Loeffler used to go down to the docks and buy wood from South America and the East from the sea captains. The young men were as foolish about their house as a bridal pair. Zichec, the young cabinet-maker, devised every sort of convenience, and Rosicky kept their clothes in order. At night and on Sundays, when the quiver of machinery underneath was still, it was the quietest place in the world, and on summer nights all the sea winds blew in. Zichec often practised on his flute in the evening. They were both fond of music and went to the opera together. Rosicky thought he wanted to live like that for ever.

But as the years passed, all alike, he began to get a little restless. When spring came round, he would begin to feel fretted, and he got to drinking. He was likely to drink too much of a Saturday night. On Sunday he was languid and heavy, getting over his spree. On Monday he plunged into work again. So he never had time to figure out what ailed him, though he knew something did. When the grass turned green in Park Place, and the lilac hedge at the back of Trinity churchyard put out its blossoms, he was tormented by a longing to run away. That was why he drank too much; to get a temporary illusion of freedom and wide horizons.

Rosicky, the old Rosicky, could remember as if it were yesterday the day when the young Rosicky found out what was the matter with him. It was on a Fourth of July afternoon, and he was sitting in Park Place in the sun. The lower part of New York was empty. Wall Street, Liberty Street, Broadway, all empty. So much stone and asphalt with nothing going on, so many empty windows. The emptiness was intense, like the stillness in a great factory when the machinery stops and the belts and bands cease running. It was too great a change, it took all the strength out of one. Those blank buildings, without the steam of life pouring through them, were like empty jails. It struck young Rosicky that this was the trouble with big cities; they built you in from the earth itself, cemented you away from any contact with the ground. You lived in an unnatural world, like the fish in an aquarium, who were probably much more comfortable than they ever were in the sea.

On that very day he began to think seriously about the articles he had read in the Bohemian papers, describing prosperous Czech farming communities in the

West. He believed he would like to go out there as a farm hand; it was hardly possible that he could ever have land of his own. His people had always been workmen; his father and grandfather had worked in shops. His mother's parents had lived in the country, but they rented their farm and had a hard time to get along. Nobody in his family had ever owned any land,—that belonged to a different station of life altogether. Anton's mother died when he was little, and he was sent into the country to her parents. He stayed with them until he was twelve, and formed those ties with the earth and the farm animals and growing things which are never made at all unless they are made early. After his grandfather died, he went back to live with his father and stepmother, but she was very hard on him, and his father helped him to get passage to London.

After that Fourth of July day in Park Place, the desire to return to the country never left him. To work on another man's farm would be all he asked; to see the sun rise and set and to plant things and watch them grow. He was a very simple man. He was like a tree that has not many roots, but one tap-root that goes down deep. He subscribed for a Bohemian paper printed in Chicago, then for one printed in Omaha. His mind got farther and farther west. He began to save a little money to buy his liberty. When he was thirty-five, there was a great meeting in New York of Bohemian athletic societies, and Rosicky left the tailor shop and went home with the Omaha delegates to try his fortune in another part of the world.

IV

Perhaps the fact that his own youth was well over before he began to have a family was one reason why

Rosicky was so fond of his boys. He had almost a grandfather's indulgence for them. He had never had to worry about any of them—except, just now, a little about Rudolph.

On Saturday night the boys always piled into the Ford, took little Josephine, and went to town to the moving-picture show. One Saturday morning they were talking at the breakfast table about starting early that evening, so that they would have an hour or so to see the Christmas things in the stores before the show began. Rosicky looked down the table.

"I hope you boys ain't disappointed, but I want you to let me have de car tonight. Maybe some of you can go in with de neighbours."

Their faces fell. They worked hard all week, and they were still like children. A new jack-knife or a box of candy pleased the older ones as much as the little fellow.

"If you and Mother are going to town," Frank said, "maybe you could take a couple of us along with you, anyway."

"No, I want to take de car down to Rudolph's, and let him an' Polly go in to de show. She don't git into town enough, an' I'm afraid she's gettin' lonesome, an' he can't afford no car yet."

That settled it. The boys were a good deal dashed. Their father took another piece of apple-cake and went on: "Maybe next Saturday night de two little fellers can go along wid dem."

"Oh, is Rudolph going to have the car every Saturday night?"

Rosicky did not reply at once; then he began to speak seriously: "Listen, boys; Polly ain't lookin' so good. I don't like to see nobody lookin' sad. It comes hard fur a town girl to be a farmer's wife. I don't want no trouble to start in Rudolph's family. When it starts, it ain't so easy to stop. An American girl don't git used to our ways all at once. I like to tell Polly she and Rudolph can have the car every Saturday night till after New Year's, if it's all right with you boys."

"Sure it's all right, Papa," Mary cut in. "And it's good you thought about that. Town girls is used to more than country girls. I lay awake nights, scared she'll make Rudolph discontented with the farm."

The boys put as good a face on it as they could. They surely looked forward to their Saturday nights in town. That evening Rosicky drove the car the half-mile down to Rudolph's new, bare little house.

Polly was in a short-sleeved gingham dress, clearing away the supper dishes. She was a trim, slim little thing, with blue eyes and shingled yellow hair, and her eyebrows were reduced to a mere brush-stroke, like Miss Pearl's.

"Good evening, Mr. Rosicky. Rudolph's at the barn, I guess." She never called him father, or Mary mother. She was sensitive about having married a foreigner. She never in the world would have done it if Rudolph hadn't been such a handsome, persuasive fellow and such a gallant lover. He had graduated in her class in the high school in town, and their friendship began in the ninth grade.

Rosicky went in, though he wasn't exactly asked. "My boys ain't goin' to town tonight, an' I brought de car over fur you two to go in to de picture show."

Polly, carrying dishes to the sink, looked over her shoulder at him. "Thank you. But I'm late with my work tonight, and pretty tired. Maybe Rudolph would like to go in with you."

"Oh, I don't go to de shows! I'm too old-fashioned. You won't feel so tired after you ride in de air a ways.

It's a nice clear night, an' it ain't cold. You go an' fix yourself up, Polly, an' I'll wash de dishes an' leave everything nice fur you."

Polly blushed and tossed her bob. "I couldn't let you do that, Mr. Rosicky. I wouldn't think of it."

Rosicky said nothing. He found a bib apron on a nail behind the kitchen door. He slipped it over his head and then took Polly by her two elbows and pushed her gently toward the door of her own room. "I washed up de kitchen many times for my wife, when de babies was sick or somethin'. You go an' make yourself look nice. I like you to look prettier'n any of dem town girls when you go in. De young folks must have some fun, an' I'm goin' to look out fur you, Polly."

That kind, reassuring grip on her elbows, the old man's funny bright eyes, made Polly want to drop her head on his shoulder for a second. She restrained herself, but she lingered in his grasp at the door of her room, murmuring tearfully: "You always lived in the city when you were young, didn't you? Don't you ever get lonesome out here?"

As she turned round to him, her hand fell naturally into his, and he stood holding it and smiling into her face with his peculiar, knowing, indulgent smile without a shadow of reproach in it. "Dem big cities is all right fur de rich, but dey is terrible hard fur de poor."

"I don't know. Sometimes I think I'd like to take a chance. You lived in New York, didn't you?"

"An' London. Da's bigger still. I learned my trade dere. Here's Rudolph comin', you better hurry."

"Will you tell me about London some time?"

"Maybe. Only I ain't no talker, Polly. Run an' dress yourself up."

The bedroom door closed behind her, and Rudolph

came in from the outside, looking anxious. He had seen the car and was sorry any of his family should come just then. Supper hadn't been a very pleasant occasion. Halting in the doorway, he saw his father in a kitchen apron, carrying dishes to the sink. He flushed crimson and something flashed in his eye. Rosicky held up a warning finger.

"I brought de car over fur you an' Polly to go to de picture show, an' I made her let me finish here so you won't be late. You go put on a clean shirt, quick!"

"But don't the boys want the car, Father?"

"Not tonight dey don't." Rosicky fumbled under his apron and found his pants pocket. He took out a silver dollar and said in a hurried whisper: "You go an' buy dat girl some ice cream an' candy tonight, like you was courtin'. She's awful good friends wid me."

Rudolph was very short of cash, but he took the money as if it hurt him. There had been a crop failure all over the country. He had more than once been sorry he'd married this year.

In a few minutes the young people came out, looking clean and a little stiff. Rosicky hurried them off, and then he took his own time with the dishes. He scoured the pots and pans and put away the milk and swept the kitchen. He put some coal in the stove and shut off the draughts, so the place would be warm for them when they got home late at night. Then he sat down and had a pipe and listened to the clock tick.

Generally speaking, marrying an American girl was certainly a risk. A Czech should marry a Czech. It was lucky that Polly was the daughter of a poor widow woman; Rudolph was proud, and if she had a prosperous family to throw up at him, they could never make it go. Polly was one of four sister, and they all worked; one was book-keeper in the bank, one taught music, and Polly and her younger sisters had been clerks, like Miss Pearl. All four of them were musical, had pretty voices, and sang in the Methodist choir, which the eldest sister directed.

Polly missed the sociability of a store position. She missed the choir, and the company of her sisters. She didn't dislike housework, but she disliked so much of it. Rosicky was a little anxious about this pair. He was afraid Polly would grow so discontented that Rudy would quit the farm and take a factory job in Omaha. He had worked for a winter up there, two years ago, to get money to marry on. He had done very well, and they would always take him back at the stockyards. But to Rosicky that meant the end of everything for his son. To be a landless man was to be a wage-earner, a slave, all your life; to have nothing, to be nothing.

Rosicky thought he would come over and do a little carpentering for Polly after the New Year. He guessed she needed jollying. Rudolph was a serious sort of chap, serious in love and serious about his work.

Rosicky shook out his pipe and walked home across the fields. Ahead of him the lamplight shone from his kitchen windows. Suppose he were still in a tailor shop on Vesey Street, with a bunch of pale, narrow-chested sons working on machines, all coming home tired and sullen to eat supper in a kitchen that was a parlour also; with another crowded, angry family quarrelling just across the dumb-waiter shaft, and squeaking pulleys at the windows where dirty washings hung on dirty lines above a court full of old brooms and mops and ash-cans....

He stopped by the windmill to look up at the frosty winter stars and draw a long breath before he went inside. That kitchen with the shining windows was dear to him; but the sleeping fields and bright stars and the noble darkness were dearer still.

V

On the day before Christmas the weather set in very cold; no snow, but a bitter, biting wind that whistled and sang over the flat land and lashed one's face like fine wires. There was baking going on in the Rosicky kitchen all day, and Rosicky sat inside, making over a coat that Albert had outgrown into an overcoat for John. Mary had a big red geranium in bloom for Christmas, and a row of Jerusalem cherry trees, full of berries. It was the first year she had ever grown these; Doctor Ed brought her the seeds from Omaha when he went to some medical convention. They reminded Rosicky of plants he had seen in England; and all afternoon, as he stitched, he sat thinking about those two years in London, which his mind usually shrank from even after all this while.

He was a lad of eighteen when he dropped down into London, with no money and no connexions except the address of a cousin who was supposed to be working at a confectioner's. When he went to the pastry shop, however, he found that the cousin had gone to America. Anton tramped the streets for several days, sleeping in doorways and on the Embankment, until he was in utter despair. He knew no English, and the sound of the strange language all about him confused him. By chance he met a poor German tailor who had learned his trade in Vienna, and could speak a little Czech. This tailor, Lifschnitz, kept a repair shop in a Cheapside basement, underneath a cobbler. He didn't much need an apprentice, but he was sorry for the boy and took him in for no wages but his keep and what he could pick up. The pickings were supposed to be coppers given you when you took work home to a customer. But most of the customers called for their clothes themselves, and the coppers that came Anton's way were very few. He had, however, a place to sleep. The tailor's family lived upstairs in three rooms; a kitchen, a bedroom, where Lifschnitz and his wife and five children slept, and a living-room. Two corners of this living-room were curtained off for lodgers; in one Rosicky slept on an old horsehair sofa, with a feather quilt to wrap himself in. The other corner was rented to a wretched, dirty boy, who was studying the violin. He actually practised there. Rosicky was dirty, too. There was no way to be anything else. Mrs. Lifschnitz got the water she cooked and washed with from a pump in a brick court, four flights down. There were bugs in the place, and multitudes of fleas, though the poor woman did the best she could. Rosicky knew she often went empty to give another potato or a spoonful of dripping to the two hungry, sad-eyed boys who lodged with her. He used to think he would never get out of there, never get a clean shirt to his back again. What would he do, he wondered, when his clothes actually dropped to pieces and the worn cloth wouldn't hold patches any longer?

It was still early when the old farmer put aside his sewing and his recollections. The sky had been a dark grey all day, with not a gleam of sun, and the light failed at four o'clock. He went to shave and change his shirt while the turkey was roasting. Rudolph and Polly were coming over for supper.

After supper they sat round in the kitchen, and the

younger boys were saying how sorry they were it hadn't snowed. Everybody was sorry. They wanted a deep snow that would lie long and keep the wheat warm, and leave the ground soaked when it melted.

"Yes, sir!" Rudolph broke out fiercely; "if we have another dry year like last year, there's going to be hard times in this country."

Rosicky filled his pipe. "You boys don't know what hard times is. You don't owe nobody, you got plenty to eat an' keep warm, an' plenty water to keep clean. When you got them, you can't have it very hard."

Rudolph frowned, opened and shut his big right hand, and dropped it clenched upon his knee. "I've got to have a good deal more than that, Father, or I'll quit this farming gamble. I can always make good wages railroading, or at the packing house, and be sure of my money."

"Maybe so," his father answered dryly.

Mary, who had just come in from the pantry and was wiping her hands on the roller towel, thought Rudy and his father were getting too serious. She brought her darning-basket and sat down in the middle of the group.

"I ain't much afraid of hard times, Rudy," she said heartily. "We've had a plenty, but we've always come through. Your father wouldn't never take nothing very hard, not even hard times. I got a mind to tell you a story on him. Maybe you boys can't hardly remember the year we had that terrible hot wind, that burned everything up on the Fourth of July? All the corn an' the gardens. An' that was in the days when we didn't have alfalfa yet,—I guess it wasn't invented.

"Well, that very day your father was out cultivatin' corn, and I was here in the kitchen makin' plum preserves. We had bushels of plums that year. I noticed it was terrible hot, but it's always hot in the kitchen when you're preservin', an' I was too busy with my plums to mind. Anton come in from the field about three o'clock, an' I asked him what was the matter.

"'Nothin',' he says, 'but it's pretty hot, an' I think I won't work no more today.' He stood round for a few minutes, an' then he says: 'Ain't you near through? I want you should git up a nice supper for us tonight. It's Fourth of July.'

"I told him to git along, that I was right in the middle of preservin', but the plums would taste good on hot biscuit. 'I'm goin' to have fried chicken, too,' he says, and he went off an' killed a couple. You three oldest boys was little fellers, playin' round outside, real hot an' sweaty, an' your father took you to the horse tank down by the windmill an' took off your clothes an' put you in. Them two box-elder trees was little then, but they made shade over the tank. Then he took off all his own clothes, an' got in with you. While he was playin' in the water with you, the Methodist preacher drove into our place to say how all the neighbours was goin' to meet at the schoolhouse that night, to pray for rain. He drove right to the windmill, of course, and there was your father and you three with no clothes on. I was in the kitchen door, an' I had to laugh, for the preacher acted like he ain't never seen a naked man before. He surely was embarrassed, an' your father couldn't git to his clothes; they was all hangin' up on the windmill to let the sweat dry out of 'em. So he laid in the tank where he was, an' put one of you boys on top of him to cover him up a little, an' talked to the preacher.

"When you got through playin' in the water, he put clean clothes on you and a clean shirt on himself, an' by that time I'd begun to get supper. He says: 'It's too hot in here to eat comfortable. Let's have a picnic in the orchard. We'll eat our supper behind the mulberry hedge, under them linden trees.'

"So he carried our supper down, an' a bottle of my wild-grape wine, an' everything tasted good, I can tell you. The wind got cooler as the sun was goin' down, and it turned out pleasant, only I noticed how the leaves was curled up on the linden trees. That made me think, an' I asked your father if that hot wind all day hadn't been terrible hard on the gardens an' the corn.

" 'Corn,' he says, 'there ain't no corn.'

" 'What you talkin' about?' I said. 'Ain't we got forty acres?'

" 'We ain't got an ear,' he says, 'nor nobody else ain't got none. All the corn in this country was cooked by three o'clock today, like you'd roasted it in an oven.'

" 'You mean you won't get no crop at all?' I asked him. I couldn't believe it, after he'd worked so hard.

" 'No crop this year,' he says. 'That's why we're havin' a picnic. We might as well enjoy what we got.'

"An' that's how your father behaved, when all the neighbours was so discouraged they couldn't look you in the face. An' we enjoyed ourselves that year, poor as we was, an' our neighbours wasn't a bit better off for bein' miserable. Some of 'em grieved till they got poor digestions and couldn't relish what they did have."

The younger boys said they thought their father had the best of it. But Rudolph was thinking that, all the same, the neighbours had managed to get ahead more, in the fifteen years since that time. There must be something wrong about his father's way of doing things. He wished he knew what was going on in the back of Polly's mind. He knew she liked his father, but he knew, too, that she was afraid of something. When his mother sent over coffee-cake or prune tarts or a loaf of fresh bread, Polly seemed to regard them with a certain suspicion. When she observed to him that his brothers had nice manners, her tone implied that it was remarkable they should have. With his mother she was stiff and on her guard. Mary's hearty frankness and gusts of good humour irritated her. Polly was afraid of being unusual or conspicuous in any way, of being "ordinary," as she said!

When Mary had finished her story, Rosicky laid aside his pipe.

"You boys like me to tell you about some of dem hard times I been through in London?" Warmly encouraged, he sat rubbing his forehead along the deep creases. It was bothersome to tell a long story in English (he nearly always talked to the boys in Czech), but he wanted Polly to hear this one.

"Well, you know about dat tailor shop I worked in in London? I had one Christmas dere I ain't never forgot. Times was awful bad before Christmas; de boss ain't got much work, an' have it awful hard to pay his rent. It ain't so much fun, bein' poor in a big city like London, I'll say! All de windows is full of good t'ings to eat, an' all de pushcarts in de streets is full, an' you smell 'em all de time, an' you ain't got no money,—not a damn bit. I didn't mind de cold so much, though I didn't have no overcoat, chust a short jacket I'd outgrowed so it wouldn't meet on me, an' my hands was chapped raw. But I always had a good appetite, like you all know, an' de sight of dem pork pies in de windows was awful fur me!

"Day before Christmas was terrible foggy dat year, an' dat fog gits into your bones and makes you all damp like. Mrs. Lifschnitz didn't give us nothin' but a little bread an' drippin' for supper, because she was savin' to try for to give us a good dinner on Christmas Day. After supper de boss say I can go an' enjoy myself, so I went into de streets to listen to de Christmas singers. Dey sing old songs an' make very nice music, an' I run round after dem a good ways, till I got awful hungry. I t'ink maybe if I go home, I can sleep till morning an' forgit my belly.

"I went into my corner real quiet, and roll up in my fedder quilt. But I ain't got my head down, till I smell somet'ing good. Seem like it git stronger an' stronger, an' I can't git to sleep noway. I can't understand dat smell. Dere was a gas light in a hall across de court, dat always shine in at my window a little. I got up an' look round. I got a little wooden box in my corner fur a stool, 'cause I ain't got no chair. I picks up dat box, and under it dere is a roast goose on a platter! I can't believe my eyes. I carry it to de window where de light comes in, an' touch it and smell it to find out, an' den I taste it to be sure. I say, I will eat chust one little bite of dat goose, so I can go to sleep, and tomorrow I won't eat none at all. But I tell you, boys, when I stop, one half of dat goose was gone!"

The narrator bowed his head, and the boys shouted. But little Josephine slipped behind his chair and kissed him on the neck beneath his ear.

"Poor little Papa, I don't want him to be hungry!"

"Da's long ago, child. I ain't never been hungry since I had your mudder to cook fur me."

"Go on and tell us the rest, please," said Polly.

"Well, when I come to realize what I done, of course, I felt terrible. I felt better in de stomach, but very bad in de heart. I set on my bed wid dat platter on my knees, an' it all come to me; how hard dat poor woman save to buy dat goose, and how she get some neighbour to cook it dat got more fire, an' how she put it in my corner to keep it away from dem hungry children. Dey was a old carpet hung up to shut my corner off, an' de children wasn't allowed to go in dere. An' I know she put it in my corner because she trust me more'n she did de violin boy. I can't stand it to face her after I spoil de Christmas. So I put on my shoes and go out into de city. I tell myself I better throw myself in de river; but I guess I ain't dat kind of a boy.

"It was after twelve o'clock, an' terrible cold, an' I start out to walk about London all night. I walk along de river awhile, but dey was lots of drunks all along; men, and women too. I chust move along to keep away from de police. I git onto de Strand, an' den over to New Oxford Street, where dere was a big German restaurant on de ground floor, wid big windows all fixed up fine, an' I could see de people havin' parties inside. While I was lookin' in, two men and two ladies come out, laughin' and talkin' and feelin' happy about all dey been eatin' an' drinkin', and dey was speakin' Czech,—not like de Austrians, but like de home folks talk it.

"I guess I went crazy, an' I done what I ain't never done before nor since. I went right up to dem gay people an' begun to beg dem: 'Fellow-countrymen, for God's sake give me money enough to buy a goose!'

"Dey laugh, of course, but de ladies speak awful kind to me, an' dey take me back into de restaurant and give me hot coffee and cakes, an' make me tell all about how I happened to come to London, an' what I was doin' dere. Dey take my name and where I work down on paper, an' both of dem ladies give me ten shillings.

"De big market at Covent Garden ain't very far away, an' by dat time it was open. I go dere an' buy a big goose an' some pork pies, an' potatoes and onions, an' cakes an' oranges fur de children,—all I could carry! When I git home, everybody is still asleep. I pile all I bought on de kitchen table, an' go in an' lay down on my bed, an' I ain't waken up till I hear dat woman scream when she come out into her kitchen. My goodness, but she was surprise! She laugh an' cry at de same time, an' hug me and waken all de children. She ain't stop fur no breakfast; she git de Christmas dinner ready dat morning, and we all sit down an' eat all we can hold. I ain't never seen dat violin boy have all he can hold before.

"Two three days after dat, de two men come to hunt me up, an' dey ask my boss, and he give me a good report an' tell dem I was a steady boy all right. One of dem Bohemians was very smart an' run a Bohemian newspaper in New York, an' de odder was a rich man, in de importing business, an' dey been travelling togedder. Dey told me how t'ings was easier in New York, an' offered to pay my passage when dey was goin' home soon on a boat. My boss say to me: 'You go. You ain't got no chance here, an' I like to see you git ahead, fur you always been a good boy to my woman, and fur dat fine Christmas dinner you give us all.' An' da's how I got to New York."

That night when Rudolph and Polly, arm in arm, were running home across the fields with the bitter wind at their backs, his heart leaped for joy when she said she thought they might have his family come over for supper on New Year's Eve. "Let's get up a nice supper, and not let your mother help at all; make her be company for once."

"That would be lovely of you, Polly," he said humbly. He was a very simple, modest boy, and he, too, felt vaguely that Polly and her sisters were more experienced and worldly than his people.

VI

The winter turned out badly for farmers. It was bitterly cold, and after the first light snows before Christmas there was no snow at all,—and no rain. March was as bitter as February. On those days when the wind fairly punished the country, Rosicky sat by his window. In the fall he and the boys had put in a big wheat planting, and now the seed had frozen in the ground. All that land would have to be ploughed up and planted over again, planted in corn. It had happened before, but he was younger then, and he never worried about what had to be. He was sure of himself and of Mary; he knew they could bear what they had to bear, that they would always pull through somehow. But he was not so sure about the young ones, and he felt troubled because Rudolph and Polly were having such a hard start.

Sitting beside his flowering window while the panes rattled and the wind blew in under the door, Rosicky gave himself to reflection as he had not done since those Sundays in the loft of the furniture-factory in New York, long ago. Then he was trying to find what he wanted in life for himself; now he was trying to find what he wanted for his boys, and why it was he so hungered to feel sure they would be here, working this very land, after he was gone.

They would have to work hard on the farm, and probably they would never do much more than make a living. But if he could think of them as staying here on the land, he wouldn't have to fear any great unkindness for them. Hardships, certainly; it was a hardship to have the wheat freeze in the ground when seed was so high; and to have to sell your stock because you had no feed. But there would be other years when everything came along right, and you caught up. And what you had was your own. You didn't have to choose between bosses and strikers, and go wrong either way. You didn't have to do with dishonest and cruel people. They were the only things in his experience he had found terrifying and horrible; the look in the eyes of a dishonest and crafty man, of a scheming and rapacious woman.

In the country, if you had a mean neighbour, you could keep off his land and make him keep off yours. But in the city, all the foulness and misery and brutality of your neighbours was part of your life. The worst things he had come upon in his journey through the world were human,—depraved and poisonous specimens of man. To this day he could recall certain terrible faces in the London streets. There were mean people everywhere, to be sure, even in their own country town here. But they weren't tempered, hardened, sharpened, like the treacherous people in cities who live by grinding or cheating or poisoning their fellowmen. He had helped to bury two of his fellow-workmen in the tailoring trade, and he was distrustful of the organized industries that see one out of the world in big cities. Here, if you were sick, you had Doctor Ed to look after you; and if you died, fat Mr. Haycock, the kindest man in the world, buried you.

It seemed to Rosicky that for good, honest boys like his, the worst they could do on the farm was better than the best they would be likely to do in the city. If he'd had a mean boy, now, one who was crooked and sharp and tried to put anything over on his brothers, then town would be the place for him. But he had no such boy. As for Rudolph, the discontented one, he would give the shirt off his back to anyone who touched his heart. What Rosicky really hoped for his boys was that they could get through the world without ever knowing much about the cruelty of human beings. "Their mother and me ain't prepared them for that," he sometimes said to himself.

These thoughts brought him back to a grateful consideration of his own case. What an escape he had had, to be sure! He, too, in his time, had had to take money for repair work from the hand of a hungry child who let it go so wistfully; because it was money due his boss. And now, in all these years, he had never had to take a cent from anyone in bitter need,—never had to look at the face of a woman become like a wolf's from struggle and famine. When he thought of these things, Rosicky would put on his cap and jacket and slip down to the barn and give his work-horses a little extra oats, letting them eat it out of his hand in their slobbery fashion. It was his way of expressing what he felt, and made him chuckle with pleasure.

The spring came warm, with blue skies,—but dry, dry as a bone. The boys began ploughing up the wheat-fields to plant them over in corn. Rosicky would stand at the fence corner and watch them, and the earth was so dry it blew up in clouds of brown dust that hid the horses and the sulky plough and the driver. It was a bad outlook.

The big alfalfa-field that lay between the home place and Rudolph's came up green, but Rosicky was worried because during that open windy winter a great many Russian thistle plants had blown in there and lodged. He kept asking the boys to rake them out; he was afraid their seed would root and "take the alfalfa." Rudolph said that was nonsense. The boys were working so hard planting corn, their father felt he couldn't insist about the thistles, but he set great store by that big alfalfa-field. It was a feed you could depend on,—and there was some deeper reason, vague, but strong. The peculiar green of that clover woke early memories in old Rosicky, went back to something in his childhood in the old world. When he was a little boy, he had played in fields of that strong blue-green colour.

One morning, when Rudolph had gone to town in the car, leaving a work-team idle in his barn, Rosicky went over to his son's place, put the horses to the buggy-rake, and set about quietly raking up those thistles. He behaved with guilty caution, and rather enjoyed stealing a march on Doctor Ed, who was just then taking his first vacation in seven years of practice and was attending a clinic in Chicago. Rosicky got the thistles raked up, but did not stop to burn them. That would take some time, and his breath was pretty short, so he thought he had better get the horses back to the barn.

He got them into the barn and to their stalls, but the pain had come on so sharp in his chest that he didn't try to take the harness off. He started for the house, bending lower with every step. The cramp in his chest was shutting him up like a jack-knife. When he reached the windmill, he swayed and caught at the ladder. He saw Polly coming down the hill, running with the swiftness of a slim greyhound. In a flash she had her shoulder under his armpit.

"Lean on me, Father, hard! Don't be afraid. We can get to the house all right."

Somehow they did, though Rosicky became blind with pain; he could keep on his legs, but he couldn't steer his course. The next thing he was conscious of was lying on Polly's bed, and Polly bending over him wringing out bath towels in hot water and putting them on his chest. She stopped only to throw coal into the stove, and she kept the tea-kettle and the black pot going. She put these hot applications on him for nearly an hour, she told him afterwards, and all that time he was drawn up stiff and blue, with the sweat pouring off him.

As the pain gradually loosed its grip, the stiffness went out of his jaws, the black circles round his eyes disappeared, and a little of his natural colour came back. When his daughter-in-law buttoned his shirt over his chest at last, he sighed.

"Da's fine, de way I feel now, Polly. It was a awful bad spell, an' I was so sorry it all come on you like it did."

Polly was flushed and excited. "Is the pain really gone? Can I leave you long enough to telephone over to your place?"

Rosicky's eyelids fluttered. "Don't telephone, Polly. It ain't no use to scare my wife. It's nice and quiet here, an' if I ain't too much trouble to you, just let me lay still till I feel like myself. I ain't got no pain now. It's nice here."

Polly bent over him and wiped the moisture from his face. "Oh, I'm so glad it's over!" she broke out impulsively. "It just broke my heart to see you suffer so, Father."

Rosicky motioned her to sit down on the chair where the tea-kettle had been, and looked up at her with that lively affectionate gleam in his eyes. "You was awful good to me, I won't never forget dat. I hate it to be sick on you like dis. Down at de barn I say to myself, dat young girl ain't had much experience in sickness, I don't want to scare her, an' maybe she's got a baby comin' or somet'ing."

Polly took his hand. He was looking at her so intently and affectionately and confidingly; his eyes seemed to caress her face, to regard it with pleasure. She frowned with her funny streaks of eyebrows, and then smiled back at him.

"I guess maybe there is something of that kind going to happen. But I haven't told anyone yet, not my mother or Rudolph. You'll be the first to know."

His hand pressed hers. She noticed that it was warm again. The twinkle in his yellow-brown eyes seemed to come nearer.

"I like mighty well to see dat little child, Polly," was all he said. Then he closed his eyes and lay half-smiling. But Polly sat still, thinking hard. She had a sudden feeling that nobody in the world, not her mother, not Rudolph, or anyone, really loved her as much as old Rosicky did. It perplexed her. She sat frowning and trying to puzzle it out. It was as if Rosicky had a special gift for loving people, something that was like an ear for music or an eye for colour. It was quiet, unobtrusive; it was merely there. You saw it in his eyes,—perhaps that was why they were merry. You felt it in his hands, too. After he dropped off to sleep, she sat holding his warm, broad, flexible brown hand. She had never seen another in the least like it. She wondered if it wasn't a kind of gypsy hand, it was so alive and quick and light in its communications,— very strange in a farmer. Nearly all the farmers she knew had huge lumps of fists, like mauls, or they were knotty and bony and uncomfortable-looking, with stiff fingers. But Rosicky's was like quicksilver, flexible, muscular, about the colour of a pale cigar, with deep, deep creases across the palm. It wasn't nervous, it wasn't a stupid lump; it was a warm brown human hand, with some cleverness in it, a great deal of generosity, and something else which Polly could only call "gypsy-like,"—something nimble and lively and sure, in the way that animals are.

Polly remembered that hour long afterwards; it had been like an awakening to her. It seemed to her that she had never learned so much about life from anything as from old Rosicky's hand. It brought her to herself; it communicated some direct and untranslatable message.

When she heard Rudolph coming in the car, she ran out to meet him.

"Oh, Rudy, your father's been awful sick! He raked up those thistles he's been worrying about, and afterwards he could hardly get to the house. He suffered so I was afraid he was going to die."

Rudolph jumped to the ground. "Where is he now?"

"On the bed. He's asleep. I was terribly scared, because, you know, I'm so fond of your father." She slipped her arm through his and they went into the house. That afternoon they took Rosicky home and put him to bed, though he protested that he was quite well again.

The next morning he got up and dressed and sat down to breakfast with his family. He told Mary that his coffee tasted better than usual to him, and he warned the boys not to bear any tales to Doctor Ed when he got home. After breakfast he sat down by his window to do some patching and asked Mary to thread several needles for him before she went to feed her chickens,—her eyes were better than his, and her hands steadier. He lit his pipe and took up John's overalls. Mary had been watching him anxiously all morning, and as she went out of the door with her bucket of scraps, she saw that he was smiling. He was thinking, indeed, about Polly, and how he might never have known what a tender heart she had if he hadn't got sick over there. Girls nowadays didn't wear their heart on their sleeve. But now he knew Polly would make a fine woman after the foolishness wore off. Either a woman had that sweetness at her heart or she hadn't. You couldn't always tell by the look of them; but if they had that, everything came out right in the end.

After he had taken a few stitches, the cramp began in his chest, like yesterday. He put his pipe cautiously down on the window-sill and bent over to ease the pull. No use,—he had better try to get to his bed if he could. He rose and groped his way across the familiar floor, which was rising and falling like the deck of a ship. At the door he fell. When Mary came in, she found him lying there, and the moment she touched him she knew that he was gone.

Doctor Ed was away when Rosicky died, and for the first few weeks after he got home he was hard driven. Every day he said to himself that he must get out to see that family that had lost their father. One soft, warm moonlight night in early summer he started for the farm. His mind was on other things, and not until his road ran by the graveyard did he realize that Rosicky wasn't over there on the hill where the red lamplight shone, but here, in the moonlight. He stopped his car, shut off the engine, and sat there for a while.

A sudden hush had fallen on his soul. Everything here seemed strangely moving and significant, though signifying what, he did not know. Close by the wire fence stood Rosicky's mowing-machine, where one of the boys had been cutting hay that afternoon; his own work-horses had been going up and down there. The new-cut hay perfumed all the night air. The moonlight silvered the long, billowy grass that grew over the graves and hid the fence; the few little evergreens stood out black in it, like shadows in a pool. The sky was very blue and soft, the stars rather faint because the moon was full.

For the first time it struck Doctor Ed that this was really a beautiful graveyard. He thought of city cemeteries; acres of shrubbery and heavy stone, so arranged and lonely and unlike anything in the living world. Cities of the dead, indeed; cities of the forgotten, of the "put away." But this was open and free, this little square of long grass which the wind for ever stirred. Nothing but the sky overhead, and the many-coloured fields running on until they met that sky. The horses worked here in summer; the neighbours passed on their way to town; and over yonder, in the corn-field, Rosicky's own cattle would be eating fodder as winter came on. Nothing could be more undeathlike than this place; nothing could be more right for a man who had helped to do the work of great cities and had always longed for the open country and had got to it at last. Rosicky's life seemed to him complete and beautiful.

OLD MRS. HARRIS

I

Mrs. David Rosen, cross-stitch in hand, sat looking out of the window across her own green lawn to the ragged, sunburned back yard of her neighbours on the right. Occasionally she glanced anxiously over her shoulder toward her shining kitchen, with a black and white linoleum floor in big squares, like a marble pavement.

"Will dat woman never go?" she muttered impatiently, just under her breath. She spoke with a slight accent—it affected only her *th*'s, and, occasionally, the letter *v*. But people in Skyline thought this unfortunate, in a woman whose superiority they recognized.

Mrs. Rosen ran out to move the sprinkler to another spot on the lawn, and in doing so she saw what she had been waiting to see. From the house next door a tall, handsome woman emerged, dressed in white broadcloth and a hat with white lilacs; she carried a sunshade and walked with a free, energetic step, as if she were going out on a pleasant errand.

Mrs. Rosen darted quickly back into the house, lest her neighbour should hail her and stop to talk. She herself was in her kitchen housework dress, a crisp blue chambray which fitted smoothly over her tightly corseted figure, and her lustrous black hair was done in two smooth braids, wound flat at the back of her head, like a braided rug. She did not stop for a hat— her dark, ruddy, salmon-tinted skin had little to fear from the sun. She opened the half-closed oven door and took out a symmetrically plaited coffee-cake, beautifully browned, delicately peppered over with poppy seeds, with sugary margins about the twists. On the kitchen table a tray stood ready with cups and saucers. She wrapped the cake in a napkin, snatched up a little French coffee-pot with a black wooden handle, and ran across her green lawn, through the alleyway and the sandy, unkept yard next door, and entered her neighbour's house by the kitchen.

The kitchen was hot and empty, full of untempered afternoon sun. A door stood open into the next room; a cluttered, hideous room, yet somehow homely. There, beside a goods-box covered with figured oilcloth, stood an old woman in a brown calico dress, washing her hot face and neck at a tin basin. She stood with her feet wide apart, in an attitude of profound weariness. She started guiltily as the visitor entered.

"Don't let me disturb you, Grandma," called Mrs. Rosen. "I always have my coffee at dis hour in the afternoon. I was just about to sit down to it when I thought: 'I will run over and see if Grandma Harris won't take a cup with me.' I hate to drink my coffee alone."

Grandma looked troubled,—at a loss. She folded her towel and concealed it behind a curtain hung across the corner of the room to make a poor sort of closet. The old lady was always composed in manner, but it was clear that she felt embarrassment.

"Thank you, Mrs. Rosen. What a pity Victoria just this minute went down town!"

"But dis time I came to see you yourself, Grandma. Don't let me disturb you. Sit down there in your own rocker, and I will put my tray on this little chair between us, so!"

Mrs. Harris sat down in her black wooden rocking-chair with curved arms and a faded cretonne pillow on the wooden seat. It stood in the corner beside a narrow spindle-frame lounge. She looked on silently while Mrs. Rosen uncovered the cake and delicately broke it with her plump, smooth, dusky-red hands. The old lady did not seem pleased,—seemed uncertain and apprehensive, indeed. But she was not fussy or fidgety. She had the kind of quiet, intensely quiet, dignity that comes from complete resignation to the chances of life. She watched Mrs. Rosen's deft hands out of grave, steady brown eyes.

"Dis is Mr. Rosen's favourite coffee-cake, Grandma, and I want you to try it. You are such a good cook yourself, I would like your opinion of my cake."

"It's very nice, ma'am," said Mrs. Harris politely, but without enthusiasm.

"And you aren't drinking your coffee; do you like more cream in it?"

"No, thank you. I'm letting it cool a little. I generally drink it that way."

"Of course she does," thought Mrs. Rosen, "since

she never has her coffee until all the family are done breakfast!"

Mrs. Rosen had brought Grandma Harris coffee-cake time and again, but she knew that Grandma merely tasted it and saved it for her daughter Victoria, who was as fond of sweets as her own children, and jealous about them, moreover,—couldn't bear that special dainties should come into the house for any-one but herself. Mrs. Rosen, vexed at her failures, had determined that just once she would take a cake to "de old lady Harris," and with her own eyes see her eat it. The result was not all she had hoped. Receiving a visitor alone, unsupervised by her daughter, having cake and coffee that should properly be saved for Vic-toria, was all so irregular that Mrs. Harris could not enjoy it. Mrs. Rosen doubted if she tasted the cake as she swallowed it,—certainly she ate it without relish, as a hollow form. But Mrs. Rosen enjoyed her own cake, at any rate, and she was glad of an opportunity to sit quietly and look at Grandmother, who was more interesting to her than the handsome Victoria.

It was a queer place to be having coffee, when Mrs. Rosen liked order and comeliness so much: a hideous, cluttered room, furnished with a rocking-horse, a sewing-machine, an empty baby-buggy. A walnut table stood against a blind window, piled high with old magazines and tattered books, and children's caps and coats. There was a wash-stand (two wash-stands, if you counted the oilcloth-covered box as one). A corner of the room was curtained off with some black-and-red-striped cotton goods, for a clothes closet. In another corner was the wooden lounge with a thin mattress and a red calico spread which was Grandma's bed. Beside it was her wooden rocking-chair, and the little splint-bottom chair with the legs sawed short on which her darning-basket usually stood, but which Mrs. Rosen was now using for a tea-table.

The old lady was always impressive, Mrs. Rosen was thinking,—one could not say why. Perhaps it was the way she held her head,—so simply, unprotesting and unprotected; or the gravity of her large, deep-set brown eyes, a warm, reddish brown, though their look, always direct, seemed to ask nothing and hope for nothing. They were not cold, but inscrutable, with no kindling gleam of intercourse in them. There was the kind of nobility about her head that there is about an old lion's: an absence of self-consciousness, vanity, preoccupation—something absolute. Her grey hair was parted in the middle, wound in two little horns over her ears, and done in a little flat knot behind. Her mouth was large and composed,—resigned, the corners drooping. Mrs. Rosen had very seldom heard her laugh (and then it was a gentle, polite laugh which meant only politeness). But she had observed that whenever Mrs. Harris's grandchildren were about, tumbling all over her, asking for cookies, teasing her to read to them, the old lady looked happy.

As she drank her coffee, Mrs. Rosen tried one subject after another to engage Mrs. Harris's attention.

"Do you feel this hot weather, Grandma? I am afraid you are over the stove too much. Let those naughty children have a cold lunch occasionally."

"No'm, I don't mind the heat. It's apt to come on like this for a spell in May. I don't feel the stove. I'm accustomed to it."

"Oh, so am I! But I get very impatient with my cooking in hot weather. Do you miss your old home in Tennessee very much, Grandma?"

"No'm, I can't say I do. Mr. Templeton thought

Colorado was a better place to bring up the children."

"But you had things much more comfortable down there, I'm sure. These little wooden houses are too hot in summer."

"Yes'm, we were more comfortable. We had more room."

"And a flower-garden, and beautiful old trees, Mrs. Templeton told me."

"Yes'm, we had a great deal of shade."

Mrs. Rosen felt that she was not getting anywhere. She almost believed that Grandma thought she had come on an equivocal errand, to spy out something in Victoria's absence. Well, perhaps she had! Just for once she would like to get past the others to the real grandmother,—and the real grandmother was on her guard, as always. At this moment she heard a faint miaow. Mrs. Harris rose, lifting herself by the wooden arms of her chair, said: "Excuse me," went into the kitchen, and opened the screen door.

In walked a large, handsome, thickly furred Maltese cat, with long whiskers and yellow eyes and a white star on his breast. He preceded Grandmother, waited until she sat down. Then he sprang up into her lap and settled himself comfortably in the folds of her full-gathered calico skirt. He rested his chin in his deep bluish fur and regarded Mrs. Rosen. It struck her that he held his head in just the way Grandmother held hers. And Grandmother now became more alive, as if some missing part of herself were restored.

"This is Blue Boy," she said, stroking him. "In winter, when the screen door ain't on, he lets himself in. He stands up on his hind legs and presses the thumb-latch with his paw, and just walks in like anybody."

"He's your cat, isn't he, Grandma?" Mrs. Rosen

couldn't help prying just a little; if she could find but a single thing that was Grandma's own!

"He's our cat," replied Mrs. Harris. "We're all very fond of him. I expect he's Vickie's more'n anybody's."

"Of course!" groaned Mrs. Rosen to herself. "Dat Vickie is her mother over again."

Here Mrs. Harris made her first unsolicited remark. "If you was to be troubled with mice at any time, Mrs. Rosen, ask one of the boys to bring Blue Boy over to you, and he'll clear them out. He's a master mouser." She scratched the thick blue fur at the back of his neck, and he began a deep purring. Mrs. Harris smiled. "We call that spinning, back with us. Our children still say: 'Listen to Blue Boy spin,' though none of 'em is ever heard a spinning-wheel—except maybe Vickie remembers."

"Did you have a spinning-wheel in your own house, Grandma Harris?"

"Yes'm. Miss Sadie Crummer used to come and spin for us. She was left with no home of her own, and it was to give her something to do, as much as anything, that we had her. I spun a good deal myself, in my young days." Grandmother stopped and put her hands on the arms of her chair, as if to rise. "Did you hear a door open? It might be Victoria."

"No, it was the wind shaking the screen door. Mrs. Templeton won't be home yet. She is probably in my husband's store this minute, ordering him about. All the merchants down town will take anything from your daughter. She is very popular wid de gentlemen, Grandma."

Mrs. Harris smiled complacently. "Yes'm. Victoria was always much admired."

At this moment a chorus of laughter broke in upon the warm silence, and a host of children, as it seemed to Mrs. Rosen, ran through the yard. The hand-pump on the back porch, outside the kitchen door, began to scrape and gurgle.

"It's the children, back from school," said Grandma. "They are getting a cool drink."

"But where is the baby, Grandma?"

"Vickie took Hughie in his cart over to Mr. Holliday's yard, where she studies. She's right good about minding him."

Mrs. Rosen was glad to hear that Vickie was good for something.

Three little boys came running in through the kitchen; the twins, aged ten, and Ronald, aged six, who went to kindergarten. They snatched off their caps and threw their jackets and school bags on the table, the sewing-machine, the rocking-horse.

"Howdy do, Mrs. Rosen." They spoke to her nicely. They had nice voices, nice faces, and were always courteous, like their father. "We are going to play in our back yard with some of the boys, Gram'ma," said one of the twins respectfully, and they ran out to join a troop of schoolmates who were already shouting and racing over that poor trampled back yard, strewn with velocipedes and croquet mallets and toy wagons, which was such an eyesore to Mrs. Rosen.

Mrs. Rosen got up and took her tray.

"Can't you stay a little, ma'am? Victoria will be here any minute."

But her tone let Mrs. Rosen know that Grandma really wished her to leave before Victoria returned.

A few moments after Mrs. Rosen had put the tray down in her own kitchen, Victoria Templeton came up the wooden sidewalk, attended by Mr. Rosen, who had quitted his store half an hour earlier than usual for the pleasure of walking home with her. Mrs. Templeton stopped by the picket fence to smile at the children playing in the back yard,—and it was a real smile, she was glad to see them. She called Ronald over to the fence to give him a kiss. He was hot and sticky.

"Was your teacher nice today? Now run in and ask Grandma to wash your face and put a clean waist on you."

II

That night Mrs. Harris got supper with an effort— had to drive herself harder than usual. Mandy, the bound girl they had brought with them from the South, noticed that the old lady was uncertain and short of breath. The hours from two to four, when Mrs. Harris usually rested, had not been at all restful this afternoon. There was an understood rule that Grandmother was not to receive visitors alone. Mrs. Rosen's call, and her cake and coffee, were too much out of the accepted order. Nervousness had prevented the old lady from getting any repose during her visit.

After the rest of the family had left the supper table, she went into the dining-room and took her place, but she ate very little. She put away the food that was left, and then, while Mandy washed the dishes, Grandma sat down in her rocking-chair in the dark and dozed.

The three little boys came in from playing under the electric light (arc lights had been but lately installed in Skyline) and began begging Mrs. Harris to read *Tom Sawyer* to them. Grandmother loved to read, anything at all, the Bible or the continued story in the Chicago weekly paper. She roused herself, lit her brass "safety lamp," and pulled her black rocker out of its corner to the wash-stand (the table was too far away from her corner, and anyhow it was completely covered with coats and school satchels). She put on her old-fashioned silver-rimmed spectacles and began to read. Ronald lay down on Grandmother's lounge bed, and the twins, Albert and Adelbert, called Bert and Del, sat down against the wall, one on a low box covered with felt, and the other on the little sawed-off chair upon which Mrs. Rosen had served coffee. They looked intently at Mrs. Harris, and she looked intently at the book.

Presently Vickie, the oldest grandchild, came in. She was fifteen. Her mother was entertaining callers in the parlour, callers who didn't interest Vickie, so she was on her way up to her own room by the kitchen stairway.

Mrs. Harris looked up over her glasses. "Vickie, maybe you'd take the book awhile, and I can do my darning."

"All right," said Vickie. Reading aloud was one of the things she would always do toward the general comfort. She sat down by the wash-stand and went on with the story. Grandmother got her darning-basket and began to drive her needle across great knee-holes in the boys' stockings. Sometimes she nodded for a moment, and her hands fell into her lap. After a while the little boy on the lounge went to sleep. But the twins sat upright, their hands on their knees, their round brown eyes fastened upon Vickie, and when there was anything funny, they giggled. They were chubby, dark-skinned little boys, with round jolly faces, white teeth, and yellow-brown eyes that were always bubbling with fun unless they were sad,—even then their eyes never got red or weepy. Their tears sparkled and fell; left no trace but a streak on the cheeks, perhaps.

Presently old Mrs. Harris gave out a long snore of utter defeat. She had been overcome at last. Vickie put down the book. "That's enough for tonight. Grandmother's sleepy, and Ronald's fast asleep. What'll we do with him?"

"Bert and me'll get him undressed," said Adelbert. The twins roused the sleepy little boy and prodded him up the back stairway to the bare room without window blinds, where he was put into his cot beside their double bed. Vickie's room was across the narrow hallway; not much bigger than a closet, but, anyway, it was her own. She had a chair and an old dresser, and beside her bed was a high stool which she used as a lamp-table,—she always read in bed.

After Vickie went upstairs, the house was quiet. Hughie, the baby, was asleep in his mother's room, and Victoria herself, who still treated her husband as if he were her "beau," had persuaded him to take her down town to the ice-cream parlour. Grandmother's room, between the kitchen and the dining-room, was rather like a passage-way; but now that the children were upstairs and Victoria was off enjoying herself somewhere, Mrs. Harris could be sure of enough privacy to undress. She took off the calico cover from her lounge bed and folded it up, put on her nightgown and white nightcap.

Mandy, the bound girl, appeared at the kitchen door.

"Miz' Harris," she said in a guarded tone, ducking her head, "you want me to rub your feet for you?"

For the first time in the long day the old woman's low composure broke a little. "Oh, Mandy, I would take it kindly of you!" she breathed gratefully.

That had to be done in the kitchen; Victoria didn't like anybody slopping about. Mrs. Harris put an old checked shawl round her shoulders and followed Mandy. Beside the kitchen stove Mandy had a little wooden tub full of warm water. She knelt down and untied Mrs. Harris's garter strings and took off her flat cloth slippers and stockings.

"Oh, Miz' Harris, your feet an' legs is swelled turrible tonight!"

"I expect they air, Mandy. They feel like it."

"Pore soul!" murmured Mandy. She put Grandma's feet in the tub and, crouching beside it, slowly, slowly rubbed her swollen legs. Mandy was tired, too. Mrs. Harris sat in her nightcap and shawl, her hands crossed in her lap. She never asked for this greatest solace of the day; it was something that Mandy gave, who had nothing else to give. If there could be a comparison in absolutes, Mandy was the needier of the two,—but she was younger. The kitchen was quiet and full of shadow, with only the light from an old lantern. Neither spoke. Mrs. Harris dozed from comfort, and Mandy herself was half asleep as she performed one of the oldest rites of compassion.

Although Mrs. Harris's lounge had no springs, only a thin cotton mattress between her and the wooden slats, she usually went to sleep as soon as she was in bed. To be off her feet, to lie flat, to say over the psalm beginning: *"The Lord is my shepherd,"* was comfort enough. About four o'clock in the morning, however, she would begin to feel the hard slats under her, and the heaviness of the old home-made quilts, with weight but little warmth, on top of her. Then she would reach under her pillow for her little comforter (she called it that to herself) that Mrs. Rosen had given her. It was a tan sweater of very soft brushed wool, with one sleeve torn and ragged. A young nephew from Chicago had spent a fortnight with Mrs. Rosen last summer and had left this behind him. One morning, when Mrs. Harris went out to the stable at the back of the yard to pat Buttercup, the cow, Mrs. Rosen ran across the alley-way.

"Grandma Harris," she said, coming into the shelter of the stable, "I wonder if you could make any use of this sweater Sammy left? The yarn might be good for your darning."

Mrs. Harris felt of the article gravely. Mrs. Rosen thought her face brightened. "Yes'm, indeed I could use it. I thank you kindly."

She slipped it under her apron, carried it into the house with her, and concealed it under her mattress. There she had kept it ever since. She knew Mrs. Rosen understood how it was; that Victoria couldn't bear to have anything come into the house that was not for her to dispose of.

On winter nights, and even on summer nights after the cocks began to crow, Mrs. Harris often felt cold and lonely about the chest. Sometimes her cat, Blue Boy, would creep in beside her and warm that aching spot. But on spring and summer nights he was likely to be abroad skylarking, and this little sweater had become the dearest of Grandmother's few possessions. It was kinder to her, she used to think, as she wrapped it about her middle, than any of her own children had been. She had married at eighteen and had had eight children; but some died, and some were, as she said, scattered.

After she was warm in that tender spot under the ribs, the old woman could lie patiently on the slats, waiting for daybreak; thinking about the comfortable rambling old house in Tennessee, its feather beds and hand-woven rag carpets and splint-bottom chairs, the mahogany sideboard, and the marble-top parlour table; all that she had left behind to follow Victoria's fortunes.

She did not regret her decision; indeed, there had been no decision. Victoria had never once thought it possible that Ma should not go wherever she and the children went, and Mrs. Harris had never thought it possible. Of course she regretted Tennessee, though she would never admit it to Mrs. Rosen:—the old neighbours, the yard and garden she had worked in all her life, the apple trees she had planted, the lilac arbour, tall enough to walk in, which she had clipped and shaped so many years. Especially she missed her lemon tree, in a tub on the front porch, which bore little lemons almost every summer, and folks would come for miles to see it.

But the road had led westward, and Mrs. Harris didn't believe that women, especially old women, could say when or where they would stop. They were tied to the chariot of young life, and had to go where it went, because they were needed. Mrs. Harris had gathered from Mrs. Rosen's manner, and from comments she occasionally dropped, that the Jewish people had an altogether different attitude toward their old folks; therefore her friendship with this kind neighbour was almost as disturbing as it was pleasant. She didn't want Mrs. Rosen to think that she was "put upon," that there was anything unusual or pitiful in her lot. To be pitied was the deepest hurt anybody could know. And if Victoria once suspected Mrs. Rosen's indignation, it would be all over. She would freeze her neighbour out, and that friendly voice, that quick pleasant chatter with the little foreign twist, would thenceforth be heard only at a distance, in the alley-way or across the fence. Victoria had a good heart, but she was terribly proud and could not bear the least criticism.

As soon as the grey light began to steal into the room, Mrs. Harris would get up softly and wash at the basin on the oilcloth-covered box. She would wet her hair above her forehead, comb it with a little bone comb set in a tin rim, do it up in two smooth little horns over her ears, wipe the comb dry, and put it away in the pocket of her full-gathered calico skirt. She left nothing lying about. As soon as she was dressed, she made her bed, folding her nightgown and nightcap under the pillow, the sweater under the mattress. She smoothed the heavy quilts, and drew the red calico spread neatly over all. Her towel was hung on its special nail behind the curtain. Her soap she kept in a tin tobacco-box; the children's soap was in a crockery saucer. If her soap or towel got mixed up with the children's, Victoria was always sharp about it. The little rented house was much too small for the family, and Mrs. Harris and her "things" were almost required to be invisible. Two clean calico dresses hung in the curtained corner; another was on her back, and a fourth was in the wash. Behind the curtain there was always a good supply of aprons; Victoria bought them at church fairs, and it was a great satisfaction to Mrs. Harris to put on a clean one whenever she liked. Upstairs, in Mandy's attic room over the kitchen, hung a black cashmere dress and a black bonnet with a long crêpe veil, for the rare occasions when Mr. Templeton hired a double buggy and horses and drove his family to a picnic or to Decoration Day exercises. Mrs. Harris rather dreaded these drives, for Victoria was usually cross afterwards.

When Mrs. Harris went out into the kitchen to get

breakfast, Mandy always had the fire started and the water boiling. They enjoyed a quiet half-hour before the little boys came running down the stairs, always in a good humour. In winter the boys had their breakfast in the kitchen, with Vickie. Mrs. Harris made Mandy eat the cakes and fried ham the children left, so that she would not fast so long. Mr. and Mrs. Templeton breakfasted rather late, in the dining-room, and they always had fruit and thick cream,—a small pitcher of the very thickest was for Mrs. Templeton. The children were never fussy about their food. As Grandmother often said feelingly to Mrs. Rosen, they were as little trouble as children could possibly be. They sometimes tore their clothes, of course, or got sick. But even when Albert had an abscess in his ear and was in such pain, he would lie for hours on Grandmother's lounge with his cheek on a bag of hot salt, if only she or Vickie would read aloud to him.

"It's true, too, what de old lady says," remarked Mrs. Rosen to her husband one night at supper, "dey are nice children. No one ever taught them anything, but they have good instincts, even dat Vickie. And think, if you please, of all the self-sacrificing mothers we know,—Fannie and Esther, to come near home; how they have planned for those children from infancy and given them every advantage. And now ingratitude and coldness is what dey meet with."

Mr. Rosen smiled his teasing smile. "Evidently your sister and mine have the wrong method. The way to make your children unselfish is to be comfortably selfish yourself."

"But dat woman takes no more responsibility for her children than a cat takes for her kittens. Nor does poor young Mr. Templeton, for dat matter. How can he expect to get so many children started in life, I ask you? It is not at all fair!"

Mr. Rosen sometimes had to hear altogether too much about the Templetons, but he was patient, because it was a bitter sorrow to Mrs. Rosen that she had no children. There was nothing else in the world she wanted so much.

III

Mrs. Rosen in one of her blue working dresses, the indigo blue that became a dark skin and dusky red cheeks with a tone of salmon colour, was in her shining kitchen, washing her beautiful dishes—her neighbours often wondered why she used her best china and linen every day—when Vickie Templeton came in with a book under her arm.

"Good day, Mrs. Rosen. Can I have the second volume?"

"Certainly. You know where the books are." She spoke coolly, for it always annoyed her that Vickie never suggested wiping the dishes or helping with such household work as happened to be going on when she dropped in. She hated the girl's bringing-up so much that sometimes she almost hated the girl.

Vickie strolled carelessly through the dining-room into the parlour and opened the doors of one of the big bookcases. Mr. Rosen had a large library, and a great many unusual books. There was a complete set of the Waverley Novels in German, for example; thick, dumpy little volumes bound in tooled leather, with very black type and dramatic engravings printed on wrinkled, yellowing pages. There were many French books, and some of the German classics done into English, such as Coleridge's translation of Schiller's *Wallenstein*.

Of course no other house in Skyline was in the least like Mrs. Rosen's; it was the nearest thing to an art gallery and a museum that the Templetons had ever seen. All the rooms were carpeted alike (that was very unusual), with a soft velvet carpet, little blue and rose flowers scattered on a rose-grey ground. The deep chairs were upholstered in dark blue velvet. The walls were hung with engravings in pale gold frames: some of Raphael's "Hours," a large soft engraving of a castle on the Rhine, and another of cypress trees about a Roman ruin, under a full moon. There were a number of water-colour sketches, made in Italy by Mr. Rosen himself when he was a boy. A rich uncle had taken him abroad as his secretary. Mr. Rosen was a reflective, unambitious man, who didn't mind keeping a clothing-store in a little Western town, so long as he had a great deal of time to read philosophy. He was the only unsuccessful member of a large, rich Jewish family.

Last August, when the heat was terrible in Skyline, and the crops were burned up on all the farms to the north, and the wind from the pink and yellow sand-hills to the south blew so hot that it singed the few green lawns in the town, Vickie had taken to dropping in upon Mrs. Rosen at the very hottest part of the afternoon. Mrs. Rosen knew, of course, that it was probably because the girl had no other cool and quiet place to go—her room at home under the roof would be hot enough! Now, Mrs. Rosen liked to undress and take a nap from three to five,—if only to get out of her tight corsets, for she would have an hourglass figure at any cost. She told Vickie firmly that she was welcome to come if she would read in the parlour with the blind up only a little way, and would be as still as a mouse. Vickie came, meekly enough, but she seldom read. She would take a sofa pillow and lie down on the soft carpet and look up at the pictures in the dusky room, and feel a happy, pleasant excitement from the heat and glare outside and the deep shadow and quiet within. Curiously enough, Mrs. Rosen's house never made her dissatisfied with her own; she thought that very nice, too.

Mrs. Rosen, leaving her kitchen in a state of such perfection as the Templetons were unable to sense or to admire, came into the parlour and found her visitor sitting cross-legged on the floor before one of the bookcases.

"Well, Vickie, and how did you get along with *Wilhelm Meister?*"

"I like it," said Vickie.

Mrs. Rosen shrugged. The Templetons always said that; quite as if a book or a cake were lucky to win their approbation.

"Well, *what* did you like?"

"I guess I liked all that about the theatre and Shakspere best."

"It's rather celebrated," remarked Mrs. Rosen dryly. "And are you studying every day? Do you think you will be able to win that scholarship?"

"I don't know. I'm going to try awful hard."

Mrs. Rosen wondered whether any Templeton knew how to try very hard. She reached for her workbasket and began to do cross-stitch. It made her nervous to sit with folded hands.

Vickie was looking at a German book in her lap, an illustrated edition of *Faust*. She had stopped at a very German picture of Gretchen entering the church, with

Faustus gazing at her from behind a rose tree, Mephisto at his shoulder.

"I wish I could read this," she said, frowning at the black Gothic text. "It's splendid, isn't it?"

Mrs. Rosen rolled her eyes upward and sighed. "Oh, my dear, one of de world's masterpieces!"

That meant little to Vickie. She had not been taught to respect masterpieces, she had no scale of that sort in her mind. She cared about a book only because it took hold of her.

She kept turning over the pages. Between the first and second parts, in this edition, there was inserted the *Dies Iræ* hymn in full. She stopped and puzzled over it for a long while.

"Here is something I can read," she said, showing the page to Mrs. Rosen.

Mrs. Rosen looked up from her cross-stitch. "There you have the advantage of me. I do not read Latin. You might translate it for me."

Vickie began:

> "Day of wrath, upon that day
> The world to ashes melts away,
> As David and the Sibyl say.

"But that don't give you the rhyme; every line ought to end in two syllables."

"Never mind if it doesn't give the metre," corrected Mrs. Rosen kindly; "go on, if you can."

Vickie went on stumbling through the Latin verses, and Mrs. Rosen sat watching her. You couldn't tell about Vickie. She wasn't pretty, yet Mrs. Rosen found her attractive. She liked her sturdy build, and the steady vitality that glowed in her rosy skin and dark blue eyes—even gave a springy quality to her curly reddish-brown hair, which she still wore in a single braid down her back. Mrs. Rosen liked to have Vickie about because she was never listless or dreamy or apathetic. A half-smile nearly always played about her lips and eyes, and it was there because she was pleased with something, not because she wanted to be agreeable. Even a half-smile made her cheeks dimple. She had what her mother called "a happy disposition."

When she finished the verses, Mrs. Rosen nodded approvingly. "Thank you, Vickie. The very next time I go to Chicago, I will try to get an English translation of *Faust* for you."

"But I want to read this one." Vickie's open smile darkened. "What I want is to pick up any of these books and just read them, like you and Mr. Rosen do."

The dusky red of Mrs. Rosen's cheeks grew a trifle deeper. Vickie never paid compliments, absolutely never; but if she really admired anyone, something in her voice betrayed it so convincingly that one felt flattered. When she dropped a remark of this kind, she added another link to the chain of responsibility which Mrs. Rosen unwillingly bore and tried to shake off—the irritating sense of being somehow responsible for Vickie, since, God knew, no one else felt responsible.

Once or twice, when she happened to meet pleasant young Mr. Templeton alone, she had tried to talk to him seriously about his daughter's future. "She has finished de school here, and she should be getting training of some sort; she is growing up," she told him severely.

He laughed and said in his way that was so honest, and so disarmingly sweet and frank: "Oh, don't remind me, Mrs. Rosen! I just pretend to myself she isn't. I want to keep my little daughter as long as I can." And there it ended.

Sometimes Vickie Templeton seemed so dense, so utterly unperceptive, that Mrs. Rosen was ready to wash her hands of her. Then some queer streak of sensibility in the child would make her change her mind. Last winter, when Mrs. Rosen came home from a visit to her sister in Chicago, she brought with her a new cloak of the sleeveless dolman type, black velvet, lined with grey and white squirrel skins, a grey skin next a white. Vickie, so indifferent to clothes, fell in love with that cloak. Her eyes followed it with delight whenever Mrs. Rosen wore it. She found it picturesque, romantic. Mrs. Rosen had been captivated by the same thing in the cloak, and had bought it with a shrug, knowing it would be quite out of place in Skyline; and Mr. Rosen, when she first produced it from her trunk, had laughed and said: "Where did you get that?—out of *Rigoletto?*" It looked like that—but how could Vickie know?

Vickie's whole family puzzled Mrs. Rosen; their feelings were so much finer than their way of living. She bought milk from the Templetons because they kept a cow—which Mandy milked,—and every night one of the twins brought the milk to her in a tin pail. Whichever boy brought it, she always called him Albert—she thought Adelbert a silly, Southern name.

One night when she was fitting the lid on an empty pail, she said severely:

"Now, Albert, I have put some cookies for Grandma in this pail, wrapped in a napkin. And they are for Grandma, remember, not for your mother or Vickie."

"Yes'm."

When she turned to him to give him the pail, she saw two full crystal globes in the little boy's eyes, just ready to break. She watched him go softly down the path and dash those tears away with the back of his hand. She was sorry. She hadn't thought the little boys realized that their household was somehow a queer one.

Queer or not, Mrs. Rosen liked to go there better than to most houses in the town. There was something easy, cordial, and carefree in the parlour that never smelled of being shut up, and the ugly furniture looked hospitable. One felt a pleasantness in the human relationships. These people didn't seem to know there were such things as struggle or exactness or competition in the world. They were always genuinely glad to see you, had time to see you, and were usually gay in mood—all but Grandmother, who had the kind of gravity that people who take thought of human destiny must have. But even she liked light-heartedness in others; she drudged, indeed, to keep it going.

There were houses that were better kept, certainly, but the housekeepers had no charm, no gentleness of manner, were like hard little machines, most of them; and some were grasping and narrow. The Templetons were not selfish or scheming. Anyone could take advantage of them, and many people did. Victoria might eat all the cookies her neighbour sent in, but she would give away anything she had. She was always ready to lend her dresses and hats and bits of jewellery for the school theatricals, and she never worked people for favours.

As for Mr. Templeton (people usually called him "young Mr. Templeton"), he was too delicate to collect his just debts. His boyish, eager-to-please manner, his fair complexion and blue eyes and young face, made him seem very soft to some of the hard old money-grubbers on Main Street, and the fact that he always said "Yes, sir," and "No, sir," to men older than himself furnished a good deal of amusement to by-standers.

Two years ago, when this Templeton family came to Skyline and moved into the house next door, Mrs. Rosen was inconsolable. The new neighbours had a lot of children, who would always be making a racket. They put a cow and a horse into the empty barn, which would mean dirt and flies. They strewed their back yard with packing-cases and did not pick them up.

She first met Mrs. Templeton at an afternoon card party, in a house at the extreme north end of the town, fully half a mile away, and she had to admit that her new neighbour was an attractive woman, and that there was something warm and genuine about her. She wasn't in the least willowy or languishing, as Mrs. Rosen had usually found Southern ladies to be. She was high-spirited and direct; a trifle imperious, but with a shade of diffidence, too, as if she were trying to adjust herself to a new group of people and to do the right thing.

While they were at the party, a blinding snowstorm came on, with a hard wind. Since they lived next door to each other, Mrs. Rosen and Mrs. Templeton struggled homeward together through the blizzard. Mrs. Templeton seemed delighted with the rough weather; she laughed like a big country girl whenever she made a mis-step off the obliterated sidewalk and sank up to her knees in a snow-drift.

"Take care, Mrs. Rosen," she kept calling, "keep to the right! Don't spoil your nice coat. My, ain't this real winter? We never had it like this back with us."

When they reached the Templetons' gate, Victoria wouldn't hear of Mrs. Rosen's going farther. "No, indeed, Mrs. Rosen, you come right in with me and get dry, and Ma'll make you a hot toddy while I take the baby."

By this time Mrs. Rosen had begun to like her neighbour, so she went in. To her surprise, the parlour was neat and comfortable—the children did not strew things about there, apparently. The hard-coal burner threw out a warm red glow. A faded, respectable Brussels carpet covered the floor, an old-fashioned wooden clock ticked on the walnut bookcase. There were a few easy chairs, and no hideous ornaments about. She rather liked the old oil-chromos on the wall: "Hagar and Ishmael in the Wilderness," and "The Light of the World." While Mrs. Rosen dried her feet on the nickel base of the stove, Mrs. Templeton excused herself and withdrew to the next room,— her bedroom,—took off her silk dress and corsets, and put on a white challis négligée. She reappeared with the baby, who was not crying, exactly, but making eager, passionate, gasping entreaties,—faster and faster, tenser and tenser, as he felt his dinner nearer and nearer and yet not his.

Mrs. Templeton sat down in a low rocker by the stove and began to nurse him, holding him snugly but carelessly, still talking to Mrs. Rosen about the card party, and laughing about their wade home through the snow. Hughie, the baby, fell to work so fiercely that beads of sweat came out all over his flushed forehead. Mrs. Rosen could not help admiring him and his mother. They were so comfortable and complete. When he was changed to the other side, Hughie resented the interruption a little; but after a time he became soft and bland, as smooth as oil, indeed; began looking about him as he drew in his milk. He finally dropped the nipple from his lips altogether, turned on his mother's arm, and looked inquiringly at Mrs. Rosen.

"What a beautiful baby!" she exclaimed from her heart. And he was. A sort of golden baby. His hair was like sunshine, and his long lashes were gold over such gay blue eyes. There seemed to be a gold glow in his soft pink skin, and he had the smile of a cherub.

"We think he's a pretty boy," said Mrs. Templeton. "He's the prettiest of my babies. Though the twins were mighty cunning little fellows. I hated the idea of twins, but the minute I saw them, I couldn't resist them."

Just then old Mrs. Harris came in, walking widely in her full-gathered skirt and felt-soled shoes, bearing a tray with two smoking goblets upon it.

"This is my mother, Mrs. Harris, Mrs. Rosen," said Mrs. Templeton.

"I'm glad to know you, ma'am," said Mrs. Harris. "Victoria, let me take the baby, while you two ladies have your toddy."

"Oh, don't take him away, Mrs. Harris, please!" cried Mrs. Rosen.

The old lady smiled. "I won't. I'll set right here. He never frets with his grandma."

When Mrs. Rosen had finished her excellent drink, she asked if she might hold the baby, and Mrs. Harris placed him on her lap. He made a few rapid boxing motions with his two fists, then braced himself on his heels and the back of his head, and lifted himself up in an arc. When he dropped back, he looked up at Mrs. Rosen with his most intimate smile. "See what a smart boy I am!"

When Mrs. Rosen walked home, feeling her way

through the snow by following the fence, she knew she could never stay away from a house where there was a baby like that one.

IV

Vickie did her studying in a hammock hung between two tall cottonwood trees over in the Roadmaster's green yard. The Roadmaster had the finest yard in Skyline, on the edge of the town, just where the sandy plain and the sage-brush began. His family went back to Ohio every summer, and Bert and Del Templeton were paid to take care of his lawn, to turn the sprinkler on at the right hours and to cut the grass. They were really too little to run the heavy lawn-mower very well, but they were able to manage because they were twins. Each took one end of the handle-bar, and they pushed together like a pair of fat Shetland ponies. They were very proud of being able to keep the lawn so nice, and worked hard on it. They cut Mrs. Rosen's grass once a week, too, and did it so well that she wondered why in the world they never did anything about their own yard. They didn't have city water, to be sure (it was expensive), but she thought they might pick up a few velocipedes and iron hoops, and dig up the messy "flower-bed," that was even uglier than the naked gravel spots. She was particularly offended by a deep ragged ditch, a miniature arroyo, which ran across the back yard, serving no purpose and looking very dreary.

One morning she said craftily to the twins, when she was paying them for cutting her grass:

"And, boys, why don't you just shovel the sand-pile by your fence into dat ditch, and make your back yard smooth?"

"Oh, no, ma'am," said Adelbert with feeling. "We like to have a ditch to build bridges over!"

Ever since vacation began, the twins had been busy getting the Roadmaster's yard ready for the Methodist lawn party. When Mrs. Holliday, the Roadmaster's wife, went away for the summer, she always left a key with the Ladies' Aid Society and invited them to give their ice-cream social at her place.

This year the date set for the party was June fifteenth. The day was a particularly fine one, and as Mr. Holliday himself had been called to Cheyenne on railroad business, the twins felt personally responsible for everything. They got out to the Holliday place early in the morning, and stayed on guard all day. Before noon the drayman brought a wagonload of card-tables and folding chairs, which the boys placed in chosen spots under the cottonwood trees. In the afternoon the Methodist ladies arrived and opened up the kitchen to receive the freezers of home-made ice-cream, and the cakes which the congregation donated. Indeed, all the good cake-bakers in town were expected to send a cake. Grandma Harris baked a white cake, thickly iced and covered with freshly grated coconut, and Vickie took it over in the afternoon.

Mr. and Mrs. Rosen, because they belonged to no church, contributed to the support of all, and usually went to the church suppers in winter and the socials in summer. On this warm June evening they set out early, in order to take a walk first. They strolled along the hard gravelled road that led out through the sage toward the sand-hills; tonight it led toward the moon, just rising over the sweep of dunes. The sky was almost as blue as at midday, and had that look of being very near and very soft which it has in desert countries. The moon, too, looked very near, soft and bland

and innocent. Mrs. Rosen admitted that in the Adirondacks, for which she was always secretly homesick in summer, the moon had a much colder brilliance, seemed farther off and made of a harder metal. This moon gave the sage-brush plain and the drifted sandhills the softness of velvet. All countries were beautiful to Mr. Rosen. He carried a country of his own in his mind, and was able to unfold it like a tent in any wilderness.

When they at last turned back toward the town, they saw groups of people, women in white dresses, walking toward the dark spot where the paper lanterns made a yellow light underneath the cottonwoods. High above, the rustling tree-tops stirred free in the flood of moonlight.

The lighted yard was surrounded by a low board fence, painted the dark red Burlington colour, and as the Rosens drew near, they noticed four children standing close together in the shadow of some tall elder bushes just outside the fence. They were the poor Maude children; their mother was the washwoman, the Rosens' laundress and the Templetons'. People said that every one of those children had a different father. But good laundresses were few, and even the members of the Ladies' Aid were glad to get Mrs. Maude's services at a dollar a day, though they didn't like their children to play with hers. Just as the Rosens approached, Mrs. Templeton came out from the lighted square, leaned over the fence, and addressed the little Maudes.

"I expect you children forgot your dimes, now didn't you? Never mind, here's a dime for each of you, so come along and have your ice-cream."

The Maudes put out small hands and said: "Thank you," but not one of them moved.

"Come along, Francie." (The oldest girl was named Frances.) "Climb right over the fence." Mrs. Templeton reached over and gave her a hand, and the little boys quickly scrambled after their sister. Mrs. Templeton took them to a table which Vickie and the twins had just selected as being especially private—they liked to do things together.

"Here, Vickie, let the Maudes sit at your table, and take care they get plenty of cake."

The Rosens had followed close behind Mrs. Templeton, and Mr. Rosen now overtook her and said in his most courteous and friendly manner: "Good evening, Mrs. Templeton. Will you have ice-cream with us?" He always used the local idioms, though his voice and enunciation made them sound altogether different from Skyline speech.

"Indeed I will, Mr. Rosen. Mr. Templeton will be late. He went out to his farm yesterday, and I don't know just when to expect him."

Vickie and the twins were disappointed at not having their table to themselves, when they had come early and found a nice one; but they knew it was right to look out for the dreary little Maudes, so they moved close together and made room for them. The Maudes didn't cramp them long. When the three boys had eaten the last crumb of cake and licked their spoons, Francie got up and led them to a green slope by the fence, just outside the lighted circle. "Now set down, and watch and see how folks do," she told them. The boys looked to Francie for commands and support. She was really Amos Maude's child, born before he ran away to the Klondike, and it had been rubbed into them that this made a difference.

The Templeton children made their ice-cream linger out, and sat watching the crowd. They were glad to see their mother go to Mr. Rosen's table, and noticed how nicely he placed a chair for her and insisted upon putting a scarf about her shoulders. Their mother was wearing her new dotted Swiss, with many ruffles, all edged with black ribbon, and wide ruffly sleeves. As the twins watched her over their spoons, they thought how much prettier their mother was than any of the other women, and how becoming her new dress was. The children got as much satisfaction as Mrs. Harris out of Victoria's good looks.

Mr. Rosen was well pleased with Mrs. Templeton and her new dress, and with her kindness to the little Maudes. He thought her manner with them just right, —warm, spontaneous, without anything patronizing. He always admired her way with her own children, though Mrs. Rosen thought it was too casual. Being a good mother, he believed, was much more a matter of physical poise and richness than of sentimentalizing and reading doctor-books. Tonight he was more talkative than usual, and in his quiet way made Mrs. Templeton feel his real friendliness and admiration. Unfortunately, he made other people feel it, too.

Mrs. Jackson, a neighbour who didn't like the Templetons, had been keeping an eye on Mr. Rosen's table. She was a stout square woman of imperturbable calm, effective in regulating the affairs of the community because she never lost her temper, and could say the most cutting things in calm, even kindly, tones. Her face was smooth and placid as a mask, rather good-humoured, and the fact that one eye had a cast and looked askance made it the more difficult to see through her intentions. When she had been lingering about the Rosens' table for some time, studying Mr. Rosen's pleasant attentions to Mrs. Templeton, she brought up a trayful of cake.

"You folks are about ready for another helping," she remarked affably.

Mrs. Rosen spoke. "I want some of Grandma Harris's cake. It's a white coconut, Mrs. Jackson."

"How about you, Mrs. Templeton, would you like some of your own cake?"

"Indeed I would," said Mrs. Templeton heartily. "Ma said she had good luck with it. I didn't see it. Vickie brought it over."

Mrs. Jackson deliberately separated the slices on her tray with two forks. "Well," she remarked with a chuckle that really sounded amiable, "I don't know but I'd like my cakes, if I kept somebody in the kitchen to bake them for me."

Mr. Rosen for once spoke quickly. "If I had a cook like Grandma Harris in my kitchen, I'd live in it!" he declared.

Mrs. Jackson smiled. "I don't know as we feel like that, Mrs. Templeton? I tell Mr. Jackson that my idea of coming up in the world would be to forget I had a cook-stove, like Mrs. Templeton. But we can't all be lucky."

Mr. Rosen could not tell how much was malice and how much was stupidity. What he chiefly detected was self-satisfaction; the craftiness of the coarse-fibred country girl putting catch questions to the teacher. Yes, he decided, the woman was merely showing off,—she regarded it as an accomplishment to make people uncomfortable.

Mrs. Templeton didn't at once take it in. Her training was all to the end that you must give a guest everything you have, even if he happens to be your worst enemy, and that to cause anyone embarrassment is a frightful and humiliating blunder. She felt hurt without knowing just why, but all evening it kept growing clearer to her that this was another of those thrusts from the outside which she couldn't understand. The neighbours were sure to take sides against her, apparently, if they came often to see her mother.

Mr. Rosen tried to distract Mrs. Templeton, but he could feel the poison working. On the way home the children knew something had displeased or hurt their mother. When they went into the house, she told them to go upstairs at once, as she had a headache. She was severe and distant. When Mrs. Harris suggested making her some peppermint tea, Victoria threw up her chin.

"I don't want anybody waiting on me. I just want to be let alone." And she withdrew without saying good-night, or "Are you all right, Ma?" as she usually did.

Left alone, Mrs. Harris sighed and began to turn down her bed. She knew, as well as if she had been at the social, what kind of thing had happened. Some of those prying ladies of the Woman's Relief Corps, or the Woman's Christian Temperance Union, had been intimating to Victoria that her mother was "put upon." Nothing ever made Victoria cross but criticism. She was jealous of small attentions paid to Mrs. Harris, because she felt they were paid "behind her back" or "over her head," in a way that implied reproach to her. Victoria had been a belle in their own town in Tennessee, but here she was not very popular, no matter how many pretty dresses she wore, and she couldn't bear it. She felt as if her mother and Mr. Templeton must be somehow to blame; at least they ought to protect her from whatever was disagreeable —they always had!

V

Mrs. Harris wakened at about four o'clock, as usual, before the house was stirring, and lay thinking about their position in this new town. She didn't know why the neighbours acted so; she was as much in the dark as Victoria. At home, back in Tennessee, her place in the family was not exceptional, but perfectly regular. Mrs. Harris had replied to Mrs. Rosen, when that lady asked why in the world she didn't break Vickie in to help her in the kitchen: "We are only young once, and trouble comes soon enough." Young girls, in the South, were supposed to be carefree and foolish; the fault Grandmother found in Vickie was that she wasn't foolish enough. When the foolish girl married and began to have children, everything else must give way to that. She must be humoured and given the best of everything, because having children was hard on a woman, and it was the most important thing in the world. In Tennessee every young married woman in good circumstances had an older woman in the house, a mother or mother-in-law or an old aunt, who managed the household economies and directed the help.

That was the great difference; in Tennessee there had been plenty of helpers. There was old Miss Sadie Crummer, who came to the house to spin and sew and mend; old Mrs. Smith, who always arrived to help at butchering- and preserving-time; Lizzie, the coloured girl, who did the washing and who ran in every day to help Mandy. There were plenty more, who came whenever one of Lizzie's barefoot boys ran to fetch them. The hills were full of solitary old women, or women but slightly attached to some household, who were glad to come to Miz' Harris's for good food and a warm bed, and the little present that either Mrs. Harris or Victoria slipped into their carpet-sack when they went away.

To be sure, Mrs. Harris, and the other women of her age who managed their daughter's house, kept in the background; but it was their own background, and they ruled it jealously. They left the front porch and the parlour to the young married couple and their young friends; the old women spent most of their lives in the kitchen and pantries and back dining-room. But there they ordered life to their own taste, entertained their friends, dispensed charity, and heard the troubles of the poor. Moreover, back there it was Grandmother's own house they lived in. Mr. Templeton came of a superior family and had what Grandmother called "blood," but no property. He never so much as mended one of the steps to the front porch without consulting Mrs. Harris. Even "back home," in the aristocracy, there were old women who went on living like young ones,—gave parties and drove out in their carriage and "went North" in the summer. But among the middle-class people and the country-folk, when a woman was a widow and had married daughters, she considered herself an old woman and wore full-gathered black dresses and a black bonnet and became a housekeeper. She accepted this estate unprotestingly, almost gratefully.

The Templetons' troubles began when Mr. Templeton's aunt died and left him a few thousand dollars, and he got the idea of bettering himself. The twins were little then, and he told Mrs. Harris his boys would have a better chance in Colorado—everybody was going West. He went alone first, and got a good position with a mining company in the mountains of southern Colorado. He had been book-keeper in the bank in his home town, had "grown up in the bank," as they said. He was industrious and honourable, and the managers of the mining company liked him, even if they laughed at his polite, soft-spoken manners. He could have held his position indefinitely, and maybe got a promotion. But the altitude of that mountain town was too high for his family. All the children were sick there; Mrs. Templeton was ill most of the time and nearly died when Ronald was born. Hillary Templeton lost his courage and came north to the flat, sunny, semi-arid country between Wray and Cheyenne, to work for an irrigation project. So far, things had not gone well with him. The pinch told on everyone, but most on Grandmother. Here, in Skyline, she had all her accustomed responsibilities, and no helper but Mandy. Mrs. Harris was no longer living in a feudal society, where there were plenty of landless people glad to render service to the more fortunate, but in a snappy little Western democracy, where every man was as good as his neighbour and out to prove it.

Neither Mrs. Harris nor Mrs. Templeton understood just what was the matter; they were hurt and dazed, merely. Victoria knew that here she was censured and criticized, she who had always been so admired and envied! Grandmother knew that these meddlesome "Northerners" said things that made Victoria suspicious and unlike herself; made her unwilling that Mrs. Harris should receive visitors alone, or accept marks of attention that seemed offered in compassion for her state.

These women who belonged to clubs and Relief Corps lived differently, Mrs. Harris knew, but she herself didn't like the way they lived. She believed that somebody ought to be in the parlour, and somebody in the kitchen. She wouldn't for the world have had

Victoria go about every morning in a short gingham dress, with bare arms, and a dust-cap on her head to hide the curling-kids, as these brisk housekeepers did. To Mrs. Harris that would have meant real poverty, coming down in the world so far that one could no longer keep up appearances. Her life was hard now, to be sure, since the family went on increasing and Mr. Templeton's means went on decreasing; but she certainly valued respectability above personal comfort, and she could go on a good way yet if they always had a cool pleasant parlour, with Victoria properly dressed to receive visitors. To keep Victoria different from these "ordinary" women meant everything to Mrs. Harris. She realized that Mrs. Rosen managed to be mistress of any situation, either in kitchen or parlour, but that was because she was "foreign." Grandmother perfectly understood that their neighbour had a superior cultivation which made everything she did an exercise of skill. She knew well enough that their own ways of cooking and cleaning were primitive beside Mrs. Rosen's.

If only Mr. Templeton's business affairs would look up, they could rent a larger house, and everything would be better. They might even get a German girl to come in and help,—but now there was no place to put her. Grandmother's own lot could improve only with the family fortunes—any comfort for herself, aside from that of the family, was inconceivable to her; and on the other hand she could have no real unhappiness while the children were well, and good, and fond of her and their mother. That was why it was worth while to get up early in the morning and make her bed neat and draw the red spread smooth. The little boys loved to lie on her lounge and her pillows when they were tired. When they were sick, Ronald and Hughie

wanted to be in her lap. They had no physical shrinking from her because she was old. And Victoria was
never jealous of the children's wanting to be with her
so much; that was a mercy!

Sometimes, in the morning, if her feet ached more
than usual, Mrs. Harris felt a little low. (Nobody did
anything about broken arches in those days, and the
common endurance test of old age was to keep going
after every step cost something.) She would hang up
her towel with a sigh and go into the kitchen, feeling
that it was hard to make a start. But the moment she
heard the children running down the uncarpeted back
stairs, she forgot to be low. Indeed, she ceased to be
an individual, an old woman with aching feet; she became part of a group, became a relationship. She was
drunk up into their freshness when they burst in upon
her, telling her about their dreams, explaining their
troubles with buttons and shoe-laces and underwear
shrunk too small. The tired, solitary old woman
Grandmother had been at daybreak vanished; suddenly the morning seemed as important to her as it
did to the children, and the mornings ahead stretched
out sunshiny, important.

VI

The day after the Methodist social, Blue Boy didn't
come for his morning milk; he always had it in a clean
saucer on the covered back porch, under the long
bench where the tin wash-tubs stood ready for Mrs.
Maude. After the children had finished breakfast,
Mrs. Harris sent Mandy out to look for the cat.

The girl came back in a minute, her eyes big.

"Law me, Miz' Harris, he's awful sick. He's a-layin'

in the straw in the barn. He's swallered a bone, or havin' a fit or somethin'."

Grandmother threw an apron over her head and went out to see for herself. The children went with her. Blue Boy was retching and choking, and his yellow eyes were filled up with rheum.

"Oh, Gram'ma, what's the matter?" the boys cried.

"It's the distemper. How could he have got it?" Her voice was so harsh that Ronald began to cry. "Take Ronald back to the house, Del. He might get bit. I wish I'd kept my word and never had a cat again!"

"Why, Gram'ma!" Albert looked at her. "Won't Blue Boy get well?"

"Not from the distemper, he won't."

"But Gram'ma, can't I run for the veter'nary?"

"You gather up an armful of hay. We'll take him into the coal-house, where I can watch him."

Mrs. Harris waited until the spasm was over, then picked up the limp cat and carried him to the coal-shed that opened off the back porch. Albert piled the hay in one corner—the coal was low, since it was summer—and they spread a piece of old carpet on the hay and made a bed for Blue Boy. "Now you run along with Adelbert. There'll be a lot of work to do on Mr. Holliday's yard, cleaning up after the sociable. Mandy an' me'll watch Blue Boy. I expect he'll sleep for a while."

Albert went away regretfully, but the drayman and some of the Methodist ladies were in Mr. Holliday's yard, packing chairs and tables and ice-cream freezers into the wagon, and the twins forgot the sick cat in their excitement. By noon they had picked up the last paper napkin, raked over the gravel walks where the salt from the freezers had left white patches, and hung the hammock in which Vickie did her studying back in its place. Mr. Holliday paid the boys a dollar a week for keeping up the yard, and they gave the money to their mother—it didn't come amiss in a family where actual cash was so short. She let them keep half the sum Mrs. Rosen paid for her milk every Saturday, and that was more spending money than most boys had. They often made a few extra quarters by cutting grass for other people, or by distributing handbills. Even the disagreeable Mrs. Jackson next door had remarked over the fence to Mrs. Harris: "I do believe Bert and Del are going to be industrious. They must have got it from you, Grandma."

The day came on very hot, and when the twins got back from the Roadmaster's yard, they both lay down on Grandmother's lounge and went to sleep. After dinner they had a rare opportunity; the Roadmaster himself appeared at the front door and invited them to go up to the next town with him on his railroad velocipede. That was great fun: the velocipede always whizzed along so fast on the bright rails, the gasoline engine puffing; and grasshoppers jumped up out of the sage-brush and hit you in the face like sling-shot bullets. Sometimes the wheels cut in two a lazy snake who was sunning himself on the track, and the twins always hoped it was a rattler and felt they had done a good work.

The boys got back from their trip with Mr. Holliday late in the afternoon. The house was cool and quiet. Their mother had taken Ronald and Hughie down town with her, and Vickie was off somewhere. Grandmother was not in her room, and the kitchen was empty. The boys went out to the back porch to pump a drink. The coal-shed door was open, and inside, on a low stool, sat Mrs. Harris beside her cat. Bert and Del didn't stop to get a drink; they felt ashamed that they had gone off for a gay ride and forgotten Blue Boy. They sat down on a big lump of coal beside Mrs. Harris. They would never have known that this miserable rumpled animal was their proud tom. Presently he went off into a spasm and began to froth at the mouth.

"Oh, Gram'ma, can't you do anything?" cried Albert, struggling with his tears. "Blue Boy was such a good cat,—why has he got to suffer?"

"Everything that's alive has got to suffer," said Mrs. Harris. Albert put out his hand and caught her skirt, looking up at her beseechingly, as if to make her unsay that saying, which he only half understood. She patted his hand. She had forgot she was speaking to a little boy.

"Where's Vickie?" Adelbert asked aggrievedly. "Why don't she do something? He's part her cat."

Mrs. Harris sighed. "Vickie's got her head full of things lately; that makes people kind of heartless."

The boys resolved they would never put anything into their heads, then!

Blue Boy's fit passed, and the three sat watching their pet that no longer knew them. The twins had not seen much suffering; Grandmother had seen a great deal. Back in Tennessee, in her own neighbourhood, she was accounted a famous nurse. When any of the poor mountain people were in great distress, they always sent for Miz' Harris. Many a time she had gone into a house where five or six children were all down with scarlet fever or diphtheria, and done what she could. Many a child and many a woman she had laid out and got ready for the grave. In her primitive community the undertaker made the coffin,—he did nothing more. She had seen so much misery that she wondered herself why it hurt so to see her tom-cat die.

She had taken her leave of him, and she got up from her stool. She didn't want the boys to be too much distressed.

"Now you boys must wash and put on clean shirts. Your mother will be home pretty soon. We'll leave Blue Boy; he'll likely be easier in the morning." She knew the cat would die at sundown.

After supper, when Bert looked into the coal-shed and found the cat dead, all the family were sad. Ronald cried miserably, and Hughie cried because Ronald did. Mrs. Templeton herself went out and looked into the shed, and she was sorry, too. Though she didn't like cats, she had been fond of this one.

"Hillary," she told her husband, "when you go down town tonight, tell the Mexican to come and get that cat early in the morning, before the children are up."

The Mexican had a cart and two mules, and he hauled away tin cans and refuse to a gully out in the sage-brush.

Mrs. Harris gave Victoria an indignant glance when she heard this, and turned back to the kitchen. All evening she was gloomy and silent. She refused to read aloud, and the twins took Ronald and went mournfully out to play under the electric light. Later, when they had said good-night to their parents in the parlour and were on their way upstairs, Mrs. Harris followed them into the kitchen, shut the door behind her, and said indignantly:

"Air you two boys going to let that Mexican take Blue Boy and throw him onto some trash-pile?"

The sleepy boys were frightened at the anger and bitterness in her tone. They stood still and looked up at her, while she went on:

"You git up early in the morning, and I'll put him in

a sack, and one of you take a spade and go to that crooked old willer tree that grows just where the sand creek turns off the road, and you dig a little grave for Blue Boy, an' bury him right."

They had seldom seen such resentment in their grandmother. Albert's throat choked up, he rubbed the tears away with his fist.

"Yes'm, Gram'ma, we will, we will," he gulped.

VII

Only Mrs. Harris saw the boys go out next morning. She slipped a bread-and-butter sandwich into the hand of each, but she said nothing, and they said nothing.

The boys did not get home until their parents were ready to leave the table. Mrs. Templeton made no fuss, but told them to sit down and eat their breakfast. When they had finished, she said commandingly:

"Now you march into my room." That was where she heard explanations and administered punishment. When she whipped them, she did it thoroughly.

She followed them and shut the door.

"Now, what were you boys doing this morning?"

"We went off to bury Blue Boy."

"Why didn't you tell me you were going?"

They looked down at their toes, but said nothing. Their mother studied their mournful faces, and her overbearing expression softened.

"The next time you get up and go off anywhere, you come and tell me beforehand, do you understand?"

"Yes'm."

She opened the door, motioned them out, and went with them into the parlour. "I'm sorry about your cat, boys," she said. "That's why I don't like to have cats around; they're always getting sick and dying. Now run along and play. Maybe you'd like to have a circus in the back yard this afternoon? And we'll all come."

The twins ran out in a joyful frame of mind. Their grandmother had been mistaken; their mother wasn't indifferent about Blue Boy, she was sorry. Now everything was all right, and they could make a circus ring.

They knew their grandmother got put out about strange things, anyhow. A few months ago it was because their mother hadn't asked one of the visiting preachers who came to the church conference to stay with them. There was no place for the preacher to sleep except on the folding lounge in the parlour, and no place for him to wash—he would have been very uncomfortable, and so would all the household. But Mrs. Harris was terribly upset that there should be a conference in the town, and they not keeping a preacher! She was quite bitter about it.

The twins called in the neighbour boys, and they made a ring in the back yard, around their turning-bar. Their mother came to the show and paid admission, bringing Mrs. Rosen and Grandma Harris. Mrs. Rosen thought if all the children in the neighbourhood were to be howling and running in a circle in the Templetons' back yard, she might as well be there, too, for she would have no peace at home.

After the dog races and the Indian fight were over, Mrs. Templeton took Mrs. Rosen into the house to revive her with cake and lemonade. The parlour was cool and dusky. Mrs. Rosen was glad to get into it after sitting on a wooden bench in the sun. Grandmother stayed in the parlour with them, which was unusual. Mrs. Rosen sat waving a palm-leaf fan,—she felt the heat very much, because she wore her stays so tight—while Victoria went to make the lemonade.

"De circuses are not so good, widout Vickie to manage them, Grandma," she said.

"No'm. The boys complain right smart about losing Vickie from their plays. She's at her books all the time now. I don't know what's got into the child."

"If she wants to go to college, she must prepare herself, Grandma. I am agreeably surprised in her. I didn't think she'd stick to it."

Mrs. Templeton came in with a tray of tumblers and the glass pitcher all frosted over. Mrs. Rosen wistfully admired her neighbour's tall figure and good carriage; she was wearing no corsets at all today under her flowered organdie afternoon dress, Mrs. Rosen had noticed, and yet she could carry herself so smooth and straight,—after having had so many children, too! Mrs. Rosen was envious, but she gave credit where credit was due.

When Mrs. Templeton brought in the cake, Mrs. Rosen was still talking to Grandmother about Vickie's studying. Mrs. Templeton shrugged carelessly.

"There's such a thing as overdoing it. Mrs. Rosen," she observed as she poured the lemonade. "Vickie's very apt to run to extremes."

"But, my dear lady, she can hardly be too extreme in dis matter. If she is to take a competitive examination with girls from much better schools than ours, she will have to do better than the others, or fail; no two ways about it. We must encourage her."

Mrs. Templeton bridled a little. "I'm sure I don't interfere with her studying, Mrs. Rosen. I don't see where she got this notion, but I let her alone."

Mrs. Rosen accepted a second piece of chocolate cake. "And what do you think about it, Grandma?"

Mrs. Harris smiled politely. "None of our people,

or Mr. Templeton's either, ever went to college. I expect it is all on account of the young gentleman who was here last summer."

Mrs. Rosen laughed and lifted her eyebrows. "Something very personal in Vickie's admiration for Professor Chalmers we think, Grandma? A very sudden interest in de sciences, I should say!"

Mrs. Templeton shrugged. "You're mistaken, Mrs. Rosen. There ain't a particle of romance in Vickie."

"But there are several kinds of romance, Mrs. Templeton. She may not have your kind."

"Yes'm, that's so," said Mrs. Harris in a low, grateful voice. She thought that a hard word Victoria had said of Vickie.

"I didn't see a thing in that Professor Chalmers, myself," Victoria remarked. "He was a gawky kind of fellow, and never had a thing to say in company. Did you think he amounted to much?"

"Oh, widout doubt Doctor Chalmers is a very scholarly man. A great many brilliant scholars are widout de social graces, you know." When Mrs. Rosen, from a much wider experience, corrected her neighbour, she did so somewhat playfully, as if insisting upon something Victoria capriciously chose to ignore.

At this point old Mrs. Harris put her hands on the arms of the chair in preparation to rise. "If you ladies will excuse me, I think I will go and lie down a little before supper." She rose and went heavily out on her felt soles. She never really lay down in the afternoon, but she dozed in her own black rocker. Mrs. Rosen and Victoria sat chatting about Professor Chalmers and his boys.

Last summer the young professor had come to Skyline with four of his students from the University of

Michigan, and had stayed three months, digging for fossils out in the sand-hills. Vickie had spent a great many mornings at their camp. They lived at the town hotel, and drove out to their camp every day in a light spring-wagon. Vickie used to wait for them at the edge of the town, in front of the Roadmaster's house, and when the spring-wagon came rattling along, the boys would call: "There's our girl!" slow the horses, and give her a hand up. They said she was their mascot, and were very jolly with her. They had a splendid summer,—found a great bed of fossil elephant bones, where a whole herd must once have perished. Later on they came upon the bones of a new kind of elephant, scarcely larger than a pig. They were greatly excited about their finds, and so was Vickie. That was why they liked her. It was they who told her about a memorial scholarship at Ann Arbor, which was open to any girl from Colorado.

VIII

In August Vickie went down to Denver to take her examinations. Mr. Holliday, the Roadmaster, got her a pass, and arranged that she should stay with the family of one of his passenger conductors.

For three days she wrote examination papers along with other contestants, in one of the Denver high schools, proctored by a teacher. Her father had given her five dollars for incidental expenses, and she came home with a box of mineral specimens for the twins, a singing top for Ronald, and a toy burro for Hughie.

Then began days of suspense that stretched into weeks. Vickie went to the post-office every morning, opened her father's combination box, and looked over the letters, long before he got down town,—always hoping there might be a letter from Ann Arbor. The night mail came in at six, and after supper she hurried to the post-office and waited about until the shutter at the general-delivery window was drawn back, a signal that the mail had all been "distributed." While the tedious process of distribution was going on, she usually withdrew from the office, full of joking men and cigar smoke, and walked up and down under the big cottonwood trees that overhung the side street. When the crowd of men began to come out, then she knew the mail-bags were empty, and she went in to get whatever letters were in the Templeton box and take them home.

After two weeks went by, she grew downhearted. Her young professor, she knew, was in England on his vacation. There would be no one at the University of Michigan who was interested in her fate. Perhaps the fortunate contestant had already been notified of her success. She never asked herself, as she walked up and down under the cottonwoods on those summer nights, what she would do if she didn't get the scholarship. There was no alternative. If she didn't get it, then everything was over.

During the weeks when she lived only to go to the post-office, she managed to cut her finger and get ink into the cut. As a result, she had a badly infected hand and had to carry it in a sling. When she walked her nightly beat under the cottonwoods, it was a kind of comfort to feel that finger throb; it was companionship, made her case more complete.

The strange thing was that one morning a letter came, addressed to Miss Victoria Templeton; in a long envelope such as her father called "legal size," with "University of Michigan" in the upper left-hand corner. When Vickie took it from the box, such a wave of fright and weakness went through her that she could scarcely get out of the post-office. She hid the letter under her striped blazer and went a weak, uncertain trail down the sidewalk under the big trees. Without seeing anything or knowing what road she took, she got to the Roadmaster's green yard and her hammock, where she always felt not on the earth, yet of it.

Three hours later, when Mrs. Rosen was just tasting one of those clear soups upon which the Templetons thought she wasted so much pains and good meat, Vickie walked in at the kitchen door and said in a low but somewhat unnatural voice:

"Mrs. Rosen, I got the scholarship."

Mrs. Rosen looked up at her sharply, then pushed the soup back to a cooler part of the stove.

"What is dis you say, Vickie? You have heard from de University?"

"Yes'm. I got the letter this morning." She produced it from under her blazer.

Mrs. Rosen had been cutting noodles. She took Vickie's face in two hot, plump hands that were still floury, and looked at her intently. "Is dat true, Vickie? No mistake? I am delighted—and surprised! Yes, surprised. Den you will *be* something, you won't just sit on de front porch." She squeezed the girl's round, good-natured cheeks, as if she could mould them into something definite then and there. "Now you must stay for lunch and tell us all about it. Go in and announce yourself to Mr. Rosen."

Mr. Rosen had come home for lunch and was sitting, a book in his hand, in a corner of the darkened front parlour where a flood of yellow sun streamed in under the dark green blind. He smiled his friendly smile at Vickie and waved her to a seat, making her understand that he wanted to finish his paragraph. The dark engraving of the pointed cypresses and the Roman tomb was on the wall just behind him.

Mrs. Rosen came into the back parlour, which was the dining-room, and began taking things out of the silver-drawer to lay a place for their visitor. She spoke to her husband rapidly in German.

He put down his book, came over, and took Vickie's hand.

"Is is true, Vickie? Did you really win the scholarship?"

"Yes, sir."

He stood looking down at her through his kind, remote smile,—a smile in the eyes, that seemed to come up through layers and layers of something— gentle doubts, kindly reservations.

"Why do you want to go to college, Vickie?" he asked playfully.

"To learn," she said with surprise.

"But why do you want to learn? What do you want to do with it?"

"I don't know. Nothing, I guess."

"Then what do you want it for?"

"I don't know. I just want it."

For some reason Vickie's voice broke there. She had been terribly strung up all morning, lying in the hammock with her eyes tight shut. She had not been home at all, she had wanted to take her letter to the Rosens first. And now one of the gentlest men she knew made her choke by something strange and presageful in his voice.

"Then if you want it without any purpose at all, you will not be disappointed." Mr. Rosen wished to distract her and help her to keep back the tears. "Listen: a great man once said: '*Le but n'est rien; le chemin, c'est tout.*' That means: 'The end is nothing, the road is all.' Let me write it down for you and give you your first French lesson."

He went to the desk with its big silver inkwell, where he and his wife wrote so many letters in several languages, and inscribed the sentence on a sheet of purple paper, in his delicately shaded foreign script, signing under it a name: *J. Michelet.* He brought it back and shook it before Vickie's eyes. "There, keep it to remember me by. Slip it into the envelope with your college credentials,—that is a good place for it." From his deliberate smile and the twitch of one eyebrow, Vickie knew he meant her to take it along as an antidote, a corrective for whatever colleges might do to her. But she had always known that Mr. Rosen was wiser than professors.

Mrs. Rosen was frowning, she thought that sentence a bad precept to give any Templeton. Moreover, she always promptly called her husband back to earth when he soared a little; though it was exactly for this transcendental quality of mind that she reverenced him in her heart, and thought him so much finer than any of his successful brothers.

"Luncheon is served," she said in the crisp tone that put people in their places. "And Miss Vickie, you are to eat your tomatoes with an oil dressing, as we do. If you are going off into the world, it is quite time you learn to like things that are everywhere accepted."

Vickie said: "Yes'm," and slipped into the chair Mr. Rosen had placed for her. Today she didn't care what she ate, though ordinarily she thought a French dressing tasted a good deal like castor oil.

IX

Vickie was to discover that nothing comes easily in this world. Next day she got a letter from one of the jolly students of Professor Chalmers's party, who was watching over her case in his chief's absence. He told her the scholarship meant admission to the freshman class without further examinations, and two hundred dollars toward her expenses; she would have to bring along about three hundred more to put her through the year.

She took this letter to her father's office. Seated in his revolving desk-chair, Mr. Templeton read it over several times and looked embarrassed.

"I'm sorry, daughter," he said at last, "but really, just now, I couldn't spare that much. Not this year. I expect next year will be better for us."

"But the scholarship is for this year, Father. It wouldn't count next year. I just have to go in September."

"I really ain't got it, daughter." He spoke, oh so kindly! He had lovely manners with his daughter and his wife. "It's just all I can do to keep the store bills paid up. I'm away behind with Mr. Rosen's bill. Couldn't you study here this winter and get along about as fast? It isn't that I wouldn't like to let you have the money if I had it. And with young children, I can't let my life insurance go."

Vickie didn't say anything more. She took her letter and wandered down Main Street with it, leaving young Mr. Templeton to a very bad half-hour.

At dinner Vickie was silent, but everyone could see she had been crying. Mr. Templeton told *Uncle Remus* stories to keep up the family morale and make the giggly twins laugh. Mrs. Templeton glanced covertly at her daughter from time to time. She was sometimes a little afraid of Vickie, who seemed to her to have a hard streak. If it were a love-affair that the girl was crying about, that would be so much more natural—and more hopeful!

At two o'clock Mrs. Templeton went to the Afternoon Euchre Club, the twins were to have another ride with the Roadmaster on his velocipede, the little boys took their nap on their mother's bed. The house was empty and quiet. Vickie felt an aversion for the hammock under the cottonwoods where she had been betrayed into such bright hopes. She lay down on her grandmother's lounge in the cluttered play-room and turned her face to the wall.

When Mrs. Harris came in for her rest and began to wash her face at the tin basin, Vickie got up. She wanted to be alone. Mrs. Harris come over to her while she was still sitting on the edge of the lounge.

"What's the matter, Vickie child?" She put her hand on her grand-daughter's shoulder, but Vickie shrank away. Young misery is like that, sometimes.

"Nothing. Except that I can't go to college after all. Papa can't let me have the money."

Mrs. Harris settled herself on the faded cushions of her rocker. "How much is it? Tell me about it, Vickie. Nobody's around."

Vickie told her what the conditions were, briefly and dryly, as if she were talking to an enemy. Everyone was an enemy; all society was against her. She told her grandmother the facts and then went upstairs, refusing to be comforted.

Mrs. Harris saw her disappear through the kitchen door, and then sat looking at the door, her face grave, her eyes stern and sad. A poor factory-made piece of joiner's work seldom has to bear a look of such intense, accusing sorrow; as if the flimsy pretence of "grained" yellow pine were the door shut against all young aspiration.

X

Mrs. Harris had decided to speak to Mr. Templeton, but opportunities for seeing him alone were not frequent. She watched out of the kitchen window, and when she next saw him go into the barn to fork down hay for his horse, she threw an apron over her head and followed him. She waylaid him as he came down from the hayloft.

"Hillary, I want to see you about Vickie. I was wondering if you could lay hand on any of the money you got for the sale of my house back home."

Mr. Templeton was nervous. He began brushing his trousers with a little whisk-broom he kept there, hanging on a nail.

"Why, no'm, Mrs. Harris. I couldn't just conveniently call in any of it right now. You know we had to use part of it to get moved up here from the mines."

"I know. But I thought if there was any left you could get at, we could let Vickie have it. A body'd like to help the child."

"I'd like to, powerful well, Mrs. Harris. I would, indeedy. But I'm afraid I can't manage it right now. The fellers I've loaned to can't pay up this year. Maybe next year—" He was like a little boy trying to escape a scolding, though he had never had a nagging word from Mrs. Harris.

She looked downcast, but said nothing.

"It's all right, Mrs. Harris," he took on his brisk

business tone and hung up the brush. "The money's perfectly safe. It's well invested."

Invested; that was a word men always held over women, Mrs. Harris thought, and it always meant they could have none of their own money. She sighed deeply.

"Well, if that's the way it is—" She turned away and went back to the house on her flat heelless slippers, just in time; Victoria was at that moment coming out to the kitchen with Hughie.

"Ma," she said, "can the little boy play out here, while I go down town?"

XI

For the next few days Mrs. Harris was very sombre, and she was not well. Several times in the kitchen she was seized with what she called giddy spells, and Mandy had to help her to a chair and give her a little brandy.

"Don't you say nothin', Mandy," she warned the girl. But Mandy knew enough for that.

Mrs. Harris scarcely noticed how her strength was failing, because she had so much on her mind. She was very proud, and she wanted to do something that was hard for her to do. The difficulty was to catch Mrs. Rosen alone.

On the afternoon when Victoria went to her weekly euchre, the old lady beckoned Mandy and told her to run across the alley and fetch Mrs. Rosen for a minute.

Mrs. Rosen was packing her trunk, but she came at once. Grandmother awaited her in her chair in the play-room.

"I take it very kindly of you to come, Mrs. Rosen.

I'm afraid it's warm in here. Won't you have a fan?" She extended the palm leaf she was holding.

"Keep it yourself, Grandma. You are not looking very well. Do you feel badly, Grandma Harris?" She took the old lady's hand and looked at her anxiously.

"Oh, no, ma'am! I'm as well as usual. The heat wears on me a little, maybe. Have you seen Vickie lately, Mrs. Rosen?"

"Vickie? No. She hasn't run in for several days. These young people are full of their own affairs, you know."

"I expect she's backward about seeing you, now that she's so discouraged."

"Discouraged? Why, didn't the child get her scholarship after all?"

"Yes'm, she did. But they write her she has to bring more money to help her out; three hundred dollars. Mr. Templeton can't raise it just now. We had so much sickness in that mountain town before we moved up here, he got behind. Pore Vickie's downhearted."

"Oh, that is too bad! I expect you've been fretting over it, and that is why you don't look like yourself. Now what can we do about it?"

Mrs. Harris sighed and shook her head. "Vickie's trying to muster courage to go around to her father's friends and borrow from one and another. But we ain't been here long,—it ain't like we had old friends here. I hate to have the child do it."

Mrs. Rosen looked perplexed. "I'm sure Mr. Rosen would help her. He takes a great interest in Vickie."

"I thought maybe he could see his way to. That's why I sent Mandy to fetch you."

"That was right, Grandma. Now let me think." Mrs. Rosen put up her plump red-brown hand and leaned her chin upon it. "Day after tomorrow I am

going to run on to Chicago for my niece's wedding."
She saw her old friend's face fall. "Oh, I shan't be
gone long; ten days, perhaps. I will speak to Mr.
Rosen tonight, and if Vickie goes to him after I am off
his hands, I'm sure he will help her."

Mrs. Harris looked up at her with solemn gratitude.
"Vickie ain't the kind of girl would forget anything
like that, Mrs. Rosen. Nor I wouldn't forget it."

Mrs. Rosen patted her arm. "Grandma Harris," she
exclaimed, "I will just ask Mr. Rosen to do it for you!
You know I care more about the old folks than the
young. If I take this worry off your mind, I shall go
away to the wedding with a light heart. Now dismiss
it. I am sure Mr. Rosen can arrange this himself for
you, and Vickie won't have to go about to these people here, and our gossipy neighbours will never be the
wiser." Mrs. Rosen poured this out in her quick, au-
thoritative tone, converting her *th*'s into *d*'s, as she did
when she was excited.

Mrs. Harris's red-brown eyes slowly filled with
tears,—Mrs. Rosen had never seen that happen before. But she simply said, with quiet dignity: "Thank
you, ma'am. I wouldn't have turned to nobody else."

"That means I am an old friend already, doesn't it,
Grandma? And that's what I want to be. I am very
jealous where Grandma Harris is concerned!" She
lightly kissed the back of the purple-veined hand she
had been holding, and ran home to her packing.
Grandma sat looking down at her hand. How easy it
was for these foreigners to say what they felt!

XII

Mrs. Harris knew she was failing. She was glad to be
able to conceal it from Mrs. Rosen when that kind

neighbour dashed in to kiss her good-bye on the morning of her departure for Chicago. Mrs. Templeton was, of course, present, and secrets could not be discussed. Mrs. Rosen, in her stiff little brown travelling-hat, her hands tightly gloved in brown kid, could only wink and nod to Grandmother to tell her all was well. Then she went out and climbed into the "hack" bound for the depot, which had stopped for a moment at the Templetons' gate.

Mrs. Harris was thankful that her excitable friend hadn't noticed anything unusual about her looks, and, above all, that she had made no comment. She got through the day, and that evening, thank goodness, Mr. Templeton took his wife to hear a company of strolling players sing *The Chimes of Normandy* at the Opera House. He loved music, and just now he was very eager to distract and amuse Victoria. Grandma sent the twins out to play and went to bed early.

Next morning, when she joined Mandy in the kitchen, Mandy noticed something wrong.

"You set right down, Miz' Harris, an' let me git you some whisky. Deed, ma'am, you look awful porely. You ought to tell Miss Victoria an' let her send for the doctor."

"No, Mandy, I don't want no doctor. I've seen more sickness than ever he has. Doctors can't do no more than linger you out, an' I've always prayed I wouldn't last to be a burden. You git me some whisky in hot water, and pour it on a piece of toast. I feel real empty."

That afternoon when Mrs. Harris was taking her rest, for once she lay down upon her lounge. Vickie came in, tense and excited, and stopped for a moment.

"It's all right, Grandma. Mr. Rosen is going to lend

me the money. I won't have to go to anybody else. He won't ask Father to endorse my note, either. He'll just take my name." Vickie rather shouted this news at Mrs. Harris, as if the old lady were deaf, or slow of understanding. She didn't thank her; she didn't know her grandmother was in any way responsible for Mr. Rosen's offer, though at the close of their interview he had said: "We won't speak of our arrangement to anyone but your father. And I want you to mention it to the old lady Harris. I know she has been worrying about you."

Having brusquely announced her news, Vickie hurried away. There was so much to do about getting ready, she didn't know where to begin. She had no trunk and no clothes. Her winter coat, brought two years ago, was so outgrown that she couldn't get into it. All her shoes were run over at the heel and must go to the cobbler. And she had only two weeks in which to do everything! She dashed off.

Mrs. Harris sighed and closed her eyes happily. She thought with modest pride that with people like the Rosens she had always "got along nicely." It was only with the ill-bred and unclassified, like this Mrs. Jackson next door, that she had disagreeable experiences. Such folks, she told herself, had come out of nothing and knew no better. She was afraid this inquisitive woman might find her ailing and come prying round with unwelcome suggestions.

Mrs. Jackson did, indeed, call that very afternoon, with a miserable contribution of veal-loaf as an excuse (all the Templetons hated veal), but Mandy had been forewarned, and she was resourceful. She met Mrs. Jackson at the kitchen door and blocked the way.

"Sh-h-h, ma'am, Miz' Harris is asleep, havin' her nap. No'm, she ain't porely, she's as usual. But Hughie had the colic last night when Miss Victoria was at the show, an' kep' Miz' Harris awake."

Mrs. Jackson was loath to turn back. She had really come to find out why Mrs. Rosen drove away in the depot hack yesterday morning. Except at church socials, Mrs. Jackson did not meet people in Mrs. Rosen's set.

The next day, when Mrs. Harris got up and sat on the edge of her bed, her head began to swim, and she lay down again. Mandy peeped into the play-room as soon as she came downstairs, and found the old lady still in bed. She leaned over her and whispered:

"Ain't you feelin' well, Miz' Harris?"

"No, Mandy, I'm right porely," Mrs. Harris admitted.

"You stay where you air, ma'am. I'll git the breakfast fur the chillun, an' take the other breakfast in fur Miss Victoria an' Mr. Templeton." She hurried back to the kitchen, and Mrs. Harris went to sleep.

Immediately after breakfast Vickie dashed off about her own concerns, and the twins went to cut grass while the dew was still on it. When Mandy was taking the other breakfast into the dining-room, Mrs. Templeton came through the play-room.

"What's the matter, Ma? Are you sick?" she asked in an accusing tone.

"No, Victoria, I ain't sick. I had a little giddy spell, and I thought I'd lay still."

"You ought to be more careful what you eat, Ma. If you're going to have another bilious spell, when everything is so upset anyhow, I don't know what I'll do!" Victoria's voice broke. She hurried back into her bedroom, feeling bitterly that there was no place in that house to cry in, no spot where one could be alone, even with misery; that the house and the people in it were choking her to death.

Mrs. Harris sighed and closed her eyes. Things did seem to be upset, though she didn't know just why. Mandy, however, had her suspicions. While she waited on Mr. and Mrs. Templeton at breakfast, narrowly observing their manner toward each other and Victoria's swollen eyes and desperate expression, her suspicions grew stronger.

Instead of going to his office, Mr. Templeton went to the barn and ran out the buggy. Soon he brought out Cleveland, the black horse, with his harness on. Mandy watched from the back window. After he had hitched the horse to the buggy, he came into the kitchen to wash his hands. While he dried them on the roller towel, he said in his most business-like tone:

"I likely won't be back tonight, Mandy. I have to go out to my farm, and I'll hardly get through my business there in time to come home."

Then Mandy was sure. She had been through these times before, and at such a crisis poor Mr. Templeton was always called away on important business. When he had driven out through the alley and up the street past Mrs. Rosen's, Mandy left her dishes and went in to Mrs. Harris. She bent over and whispered low:

"Miz' Harris, I 'spect Miss Victoria's done found out she's goin' to have another baby! It looks that way. She's gone back to bed."

Mrs. Harris lifted a warning finger. "Sh-h-h!"

'Oh yes'm, I won't say nothin'. I never do."

Mrs. Harris tried to face this possibility, but her

mind didn't seem strong enough—she dropped off into another doze.

All that morning Mrs. Templeton lay on her bed alone, the room darkened and a handkerchief soaked in camphor tied round her forehead. The twins had taken Ronald off to watch them cut grass, and Hughie played in the kitchen under Mandy's eye.

Now and then Victoria sat upright on the edge of the bed, beat her hands together softly and looked desperately at the ceiling, then about at those frail, confining walls. If only she could meet the situation with violence, fight it, conquer it! But there was nothing for it but stupid animal patience. She would have to go through all that again, and nobody, not even Hillary, wanted another baby,—poor as they were, and in this overcrowded house. Anyhow, she told herself, she was ashamed to have another baby, when she had a daughter old enough to go to college! She was sick of it all; sick of dragging this chain of life that never let her rest and periodically knotted and overpowered her; made her ill and hideous for months, and then dropped another baby into her arms. She had had babies enough; and there ought to be an end to such apprehensions some time before you were old and ugly.

She wanted to run away, back to Tennessee, and lead a free, gay life, as she had when she was first married. She could do a great deal more with freedom than ever Vickie could. She was still young, and she was still handsome; why must she be forever shut up in a little cluttered house with children and fresh babies and an old woman and a stupid bound girl and a husband who wasn't very successful? Life hadn't brought her what she expected when she married Hillary Templeton; life hadn't used her right. She had tried to keep up appearances, to dress well with very little to do it on, to keep young for her husband and children. She had tried, she had tried! Mrs. Templeton buried her face in the pillow and smothered the sobs that shook the bed.

Hillary Templeton, on his drive out through the sagebrush, up into the farming country that was irrigated from the North Platte, did not feel altogether cheerful, though he whistled and sang to himself on the way. He was sorry Victoria would have to go through another time. It was awkward just now, too, when he was so short of money. But he was naturally a cheerful man, modest in his demands upon fortune, and easily diverted from unpleasant thoughts. Before Cleveland had travelled half the eighteen miles to the farm, his master was already looking forward to a visit with his tenants, an old German couple who were fond of him because he never pushed them in a hard year—so far, all the years had been hard—and he sometimes brought them bananas and such delicacies from town.

Mrs. Heyse would open her best preserves for him, he knew, and kill a chicken, and tonight he would have a clean bed in her spare room. She always put a vase of flowers in his room when he stayed overnight with them, and that pleased him very much. He felt like a youth out there, and forgot all the bills he had somehow to meet, and the loans he had made and couldn't collect. The Heyses kept bees and raised turkeys, and had honeysuckle vines running over the front porch. He loved all those things. Mr. Templeton touched Cleveland with the whip, and as they sped along into the grass country, sang softly:

"Old Jesse was a gem'man,
Way down in Tennessee."

XIII

Mandy had to manage the house herself that day, and
she was not at all sorry. There wasn't a great deal of
variety in her life, and she felt very important taking
Mrs. Harris's place, giving the children their dinner,
and carrying a plate of milk toast to Mrs. Templeton.
She was worried about Mrs. Harris, however, and remarked to the children at noon that she thought
somebody ought to "set" with their grandma. Vickie
wasn't home for dinner. She had her father's office to
herself for the day and was making the most of it,
writing a long letter to Professor Chalmers. Mr. Rosen
had invited her to have dinner with him at the hotel
(he boarded there when his wife was away), and that
was a great honour.

When Mandy said someone ought to be with the
old lady, Bert and Del offered to take turns. Adelbert
went off to rake up the grass they had been cutting all
morning, and Albert sat down in the play-room. It
seemed to him his grandmother looked pretty sick. He
watched her while Mandy gave her toast-water with
whisky in it, and thought he would like to make the
room look a little nicer. While Mrs. Harris lay with
her eyes closed, he hung up the caps and coats lying
about, and moved away the big rocking-chair that
stood by the head of Grandma's bed. There ought to
be a table there, he believed, but the small tables in
the house all had something on them. Upstairs, in the
room where he and Adelbert and Ronald slept, there
was a nice clean wooden crackerbox, on which they
sat in the morning to put on their shoes and stockings.

He brought this down and stood it on end at the head of Grandma's lounge, and put a clean napkin over the top of it.

She opened her eyes and smiled at him. "Could you git me a tin of fresh water, honey?"

He went to the back porch and pumped till the water ran cold. He gave it to her in a tin cup as she had asked, but he didn't think that was the right way. After she dropped back on the pillow, he fetched a glass tumbler from the cupboard, filled it, and set it on the table he had just manufactured. When Grandmother drew a red cotton handkerchief from under her pillow and wiped the moisture from her face, he ran upstairs again and got one of his Sunday-school handkerchiefs, linen ones, that Mrs. Rosen had given him and Del for Christmas. Having put this in Grandmother's hand and taken away the crumpled red one, he could think of nothing else to do—except to darken the room a little. The windows had no blinds, but flimsy cretonne curtains tied back,—not really tied, but caught back over nails driven into the sill. He loosened them and let them hang down over the bright afternoon sunlight. Then he sat down on the low sawed-off chair and gazed about, thinking that now it looked quite like a sick-room.

It was hard for a little boy to keep still.

"Would you like me to read *Joe's Luck* to you, Gram'ma?" he said presently.

"You might, Bertie."

He got the "boy's book" she had been reading aloud to them, and began where she had left off. Mrs. Harris liked to hear his voice and she liked to look at him when she opened her eyes from time to time. She did not follow the story. In her mind she was repeating a passage from the second part of *Pilgrim's Prog-*

ress, which she had read aloud to the children so many times; the passage where Christiana and her band come to the arbour on the Hill of Difficulty: *"Then said Mercy, how sweet is rest to them that labour."*

At about four o'clock Adelbert came home, hot and sweaty from raking. He said he had got in the grass and taken it to their cow, and if Bert was reading, he guessed he'd like to listen. He dragged the wooden rocking-chair up close to Grandma's bed and curled up in it.

Grandmother was perfectly happy. She and the twins were about the same age; they had in common all the realest and truest things. The years between them and her, it seemed to Mrs. Harris, were full of trouble and unimportant. The twins and Ronald and Hughie were important. She opened her eyes.

"Where is Hughie?" she asked.

"I guess he's asleep. Mother took him into her bed."

"And Ronald?"

"He's upstairs with Mandy. There ain't nobody in the kitchen now."

"Then you might git me a fresh drink, Del."

"Yes'm, Gram'ma." He tiptoed out to the pump in his brown canvas sneakers.

When Vickie came home at five o'clock, she went to her mother's room, but the door was locked—a thing she couldn't remember ever happening before. She went into the play-room—old Mrs. Harris was asleep, with one of the twins on guard, and he held up a warning finger. She went into the kitchen. Mandy was making biscuits, and Ronald was helping her to cut them out.

"What's the matter, Mandy? Where is everybody?"

"You know your papa's away, Miss Vickie; an' your mama's got a headache, an' Miz' Harris has had a bad spell. Maybe I'll just fix supper for you an' the boys in the kitchen, so you won't all have to be runnin' through her room."

"Oh, very well," said Vickie bitterly, and she went upstairs. Wasn't it just like them all to go and get sick, when she had now only two weeks to get ready for school, and no trunk and no clothes or anything? Nobody but Mr. Rosen seemed to take the least interest, "when my whole life hangs by a thread," she told herself fiercely. What were families for, anyway?

After supper Vickie went to her father's office to read; she told Mandy to leave the kitchen door open, and when she got home she would go to bed without disturbing anybody. The twins ran out to play under the electric light with the neighbour boys for a little while, then slipped softly up the back stairs to their room. Mandy came to Mrs. Harris after the house was still.

"Kin I rub your legs fur you, Miz' Harris?"

"Thank you, Mandy. And you might get me a clean nightcap out of the press."

Mandy returned with it.

"Lawsie me! But your legs is cold, ma'am!"

"I expect it's about time, Mandy," murmured the old lady. Mandy knelt on the floor and set to work with a will. It brought the sweat out on her, and at last she sat up and wiped her face with the back of her hand.

"I can't seem to git no heat into 'em, Miz' Harris. I got a hot flat-iron on the stove; I'll wrap it in a piece of old blanket and put it to your feet. Why didn't you have the boys tell me you was cold, pore soul?"

Mrs. Harris did not answer. She thought it was probably a cold that neither Mandy nor the flat-iron could do much with. She hadn't nursed so many people back in Tennessee without coming to know certain signs.

After Mandy was gone, she fell to thinking of her blessings. Every night for years, when she said her prayers, she had prayed that she might never have a long sickness or be a burden. She dreaded the heartache and humiliation of being helpless on the hands of people who would be impatient under such a care. And now she felt certain that she was going to die tonight, without troubling anybody.

She was glad Mrs. Rosen was in Chicago. Had she been at home, she would certainly have come in, would have seen that her old neighbour was very sick, and bustled about. Her quick eye would have found out all Grandmother's little secrets: how hard her bed was, that she had no proper place to wash, and kept her comb in her pocket; that her nightgowns were patched and darned. Mrs. Rosen would have been indignant, and that would have made Victoria cross. She didn't have to see Mrs. Rosen again to know that Mrs. Rosen thought highly of her and admired her— yes, admired her. Those funny little pats and arch pleasantries had meant a great deal to Mrs. Harris.

It was a blessing that Mr. Templeton was away, too. Appearances had to be kept up when there was a man in the house; and he might have taken it into his head to send for the doctor, and stir everybody up. Now everything would be so peaceful. *"The Lord is my shepherd,"* she whispered gratefully. "Yes, Lord, I always spoiled Victoria. She was so much the prettiest. But nobody won't ever be the worse for it: Mr. Templeton will always humour her, and the children love her more than most. They'll always be good to her; she has that way with her."

Grandma fell to remembering the old place at home: what a dashing, high-spirited girl Victoria was, and how proud she had always been of her; how she used to hear her laughing and teasing out in the lilac arbour when Hillary Templeton was courting her. Toward morning all these pleasant reflections faded out. Mrs. Harris felt that she and her bed were softly sinking, through the darkness to a deeper darkness.

Old Mrs. Harris did not really die that night, but she believed she did. Mandy found her unconscious in the morning. Then there was a great stir and bustle; Victoria, and even Vickie, were startled out of their intense self-absorption. Mrs. Harris was hastily carried out of the play-room and laid in Victoria's bed, put into one of Victoria's best nightgowns. Mr. Templeton was sent for, and the doctor was sent for. The inquisitive Mrs. Jackson from next door got into the house at last,—installed herself as nurse, and no one had the courage to say her nay. But Grandmother was out of it all, never knew that she was the object of so much attention and excitement. She died a little while after Mr. Templeton got home.

Thus Mrs. Harris slipped out of the Templetons' story; but Victoria and Vickie had still to go on, to follow the long road that leads through things unguessed at and unforeseeable. When they are old, they will come closer and closer to Grandma Harris. They will think a great deal about her, and remember things they never noticed; and their lot will be more or less like hers. They will regret that they heeded her so little; but they, too, will look into the eager, unseeing eyes of young people and feel themselves alone. They will say to themselves: "I was heartless, because I was young and strong and wanted things so much. But now I know."

THE NOVEL
DÉMEUBLÉ

The novel, for a long while, has been over-furnished. The property-man has been so busy on its pages, the importance of material objects and their vivid presentation have been so stressed, that we take it for granted whoever can observe, and can write the English language, can write a novel. Often the latter qualification is considered unnecessary.

In any discussion of the novel, one must make it clear whether one is talking about the novel as a form of amusement, or as a form of art; since they serve very different purposes and in very different ways. One does not wish the egg one eats for breakfast, or the morning paper, to be made of the stuff of immortality. The novel manufactured to entertain great multitudes of people must be considered exactly like a cheap soap or a cheap perfume, or cheap furniture. Fine quality is a distinct disadvantage in articles made for great numbers of people who do not want quality but quantity, who do not want a thing that "wears," but who want change,—a succession of new things that are quickly threadbare and can be lightly thrown away. Does anyone pretend that if the Woolworth store windows were piled high with Tanagra figurines at ten cents, they could for a moment compete with Kewpie brides in the popular esteem? Amusement is one thing; enjoyment of art is another.

Every writer who is an artist knows that his "power of observation," and his "power of description," form but a low part of his equipment. He must have both, to be sure; but he knows that the most trivial of writers often have a very good observation. Mérimée said in his remarkable essay on Gogol: "L'art de choisir parmi les innombrables traits que nous offre la nature est, après tout, bien plus difficile que celui de les observer avec attention et de les rendre avec exactitude."

There is a popular superstition that "realism" asserts itself in the cataloguing of a great number of material objects, in explaining mechanical processes, the methods of operating manufactories and trades, and in minutely and unsparingly describing physical sensations. But is not realism, more than it is anything else, an attitude of mind on the part of the writer toward his material, a vague indication of the sympathy and candour with which he accepts, rather than chooses, his theme? Is the story of a banker, who is unfaithful to his wife and who ruins himself by speculation in trying to gratify the caprices of his mistresses, at all reinforced by a masterly exposition of banking, our whole system of credits, the methods of the Stock Exchange? Of course, if the story is thin, these things do reinforce it in a sense,—any amount of red meat thrown into the scale to make the beam dip. But are the banking system and the Stock Exchange worth being written about at all? Have such things any proper place in imaginative art?

The automatic reply to this question is the name of Balzac. Yes, certainly, Balzac tried out the value of literalness in the novel, tried it out to the uttermost, as Wagner did the value of scenic literalness in the music drama. He tried it, too, with the passion of discovery, with the inflamed zest of an unexampled curiosity. If the heat of that furnace could not give hardness and sharpness to material accessories, no other brain will ever do it. To reproduce on paper the actual city of Paris; the houses, the upholstery, the food, the wines, the game of pleasure, the game of business, the game of finance: a stupendous ambition—but, after all, unworthy of an artist. In exactly so far as he succeeded in pouring out on his pages that mass of brick and mortar and furniture and proceedings in bankruptcy, in exactly so far he defeated his end. The things by which he still lives, the types of greed and avarice and ambition and vanity and lost innocence of heart which he created—are as vital today as they were then. But their material surroundings, upon which he expended such labour and pains . . . the eye glides over them. We have had too much of the interior decorator and the "romance of business" since his day. The city he built on paper is already crumbling. Stevenson said he wanted to blue-pencil a great deal of Balzac's "presentation"—and he loved him beyond all modern novelists. But where is the man who could cut one sentence from the stories of Mérimée? And who wants any more detail as to how Carmencita and her fellow factory-girls made cigars? Another sort of novel? Truly. Isn't it a better sort?

In this discussion another great name naturally occurs. Tolstoi was almost as great a lover of material things as Balzac, almost as much interested in the way dishes were cooked, and people were dressed, and houses were furnished. But there is this determining difference: the clothes, the dishes, the haunting interiors of those old Moscow houses, are always so much a part of the emotions of the people that they are perfectly synthesized; they seem to exist, not so much in the author's mind, as in the emotional penumbra of the characters themselves. When it is fused like this, literalness ceases to be literalness—it is merely part of the experience.

If the novel is a form of imaginative art, it cannot be at the same time a vivid and brilliant form of journalism. Out of the teeming, gleaming stream of the present it must select the eternal material of art. There are hopeful signs that some of the younger writers are trying to break away from mere verisimilitude, and, following the development of modern painting, to interpret imaginatively the material and social investiture of their characters; to present their scene by suggestion rather than by enumeration. The higher processes of art are all processes of simplification. The novelist must learn to write, and then he must unlearn it; just as the modern painter learns to draw, and then learns when utterly to disregard his accomplishment, when to subordinate it to a higher and truer effect. In this direction only, it seems to me, can the novel develop into anything more varied and perfect than all the many novels that have gone before.

One of the very earliest American romances might well serve as a suggestion to later writers. In *The Scarlet Letter* how truly in the spirit of art is the mise-en-scène presented. That drudge, the theme-writing high-school student, could scarcely be sent there for information regarding the manners and dress and interiors of Puritan society. The material investiture of the story is presented as if unconsciously; by the reserved, fastidious hand of an artist, not by the gaudy fingers of a showman or the mechanical industry of a department-store window-dresser. As I remember it, in the twilight melancholy of that book, in its consistent mood, one can scarcely see the actual surroundings of the people; one feels them, rather, in the dusk.

Whatever is felt upon the page without being specifically named there—that, one might say, is created. It is the inexplicable presence of the thing not named, of the overtone divined by the ear but not heard by it, the verbal mood, the emotional aura of the fact or the thing or the deed, that gives high quality to the novel or the drama, as well as to poetry itself.

Literalness, when applied to the presenting of mental reactions and of physical sensations, seems to be no more effective than when it is applied to material things. A novel crowded with physical sensations is no less a catalogue than one crowded with furniture. A book like *The Rainbow* by D. H. Lawrence sharply reminds one how vast a distance lies between emotion and mere sensory reactions. Characters can be almost dehumanized by a laboratory study of the behaviour of their bodily organs under sensory stimuli—can be reduced, indeed, to mere animal pulp. Can one imagine anything more terrible than the story of *Romeo and Juliet* rewritten in prose by D. H. Lawrence?

How wonderful it would be if we could throw all the furniture out of the window; and along with it, all the meaningless reiterations concerning physical sensations, all the tiresome old patterns, and leave the room as bare as the stage of a Greek theatre, or as that house into which the glory of Pentecost descended; leave the scene bare for the play of emotions, great and little—for the nursery tale, no less than the tragedy, is killed by tasteless amplitude. The elder Dumas enunciated a great principle when he said that to make a drama, a man needed one passion, and four walls.

CHRONOLOGY

1873   Willa Cather is born December 7, the first child of Charles and Virginia Cather. She is christened Wilella; "Willa" is the name she will give to herself.

1879   The young Willa Cather witnesses the dramatic reunion between a Cather family servant and her daughter Nancy, an ex-slave who had escaped to Canada before the Civil War. (Sixty years later, Cather will draw upon this memory for *Sapphira and the Slave Girl*, her last novel.)

1883   The Charles Cather family moves to Nebraska, arriving in April. For the next seventeen months they will live in a farmhouse on the Divide, the plains between the Republican and the Blue rivers and between the Blue and the Platte.

1884 The Cathers move to Red Cloud in September.

1890 Willa Cather leaves Red Cloud for Lincoln in September. She will spend a year doing additional preparation necessary before enrolling in the University of Nebraska.

1891 Willa Cather's career as a published writer begins in March, when her English professor arranges for the newspaper publication of Cather's essay, "The Personal Characteristics of Thomas Carlyle."

1893 Cather begins to write on a regular basis for the *Nebraska State Journal*. Her first column appears on November 5.

1895 Cather meets Stephen Crane when he visits Lincoln in February. In March she travels to Chicago where she hears grand opera for the first time. On June 12, she graduates from the University of Nebraska with a Bachelor of Arts.

1896 Cather travels to Pittsburgh in June to edit the *Home Monthly*.

1897 Cather resigns from the *Home Monthly* and in September begins work as telegraph editor of the Pittsburgh *Daily Leader*. Her job is to read cables and expand them into printable stories.

1898 Cather meets and becomes friendly with Ethelbert Nevin, a gifted composer upon whom she would base her 1925 portrait of Valentine Ramsay in "Uncle Valentine."

1900 Cather sells "Eric Hermannson's Soul" to *Cosmopolitan,* which publishes it in April. Cather resigns from the *Leader* later that same month.

1901 In March, Cather begins teaching at Pittsburgh's Central High School. Sometime during the year she meets Isabelle McClung.

1902 Accompanied by Isabelle McClung, Cather makes her first trip to Europe, visiting England and France.

1903 Cather moves into the McClung mansion at 1180 Murray Hill Avenue. She begins teaching at Allegheny High School in Pittsburgh. *April Twilights,* a collection of poems and her first book, is published by Richard Badger. On May 1 she meets Samuel McClure who promises to publish her stories in his magazine and to publish a collection of them in book form. During a summer visit, she meets Edith Lewis in Nebraska.

1905 *The Troll Garden* is published by McClure, Phillips, and Company. On December 5, Cather attends the gala party at Delmonico's in New York to celebrate Mark Twain's seventieth birthday.

1906 Cather leaves Pittsburgh for New York, where she joins the staff of *McClure's Magazine.*

1908 Cather meets Sarah Orne Jewett. In April Cather travels to France and Italy with Isabelle McClung.

1909 Cather goes to Europe in May. Sarah Orne Jewett dies in June.

1911 With Isabelle McClung, Cather rents a house in Cherry Valley, New York, where she will spend three productive months in the fall writing.

1912 Her first novel, *Alexander's Bridge,* is published by Houghton Mifflin in April. Cather makes her first trip to the Southwest and resigns from *McClure's.*

1913 *O Pioneers!* is published. With Edith Lewis,

Cather rents an apartment at 5 Bank Street in Greenwich Village. Lewis will be Cather's companion for the next thirty-four years.

1915   *The Song of the Lark* is published in October. On November 12, Judge McClung dies in Pittsburgh.

1916   The McClung mansion is sold. Isabelle McClung marries Jan Hambourg on April 3.

1918   *My Antonia* is published in September.

1920   *Youth and the Bright Medusa,* Cather's second collection of stories, is published by Alfred A. Knopf—who will remain Cather's publisher for the rest of her life.

1922   In later years, Cather would claim, "the world broke in two in 1922 or thereabout." During the summer, Cather lectures at Bread Loaf, Vermont. *One of Ours* is published. Along with her parents, Cather is confirmed in the Episcopal Church on December 27.

1923   Cather receives a Pulitzer Prize for *One of Ours. A Lost Lady* is published. Leon Bakst paints Cather's portrait.

1925   *The Professor's House* is published in September.

1926   *My Mortal Enemy* is published in March by *McCall's.* It is published as a book by Knopf in October. Cather buys land on Grand Manan Island and arranges for a cottage to be built for her there.

1927   *Death Comes for the Archbishop* is published. Cather is forced to give up her Bank Street apartment.

1928   Charles Cather dies in March. In June Cather receives an honorary degree from Columbia.

1930   In March, Cather travels to California to see

her mother, who is ill there. During the summer, she visits Europe where she meets Yehudi Menuhin in Paris and Mme. Franklin Grout in Aix-les-Bains.

1931 Cather receives honorary degrees from the University of California and Princeton. *Shadows on the Rock* is published in August. Virginia Cather dies in September.

1932 *Obscure Destinies* is published in August. In November, Cather leases an apartment at 570 Park Avenue; this will be her home for the rest of her life.

1935 *Lucy Gayheart* is published in August.

1936 Cather publishes her first collection of essays, *Not Under Forty.*

1938 In April Cather revisits Virginia in preparation for a new novel. Cather's brother Douglass dies of a heart attack in June. Isabelle McClung Hambourg dies in October.

1940 *Sapphira and the Slave Girl* is published in December.

1944 Cather receives the gold medal for fiction awarded once every ten years by the National Institute of Arts and Letters.

1947 On April 24, Willa Cather dies in her New York apartment.

1948 *The Old Beauty and Others,* Cather's fourth collection of stories, is published posthumously.

BIBLIOGRAPHY

There is no definitive edition of Cather's collected work. Between 1937 and 1941, Houghton Mifflin published *The Novels and Stories of Willa Cather* and this is called the Library Edition. It omits most of Cather's short fiction, however, and includes extensive revisions made by Cather as she reconsidered her published works. (For example, the conclusion of "A Wagner Matinee," changes from "She burst into tears and sobbed pleadingly. 'I don't want to go, Clark, I don't want to go!'" to "She turned to me with a sad little smile. 'I don't want to go, Clark. I suppose we must.'" Most Cather scholars agree that this revision weakens the power of the original story.) Other editions of Cather's work published during her lifetime also include substantial changes. For the 1932 reissue of *The Song of the Lark*, for example, Cather cut approximately seven thousand words in response to criticism that the original novel was too long.

Anyone interested in Cather should begin by reading the original editions of her work, the publication dates for which can be found in the Chronology (pages 331–335). There have been many reprintings of these editions, and Cather's original publishers, Houghton Mifflin and Alfred A. Knopf (which is now owned by Random House), keep most of her titles available in paperback. Several important volumes of Cather's work are available in scholarly editions from the University of Nebraska Press.

The standard collection of Cather's early stories is *Willa Cather's Collected Short Fiction 1892–1912;* edited by Virginia Faulkner with an excellent introduction by Mildred Bennett, it was first published in 1965 and then revised for reissue in 1970. *Uncle Valentine and Other Stories: Willa Cather's Uncollected Short Fiction, 1915–1929,* edited with an introduction by Bernice Slote, has a valuable appendix that records variants between "Coming, Eden Bower!" and "Coming, Aphrodite!" the magazine and book versions of an important story from 1920. Slote also edited for Nebraska a 1966 selection of Cather's reviews, *The Kingdom of Art: Willa Cather's First Principles and Critical Statements 1893–1896.* In 1970, this volume was supplemented by *The World and the Parish: Willa Cather's Articles and Reviews, 1893–1902,* two volumes edited by William M. Curtin. Nebraska has also published a definitive edition of *April Twilights,* edited by Bernice Slote (1968), and a variorum edition of *The Troll Garden,* edited by James Woodress (1983). (The three *Troll Garden* stories reprinted in *Great Short Works of Willa Cather* are taken from this scholarly edition.) *Willa Cather: A Bibliography* by Joan Crane (Lincoln: University of Nebraska Press, 1982) provides a detailed history of Cather's published works.

Because Cather's will prohibits the publication of her letters, they are not available in print except for the handful she chose to publish in various newspapers and magazines. Collections of her letters can be read (but not quoted) in Lincoln at the University of Nebraska Library and the Nebraska State Historical Society and, in Red Cloud, at the Willa Cather Historical Center. Other important letter collections are at the Beinecke Rare Book and Manuscript Library, Yale University, New Haven, Connecticut; Columbia University Library, New York, New York; Guy Baily Memorial Library, University of Vermont, Burlington; Houghton Library, Harvard University, Cambridge, Massachusetts; Huntington Library, San Marino, California; New York Public Library, New York, New York; Newberry Library, Chicago, Illinois; Pierpont Morgan Library, New York, New York; and the University of Virginia Library, Charlottesville, Virginia.

The most reliable biography of Cather is James Woodress's *Willa Cather: A Literary Life* (Lincoln: University of Nebraska Press, 1987). This scholarly work is likely to remain for many years the standard against which any other biography of Cather must be measured. It supersedes his earlier *Willa Cather: Her Life and Art,* published in 1970 and reissued in 1975. Several earlier works are still useful, however. *Willa Cather: A Critical Biography* by E. K. Brown (New York: Alfred A. Knopf, 1953) provided the base for much subsequent scholarship; completed by Leon Edel after Brown's untimely death, it still provides a good introduction for the general reader. Mildred Bennett's *The World of Willa Cather* (New York: Dodd, Mead & Co., 1951) remains an essential source for information about Cather's life in Nebraska. Anyone interested in Cather's life should also read two memoirs by women who knew her well: *Willa Cather Living* by Edith Lewis (New York: Alfred A. Knopf, 1953) and *Willa Cather: A Memoir* by Elizabeth Shepley Sergeant (Philadelphia: Lippincott, 1953). The 1983 biography by Phyllis C. Robinson, *Willa: The Life of Willa Cather,* is regarded as unreliable by most Cather scholars.

The single best critical work on Cather is Susan J. Rosowski's *The Voyage Perilous: Willa Cather's Romanticism* (Lincoln: University of Nebraska Press, 1986). Another important work is Sharon O'Brien's *Willa Cather: The Emerging Voice* (New York: Oxford Univesity Press, 1987). This feminist study of Cather's work through the 1913 publication of *O Pioneers!* strikes some readers as too polemical, but O'Brien is original and provocative even if she is not always convincing. A feminist view of Cather can also be found in Judith Fryer's *Felicitous Space: The Imaginative Structures of Edith Wharton and Willa Cather* (Chapel Hill: University of North Carolina Press, 1986). Two other important critical studies are Marilyn Arnold's *Willa Cather's Short Fiction* (Athens, Ohio: Ohio University Press, 1984) and David Stouck's *Willa Cather's Imagination* (Lincoln: University of Nebraska Press, 1975). Among earlier books on Cather that might still be consulted are David Daiches's *Willa Cather: A Critical Introduction* (Ithaca: Cornell University Press, 1951), John H. Randall's *The Landscape and the Looking Glass* (Boston: Houghton Mifflin, 1960), and Edward and Lillian Bloom's *Willa Cather's Gift of Sympathy* (Carbondale: Southern Illinois University Press, 1962). *Willa Cather and Her Critics,* edited by James Schroeter (Ithaca: Cornell University Press, 1967) provides a useful survey of Cather criticism, including a number of important reviews and the 1946 essay by E. K. Brown in the *Yale Review* that Cather herself liked so much that she began corresponding with Brown. Several more recent scholarly articles on Cather have been collected in *Critical Essays on Willa Cather*, edited by James J. Murphy (Boston: G. K. Hall, 1984).